APOCALYPSE ATLANTIS

Jay C. LaBarge

CONTENTS

PRINCIPLE CAST OF CHARACTERS

Dedicated to my wife Sandy, whose kind ear has listened to every iteration of every chapter, as my rambling mind formulated what is hopefully a cohesive narrative. Her patience and insightful critique have kept me on task and on track throughout. The devoted companionship she has provided on our many travels, which form the backbone of these tales, has been an unending source of joy.

People never believe in volcanos until the lava actually overtakes them.

—*George Santayana*

HISTORICAL NOTE

The reading of my youth, coupled with more recent trips to Greece, Turkey, and Crete, piqued my interest in the myths and history of the lands surrounding the Aegean Sea. Such a relatively small geographic area of the world, and yet the scene of the birth of so much art, culture, philosophy, and political thought. All of which has been handed down over the ages, influencing us even to this day.

Whether Atlantis ever truly existed or was merely an allegory of the hubris of man as told by Plato, most agree the genesis of its myth refers to the ancient Minoans. In the great historical game of "what ifs," it could be argued that if the massive eruption of Mount Thera hadn't decimated the Minoan empire, then the nascent Greek civilization of the Myceneans could not have arisen from its literal ashes. Recent DNA evidence confirms that modern Greeks are descendants of the Myceneans, with only a small portion from later migrations. If there had been no great disaster, then there would have been no ancient Greece as we know it, and no great flourishing of the Greek civilization that birthed the modern concept of democracy. And sadly, no writing of this book.

There is no doubt of the great contributions to civilization of the Minoans, as they left such a rich archeological trail for us to discover at places such as Knossos, Phaistos, Malia, Zakros, and even at Akrotiri on Santorini itself. They were a seafaring people, trading along the eastern Mediterranean with Egypt, Cyprus, Anatolia, and Mycenae. Minoan artifacts have even been found in Sicily, southern Italy, and recently as far away as Tel Kabri, Israel. Trade was their passion, but they jealously protected their routes and projected their power and influence.

The ancient Minoans mastered the bronze metallurgy the age was named after, developed a form of central government, kept written records on clay tablets, built large scale architecture and complex palaces, crafted exquisite jewelry, and utilized aqueducts and indoor plumbing. Historians agree theirs was the first true civilization of Europe.

The language they developed, Linear A, has never been deciphered despite extensive and repeated efforts to do so. Even with modern cryptology and computing methods, it still stubbornly refuses to reveal its secrets. Linear B, which was used by the ancient Myceneans to write the earliest attested form of Greek, was successfully deciphered by British linguist John Chadwick in 1952. Therefore, the words referenced and languages used in this book to lend a feel of authenticity for the time period are Mycenean where available, and Greek when not.

Scholars have not yet been able to differentiate between Minoan and Mycenean religions, as they were so intertwined. Both are used here. For the sake of the casual reader, Attica and Laconia, better known as Athens and Sparta, are collectively referred to as Mycenae. I have also chosen to denote ancient times with BC rather than BCE, as a personal preference.

The cause of the collapse of the Minoan civilization has been well documented, from both a tremendous cataclysmic event and its lingering aftereffects. The eruption of Mount Thera in the center of their trade empire not only decimated the immediate area, but even those at a great distance surrounding it. Archeological evidence points to a massive tsunami devastating the surrounding islands and the fleets and seaside communities of Crete, while killing thousands along the shorelines of the eastern Mediterranean. It so severely damaged the navy and trade fleet of the Minoans that they never recovered. They became ripe for conquest, and the Mycenean Greeks eagerly obliged.

The amount of ash released into the atmosphere from Thera resulted in a sort of nuclear winter. Fields were covered in residue, the amount of sunlight that could filter through altered. Excavated layers of sediment across the Mediterranean tell the story in minute detail. Ice core samples, tree rings, and documented accounts from civilizations as far away as China confirm of an epic event that had global ramifications.

Various sources were used to draw inspiration to depict the violent eruption of Thera in approximately 1646 BC, including Pliny the Younger's account of Vesuvius in 79 AD, eye witness accounts of Mount Tambora in 1816, Krakatoa in 1883, and Mount Pelee in 1902. Photographs and film footage of more contemporary eruptions also provided the author with a sense of the power and fury nature can unleash. These were supplemented by personal exploration of the great caldera of Yellowstone, a climb of Mount Etna, the witnessing of an eruption on Mount Stromboli, and treks to the time capsules of both Herculaneum and Pompeii to view the effects of the wrath of Vesuvius firsthand. Anyone who has seen the haunting plaster casts of victims in the Garden of the Fugitives of Pompeii, or the tangled bones in the boat houses of Herculaneum, can't help but feel the power and pathos of that cataclysmic eruption.

Several ancient myths are incorporated here, including that of the Minotaur, the Labyrinth, and the Graeae, those three sisters who had but one eye to share among them. I hope the reader will enjoy the modern retelling of the possible origins of such fascinating and enduring legends.

The Holocaust reached far and wide during WWII, and its impact on Greece was no exception. When Hitler's Italian allies faltered in their efforts at conquest, the Germans stepped in to secure the southern flank for their impending invasion of Russia. After the mainland was captured by ground invasion and Crete by airborne troops, Greece was divided into zones of occupation. Ultimately over 66,000 Jewish lives were lost. The father of the antagonist in this story is loosely based on the Mayor of Corfu at that time. His name was Kollas, and was a known collaborator to the Nazis. Nearly all the Jews of Corfu were deported to Auschwitz-Birkenau with his cooperation. Few survived.

While this book is purely a work of fiction, the events related to the eruption of Mount Thera, the Minoan civilization and its ultimate decline, and the Holocaust in Greece during WWII, are based upon the research and data available at the time of its writing.

Jay LaBarge
Syracuse, NY
April, 2022

CHAPTER 1
1646 BC, COAST OF MYCENAE

The harsh Mediterranean summer sun beat down mercilessly upon them, doubly cruel as it reflected off the water's shimmering surface into their squinting eyes stinging with sweat. The pounding on deep-throated kettle drums quickened their cadence. The slaves strained against their oars to avoid the stinging lash and the pouring of salt water on their already scarred and sunburned backs. With a single man to each oar, they had been trained to keep in perfect rhythm and pull together as one. Turning their vessel into the most lethal weapon anywhere on the Great Sea.

The galley master shouted out the closing of the distance periodically in between drumbeats. He didn't want them to completely exhaust themselves as they surged toward a target they couldn't see. Best to always save a small reserve of strength for the final push, soon to come.

Here and there the most weakened of the slaves slumped at their oar, their hearts bursting from the strain, or the meager rations and ill treatment finally taking its ultimate toll. Since they were shackled to one another and to the floor boards of the galley, there was no time to throw their limp bodies overboard in the heat of battle. Instead, their oar was simply tossed away from the ship, so as not to interfere with the rest still pumping frantically in unison. Woe be it to any surviving slave with no oar after the battle had been won. And if the battle was lost, what did it matter? Their ship would burn or sink, their chains ensuring a trip to the bottom, along with their brethren. Such was the life of a slave upon a fighting galley.

Thálassa Iremi subconsciously smiled his approval as he watched the chase from afar on his flag ship. Commander of the great fleet, he was thick-muscled with a broad, powerful chest, and could still be easily mistaken for the elite warriors he led. His skin was bronzed from the sun and sea just like the armor he wore, the crow's feet at the edges of eyes betraying his years. He now battled with his leadership and intellect.

Here they had cleverly lured the last of the pirates from their lair with a fat, slow moving merchant vessel that had proven irresistible. Thálassa had devised the grand strategy that ensured the same choreographed act was played out up and down the coasts. All around the scattered island anchorages known to be favorite haunts of the scourge of these pirates. What made the ploy deadly efficient was the genius of its simplicity. It had unfolded all over the empire within the span of just a few days, by spreading out the royal fleet to its very limits near and far with identical orders. All done before a word of warning could be passed from one pirate haven to the next.

He tilted his head, and could hear the collision of wooden ships even here. The sound carried across the water on the slightest breath of a breeze, followed by desperate shouts of men fighting for their lives and the ringing of bronze swords clashing.

By the gods it is good to be alive, and to deliver the wrath of the king, he thought. *Death to the barbarians who dare to prey upon the edges of the empire!*

He looked forward to making a very visible example of the transgressors, to strike fear into those they might inspire by their belligerent and insolent acts. Hanging them by grappling hooks, which were used to lash battling ships together, where their warriors' superior discipline and weaponry carried the day. That would ensure an appropriately lingering death. They would then be displayed at the docks of any nearby villages, and upon the prows of the victorious galleys. It would be fitting retribution indeed, the pirates impaled and gasping for air like the worthless trash fish they fed the slaves.

The empire had been built upon trade, and was well known for the quality of its craftsmen and bounty of its crops, and some would say the exquisite beauty of their women. Yet no empire expanded or maintained its dominance without the might of an armed fist. So confident was the great king that fortifications and stone walls did not surround their palaces and places of worship. No, their walls were made of wood and floated on the water, and could be sent to do the king's bidding and pacify the entire sea. And Thálassa, after many years of devoted service and the refining of his tradecraft of war, now proudly commanded that very wall of wood, the *Atlantean Navy*.

The part of the fleet that was in Thálassa's vicinity gathered around the flag ship. They slowly made their way south, to rendezvous with those ships of the empire not immediately sent back out on patrol. There would be no letting down of their collective guard, not after so great a victory had been won. Even the dark lord of the underworld seemed pleased, as some of the normally silent mountains of the land and islands of the sea made rumblings, blowing small clouds of fumes skyward in celebration. The omens were good, and sporadic plumes of bright-colored liquid stone and smoke were tossed skyward from his lair deep within the very earth itself. Surely this was signaling accolades for these masters of the sea.

As the wind picked up, the fleet sailed onward without the aid of oars, the slaves catching their collective breath. They were reorganized to balance the remaining manpower. Their dead comrades were unshackled and unceremoniously dumped into the passing waves, where dorsal fins below and scavenger birds above fought one another for their feast.

For a change, the slaves could watch vengeance meted out upon someone else, now in the form of the dazed and newly captive pirates. But that didn't always bring solace. It was often their own kinsmen being impaled and hung like scarecrows, sometimes even a familiar friend or family member. Vengeance burned deep within the soul of each slave, their callused hands bleeding and full of splinters, their ankles rubbed raw by the shackles, the sharp bones of their buttocks nearly breaking through their emaciated skin on the rough benches of the galley. Perhaps retribution wouldn't happen in their own fleeting lifetimes. But they prayed it would ultimately come down upon their oppressors with fury, and avenge their tormented souls.

The breezes continued to favor the journey, and soon the great port of the Atlanteans loomed in the distance. The slaves limbered up, believing they would have to row the galley into its berth. But no order was given, and they drifted beyond the reefs for two full days. The crew celebrated and drank wine, making sport of torturing the injured and oldest of the captives before throwing them overboard, while abusing the women their commanders gave them leave to. The warriors grumbled among themselves that the fairest were always saved unblemished for their leaders or the nobility. They lusted for the rare times when all captured women were fair game, regardless of rank.

Almost by the hour more and more ships gathered from further away, slowly drifting around the flag ship. Thálassa held counsel with each captain, and waited until he felt he had gathered enough of the great fleet to properly impress the king. He then organized a procession into the vast, concentric harbor. His ship was proudly at the vanguard as they slowly entered the port, looking up at magnificent Mount Thíra, below which sat the gleaming city of *Atlantis*.

As a final preparation, an offering was needed for the gods, to bless the victorious procession into the harbor. When the pirates from the last captured ship were asked who led them, several brave souls stood and said they did. They knew what fate was in store for their leader. They offered themselves in his stead, wishing to spare him both the pain and humiliation. But an imposing man among them would not have it, and signaled for them to sit back down. He calmly said that he alone led the insurrection, and he alone deserved their wrath. Even Thálassa had to admire the man's courage, as he uttered not a sound throughout the terrible ordeal. The pirate leader was stripped of his shirt and roughly handled to the bow,

4

where he was impaled and suspended for all to see, and left to a lingering fate.

Triumphal pennants fluttered from the top of the single-mast on Thálassa's flagship, while the slaves silently powered the craft into a massive circular harbor. As they approached the port, the clanging of bells and cymbals and thumping of drums could be heard all around. The high-pitched greeting of bare breasted women leaning out of the dockside taverns and the cheap rooms above hinted at what awaited men who had been away at sea too long. Even the ship's boys smiled, those whose small limber bodies brought up arms and foodstuffs from the dank cubby holes of the galleys, sensing their nocturnal abuse finally at an end.

The galley rowed into the circular harbor, past the docks where merchant ships unloaded, took on goods, and were repaired. It glided further to where many warships were housed, along with the barracks, mess halls, and forges. Here there was more order, and many craftsmen and merchants turned out in their finest clothing to greet the returning conquerors and gawk at the captives. Especially those unfortunate souls squirming from the prow of each galley.

Finally, Thálassa's lead flagship came to the berthing for the largest war ships, the prides of the fleet. Nobles and the richest of the merchants could be seen gazing out in admiration upon the might of their empire, the envy of the Bronze Age world they dominated. Thálassa's chest swelled with pride as he glanced at the line of sleek galleys following in his wake, at the engineering marvel of the great port, at the opulent city of Atlantis overlooking the whole of the sea from its perch on the plain before the great mountain. It was good to be home, to this land touched by the gods themselves. This night was to be a time to celebrate for them all.

Early the next day, Thálassa worked his way to the arena. It was a slow process since everyone wanted to see the man of the hour, to touch his cloak, to bestow their blessings to the hand of the king. Flowers and offerings were tossed at the feet of he and his hand-picked escorts, and many libations were offered and drank. The procession didn't quicken until the sound of drums and horns signaled the impending start of festivities. The pace picked up, and

Thálassa entered into the large arena with his escort fanning out to either side, magnificently attired in full battle regalia, their bronze helmets, breast plates, shields, and spear tips glinting in the sunlight.

The king glanced down at him from his strategically situated and shaded throne and nodded. Thálassa deeply bowed and touched the rich black earth on which he stood, and then pressed it to his forehead and lips in deference.

I am of the earth and serve only you, with every thought and every word, the ritualized reply indicated.

It was an honor that he had been invited to sit at the right side of the king. Thálassa silently thanked the gods for his continued good fortune, and the accolades and blessings that had followed. He was a man at the pinnacle of his powers, self-confident in the way of men accustomed to accomplishing great things, forged by continually overcoming great adversity.

His parents had been prescient, bestowing upon him a name which meant *Calmer of the Seas.* The king had granted him command of the whole of the empire's navy, a fleet of impressive ships which kept routes open to those who wished to trade, and subdued those who didn't. They journeyed as far as the lands of Troy and Ithaca to the north, Sidon, Tyre, and Jaffa to the east, Memphis and Nubia to the south, and Etruria and Sardinia to the west. This was a seafaring people, their empire ever expanding. It was reaching out to the edges of the known world, and pushing its boundaries beyond it.

The pirates hidden along mainland coves and backwater islands had become an increasing menace to the free flow of goods. Thálassa had aggressively pursued them to their lairs and made bloody spectacles of their leaders, the wounded, and the weak. The slave markets were now bursting with young men with strong backs, and insolent but pleasing women for any need. There had even been a few poorer Atlanteans sprinkled in among them, but they were not to be pitied for their treachery, and very public examples of them had been made in the arena. Yet for the most part the captives were *Mycenaeans,* a hardy people who inhabited the rugged hinterlands along the edges of the empire. Proud and defiant, they were independent and unbowed, even in their bondage.

Thálassa had claimed an exquisite beauty from the last ravaged village who caught his eye for his own. Tall, raven haired, and graceful, she had stood out of the chaos and carnage with her quiet, unassuming dignity. She would soon need to learn her proper place among her betters. They were lessons he looked forward to administering over the course of the voyage that lay in front of him. When he would have the honor of escorting the king by galley to his magnificent palace at Knossos, on their island country of *Kríti.*

A buzz of anticipation started to ripple throughout the crowd. Thálassa shook off his reverie and focused on the floor of the arena directly in front of him, for this was the much-anticipated main event. The captive sacrifices, acrobats, boxers, and oiled wrestlers had all provided much amusement, and no small amount of coin had traded hands based on the results.

This was something he had never witnessed on so grand a stage, with so much spectacle, in front of royalty and the great king himself. Even in his own *spiti,* or home, he had an exquisite fresco on the wall depicting this most sacred of acts. It was the most majestic physical sport of all, the personification of what it meant to be Atlantean. The sacred leaping of the bull.

She was still in a daze, it had all happened so very quickly. It seemed just minutes before that she and *Demotimos* had wandered down out of the craggy hills to the small seaside village for market day, shyly holding hands. Her chores had been done quicker than usual, while he had left the goat herds to the care of his little brothers. Their young hearts were light with the promise of a few hours of not being directly under the stern gaze of the elders, and senses were aroused when they spied a copse of woods where they could briefly steal away on the walk back. Young love with a little freedom on a sunny day held the same promise in any time, in any place. It had been so long since they had been truly alone, without a prying parent or troublesome little sibling in tow. Even her father, Xenophon, had begrudgingly given his permission.

"Yes, yes, you may go. I wasn't always this old, you know," he had said, casting his wife a wistful glance. "Even I had a young heart once."

As the enamored couple arrived along the footpath to the outskirts of the coastal fishing village, they were greeted with a sudden flurry of activity. A heavily laden merchant ship was visible just offshore past the reefs, struggling to move in becalmed seas. The currents were inching it ever closer toward the reefs despite the best efforts of its crew.

Cletus, the chieftain of the seaside village, who never forsook an opportunity to benefit his people, rallied the fighting age men to pursue the wallowing prize for her goods. Any of their Mycenaean brethren on board would be freed, any other slaves confiscated, and the rest of the crew put to the sword and the ship put to the torch.

The reach of Atlantis was much feared, and no trace must be left of any depredations against their trade fleet. Experience had been a cruel teacher up and down the coasts, and Cletus was selective in what chances he took. Consequently, their community had quietly thrived, but not so much as to draw any unwanted attention. He was already thinking about where to sink the merchant ship, in deep water where the currents couldn't reach and leave a hard-to-explain charred hulk washed upon the shoreline. That would bring the wrath of the dreaded sea people upon them, something to be avoided at all costs.

Walking into the market square, she saw the vendors hurry to put their wares away, while men hustled about, bringing hidden stashes of arms rapidly to the waterfront. The biggest ship in the harbor was quickly prepared for battle. Men were leaping upon it, arms were stowed, the lines cast, and oars slung into their rungs. Cletus counted heads onboard and shouted to the shore. More men were needed.

Demotimos abruptly found himself grabbed firmly on each arm by two strong fishermen, who ran down the dock with him and jumped onto the drifting boat just before the distance became too great. Another two men behind them sprinted hard and leapt, but didn't make it and splashed short of the mark, to the jeers of those both onboard and ashore. The two dejectedly swam back while they were showered with fish bait and waste buckets from the dock above.

"Alright you sons of the sea, grab an oar, and stroke to the drum. Put your backs into it lads, we'll make men out of you. We'll celebrate before sundown with women and wine," Cletus roared from the prow, pointing his spear forward.

Thud went the first beat on the drum. "*Pull*," arose the cry from the throats of all, the rhythm repeating and building as these rugged men of the sea and their vessel slowly gained momentum, making a direct line to the struggling merchantman. There would be bonfires along the shoreline and much rejoicing tonight, the hard, austere lives of the seaside community and the surrounding hamlets made a little brighter by this unexpected gift of bounty from the sea.

Kallistra, whose name meant *Most Beautiful*, ran down to the docks with all the other women, caught up in the nervousness and excitement of an unexpected opportunity and hopes of easy plunder. When she looked around, she saw that the whole village had turned out. The very young were working their way forward between the legs of adults to catch a glimpse of the chase, while the elders collected on the shoreline and prayed to the gods for a favorable outcome.

Her love was aboard, he was fighting with the other men, even her father would have to be proud. Perhaps he would now see fit to allow her to be betrothed, now that Demotimos had proven himself and come of age. It was a prospect that made her heart flutter, and she became a little light headed. She held her breath, stood on her tiptoes on the well-worn planks of the dock, and soon joined the chanting of everyone around her and on the shoreline.

"Pull, pull, PULL!"

The distance between the ships closed. It wouldn't be long now. Perhaps the merchant ship would surrender peacefully, or the slaves aboard would overpower the crew and there would be little bloodshed. She found herself giddy at the prospect. Indeed fortune had smiled upon her this day. She lightly kissed the blue amulet of her people that hung on her neck to ward off evil.

Please, don't let any harm come to my beloved Demos, she fervently prayed.

Abruptly a groan went up from those with the best eyesight, they saw something no one else did, at least not yet. Kallistra looked around uncomprehending, those around her likewise unknowing. Cletus had instructed his men to ignore the merchant ship, and charge toward a new threat to the whole village, to their very way of life. An Atlantean galley was approaching from around a bend in the coastline, where it had lain in wait out of sight. It had all been an elaborate ruse, the merchant ship merely bait to test the loyalty of the coastal village. Alas, they had failed miserably and shown they harbored pirates with ill intent among them.

The groans abruptly turned to wailing as the Atlantean ship came into sharper focus. This was not a mere armed escort, common upon the trade routes to protect vulnerable merchant ships. No, this was one of their great fighting ships loaded with their dreaded bronze-clad warriors, masters of all the sea. A wise tribal elder surveyed the scene while the drama played out before him and anticipated the inevitable outcome. He scrambled from the shore and desperately climbed up a railing onto the dock, waving wildly to all those gathered.

He screamed for quiet, and trembling faces stopped their lamentations and looked to him for guidance. "People, listen to me. Listen! Cletus is taking the fight to them, but only to buy us time. He is making a sacrifice so that we may flee to the hills, to where they can't follow or find us. Gather your loved ones, run now children, run. You must survive and live to fight another day. Our men must not be sacrificed in vain!"

Kallistra stood there bewildered, the chaos of the scene overwhelming her, people rushing by, shoving hysterically, small children falling off the deep end of the dock, a stampede of humanity rushing through the village to the sharp hills and unforgiving highlands beyond. The feeblest of the elders sat where they were, resigned to their fate, with no desire to flee and start anew. Their entire lives had been made here; it was all they knew; it was all they would ever know. A few other women refused to leave. They would rather suffer the fate of their men than live empty lives without them. Had they been attuned to hear the muses whispering what the fates held for them, they most assuredly would have joined the headlong rush to sanctuary well away from the shore.

Kalli wandered aimlessly to the very end of the dock. She could see that the merchant vessel was now rowing directly toward them. Out past the reefs, the Atlantean galley was surging toward the ship that held her beloved Demos. The remaining elders sat quietly, chanting and praying, while the other women on the dock started pulling out their hair, scratching at their faces with sharp nails, and slashing at their breasts. She turned toward a woman she had known her whole life, a quizzical look asking why they defaced themselves in such a manner.

"You don't want to be taken looking like that," the woman replied, casting a glance at Kalli's young, blossoming figure. "Like ripe fruit, the most delectable is the first eaten."

Kalli involuntarily shuddered. She had dressed elegantly in the hope of seducing Demos on the walk home, not to escape the sea people. She stared at the impending collision far out in the harbor. The sound reached her a long moment after she saw it, her mind's eye not quite comprehending it. She squinted, the men of her village seemed to be putting up a good fight, perhaps there was some small hope they would prevail. She strained to see Demos, but all she could make out was a ragged volley of spears thrown by the villagers. Faintly, she could make out individuals standing and challenging the Atlanteans, bravely brandishing their swords high in the air.

Then she saw a bright flash of light. The dreaded sea warriors on the galley lowered their polished shields in unison. They stood and unleashed a precise volley with their long-tipped spears that wreaked terrible destruction. Not until after the shafts imbedded into wood and flesh and men toppled into the water did she hear their anguished cries. She watched in horror when grappling hooks were tossed and pulled their village ship in tight in a vicelike death grip, like the water spiders at the docks did to unsuspecting minnows. The Atlanteans formed and rushed aboard en masse, quickly dispatching all who offered resistance, and many who didn't.

In but a few minutes, all was quiet. The only sounds drifting across the waves were the shrieking cries of gulls, the snap of the whip, and the rhythmic stroking of the oars by slaves. When the decoy merchant ship neared the dock, the captain surveyed what spoils awaited them in the frantic little village by the sea.

CHAPTER 2

MAY 23, PRESENT DAY, YELLOWSTONE PARK

Nick had to admit, it was all pretty dazzling to him. His buddy, Eddie Sullivan, a Paleontologist, had lured him out of his winter funk to help with a dig. It was in Yellowstone National Park of all places, but it was not just any dig. This was a nearly complete adult Allosaurus. A unique find along the edges of Yellowstone, but not unheard of in greater Wyoming.

One hundred fifty million years ago he was big man on campus, Nick thought. *Thirty to forty feet long, maybe two tons. Damn glad I'm meeting him now and not then.*

He wiped at his brow and looked around. A nearby hot spring and geyser coated him in steam. It made the cold temperatures tolerable, but obscured his vision at times. Surrounding pine trees dripped water as the night ice melted from the warm vapors. Right down his neck.

Where the hell is Eddie now? Oh yeah, had to do his morning business. Off in the woods no doubt.

Nick tapped at the rock surrounding the imbedded dinosaur skull, then around a tooth. It flaked apart, allowing him to brush it away. The serrated, banana-shaped tooth of the alpha-predator came into focus. He rubbed it gently, amazed to be touching an instrument of death from the late Jurassic Age. His mind wandered, envisioning the land as it was then. Which, he realized here in Yellowstone among the hot pots and fumaroles, might not have been all that different.

"About time Ed," he said, hearing a sound behind him.

No reply, only the gurgling of the hot spring. Another sound, closer this time.

"Ok, funny guy. I'm busy here. Everything come out alright?"

A rustling sound approached him from directly behind. Intending to turn the tables, Nick jumped up and yelled.

"Boo knucklehead!"

Five feet away, staring right back at him through the steam, were two grizzly cubs.

Shit!

He gripped a trowel and coffee mug and slowly backed away. The cubs, curious, sniffed at the exposed Allosaurus bones. Smelling only rock, they looked up and started sniffing the air. The scent of breakfast on Nick's clothes smelled better. He started banging the trowel against the mug. They followed him anyway.

Not good. Not good. Where the hell is Eddie? I gotta warn him.

He kept backing up, while looking for the mother grizzly. She couldn't be far away. He hit the trowel harder against the mug. A root caught his boot, and he tumbled backwards, landing in a hot pool of water.

"Ed. Bear here! Eddie!"

He heard a loud huff, and saw her as she emerged through the steam like an apparition. Her massive head and clawed front feet showed first, then the bulk of her shoulders and front legs. The grizzly grunted loudly, swaying left and right while she looked for her cubs.

Nick scrambled to his feet and bumped into something. Their travel van, his sanctuary, was parked directly behind him. The two cubs scampered to either side of him as the mother made her charge. He turned and ran to the driver's door, fumbling with the handle. The footsteps of the massive animal reverberated closer and closer. She closed the distance with long, powerful strides.

"Look out!" he screamed, his sweaty hand slipping from the door handle.

Suddenly Eddie rushed up next to him, waving a can of bear spray back and forth, creating a wall of pepper-laced mist. The charging grizzly slowed, smelled the air, and came to a halt. She stood up, bellowing, as her two cubs ran off in back of her. She stared at Nick and Eddie, and roared defiantly at them.

Finally satisfied the threat wasn't following, she turned on all fours and ambled away.

Eddie put an arm around Nick, still panting from running down the hill.

"So, where's *your* can of bear spray, John Coulter?" he asked between gasps, invoking the name of the first white man to traverse Yellowstone.

"In the van," Nick replied sheepishly, looking at a wet spot in the crotch of his jeans

"Smart. Good safe place for it. In case a bear ever tries to ambush us from *inside* the van."

"You thanked them, right?" Nick asked.

"Absolutely. They open in a week anyway," Eddie replied. "They had no problem giving a couple of colleagues like us a room gratis. Besides, we were both a little ripe."

"Yeah. Nothing like a long hot shower."

"Hey, I thought bathing in the boiling river served us pretty well."

"It did, but don't use soap or shampoo in it, right? No pollutants allowed. I needed a good scrub down."

"No argument there my friend."

They sat on the terrace of the Old Faithful Inn, overlooking the famous geyser as the sun slowly set. There wasn't a soul in sight. They had been working the dig site near the Norris Geyser Basin for over two weeks, living out of the back of the van. A bed and shower were well overdue.

"Cheers man, thanks for asking me along," Nick said.

They clinked their insulated Yeti coffee mugs, now doubling as bourbon glasses.

"No problem. My student reinforcements don't arrive until after you vamoose. It's good to have the company. And the chance to catch up too."

They put their feet up and watched while Old Faithful gradually built up its pressure, then dazzled them with geothermal fireworks as if on cue. When the last of the steam drifted away and the sun winked out, a carpet of stars started to emerge in the velvety purple sky. Nick reached into his backpack and grabbed a bottle of local Wyoming Small Batch Bourbon Whiskey, and poured them both another generous dram.

"This is a timeless place to chase prehistory, isn't it? Pretty cool to here be in the middle of a caldera, drinking good bourbon," Eddie mused.

"Good thing your Allosaurus lies just outside the edge of it. Any closer, the eruptions would have erased it."

"Think we're due for another anytime soon?"

Nick took a long sip to contemplate. The surroundings, cool nighttime air, and the warmth trickling down his throat were an intoxicating combination. He sighed in contentment.

"Well, first off, this isn't just any caldera. It sits over a super volcano that is prone to massive eruptions. The next time it blows up, we'll share the fate of the dinosaurs."

"But not tonight?"

"Not tonight."

Eddie took a deep swig from his mug. "So then, what's the next quest for you?"

"You know, I honestly don't have a plan yet. Lots of ideas percolating, but nothing firm. We'll have to see."

It was time to vamoose back to home. To plot out his next move.

The wind blew gently, carrying the loon's haunting call down the lake toward him. He squinted as the mid-day sun cast shimmering diamonds off the waves. Nick leaned back in the Adirondack chair on the deck of the camp, putting his feet up comfortably on the railing. He took a long, slow sip of bourbon and contemplated life. Springtime always brought renewal, even to the far reaches of the upper peninsula of Northern Michigan. Despite having spent some time digging around Yellowstone, it had been a long winter. Nick's soul could use some renewing.

What historical enigma to unravel next, he wondered?

He felt the bourbon slowly warm him despite the cool evening air. Many mysteries had intrigued him since he had started to seriously contemplate his next expedition. The Treasure of the Templars, the Lost Legion of Rome, the Arc of the Covenant, the Lost Colony of Roanoke. They and many other possibilities swirled around his brain as he watched the sun ebb toward the horizon.

Less than a year ago he had solved a great archeological mystery with the discovery of a cave in Chaco Canyon containing a vast cultural treasure of the Aztecs. It included beautifully wrought gold and silver works, priceless codices documenting Aztec history, and even the mummy of the great Montezuma himself, adorned in a magnificent golden burial mask. It had all been taken out of Mexico before the Spanish could find and destroy it. The discovery had caused an international sensation. That had afforded Nick not just momentary fame, but also the connections and recognition to continue his quest to uncover further discoveries of what he deemed of historical significance. Those that rightfully belonged to all of mankind for their mutual enlightenment, and not hidden for the ages undiscovered, or ensconced in the private collections of vain, rich, and powerful men.

Maybe search for the Spanish Treasure Fleet of 1715? he pondered.

He had been fascinated with the lost fleet ever since he was just a kid. His parents had taken Nick and his brother Charlie to Florida once, to the Spanish fort at St. Augustine, then to the beaches around Stuart and Port St. Lucie, better known as the Treasure Coast. After a powerful storm had blown through and stirred up the approaches, their dad, Albert, chanced upon a Spanish piece of eight while they combed the beaches. Nick still had it, and the thrill of that find tugged at him. It would be fitting to the memory of his parents to search for those lost Spanish Galleons of long ago. But over time, several had been discovered, and he was looking for something less well known. Something in virgin archeological territory.

He closed his eyes and thought deeper. Usually, inspiration came to him when he obliquely thought about a complex problem, or when he wasn't thinking about it at all. Many an insight had come to Nick during a long, hot shower, or in the twilight of a dream, but that wasn't working for him now. It was time to force the issue. He finished the last of the bourbon and sat up. Time to get serious.

What about the Lost Tomb of Alexander the Great? That would certainly be a worthy project.

On its way to be interred in Macedon, Alexander's body had been highjacked by one of his own generals, Ptolemy I, who became ruler of Egypt after Alexander's death. Alexander had initially been buried in Memphis, and then moved to Alexandria. Over time the body was lost, with rumors speculating many possible locations. It was lost history of the highest order.

Hmm, maybe the lost Menorah from the Second Temple?

That was taken to Rome after the conquest of Jerusalem in 70 AD, carried in the triumph of Vespasian and Titus. The bas relief on the Arch of Titus in Rome, still standing, showed Roman soldiers carrying it away. It was displayed as a war trophy for centuries. But the menorah disappeared after the Vandals sacked Rome in 455 AD. An artifact of such significance, it became the symbol of Judaism since ancient times and was featured on the coat of arms of modern Israel. Its discovery would have a significant impact on both ancient history and current geopolitics.

How about Blackbeard's Treasure that has never been found?

It was rumored that Edward Teach, better known as Blackbeard, had hidden a massive cache of loot from his years of pirating the Caribbean and the Atlantic seaboard. There were clues that indicated it could be anywhere from the Chesapeake Bay to Ocracoke Island to the Caymans. The research and undersea aspect of it intrigued Nick. So did its distinctly colonial tint. He stood up and paced slowly along the porch to clarify his thoughts.

Perhaps the Treasure of the Inca?

That was an intriguing possibility that would tie in nicely with his recent Aztec and Mayan work. The Spanish conquistadors had pillaged Cuzco, but never found the vast bulk of priceless artifacts that had gone missing. They were rumored to be hidden in the mountains of Ecuador, possibly even dumped into a lake to safeguard them from the Spaniards. Many searches had been conducted, all coming up empty. That was a real prospect that Nick had a personal affinity for.

Ah, but what of everything the Nazi's had their far-reaching tentacles into?

With his grandfather having fought in WWII, Nick had developed an increasing fascination with the cultural heritage of various countries and whole peoples that had been expropriated by the Nazis. True, hidden mines containing stolen Holocaust artwork and priceless heirlooms had been discovered when the Allies rolled into Germany. And additional finds kept surfacing, even to the present day. But the priceless Amber Room stripped in its entirety from St. Petersburg, a treasure train that disappeared into thin air in the chaos of the end of the war, and submarines rumored to be carrying key personnel and bullion to South America to fund a future Fourth Reich, all had evaded discovery. Nothing was too fantastic when it came to Hitler and his henchmen, so who knew what else they had possibly taken? These were just the tip of the iceberg, and the more Nick learned, the more he was intrigued.

All things related to Nazi Germany were certainly a possibility, and it brought the added incentives of bringing him closer to the memory of his beloved grandfather. It might even deliver a measure of justice to the descendants of those who had been wronged. Retribution even, perhaps.

The problem was there was simply too much to shoot at, too

many things that fascinated him. If only he could find one that had the greatest odds of paying off. If only—

A buzz on his cell phone broke his contemplation. Nick looked at the caller ID and smiled. It was his good friend and college mentor, Dr. Storm.

"Hi Doc, what mischief are you up to now?" he inquired.

"Cheerio Nick, so good to hear your voice. I'm in Greece, at the port of Piraeus. Turns out part of an ancient ship building site was just discovered here. You know it was actually from here that their ships left for Salamis."

Nick immediately felt a twinge of jealousy. Dr. Storm was calling from Greece, of all places. He knew the history well, and could recite it chapter and verse.

"And the Greeks defeated Darius and the Persians in a great sea battle. Thus, Western civilization escaped being stillborn," Nick replied.

"Yes, yes, quite so. Well, I know you've been pondering your next project. It turns out there is much work to do here in a short time, what with sea levels slowly but steadily rising," Dr. Storm said, the excitement in his voice building. "Care to get your hands dirty with me uncovering a little ancient history?"

"Greece? For the summer?"

"Yes. And best of all, it looks like there is a perfectly preserved *trireme* buried under the silt."

"You serious?" Nick asked. "A chance to recover the ultimate weapon of the age?"

"You know, a whole one has never been found completely intact. Greece is going through very hard times right now. Think what this would do for their national pride." Dr. Storm knew Nick had a fondness for not just Greco-Roman history, but also a fascination of undersea exploration.

The offer caught Nick off guard. His mind had been immersed in the possibility of ancient mysteries all over the world. But not in the birthplace of the very concept of democracy. Not in Athens.

"When would you need me?"

"That's up to you. But yesterday would be fine," Dr. Storm replied, unconsciously humming while awaiting an answer.

"I don't know, sir. I've got some obligations that need clearing up. It's a pretty serious time commitment."

Nick wanted to add that he was hoping for a reconciliation with the love of his life, who had recently broken his heart. But that still cut a little too deep to share. Especially with someone he looked up to and admired as much as Dr. Storm.

"You wrote me that you were trying to find the next endeavor to devote your energies to. Here is one that not only fits your interests, but your skills," Dr. Storm said.

Nick sensed hesitancy from him, which was unusual. Dr. Storm was always one to articulate a well thought out argument in a very measured and reasoned way.

"I think this would be good for you Nick, in more ways than one."

"Where are you now?" Nick asked, trying to buy some time to wrestle with his conflicting thoughts. But already suspecting how this would end.

"On a lovely terrace overlooking the sea, having dinner with a dear old friend. You know, the Agean is simply enchanting at sunset."

Nick heard laughter in the background, and the clinking of glasses. Sounds of merriment and companionship, a direct contrast to his self-imposed exile in the cold isolation of upper Michigan.

"The discovery of the trireme aside, think of what this land offers," Dr. Storm continued. "The food, the wine, the people, the culture. There is much to admire and learn from here in Athens. And summer in the Aegean, well, there is simply nothing to compare it to."

"C'mon Doc, that's dirty pool. Just not fair."

"I'm not looking to be fair. I could really use you." Dr. Storm hummed for a moment more. "So, what say you, young man?"

Nick felt a rising surge of excitement. The sun winked out on the horizon and the evening air turned cold. He had been brainstorming his next potential endeavor, and in a bit of serendipity here was Dr. Storm offering him a golden opportunity. He well knew from prior experience that a project at an ancient crossroads like the Port of Piraeus might be but a window to other—possibly even greater—mysteries to unravel. And the lure of seeing his friend and the clear azure waters of the Aegean Sea was proving irresistible.

"I've got one thing I have to do first. But I'll do it on the way out. See you in a week Doc."

CHAPTER 3

1646 BC, ISLAND OF ATLANTIS

I t was such an important part of their culture that one could even see it in stars at night. The magnificent image of *Távros*, the sacred bull. Everywhere throughout the empire there were depictions of it, from massive stone horns large enough to ride between, to small figurines on a shelf or dangling from a simple necklace.

To the Atlanteans, the bull was the subject of veneration and worship, representing both the sun and the power of man over nature. The king's throne overlooking the arena sat between two such immense bull horns, signifying his relationship with the gods themselves, and his power over the peoples within the entire empire.

On the floor of the arena, the preliminaries had all been completed and the anticipation steadily building for the main event. Off to the side emerged the lithe figure of a young woman, who bowed her head to the king, and then moved with a cat-like grace toward the center of the ring. At the other end, a gate was thrust open, a whip cracking. Out sprang a black bull, disoriented and blinking hard in the bright sunlight, slowly focusing on the brightly clad figure dancing tauntingly in front of him. Dipping his head and pawing the ground, he leaned back, bellowed, and gathered his strength. Exploding in a frenzy of pent-up energy, his massive bulk launched at her.

She rocked gently on the very tips of her toes, the ground itself shaking harder the closer the bull approached. Dust rose in little tendrils before the great beast. Large clods of clay-like black dirt kicked up in its wake. The cheering crowd slowly went silent as everyone unconsciously held their breath, knowing the enormous head bowing down and waving its horns back and forth would surely impale then crush their helpless heroine.

She waited until the very last moment, the bull's head cocked so low one horn scratched the earth as he lunged upward to strike. Bending deeply, she sprang into the air, turning a somersault over the bull while the momentum of his charge took him well past the center of the arena. Confused, he looked around for her, as she bowed to each of the cardinal directions, then blew a kiss toward him.

With renewed fury the bull launched back at her, and again she waited until the very last moment. She deftly sidestepped him while swatting his hind quarter, to the laughter and amusement of the crowd. The antics continued until the bull exhausted himself. He was roped by teams of two men on opposite sides and led back out. The bull was not to be killed but instead honored, the crowd cheering for both their sacred symbol, and the athletic prowess of the young woman. She bowed deeply to the king, and made the ritualized veneration with the very soil of the floor of the arena. *I am of the earth and serve only you.*

Thálassa was spellbound by it all. He had seen the leaping of the bull performed before in smaller arenas, but never by a woman, and never quite so exquisitely. Even the normally stoic king himself couldn't suppress a slight smile of admiration. Sitting so close, Thálassa thought he caught more in the king's glance to her than mere admiration. Perhaps she would be discretely paying him a visit later.

As the cheering subsided, drums started thumping, signaling the final event was about to commence. Again, a brightly clad figure emerged into the arena, this time a tall young man, with sinewy muscles rippling beneath his taut, olive-colored skin. The gate at the far end was rattling hard, straining against its hinges. This bull needing no encouragement to venture out. Before the latch was even released, the gate burst open. An enormous white bull emerged, shaking his horns, bellowing deeply at the heavens, and pawing the ground.

Thálassa blinked his disbelieving eyes. This was the largest bull he had ever seen. The colossal beast's gaze locked onto the prancing figure before it, and leaned back before springing forward so forcefully Thálassa could feel the thudding reverberate through the stone bench upon which he sat.

Audible gasps throughout the arena could be heard. The bull hurtled forward with a speed that belied its great mass. Even the guards who stood in front of the king at ground level, fully shielded behind the stone wall encircling the arena floor, involuntarily shied away when it appeared that the mountain of flesh was headed directly at them. Instead, the young man immediately in its path bent low, and to the amazement of the crowd, reached out and grasped its horns. The bull, in its fury to gore him, violently thrust its head up. The man expertly used the leverage to leap above and perform a perfect somersault, landing softly on his feet. The bull's momentum took it directly in front of the king, where it stopped and stood, panting in all its majesty and bellowing in frustration.

Thálassa noticed the vibrations he had felt from the charging of the bull continued, even after it had stopped moving. Confused, he looked around and saw others similarly disconcerted, until he realized what was happening. It was an earth shake, an increasingly common occurrence on the island city. He glanced up at the towering mountain looming above them. Sacred *Mount Thíra*. Small clouds were coming from its very peak, almost like smoke signals from warning pyres in the time of war. The wind caught the smokey clouds, and when they drifted over the arena, small bits of whitish stone and ash began pattering down upon them. He knelt down and picked one up. It was surprisingly light and honeycombed, yet rock-hard to the touch. The bull started to run around wildly to avoid the rain of stone. The crowd started to murmur and then panic.

The king sighed and slowly stood, signaling for silence.

"It is but an omen from the gods," he said in a deep, firm voice that carried even to the far reaches of the arena. "They reveal themselves so we know they are watching us. They bless our victorious warriors with the warmth of their breath. Listen carefully to the wind, you can hear them whisper '*Long Live Atlantis*.'"

The clouds passed. The rain of stone slowed and then stopped. Those gathered talked and laughed nervously among themselves. Some started gathering a few small stones as mementos of the day and the celebration, then slowly made their way out of the arena.

Calmly walking down from his elevated throne, the king motioned for Thálassa to walk alongside. The king grasped his shoulder firmly.

"*Návarchos,*" he said, speaking to the admiral of his fleet and warriors. "Prepare the ships. We leave for Knossos at first light."

Thálassa bowed, hoping no damage had been done to the ships in the harbor. It was not unusual for the gods to make their presence known. In fact, it was so common lately that repairing cracks in the masonry and stone walls was not done immediately. Better to let the gods finish their earth shaking so the repairs could harden properly.

He looked down toward the great circular harbor from his vantage point on the hillside of Atlantis. Small fires were starting to break out.

The forges in the docks and the hearths in the shops must have tumbled, he thought.

Thálassa caught the first whiff of smoke smelling of burning wood, distinctly different from the acrid sulphur-like odor that was the breath of the gods. He hurriedly signaled his escort to form ranks, then raced down the hillside to ensure the fires didn't spread to the docks or the precious ships tied to them below.

"Gods, I implore you, protect the fleet," he prayed aloud, out of breath as they sprinted downward.

For he, more than anyone else alive, knew that if a truly great exhale of the gods from the mountaintop above was to befall Atlantis, the wooden ships below would be their only means of deliverance.

Kalli sat unmoving in the chamber, unsure what the fates held for her. After bathing her, a young slave girl methodically brushed her hair out, then trimmed the edges to match the style favored by Atlantean women. Dark kohl was applied around her eyes, and a mirror held to her face so she could approve. Kalli was startled, having never seen a mirror. The only reflection of her own image she had ever beheld was from gazing into ponds near her home, or the water pots she filled. She had never seen anything like this, so vivid and full of color. She couldn't suppress a smile as she stared at her own delicate features framed by thick curls of black hair, and felt at the smooth olive-colored skin of her face. It was all so unreal to her.

She tried to communicate with the girl, whose dark, nearly black skin, betrayed an abduction from a distant land. The slave spoke the language of the Atlanteans haltingly, she was still learning it. But Atlantean was very similar to that which Kalli's people spoke. When Kalli was able to finally make herself understood, the slave put a finger to her lips to only whisper.

Kalli pondered her predicament and sighed. She would never see her family again. Nor her love, Demos. If he had even survived when his ship was boarded.

What could have possibly become of him? Will I ever know?

She started sobbing, the tears running freely and ruining her eye make-up. The slave girl motioned her to be quiet and still, and patiently cleaned and reapplied it.

Kalli reflected back on her abduction. It had all been so disorienting, the brilliant bronze-clad soldiers spilling upon the shores of her little village, while she stood trembling on the dock. A man of rank saw her and pulled her aside, while other women were taken into bondage or abused at the whims of the rampaging warriors. Anyone not thought to make a worthy slave was immediately put to the sword. Only a few old women were left alive when the ships departed. They were spared not out of mercy, but to tell the tale and spread fear. A warning of what became of those who defied Atlantis and harbored pirates. And old women didn't breed. When Kalli had been rowed away, an image was burnt into her memory: that of the village going up in flames, smoke curling high in the air, carrion birds descending to feast upon the scattered bodies of her kinsfolk. An entire way of life lain waste.

The slave girl put a finger under Kalli's chin, bringing her back to the present. She made her look up, and seemed to glimpse into her very soul.

"You beautiful, you their color. Someone important take you. Be submissive, not proud." The slave pulled her clothing aside to reveal her back. "Proud bring pain, proud make scars."

Kalli looked away, about to burst into tears again. The slave grabbed her by both shoulders, and shook her with surprising strength.

"Be strong, you do this. Forget home now. Home dead for me, dead for you. You endure. Survive."

Kalli composed herself, managed a smile, and put the girl's hands in hers. There was a look of gratitude and an unspoken thank you on her lips.

Kalli felt her chair rock slightly, and thought she was being pulled closer by the slave girl. But her hands weren't on the chair, they were in hers. A cat that had been asleep in the corner awoke, growled, then darted out the door. A panicked flock of birds from the waterfront flew overhead, screeching loudly. A cup fell from the table near the window, as they looked at one another, confused.

The earth trembled, lightly at first, then with more force. Pottery fell and broke, chairs overturned, startled animals cried out. They instinctively ran out into the street, away from the pieces of rock and mortar falling off the facings of buildings. A small crowd gathered, no one knowing where was safe. Overseers appeared at intersections to ensure no slaves ran away in the chaos.

Where would I even run to? Kalli thought. *There is nowhere to go. This is all the land of my enemies.*

Small scattered cracks appeared in the street, noxious fumes seeping upward and assaulting their senses. The slave girl grabbed

Kalli's hand and pointed to the mountain overlooking Atlantis. A plume of smoke had arisen from it, which was drifting with the wind. Toward them, and the docks just below. Small bits of stone started hitting her upturned face, pattering down like hail. They started increasing in size, stinging when they hit. The crowd, which had been mostly silent in awe of the spectacle, began to panic. People started screaming, running aimlessly about. There was no escape from the increasing fumes or the pummeling of airborne stones. Fires broke out from unattended hearths and toppled lamps, adding to the confusion and turmoil.

The sharp crack of a whip instinctively made Kalli turn her head. The crowd parted, two columns of soldiers briskly trotting through, then pausing. An imposing looking man in their midst, dressed in impressive battle regalia, took charge. He called to the overseers, and directed the male slaves be formed into lines from the fountains to the fires. Clay vessels were found, and water was passed hand to hand to douse the flames.

Kalli recognized him, he was the very same leader of the armada that had streamed back to Atlantis, with her and the surviving villagers as bounty. She briefly caught his eye, and he bowed his head toward her. He then deployed a few men, shouted instructions, and led the rest of the soldiers down to the docks, to the great ships.

"Put your backs into it or I'll make an offering of you," a slave driver yelled, cracking his whip on a hapless man who had dropped a heavy, slippery pot of water. Kalli could make out most of his words, and the tone of his voice made the meaning perfectly clear. The line of slaves passing water pots fell into a rhythm. One by one the scattered fires were extinguished. After a few minutes, the cloud above dissipated and the stones stopped raining down. The male slaves were marched off, while the women slaves were herded together until their owners could come for them.

Toward dusk, Kalli and the young slave girl were claimed, taken back to the house, and put to work cleaning up. In the morning she was made to sit again, and her hair was tended to and make-up reapplied. She was puzzled why such attention was paid to her, until there was a knock and two soldiers entered. They handed the mistress of the house several coins, then beckoned Kalli to come with them. She arose hesitantly, unsure of what fate awaited her. The slave girl ran to her and hugged her, whispering into her ear.

"We survivors, you and I. We will meet again, in Elysian fields."

Kalli embraced her hard, trying to hold back the tears.

"Yes, someday. But not until we do great deeds to earn our entry."

Kalli was guided down the main thoroughfare to the crowded docks, and gazed at the massive ships around the harbor. They worked their way through gangs of slaves loading the ships with provisions and trade goods, soldiers shouting directions, gulls diving for scraps, a cacophony of noise around them. They stopped in front of the largest ship in the harbor, prominent due to the great flag bearing the symbols of Atlantis fluttering above it in the breeze. It was emblazoned with the horns of the sacred bull, and a double headed axe called the *labrys*. Kalli was led aboard by her escort. She heard whistles and catcalls, not realizing they were directed at her.

A figure emerged from the far side of the galley and all noise ceased. Men came to attention, the crowded deck parting as Kalli came across. The commander of the great fleet and the king's hand walked directly over to her, and put his arm out.

"My name is Thálassa. You will personally attend to me. Welcome aboard."

Xenophon had heard the news, not daring to believe his own ears. It just wasn't possible, for the wrath of the gods to strike so suddenly, with such a terrible fury. All across the shores, and up into the hills beyond, word had spread like wildfire. For days now an exodus of wretched humanity had trickled up the foot and goat paths to the highlands and mountains, beyond the easy reach of the Atlanteans. They came seeking succor or sanctuary from relatives, or any sympathetic stranger who would take pity. There were few young men among them, only a scattering of women, and the very young or old. Only those with enough strength left to escape made it this far.

What is true and what is exaggeration? he thought. *Everything I hear seems more fantastic with the retelling. Surely what they say is not possible. What has become of my daughter?*

He finally summoned his courage to face the inevitable. He bid his bereaved wife to stay, and wandered down the path toward the sea. Carefully working his way there, all he saw was the occasional straggler begging for food, or those who had forsaken hope and collapsed by the side. Long before he reached the shore, he was assaulted by the smell of putrid flesh and stale smoke drifting upward on the breeze. Flocks of carrion birds showed him the way, calling him onward with their cruel and vile voices. Circling and descending where he must go, but dared not.

He reached the top of a hillock overlooking the village and sea, surveying the scene spread before him through disbelieving eyes. There was nothing left, only an ugly black smudge where buildings and docks had once proudly stood. Carcasses of both man and beast lay strewn about, slowly being reclaimed by scavengers and the tides. Soon it would be as if the village had never been.

"What do you want from me?" he beseeched the gods. "What more can I do? I have made the proper offerings. I have been honorable," he implored. "She is innocent. Mercy upon her I beg of you. Mercy!"

Xenophon hung his head sobbing, lost in his grief. A wind gust made something briefly brush against his foot, and he glanced downward. He jumped back when bony fingers reached out from a body he thought dead, grasping at his sandal.

An ancient woman looked up at him through dead eyes, pecked away by the birds. Overcoming his revulsion, Xenophon knelt down and looked more closely at her. Feathers and sand clung to her matted hair, dried blood trailed from her mouth. Several dead birds lay about, necks broken, half eaten.

"Mercy? The gods know not," the old woman croaked through parched lips.

He gingerly cradled her head onto his lap, and gave her a drink from his water gourd. "I have to believe they do. That they saved my daughter for a better fate than this."

She pulled the gourd to her lips with her one good hand, and drank and drank.

"Perhaps," she wheezed. "But to those who brought this pestilence upon us, I pray vengeance."

Xenophon shook his head and composed himself. "Vengeance," he murmured. "I can't trouble the gods for that. I simply pray deliverance."

She dropped the gourd and grabbed his arm sharply, trying to pull him closer. Xenophon felt her whole body start to shudder with surprising strength. "May they reap," she desperately gasped, "what they sow." With that, she emitted a last fetid breath and went limp, her battered hand relinquishing its grip, falling lifeless to the ground.

He sat contemplating the old woman and the scene before him for a few minutes, musing at the cruelness of the fates. Finally, he tried to close her eyes, but found there were no eyelids to do so. Instead, he placed small stones on them, and carefully crossed her arms. He took his time, burying her where she lay, under a pile of heavy stones. Overlooking the village from whence she and her ancestors and descendants all came. To which none would ever return.

Finished, he slowly arose, dusted himself off, and walked down the winding path to the ruins by the seashore below. Past an ever-increasing number of rotting corpses. Hoping against hope he wouldn't find his daughter Kallistra among them.

CHAPTER 4

JUNE 3, PRESENT DAY, LAKE CHARLEVOIX, MICHIGAN

He didn't sleep well that night, his mind excitedly wandering in a dozen different directions. The joy of planning an impending trip had energized Nick out of his lethargy. He was always most productive when he had concrete goals laid out in front of him. Both professionally and personally. The professional side was now congealing; Greece and the promise of adventure was beckoning. But on the personal side, not so much.

In uncovering the treasure of the Aztecs the past year, he had also found the love of his life in the person of an enchanting Navajo medicine woman named Soba. She had lineage to Montezuma, was in fact his last direct descendent, and their budding romance had blossomed. So much so it had become the fodder for tabloids, despite their best efforts to stay out of the limelight.

Nick's older brother, Charlie, had sent him a clipping that called them the Queen of the Aztecs and the Rock Hound. Which had morphed disparagingly to the Princess and the Pebble. Of course, that was the new nickname Charlie had bestowed upon him. "My little brother, the Pebble." It was funny stuff—unless it was about you.

The glare of public scrutiny had done them no favors. Soba reflected on her hereditary roots and the wishes of her ancestors, who had made it known they wanted their descendants to carry on their blood line. Unblemished. That meant with Aztec blood. Not the suspected Irish, Scottish, and French mélange that coursed through Nick's veins. No lack of suiters of the proper pedigree had sought Soba's attention, which she ignored as she searched her soul, because underneath it all, she loved Nick. But their innocent, intimate relationship could now be viewed in supermarket checkout lines. All of which had brought upon the winter of Nick's discontent, now finally receding with the melting snow pack. And with visions of the clear blue waters of the Aegean Sea off of Athens.

Knowing he couldn't sleep, Nick finally admitted defeat and got up well before the dawn to make a pot of strong coffee.

May as well be productive. I always do my best work early anyway, he thought.

Nick wandered to his dad's old office, and absentmindedly spun a large, antique looking globe. It portrayed the world as it was known in 1600, the familiar creaking sound of it spinning transporting Nick back to the more innocent time of his childhood. A time when his parents were both still alive, when he didn't yet have blood on his hands.

Looking up, he stared at a large map on the wall, bristling like a porcupine. The laminated world map was full of color-coded push pins. Each was the germ of an idea of an unsolved mystery he might pursue, every color representing a different epoch of history. His geographical hit list, his future magnum opus. He leaned closer and touched the push pins dotting the Mediterranean, then specifically those around Greece. Nick's pulse quickened and he smiled to himself. Certainly no lack of possibilities there.

Pouring a cup of coffee, he absentmindedly turned on the TV for some background noise while he packed.

Greece, gonna be hot this time of year. Need light clothes, light colors. Extra pair of swim trunks. Hiking gear, and—

A news story caught Nick's attention. He stood and grinned, recognizing the voice of the interviewee.

"It is a very unique find, a sensational opportunity that we had the good fortune to come across. Frankly it could be considered one of the holy grails of archeology for all of ancient Greece," Dr.

34

Storm commented, standing behind a podium, looking extremely official.

Nick laughed out loud. If there was ever an angle to play to get a project funded, his mentor was the maestro. In archeology circles he was called the velvet hammer. A veneer of cordiality and sophistication that always got people and corporations to willingly open their wallets. Even when they hadn't intended to.

"Perhaps you could shed some light on the significance of this discovery to our audience," a pretty, young reporter asked in an outfit that seemed a little too revealing for this type of interview.

"Of course. We suspect it is a well-preserved trireme, over 2,500 years old. 'Tri' for the three tiers of rowers who propelled it. They were the dreadnoughts and battleships of their day, hard-hitting craft designed to ram, then board their opponents. It was found near the port of Piraeus. Simply remarkable that it still exists."

"Why was this one preserved when no others have ever been found?"

"Like much that has been added to the archeological record, it was largely by chance. Perfectly preserved Viking longboats have been discovered, but only because they were purposely buried in a funeral rite. But more importantly, were buried in conditions that preserved them, that kept the organic material they were comprised of from decaying. That is what happened here. A trireme was engulfed in sediment from some type of deluge. And it was exactly the right *type* of sediment. The sediment which in turn kept out the curse of all wooden ships, namely shipworms. As well as cocooning it from the degrading effects of salt water, oxygen, and sunlight."

Nick was spellbound and sat in front of the television, his pulse quickening. This was what awaited him, what he couldn't wait to get his fingernails dirty with.

"Fascinating, Professor. But surely a ship like this doesn't get created without a blueprint from something before it. Do you care to speculate on its lineage?"

Dr. Storm stroked the point of his neatly trimmed beard in contemplation. "Well, that is the million-dollar question, isn't it? We can tell from frescos around the edges of the Adriatic, and even on

Crete, that triremes evolved from other earlier designs. Perhaps it had Minoan roots, or do I dare say—"

Another figure edged into the picture and leaned over the microphones. "I want to add that we at Hellenic Industries are proud to be the principal sponsor for this remarkable discovery," said Drakos Kollas, an immaculately groomed Greek tycoon. His sharp suit, suave demeanor, and slicked back salt and pepper hair betrayed an aristocratic bearing. The scrolling text indicated he was President and Chairman of the Board.

"For it was from here, at the very birthplace and cradle of democracy, that triremes just like this set out to defend Greece against foreign enslavement. The battle of Salamis was a turning point for the very survival of Western democracy. I think we can say, without exaggeration, that this trireme is a symbol of the very freedoms all great democratic nations enjoy today. Thank you."

"Whew," Nick said out loud to himself. It wasn't often that Dr. Storm was upstaged, but obviously this sponsor, whoever the hell he was, wanted his money's worth. Dr. Storm had told him more than once, the sponsor is always right, even when he's wrong. The morale of the story being get whatever it was you were working on out of the ground, get it to safety, and get it preserved. Before time, elements, or looters erased the find from the historical record. There would always be plenty of time for the petty back-office politics to sort themselves out later.

What else was it that Dr. Storm said once in exasperation to a jostling room full of sponsors? Oh yeah. "We have met the enemy. And they are us."

Nick bought flight tickets online, loaded up his Kindle with relevant reading material for all the fly time he would have, fired off a couple of e-mails, and finished packing.

Locking up the camp, he spied his father's work boots, in the exact same place he had last used them. His dad, Albert, had passed over a year ago, and Nick still couldn't bring himself to move them. There was still a connection there, a presence, a visceral feeling of him sitting there and unlacing them. Try as he might, Nick found he wasn't ready to break the spell and let go quite yet.

There was only one tonic for the melancholy creeping back into his soul. Nick made his way over to the Horizonvue Nursing home, and peered in on his grandmother, Ingrid. Now 97 with a mind that drifted in and out of reality, she often mistook Nick for his father through the fog of her memory. Nick took it all in stride, frankly as a compliment, and had aways shared a special bond with her. She had a habit of looking in the other rooms late at night for her long-deceased husband. Nick leaned in and gave her a kiss on the forehead.

"Mémé, I've missed you. The nurses told me you've been wandering the halls again, causing mischief."

A smile formed on her lips at the sound of his voice, and her eyes slowly fluttered open.

"Albert, how kind of you to stop in. I was just talking with your father, you know. He's roamed off. You know how he is."

"I know. He always had a bit of wanderlust. I think that is where we all got it."

"Yes, always whisking me off exploring somewhere. Such lovely times. So much to see."

"That's why I stopped by Mémé. I'm off to Greece, to see a great discovery. I'll be excited to tell you all about it when I come back."

"That sounds so nice. I look forward to it," she said, her voice starting to fade. "Do be careful deary."

She sighed and closed her eyes as the smile faded.

Go back to dreams of Grandpa and Albert, and happy times of your youth Mémé, Nick thought. *Give them my love while you're there.*

Nick held her hand and kissed her forehead again. Then he was gone.

"Hey Charlie, how's the market doing?" Nick asked when his brother answered the door. He had driven south to see him at his house in the suburbs outside of Chicago before flying out.

"OK, you know, it has its ups and downs," Charlie replied with a sparkle in his eye. It was their standard joke since Charlie was a senior partner at a multi-billion-dollar hedge fund.

"Nice to see you Pebbles. How ya been doing?"

"Fine bro, good to know I can always count on you to keep me humble."

The brothers shared a hug, and Charlie led him in to the kitchen. The kids heard their favorite uncle and came screaming at him, followed by a bounding dog. Nick took a knee and braced for the impact. Six-year-old Julien and four-year-old Yvette tackled him, Nick letting them bowl him over. They jumped on top, giggling, as the dog licked his face.

"Alright you two little crumb snatchers, you both still ticklish?" Nick rolled over and administered a good tickling. They both squealed and wiggled with delight.

Charlie's wife laughed. "Great, just like you always do. Get them all riled up then give them back to me." Sophie worked as an RN on the maternity floor of a nearby hospital. All while keeping Charlie and their two little ones on the straight and narrow, no small accomplishment.

"Hey, that's my job, isn't it?" Nick asked, getting up and giving her a peck on the cheek and a hug.

"Well, it certainly is one you take most seriously," she replied, holding him tight for a moment. "Maybe someday you could bring your own little tribe by." She missed Charlie trying to give her a look, signaling don't go there.

Nick grinned.

"Hey, I've no secrets with you two. Soba and I are on the outs right now. Not sure where it will lead, maybe it's over. Only time will tell. But right now, I've got an adventure to chase."

Charlie sheepishly held up a tabloid magazine, with a picture of Soba and a very handsome Native American man. With an inset of Nick in sunglasses walking off somewhere. The headline read:

Aztec Princess Pregnant, Keeps Bloodline Pure.
Disconsolate Rock Hound in Rehab!

"Well, at least I'm glad to see you made it out of rehab," Charlie joked. "You had me worried, you know."

Nick shook his head. "Last week I was supposedly abducted by aliens. The same ones who helped construct Aztec pyramids and drew the Nazca lines in Peru."

"Should be fun to see what happens to you next week," Sophie said in a bubbly voice. "I can't wait to find out at the grocery store!"

Looking for attention, Julien and Yvette each grabbed one of Nick's legs and sat on his shoes. Nick put his arms out like Frankenstein's monster and started walking stiff legged. The dog wasn't to be outdone, and forced his way between Nick's legs, tail wagging hard.

"Hey, what did you two both decide to name this oversized fuzz ball?" Nick asked them.

"I was going to name him Nanook, but dad said there was only one of those," Julien said. "Then I wanted to call him Topaz, but he was the wrong color. Then—"

"Wolfie!" yelled Yvette, who looked at her uncle and howled. "Awoooo!"

Wolfie naturally joined in the chorus, then Julien too.

Sophie just shook her head. She looked at Nick, put two fingers to her eyes, then pointed at him. "Yup, get them all riled up and leave me holding the bag. I've got my eyes on you mister."

"So what time is the show?" Charlie asked, giving Nick an elbow.

"Bar tender told me around nine. Why, you got a hot date or something?"

"Nope, just want to make sure I get you to the airport on time."

Nick raised a highball of bourbon to his brother. "You get me there by midnight, I'm golden. Cheers bro."

The flight across the pond to Europe was a red eye, leaving in the middle of the night. It afforded the brothers a few hours to loosen up, and more importantly, to catch up.

"Cheers back at you. So, where the hell are you headed this time?" Charlie asked.

"I'm going to Greece for a bit. Good ol' Dr. Storm called. He has a project he invited me to join."

"Sounds like a good tonic. Go see some pretty babes on the beaches. Get your mind immersed in some other things," Charlie said helpfully. "Not a bad way to get away from the paparazzi either Pebbles." And from the heartache of Soba, but he wasn't about to go there.

"Yeah, babes and beaches doesn't sound too bad about now. I suspect it will involve a lot of diving, I haven't done that in a while."

"What are you hoping to find?"

"It's already been found. Now we have to get it out. It's an ancient ship, a Greek trireme."

Charlie finished his drink and looked at Nick. "What's so special about that?"

"One has never been found. And this one is pretty complete. I'm hoping it might inspire me on to something else in the process. You open one door, there is no telling where else it may lead."

"Ah, there it is. I knew there had to be an angle for you. Although Greece in and of itself doesn't sound too bad."

Nick caught the eye of the bar tender and put up two fingers. "There's so much history scattered around there, its incredible. Just waiting to be discovered. Modern techniques make it all more probable. Especially underwater."

"So why are you flying to Germany first? Just swapping planes?"

"Because I'm gonna—" Nick began, but the band came on stage and started into a rousing rendition of *After the Thrill is Gone*, before he could finish his answer. Conversation became impossible, and the two of them settled in for more bourbon and some good live blues.

When the set ended, the conversation resumed. But with a ringing in their ears.

"You know you're getting older when you like going out, but don't have to smell like an ashtray."

"Amen to that Chuckles. Just taking a shower after a bar used to gross me out. Now we just smell like booze."

Charlie smiled at Nick and raised his glass. "You know, Sophie likes when I have a little whiskey on my breath."

"Nothing I need to hear. And hell, you've got two rug rats already."

"Yeah, well your turn next, I'm done there." Charlie looked over at the recently vacated stage. "You know, if you had your guitar, you could have jammed with them."

"Maybe," Nick said. "But I don't think they wanted walk-ons tonight. Anyway, I didn't bring it with me. Maybe I should have, always a good ice breaker. Nothing like a guitar or a puppy."

Charlie was about to say a wisecrack, and thought better of it. Nick caught his look.

"I know, I know. Soba even got to keep the damn dog."

As the band came on for the second set, Nick checked his watch. "It's time." He tipped the bartender, and they worked their way out through the crowd.

"I've got a lead on something," Nick said as Charlie drove to the airport. There was little traffic this late at night, the sky to the south well illuminated by the glow of Chicago.

"What kind of lead?"

"A tenuous one. But I'm already heading to Greece, so this is just a quick stop on the way."

Charlie looked over at Nick, raising a quizzical eyebrow. "Well? Do tell."

"Toward the end of WWII, a lot of stuff was going missing. Important cultural heritage type of stuff. That the Nazis had looted from occupied countries. I'm meeting a colleague of mine who got interested in this, we're going to root around. Maybe get lucky and find a thread to tug on."

Charlie pulled up to the departure lane at O'Hare International Airport. They both got out and Nick grabbed his things. Charlie embraced him in a bear hug.

"Good luck little brother. With everything."

"Hey, you too. Give my best to Sophie and the kids. I'll be in touch."

"Sounds good. And for the love of Pete, see if you can stay out of trouble this time. I don't want to have to fly over there to bail your ass out again."

Nick looked back and winked. But he made no promises.

CHAPTER 5

1646 BC, ISLAND OF ATLANTIS

I delivered the slaves from the last nest of pirates to Akrotiri," Yidini said. "We made an example of one who was proving difficult. Left him overhanging the docks. A warning to the others."

"Well done," Thálassa replied to his loyal second in command. "You kept some for replacements, I trust?"

"Yes Admiral, they are being brought aboard now."

Yidini glanced over at the gangplank. Six imposing looking pirates were stumbling aboard bewilderedly, chains rattling between their feet and hands. They would provide fresh, strong backs for the demanding work of manning the oars. And fill the seats of those who could no longer go on.

Thálassa walked over to them, and withdrew a wide bladed bronze sword. It had been a gift from the king, when he had been granted command of all the fleets of the empire. He tightly grasped the beautiful golden handle, and put the razor-sharp point below the chin of one particularly handsome young rogue.

"This one is a little too pretty for the galley, don't you think Yidini?"

"He won't be pretty for long," Yidini said with a conspiratorial grin. "With those good looks, I am sure he will prove most popular with his fellows.

"Yes, I suspect he will," Thálassa replied. He edged his blade into the flesh ever so slightly. "It is good you left that message at Akrotiri. I heard the slaves there were getting a bit rebellious."

The pirate slave kept his head down, but dared to glance up with his eyes. Defiance burned within them.

Thálassa flicked his wrist, and left a long, shallow cut on the slave's neck. Soon to be a permanent scar, a reminder of his disrespect.

"Always best to nip their insolence in the bud. Before it turns into something more. Like bravery."

"Yes, always sir. Your orders?"

"We will spread that same message to those who haven't heard it, after we deliver the king."

"To Knossos then?"

Thálassa put a hand on Yidini's shoulder. "Yes, make ready to sail to Kríti. King Mínōs is most anxious to get back to his family."

Yidini thumped his heart with a fist in a sharp salute, bowed, and strode off shouting orders.

Yes, the king will soon be aboard. Best to prepare and make sure all is in perfect readiness, Thálassa thought. *Time to dispense my orders.*

He left his flag ship, and spent the whole morning walking the docks with his escorts, visiting each ship in turn. He could have directed the captains to visit him, to make them show their fealty, but that wasn't his leadership style. He wanted to be among his men, see the conditions they lived in, gauge their morale. He made public showings of dispensing praise where rightly deserved, aspiring others to earn such acclaim in front of their fellows. After all, he had been one of them, had earned his position by merit alone. The power he held was an enticement to them all. Hard work and loyalty had its rewards.

One by one he met with the captains of all the ships in the vast harbor, and gave each explicit instruction. Four ships would accompany his on the voyage southward to Kríti. While protection wasn't needed given the recent actions against the pirates, he was taking no chances with his royal charge. Certain ships were designated to take trade goods and slaves to preassigned ports around the empire. They would also demonstrate what became of those who defied the king, and leave conspicuous reminders in their wake. The remainder of the ships would refit in port, and then rotate out.

All was to be action, constant motion, the great fleet projecting the power of the empire across the waves. Trade was the lifeblood of the Atlanteans, from the massive land of Kríti, to the strategically located island of Atlantis in the middle of the Great Sea, to all the lands on the outer edges of the empire and islands in between. In a maritime power you were either at sea, preparing to be at sea, or at the bottom of the sea. Thálassa would accept nothing less, and every captain knew it.

The hand of the king rubbed his temples, there was something he was forgetting. He had done all he could to prepare, his orders had been communicated. It was all now up to others to execute his plans.

Ah yes, that pretty young slave. Time to have a closer look.

He walked back to his flag ship, the crew scurrying about to prepare for the arrival of the king. Lesser royalty and nobles were being disbursed among the other vessels. Thálassa had no desire to hear any of their petty squabbling. When he was to talk strategy with the king, he wanted no untoward distractions.

Ah, there she is, standing at the far back. Looking out to sea. To her home-land, no doubt, he thought.

He made his way briskly toward her, the crowd parting, men smartly saluting with their hand to their heart and bowing.

The soft morning light bathed her in its glow. Her figure was sublime, her olive skin unblemished, her dark curly hair waving in the breeze. Thálassa was a hard man, but a fair one, he believed. He was not easily moved by emotions, had found them an encumbrance to his duties. Emotions were a useless distraction, just look at the nobles. But this creature, there was something about her. Her inno-cence, the way she carried herself, the confidence despite her tender years. Something pure, almost divine.

"What shall I call you?" he asked, startling her.

She turned and looked at him through large, deep brown eyes that had been holding back tears. Luminous eyes that looked deeply into the beholder.

"I have been known as Kallistra my whole life. Is it to be any different now?"

"No, I think not. It is a good name," he replied.

She waited for him to say more, but he was silent. He gazed at her approvingly, then grasped the railing and looked out to sea. The noise of the crew and activity of the ship distracted her, but she could tell it was a cacophony of noise well familiar to him. Kalli mustered her courage to speak.

"What is to be expected of me?" she asked.

"You will serve me," Thálassa answered. He wasn't looking for her approval. He was simply stating the reality of her new situation. He looked back at her, and saw the uncertainty in her eyes.

"And me alone. This doesn't have to be unpleasant. Frankly, most would give anything to be in your position."

She pondered that, and remembered her conversation with the slave girl who had tended to her. Better to drift with the tide than swim against it. The fates cared not for the struggles of mere mortals.

"Have you a wife, other mistresses?"

"Ha, aren't you the bold one. But since you ask directly, I will answer the same," he replied, sizing her up. "I have no wife, no time for family, only duty. The sea will always be my only mistress."

Kalli turned to face him fully. "Then what is to become of me?"

"Of that, only time will tell."

A warrior blew into a horn from atop the mast of Thálassa's flag ship.

"*Prosochí!*" Yidini called out from the deck. All aboard quickly came to attention.

An honor guard stood on either side of the gangplank, their burnished bronze shields, helmets, and spear points sparkling brightly in the sunlight. King Mínōs proudly strode aboard, nodding at those captains he recognized. Rusa, an old, trusted advisor, followed humbly in his wake. Servants and slaves with burgeoning chests of goods trailed them. Thálassa awaited the king, touched his own forehead and lips when their eyes met, then bowed slightly. The king grasped his forearm in greeting, then walked toward the stern, facing out to sea. Away from prying ears and wagging tongues.

"All is in readiness to depart, my King," Thálassa advised.

"That is good," the king replied to his trusted admiral and confidant. "The gods are restless here. They rumble, then go quiet. Then rumble yet again. It is quite strange."

"We have heard it often enough before," Thálassa said. "From Pylos to Thíra to Milatos. And many islands between."

"True, but it still concerns me. This seems more . . ." His voice trailed off. He was lost in deep thought. "More ominous. I met with the high priestess this morning and made offerings"

"Of the omens. What did they say?" Thálassa asked. He knew from personal experience they could be unerringly accurate in telling what the fates held for them. Or frustratingly obscure.

"They were neither good nor bad. But we are not about to do battle, are we? Only to take a short voyage. Let's see if the gods rest a little calmer back on Kríti."

The king gazed into the distance and noticed the four other galley ships already out beyond the harbor, awaiting them. He gave a knowing look of approval to Thálassa.

The lines were cast, and once the ship drifted far enough away from the dock, the galley slaves pushed their oars out the sides and slipped them into rungs. With the thump of a drum, all the oars were raised in readiness, except for several manned by the newest slaves. A sharp crack of the whip quickly brought those into line. Another thud on the drum indicated stroke, and the oars dipped in unison. Slowly, the ship gained momentum and worked its way out of the port.

As the awaiting galleys circled and formed a protective cordon around the flag ship, each hoisted its sail. The winds were favorable, the breath of the gods pushing them on their journey. Onward they went, passing through the harbor entrance to the great sea beyond their sacred city. Atlantis, lying majestically on the lower slope of Mount Thíra, slowly receded from view.

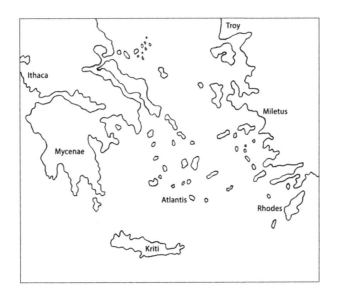

The ships settled into a comfortable rhythm, the cadence of the drum relaxed, the wind taking much of the strain off the galley slaves. The mood was light, the banter among the slaves between strokes teasing.

"The slivers plague me," one of the new slaves muttered under his breath, his hands bleeding and raw.

"Master take this wretch off the oar," a grizzled slave behind him jeered, pulling an oar to his chest. "He isn't used to such toil."

"His soft hands are meant for a different kind of stroking," another across from him mocked between strokes. "Meet with me later, lad!"

A well-muscled slave with a scarred back grunted knowingly from his bench. "Just wait you worthless she-goats." Stroke. "Until there is a battle to be won." Stroke. "When we have to catch another ship." Stroke. "Your heart feels it will burst." Stroke. "And it will." He laughed disdainfully. "It will."

There were no islands between Atlantis and Kríti, so the route they took was almost due south. Half a day out of port, a slight smell wafted on the breeze toward them. They paid no attention to it, the seas around Atlantis often gave off strange odors. They progressed further, the smell becoming stronger, assaulting their senses. It reeked of rotten eggs, much like the yellow powder found around foul vents in the earth. At the gateways to the other world. As they glided further along, the smell became nearly overpowering, mixing with the scent of death and decay.

Thálassa and the king stood at the prow, and watched the water carefully for signs. They passed over a stretch of increasingly foamy water, bubbles rising from the depths. The stench seemed to arise from them.

As they journeyed onward, the oars started hitting an occasional fish floating dead upon the surface. Soon the oars couldn't avoid hitting the filth of numerous rotted fish. They passed through hundreds, then thousands, and finally found themselves entrapped in a vast floating carpet of death. Thálassa signaled to Yidini, who ordered the cadence of the drum quickened. The other ships quickly followed suit.

"What manner of games do the gods play?" King Mínōs muttered, staring at dolphins and whales bobbing belly up within the putrid morass. Even massive squids from the greatest depths had arisen. Bloated with air, their bodies revealed themselves to carrion birds, their tangled tentacles providing favored perches.

"They warn us. But of what, I know not," Rusa said, wandering over to join them.

Thálassa held his tongue. He had passed through dead zones before, but they had been small, the fish scattered. In all his many travels upon the sea, he had never witnessed anything as vast as this. And he knew of no living mortal who had crossed the seas more than he.

The slaves stroked harder, not just in keeping with the beating of the kettle drum, but out of their own increasing fear. Viscera hung from their oars when they withdrew them from the water, the congealing mass so dense it was like rowing through sand.

Have we left the Great Sea behind? Are we now entering the very underworld itself? Thálassa thought.

Men started coughing and gagging from the unrelenting stench. The warriors could at least lean over the railing to empty their stomachs, while the slaves were forced to heave upon themselves. The whip cracked ever faster, blending with the cadence of the drum. Warriors started praying to the gods aloud, slaves pulled against their shackles, trying to leave their benches.

A breakdown of discipline would leave them floundering helplessly. Panic was on the cusp of overtaking them all, the songs of the sirens of the sea proving irresistible.

Thálassa sensed the breaking point, and climbed atop the very prow. A figurehead jutted out from there, the carved head of a bull. With one arm he grabbed it for balance, and raised his sword with his other. He spied Kallistra huddled fearfully against the mast, then looked at his warriors.

"Men of Atlantis, fear not. Have you not eaten today? The gods are merely showing us what we can harvest for dinner," he shouted, then laughed for them all to hear. He gripped the bull harder for balance. "For you alone are the masters of these seas!"

The warriors stopped their mutterings and stood a little taller. The captains started banging their shields with their swords, their men following suit. Even the slaves started gaining resolve, and the whip fell silent. The thud of the drum, the rapping of the shields, and the chants of the slaves synchronized. Nothing, in this world or the next, was going to stop them. Not with their king aboard, not without a fight. Not on *their* seas.

The king looked up at him and nodded, a knowing look of approval. He had chosen his commander well, a true leader of men. One who shined when it was darkest, one that men would rally to. He grasped Thálassa's arm when he stepped down. They would see this through together, whatever the outcome.

The rowing continued, a little progress starting to be made. Slowly the wind shifted. The heaviness of the smell started to dissipate. It was like a fog was lifting, though there was none to be seen. The quagmire of dead flesh beneath the oars began disintegrating into clots. The oars more easily broke through to the surface to gain purchase. Encouraged, the galley slaves on all the ships began to provide more power, propelling each forward more quickly. The clots became individual fish again, the foam fading to bubbles. As suddenly as they had entered into the vast floating carpet of death, so too they emerged from it.

Thálassa nodded to Yidini. He barked an order, which was repeated, and the oars came out of the water, then slid back into the ship. The slaves slumped at their seats, exhausted. The sail fluttered then filled, they could rest and regain their strength.

The king motioned to Thálassa and Rusa. They worked their way back to the stern. The warriors gathered there scattered elsewhere, affording them some privacy. They looked back at what they had traveled through, now only visible in the distance by the birds circling above it.

"Ever before in your travels?" the king asked.

"Never like that. Never that large or dense," Thálassa replied, pondering for a moment. "Certainly not with all those beasts within it."

The king started pacing in a small circle. "It is a sign. It has to be. Something momentous will occur soon."

Thálassa made no reply. He knew the king valued his counsel, perhaps above all others. It was preciously because he was a good listener. He only proffered advice when he felt he had something worthy to add. Not like the preening nobles trying to gain notice or favor.

"Offerings must be made. Significant ones," Rusa advised.

Thálassa grunted in agreement. He had grown to trust the advice Rusa offered, and would often seek his counsel. Rusa had the wisdom of many years, and had loyally served several kings.

"The fleet pursued pirates to the edges of the empire. Any indication there might be trouble brewing there? In Troy, Jaffa, or Etruria?" the king asked.

"Our trade relations are good. Delegations are coming, tribute has been received. Sidon, Tyre and Memphis are all quiet. Nubia too," Thálassa replied. "There is only one that ever worries me."

"Mycenae?"

"Yes, my King."

Thálassa raised an arm, and caught the eye of Yidini near the bow, who trotted back to join them. Yidini bowed before the king, and kept his eyes cast downward.

"Tell our king what you heard when you were chasing pirates to the north. Tell what you learned of Mycenae," Thálassa instructed.

King Mínōs tapped Yidini on the shoulder, giving him leave to stand and address him.

"We captured many pirates of Mycenaean blood. When we put the leaders under duress, we learned they were looking to do more than simply plunder," Yidini disclosed.

"How so?" the king asked.

"By organizing. Soldiers had circulated among their scattered villages, inciting and recruiting. To eliminate where they traded with us, to put our people to the sword. To gain back territory." Yidini paused. He didn't want to ramble.

The king looked to Thálassa. "You agree with this assessment?"

"His word is as mine. I have heard the same from other captains, and our spies there. I would counsel we send delegates to negotiate the peace, while we prepare for war."

The king dismissed Yidini, then rubbed his chin in contemplation. He slowly paced about.

"I believe the omens, that something of significance will soon be upon us. Let us take action rather than react to the whims of the fates. I will prepare the delegation when I get to Knossos. If nothing else, that should buy us a little time. You, Admiral, you prepare the fist."

Kalli sat huddled by the mast, terrified of what was unfolding around her. Nothing from her upbringing had ever prepared her for anything like this. Not even the worst of the tales and myths of the Mycenaeans. Stuck in a sea blanketed with creatures alive and dead, which surely smelled of the underworld, she felt the urge to wretch, tried to stifle it, but couldn't. Her bile mingled with every other odor wafting about them, absorbed by its awfulness.

She closed her eyes tightly and rubbed the pendant of her people. It hung by a string around her neck, hidden under her tunic. It was of a blue eye, meant to ward off evil spirits. She thought perhaps she should have brought a bigger pendant, and shook her head at the absurdity of her thoughts.

Then she beheld Thálassa. He stood above them all, calm in the chaos, holding a sword aloft. Their eyes met for a brief moment, and he shouted encouragement to all aboard, even the slaves. She saw the men rally to him, was transfixed at the magnetism of him, the *power* of him. The power to bend others to his will. The power to get them out of this crisis, to save his king. He wasn't of her people, was their enemy even, but she saw him for what he was. A great leader of men.

Be a willow, bend in the breeze. She pictured the face of the slave girl. *You can do this. Endure. Survive.* She looked back at Thálassa. *It need not be unpleasant*, he had said. *Most would give anything to be in your position.* She knew not where they were going, what pain and humiliation she would have to suffer, nor what the fates held for her. But she could make this work, *would* make it work, perhaps even to her advantage. And Thálassa, perhaps he might even be kind to her. It was decided then, in the midst of fear and misery unlike any she had ever known. She resolved in her mind to stay alive. To carry on her part of the bloodline of her forefathers. Whatever the costs.

As the ships slowly emerged from the chaos of the polluted seas, Kalli regained her composure. The mood on board had changed, the spell had been broken. She could sense it. The men looked approvingly at Thálassa, his words had provided encouragement and girded their courage when it was needed most. She also noticed he was in the good graces of the king, who seemed to seek his advice and trust his council. Truly he was a respected man, in a most powerful of positions.

The seas soon cleared completely, the smells dissipating to the heavens, the death and decay to the depths. Lighthearted and embarrassed laughter could be heard, even among the slaves. The oars were pulled in, and they began to move by sail alone. Pots were filled with drinking water, which servants first brought to the warriors, then to the exhausted slaves. Without being asked, Kalli picked a pot up and started passing it to the nearest slaves, shackled to the benches. Each took it from her, drank deeply, and returned it with a nod or smile of thanks.

She noticed the newest slaves were the most fatigued, being unused to these exertions. She eventually came to one slumped over his oar, who reached up with bloody hands without looking at her. He drank with greed, his eyes swollen shut from sunburn and the spray of salt water. He held the nearly empty pot back up, which she reached for with trembling hands.

Surely it can't possibly be. Why would the gods torment me so?

She nearly dropped the pot, and caught it within the folds of her tunic. She looked more closely, was about to say something, to reach down. Kalli glanced up and saw a captain staring at her, motioning for her to move along. He was looking at her with narrowed eyes and pursed lips. Was that suspicion or was it her imagination?

She held the pot carefully with both hands, moved to the next slave, and passed it to him. Without raising her head, she turned her back toward the captain, and looked up with only her eyes. At the poor soul chained to a bench, picking splinters from his hands, panting with exhaustion. At the innocent young man she had walked hand in hand with, down from the hills on market day, to the little village nestled by the sea.

At Demos.

CHAPTER 6

JUNE 6, PRESENT DAY, HAMBURG, GERMANY

The flight was so smooth Nick didn't realize they had landed at the Hamburg Airport until an attractive Lufthansa flight attendant gently nudged him awake.

"Willkommen zu Deutschland, sir."

"Danke Frau," was all Nick could manage to reply. He sat up blinking, trying to get his wits together. He had done research on the flight, until the urge to sleep overpowered him. It took him a moment to focus on where he was, to get his head around the new time zone.

Its 2 p.m. local time. I must have slept for a good four or five hours, Nick thought. *Time to meet Heinie.*

Walking out of the terminal, he made a quick call, and saw a man at the far end leaning against a car check his phone. Heinrich Schmidt's head was on a swivel before locking eyes with Nick. He smiled and waved when Nick began to walk toward him.

Nick and Heinrich had first met at UPenn, when they were both working on their masters in Historical Research & Methodology. The rock hound from Michigan and the German intellectual made an unlikely pairing, yet became close friends. About the same age, they shared a deep passion in how new technologies allowed ever more archeological discoveries to come to light across the world. They had kept in touch over the years, both interested in each other's personal and professional lives. Despite their common education, their careers had taken distinctly different paths.

The passenger loading zone was busy, so Nick quickly threw his things into the opened trunk of the Mercedes and ducked into the front seat.

"Heinrich, it's been too long," he said, giving a hearty handshake.

"Gut to see you too. You know, sie don't look anything like the tabloids portray you."

"Yeah, my brother was just telling me the same thing. Call it the curse of the Aztecs. Bring me up to date man. Your last message got me all excited."

Heinrich pulled into the traffic and drove out of Hamburg and headed northwest, toward the coast of the North Sea. Toward Cuxhaven.

"I've been working for the *Ministerium für Vermisste Soldaten*, you know, the Ministry for Missing Soldiers."

"So your career took you from archeology to forensics?"

"More like detective research than forensics. The scientific methodology I lernen prove most useful. The ministry recruited me, and I love the job. I get to bring closure to a lot of grieving relatives."

"You sound like a good German patriot."

"Ja, I like to think so. There were many gut Germans who died defending the Fatherland. Not everyone who fought was Nazi. That damn war consumed gut people from all sides."

"Sounds like rewarding work Heinie. I suspect you aren't the most popular person when you go looking out of country."

"Funny you say that. Our focus the last few years has been fate of German POWs in Russia. They took over 3 million prisoner, and 1.3 million are still unaccounted for."

Nick's mouth involuntarily hung open. "I had no idea there were that many."

"Most don't. The scale of the war on eastern front dwarfed everywhere else. It was massive. And horrific."

Nick pondered that for a moment. "Maybe it's a good thing

styles, incongruent yet perfectly charming. When they came around a bend, the Acropolis came sharply into view, dominating the city from its majestic perch even now. The classical grandeur of it—with Mount Lycabettus hovering in the background—hadn't changed in over 2,500 years.

The normally thirty-minute drive took over an hour. It didn't matter. Nick was utterly entranced.

"Time is of the essence. Now that we know exactly where the trireme lies, the clock works against us. It's cutting through the damn bureaucracy, not the excavation, that is daunting," Dr. Storm explained.

"I saw the site is near shipping lanes into the port. Is that the issue?"

"It's one of them. It sits to the north side of the port, where fortunately there is less marine traffic. If we can just get the go ahead, then tides and waves become the real enemy."

"So what are we talking, high to low variance?" Nick asked.

"About three feet plus waves. Ten feet to be safe."

"Whew," Nick whistled. "That will make for one hell of a coffer dam."

"Yes, it will. And when you allow for how far you have to drive in the pilings, potential storm surge, and water depth, you're talking nearly thirty feet. The materials have already been spec'd out."

"You were always the optimist Doc. What's the game plan?"

"First, map out the exact area to the inch and document everything. Second, build the retaining wall to keep the waters out. Third, pump it dry. Fourth, excavate. After all that, the real work of preservation begins."

"Why do I have a funny feeling I'm on map detail?"

"Because I need someone with the experience to get in there to document it accurately. To get us the exact coordinates, record it in situ, and grid it all out."

"I'm your man Doc. I've got a sneaking suspicion you're putting some pressure on the local authorities to get this rolling. You didn't perhaps leak anything to the press, did you?"

Dr. Storm smirked. "I can neither confirm nor deny. But

evidently word did get out. And once it did, I was interviewed on some of the local stations. Which were picked up by the international news services."

"I do believe I saw the famous Dr. Storm on a telecast back stateside," Nick jabbed. "Something about a symbol of Greece's glorious past, perhaps from their famous victory over the Persians, having just recently been found. An unprecedented discovery. Or so this supposed oracle of knowledge had said."

"Well, one thing I can tell you for certain young man. The city here is absolutely buzzing about it."

The hotel near the port appeared to be more like a hostel, with small rooms and cramped, shared spaces. It was chosen for its location, not its amenities, and was commonly used by transient maritime workers. After Nick dropped his things off, Dr. Storm walked him over to a nearby bar and restaurant to meet the team.

"*Kali spera*," Dr. Storm said in greetings to the assembled team. "Good afternoon. This is Nick LaBounty. Nick is going to help us document the site before we begin to excavate."

"If we ever get permission," a well-groomed older man in a tailored suit joked, extending a hand to Nick. "Stavros Nomikos, most pleased to meet you. I'm the resident head of antiquities at the National Archaeological Museum of Athens."

Nick shook his hand, and looked at the others sitting around the table. They were all drinking *ouzo*, the licorice-flavored liquor favored by Greeks.

One nodded to Nick. "Dimitris. Marine engineer."

"Yiannis," said another. "Jack of all trades."

"And master of none," cackled a grizzled mariner. "Giorgos, Marine Archeologist. At your service."

Nick spied a row of shot glasses and helped himself to one. "Pleased to meet you gentlemen. I look forward to our mutual success," he said, raising a glass in toast. "Cheers."

"*Ya mas,*" came a chorus of replies.

"Ya mas," replied Nick. He smiled inwardly. He could already tell this was a rowdy crew. Their ethos was work hard, play hard. He was going to fit right in.

The next morning started early, with a hearty breakfast of cold meats, olives, cheese, yogurt, and honey. Nick loaded up his plate, hoping it would take the edge off of all the ouzo. He wandered over to where Stavros and Dr. Storm sat, at a table with a little privacy off to one side.

"Really Philip, everyone thinks I was the one to leak it. Not that I shouldn't have," Stavros said.

"Ah Nick, please join us," Dr. Storm said, looking up and pulling out a chair. "Sometimes one has to discretely grease the wheels of bureaucracy my friend. There is simply too much traffic above the site to risk letting it sit another year. Too much of a chance of damage."

"What if the exact location got out? It would be looted before anyone even had a chance to protect it," Nick added.

Stavros put his hands up in mock surrender. "I don't disagree. Yet it puts me in an awkward position." He gave a grin. "But certainly nothing I can't handle."

Dr. Storm pushed his plate away and sat back. "Nick, you and Giorgos are going to dive the site today. Once we anchor, our secret will be out. There will be eyes all over the port looking for any diving anywhere near it."

"So how will we safeguard the site when we leave it?" Nick asked.

"I've taken care of that. We knew this eventuality would happen," Stavros said. "I've been working with the harbor *Astynomía,* how you say, Police."

"I noticed they became a whole lot more cooperative once Kollas got involved," Dr. Storm quipped.

Nick looked up from his meal. "Why does that name ring a bell?"

Stavros leaned in toward Nick and lowered his voice. "Ah, Drakos Kollas. Yes. A big name here in Greece. In the world, actually. A very wealthy industrialist, very influential in Greek politics. A Greek Nationalist, perhaps one of our best-known patriots. But not without his own controversies."

"Now I remember, I think I saw him in a newscast. Was he the one who grabbed the mic from you Doc?" Nick asked.

Dr. Storm shook his head, obviously not used to being upstaged. "Yes, that was him. He is the principal sponsor of this whole under-taking. No worries. I can always work with anyone."

"You used to say you would kiss a fat man's ass if he would sponsor a dig. Sounds like it's time to pucker up Doc." Nick laughed.

The ride out to the wreck site was smooth, except for the waves from passing cargo ships and ferries. Giorgos sat next to Nick, discussing how they would handle the upcoming dive. Dimitris piloted their well-worn research vessel, the *Poseidon*, while Yiannis prepared the dive gear. Dr. Storm and Stavros carefully watched the depth finder and sonar screen. They needed to get back to the exact coordinates, which meant fighting currents while keeping an eye out for maritime traffic. They needn't have worried. Dimitris was a seasoned hand with a deft touch.

"It was just blind luck we even found it," Giorgos excitedly told Nick. "No one was looking for it, wood never lasts this long. How do you say? Perfect conditions."

"So what turned it up?"

"Prop wash."

"Really? You're kidding. Right here? I figured this area had to have been extensively searched time and again, given the history."

Giorgos stroked his stubbled chin in contemplation. "It was. But the seas have been steadily rising over the years. The shore erosion has been creeping uphill. That recently exposed the ancient ship sheds."

"You mean the ones that housed triremes? Where they worked on them?"

"One and the same. The discovery of those led to a closer look in the harbor. The marine traffic here has grown, bigger ships, deeper drafts. The trireme we found was buried and preserved by silt."

"Dr. Storm briefed me. But this wasn't the kind of silt that slowly accumulated over the years, right?"

"That's right. There must have been some type of event on land. Something that caused a landslide, and buried the trireme underwater. In a cocoon of dirt and debris."

"When bigger ships went over it, the prop wash eventually exposed it?" Nick asked.

"Part of it. At least enough for us to find it. It's an incredible find my friend. Just wait until you touch it."

"We're here!" Stavros yelled. He looked closely at the display and the coordinates they had marked. "It should be below us right about, almost there, almost, right about . . . now."

"Mark it Yiannis," Giorgos ordered. "Before we drift."

After Dimitris placed the anchors, Yiannis hefted a specially prepared buoy over the side, the yellow line rapidly spinning out after it.

Giorgos clapped Nick on the back. "Now, we dive. I show you why Greeks ruled the world."

CHAPTER 7
1646 BC, AT SEA

King Mínōs hefted the double-bladed bronze axe toward the sun, admiring its superb balance and craftsmanship. The *labrys* was a symbol of his reign, of his people. Just like the horns of the bull, and the snake goddess worshipped throughout the empire. But it also conjured something else, something far darker. It was also what the tunnels under the palace of Knossos were called. A place of sacrifice to appease the gods. The *labyrinth*.

"If war with Mycenae is coming, we will need to stiffen our ranks. That means more swords, more shields," the king reflected.

"The trade routes should now be unthreatened. Unless we missed some small pockets of pirates," Thálassa replied.

"You would have thought, with the many blessings the gods favored us with, they would have seen fit to sprinkle a little copper and tin on our lands," the king said, "to make our fine bronze weapons."

"It could have been worse, my King. They could have sprinkled it full of ugly women."

The king clapped Thálassa on the back. "Ha, yes, you are ever the optimist. At least that's one thing we don't have to trade for."

The king glanced toward Kalli on the stern, then back at Thálassa with a smile and a raised eyebrow. "At least not all of us."

Thálassa grinned and shook his head, but kept to the business at hand. "Shipments of copper and tin from Anatolia should be arriving in a fortnight. We shall make all the arms required."

The king paced the bow of the galley, as was his habit when planning strategy. Low clouds on the horizon hinted they were approaching their great island homeland of Kríti.

"Word will get out of the rumblings above Atlantis on Thíra. Of the dead sea we passed through. We must show the gods proper piety. And we must prepare for war."

The king waved the axe to summon Rusa to join them. The old man wobbled over, using a gnarled walking stick for balance while also holding the arm of a scribe.

"Rusa, the gods have made it known through their omens that something momentous is to happen. There can be no denying that. When we land, meet with the High Priestess of Knossos. Tell her all that has happened. Ask what is required to appease the gods."

Rusa rubbed his weathered bald head in contemplation, tapping the walking stick on the deck to accentuate his voice. "I think, my King, it will be substantial."

"So be it. We shall not shortchange the gods," he replied. "Send word to my ambassadors. I want to meet with them first thing."

"As you wish," Rusa replied, bowing and retiring.

The king walked to the railing, looking ahead toward Kríti in the distance.

"Thálassa, accompany me up to Knossos. I'll gather the delegates for you to take. Drop them off at Mycenae. I don't want them suspecting we are preparing for war."

"The negotiators won't tip them off?"

"No, it's common in our dealings with them. We both dance this way and that, holding knives behind our backs. Masking it with the delivery of gifts and trade goods."

Thálassa bowed, and walked toward the mast. He caught a glimpse of Kalli, who was looking out to sea, distracted. He sensed something amiss. What it was he couldn't quite put his finger on. But something in the way she carried herself had changed.

Kalli slowly shook her head in disbelief. She still couldn't fathom that Demos was actually alive, here on the very same ship with her.

He didn't see me, couldn't see me, she thought.

She cast a sideways glance in his direction, but he was obscured by warriors milling about. She dared not walk past again and draw suspicion.

If his eyes cleared, if he saw me, how would he react? If our relationship becomes known, will he be killed?

She would avoid him for now, knowing she couldn't risk surprising or exposing him. He was a galley slave on Thálassa's flag ship, and she was Thálassa's. It was as simple as that. He wasn't going anywhere. She would bide her time, gauge Thálassa's spirit and intentions. Perhaps she could even exchange her affections for Demos's freedom. If her affections meant anything to Thálassa, which she doubted. He seemed concerned with grander things than the favors of a mere slave, which he could take easily enough if he wanted.

She overheard the crew talking, that they were headed to an island just off Kríti. A place called *Standia*. It was a place of many large coves on the lee side, to protect the ships of the fleet when they lay at anchor.

"Shaped like a great lizard," one soldier joked.

"Smells like the ass of one too," another replied.

She noticed Thálassa near the mast, who motioned to her. She made her way over. Away from the side where Demos sat chained.

"Gather my things and pack a small chest for me. We will accompany the king to Knossos," he directed. "For one night, maybe two."

She bowed her head. "Yes, my . . . ," she replied, fumbling for the right words. She made eye contact. "How am I to address you?"

"*Kýrios* will suffice."

Kalli felt her face flush, but kept her head bowed. She hadn't been sure what to expect, but the meaning was clear. Master. Making her bondage burn all the more.

"Yes, my Kýrios," she replied through clenched teeth.

She packed the great man's things as instructed. Doing so, she noticed he had brought several daggers and swords. Some were ornamental, some scarred by use. She briefly considered hiding one dagger on herself, but she was too exposed here to conceal it. Perhaps another time.

She looked up as scattered warriors started cheering, and saw the hills and mountains of Kríti looming on the horizon. She had to squint to make out the island of Standia in front, which blended in. But it too came into sharper focus as they approached, the masts of many ships in the harbors giving a sense of the size of the ports within it.

The four escort galleys peeled off one by one, the slaves onboard resuming rowing to guide their ship in as they approached the dock. Orders were barked and men started scurrying about. Items were retrieved from the hold and stacked for transfer. A gangplank from the dock was positioned, and the king and Thálassa departed, followed by Rusa and the captains.

Kalli waited until it was the servants' turn, only then stepping off. Immediately she felt dizzy, like the dock was moving beneath her. She tried to gain her balance but couldn't, felt everything spinning. She looked at the water below, and started falling.

Strong hands snatched her and held her upright. One of the king's servants, *Keos*, held her firmly and smiled.

"Have you never been aboard a ship for a long time child?" he asked.

"No, only on small fishing trips. Why does the sea move within me when I am not upon it?" She tried to stand upright, and stumbled again.

Keos couldn't stifle a laugh. "It will pass. But first we must take another voyage."

He guided her across the dock to a smaller boat, one that would shuttle them from the port of Standia across to Kríti. The king and Thálassa were already well away in another vessel. They would follow with the supplies. Once seated, the gentle motion of the boat rocking made her dizziness fade. She looked up at the dock as they sailed away, and saw the slaves being led off the galley to stretch and bathe. She saw Demos among them, getting splashed with pails of water.

I hope his sight clears soon, she thought. *He needs to know I live.*

"It is called *Heraklion*," Keos said, pointing to where they were headed. There were docks and buildings clustered about the waterfront. "We will land there, then go to a magnificent palace in the hills."

"I've never seen a palace," Kalli replied. "Have you been a slave long?"

"What, serving the king? Yes, my whole life, just like my father did before me." Keos looked around to see who might be listening. "You and I are in most favored positions. Please your master, life can be surprisingly—"

"Easy?" Kalli finished. "I am not looking for that, not after what was done to my people."

"No, I was going to say interesting. Don't judge yet. Even your own tribes fought one another, did they not?"

"They did, but now there is no one left to fight, I am afraid," Kalli replied.

"See what this culture offers, what advances they have made. Don't condemn that which you don't yet understand," Keos counseled.

Kalli leaned close and whispered under her breath. "I understand they kill what they can't have. And they can't have me."

Keos looked at her with a mix of concern and amusement, but held his tongue. This untamed young outlander would either accept her station gracefully, or find herself in a brothel. Or worse.

The great palace of Knossos was unlike anything Kalli had ever seen. Atlantis had awed her, buildings three, even four stories high. There were so many people from distant lands she couldn't even begin to count the languages spoken. The massive harbor of ships sitting beneath gleaming Atlantis and Mount Thíra was beyond description. It made her feel her people were simple, even primitive.

What did Thálassa and the king call my people? Barbarians? Yes, that was it. It was a strange word, one she had never heard before.

But even her wildest imagination and dreams hadn't prepared her for the magnificent strangeness that was Knossos. The vast palace complex was spellbinding to her disbelieving eyes. Sitting atop a hill, it was well inland of the busy trading port of Heraklion far below. Beyond which lay the lizard-shaped island of Standia with its protective harbor full of the empire's ships, ready to do the king's bidding.

As she approached the breathtaking palace, Knossos sprawled out before her. Hundreds of red ocher-colored pillars supporting layers upon layers of floors and terraces covered the entire hilltop, seemingly without end. The land around was fertile, yielding a bounty of wild game, grains, and olives. As they drew near the complex, Kalli could make out vivid murals covering the outside walls. They were full of whimsical artwork of people and fantastical beasts. The horns of the sacred bull were prominently displayed throughout, including a massive set looking out toward the valley below.

Beautifully attired people milled about, while servants discreetly worked in the background. The wealth of the empire was evident here. Kalli viewed magnificent trade goods brought from every corner. Gold from Memphis, ivory from Nubia, copper from Cyprus, and obsidian from Anatolia were but a few of the exotic goods prominently displayed. She observed that there was something about the people themselves, not arrogance, but rather a self-confidence, that seemed to define them. They enhanced their own advanced knowledge of astronomy, mathematics, and horticulture with the best of ideas from beyond their own empire. Above all, they were traders, who prospered from the free flow of goods and ideas.

It suddenly dawned on Kalli that there was no hint of any damage here. Absolutely none at all. Evidently, the rumblings of the gods of the underworld didn't reach as far as the home of the great king.

Thálassa arose early the next day to meet with the king. Working his way downward through many hallways and stairs, he was led in through a back door to the throne room. King Mīnōs sat regally upon the throne, which had been elegantly carved from a single piece of alabaster. Graceful paintings covered the walls, including two griffins looking inward toward the throne.

The king grinned when he saw Thálassa, and motioned for him to sit by his side on an ornate gypsum bench. Nobles fidgeted in a line outside the main doorway, seeking a moment or favor from the sovereign. Armed honor guards, dressed in their finest uniforms, kept them at bay until summoned.

"Weren't we just entrapped in a sea of death Thálassa?" the king said, laughing and slapping his knee.

"Yes, but thank the fates that the gods saved you for greater things," Thálassa replied.

"True, but look around you. The nobles want to drown me with their petty quarrels and grievances, though I am sure some have merit. What advice does the defender of the realm have for me?" the king inquired.

Thálassa looked out at the preening nobles, dressed in their finery, each trying to outdo the others. "Kill them all, and let the gods sort them out."

"Ha, spoken like a leader of men. If only it were that simple." The king snapped his fingers, and the first in line entered. The king glanced sideways and winked at Thálassa. "My first victim of the day."

After several hours, King Mínōs grew impatient, and dismissed all who were left. "Let us retire to meet with my advisors. Time to get to the real work of the empire."

Thálassa again found himself seated to the right of the king, at a large table with the king's advisors. Rusa was seated on the far end, and bowed his head faintly in greeting.

"What word from the high priestess?" the king asked Rusa.

Rusa stood to address the king. "I explained to her of the earth shaking on Atlantis, of the sea of death on our passage here. Just like you interpreted, she feels something momentous will soon be upon us."

"She is most wise. Her counsel has kept our people safe," the king said, spreading his arms. "Look about us, how we have prospered. What does she say we must do to appease the gods?"

"A sacrifice, my lord. From those gifted to us from the lands under your sway," Rusa replied, leaning on the table for balance. "A sacrifice to the beast of the labyrinth."

Thálassa subconsciously nodded. He had seen it done before, when the unrest of the gods demanded it. With the high priestess directing and a large crowd looking on, young men and women had been led to a gate under the palace. They were forced into the darkness of a maze of passages. To either find their way to freedom by groping along the walls, or to meet their fate upon the horns of the minotaur. The beast that was half man and half bull, and roamed under the palace complex with an insatiable blood lust. One that could only be satisfied with a sacrifice.

"How many virgins this time?" the king asked.

"Seven boys and seven girls she asks for. Unblemished in body and spirit for so great a need," Rusa replied.

"So be it. Gather them for the morrow. Make sure all domains around the empire are represented. Especially Mycenae," the king directed.

Rusa bowed and left. Two new men then entered, dressed as nobles. Thálassa could tell by their bearing these were military men, regardless of the outward trappings they wore.

"Thálassa, these are the ambassadors I want you to deliver to Mycenae. Convey them and the chests of gifts to their lands."

"Yes, my King. Anything else before I prepare to depart?" Thálassa inquired.

"Only that there will also be several people to pick up there. Our eyes and ears who have burrowed into their populace. I grant you leave after the proper offerings have been made."

Thálassa bowed, awaiting further orders. The king dismissed the rest, and motioned for Thálassa to accompany him. Together they walked out to a large courtyard overlooking the valley, out toward the sea beyond. They stood between massive stone horns of the sacred bull, pondering the omens, and what it might portend for all of Atlantis.

A great crowd had swelled, no doubt agitated by the incredible rumors they had heard. The tales had flowed from the taverns and brothels, salacious bits of gossip whispered by warriors who had escorted the king back from Atlantis. Not only of the rumblings and earth shakes under sacred Mount Thíra and Atlantis, but of fantastic monsters in the sea of death they had crossed. The gods were angry. They must be appeased.

The route to the gates of the lair under the palace were thronged by spectators on both sides. A procession slowly made its way along, led by a chanting high priestess, followed by two male and two female priests. Two columns of warriors, bedecked in their finest uniforms, marched on either side of a single file line of confused prisoners. Seven young women, followed by seven young men, dressed in bright white tunics, stumbled toward an unknown fate. Each unaware of how they had been chosen, what it was they possibly had in common with their compatriots. Ignorant of the fact that the priestess believed them to be virgins.

The crowd showered blessings upon them, reached to touch their clothes, and threw flowers along their path.

Kalli stood above the gate, several rows behind important nobles, Thálassa, and the king. The customs of these people were utterly alien to her. She had no idea if those following the priestess were to be honored, or if something far darker awaited them.

Keos sensed her confusion, and leaned over and whispered to her. "You saw the anger of the gods for yourself. In the past, if the omens were ignored, great harm came to the kingdom. But if proper offerings were made, the danger passed."

"These are . . . ," Kalli stammered, trying to find the words. "These people are to be made offerings?"

Keos put a finger to his lips. "Yes. Careful silly girl. Know your place, or you might join them."

A tear trickled down her cheek. "Always this many? Every time the underworld trembles?" she asked.

"No, I have never seen this many. The king must be greatly alarmed," Keos said, wiping her tear away. "Quiet child, now you and I must be as ghosts." He stepped away, and bowed his head.

The high priestess stopped directly in front of the king, and kissed the earth in supplication. She arose and turned to the crowd, raising her hands high. "Word has come to us. The gods whisper. They give us omens. They tell the world of the living and of the dead is out of balance."

The crowd became anxious hearing her words. Shouts could be heard from the back.

"Appease the gods!"

"Balance the world!"

King Mínōs stepped forward before the crowd. "We hear the gods. We honor them with this gift of life," he said, opening his arms toward the white-clad prisoners. He gestured toward the high priestess. "May they take this offering, and bestow blessings upon all of our kingdom."

The high priestess held two snakes high above her head, and

started chanting to the gods. The priests added their voices, while the guards closed ranks and leveled spears. The gate to the labyrinth was opened, the young men and women herded toward it. They instinctively clustered together, trying to shy away from the darkness of the tunnel. Away from the cold breath it emitted, away from their fear of the unknown. Sharp spear points forced them in despite their desperate pleading. Four guards then stood arm to arm and leveled spears, chasing them deep into the recesses. When they returned, the gate clanged shut and was locked behind them.

The restless crowd grew quiet, awaiting some sign from the gods, or lacking that from within the cave itself. Kalli held her breath and leaned in, listening. The wind rustled garments, cicadas chirped, random birds flittered about, sandals fidgeted on loose gravel, a baby cried.

Suddenly the bellow of a great bull could be heard, echoing outward. Frantic cries and screams followed, the sounds of desperate struggle within the tunnels, of hopeless anguish. After what seemed an eternity, the last of the noise faded. The crowd gradually dispersed, satisfied the anger of the gods had been fully sated. They had never seen so many offered at one time. Surely this ensured they and their loved ones were safe. That the king and all he commanded were safe. All gave thanks to their king and the high priestess as they drifted away. Relief was palatable in the air.

Kalli awaited on Thálassa, but he lingered behind. He was talking with a few of the nobles, Rusa, and the king. She saw him nod to the high priestess, some knowing glint of conspiracy exchanged. The high priestess caught Kalli looking, and held her in her gaze. There was something mysterious about the priestess, beautiful yet foreboding, with black eyes that betrayed no soul. Like the snakes she held, intertwined tightly around her arms. Kalli trembled and looked away. She gulped for air, feeling she had momentarily forgotten how to breathe. Never had she felt so alone or so far from home.

Impatient and curious, she wandered down, along the path the procession had followed, toward the entrance to the cave. No one seemed to be paying her any attention. She soon found herself peering into the gate.

What possibly lives in here, devouring the souls of the offered? What evil lurks within? she wondered.

Thinking she heard faint scratching sounds, and despite her dread, she peered between the bars. Slowly out of the shadows a solitary figure crawled toward her, toward the light. As it drew nearer, she could see it was clad in white, with bright red stains in many places. The figure saw her and reached for her. Kalli backed away, horrified. A lone hand grasped the bars of the gate, and then a second. A face looked up at her, the face of a young woman, probably her own age.

"Help me. Please."

Overcoming her fear, Kalli reached for her hands. They clasped, the girl drawing herself up upon her knees. Their eyes met, but no more words came.

The girl looked over Kalli's shoulder, recoiling in fear. Something whooshed by Kalli's ear, and the girl shrieked loudly. Her grip loosened, and her blood-soaked body fell away from the gate, collapsing unto itself.

Kalli felt a presence and turned, and saw the high priestess standing in back of her. A bloody spear was clenched in her hands.

"Render unto the gods that which is justly theirs," the priestess said.

Kalli backed away, intimidated by the ominous holy woman. She drew her hands up protectively, horrified to see they were covered in blood. As she ran back toward Thálassa she heard sinister laughter behind her, and a warning.

"Tend your master well. Lest you should befall a similar fate."

CHAPTER 8

JUNE 9, PRESENT DAY, PIRAEUS, GREECE

Nick tumbled backwards off the boat, holding his scuba mask tightly. It felt good to be in the water again, the weightlessness always exhilarating to him. Best of all, this was in the warm embrace of the Aegean Sea. He swam over to the buoy line and looked downward. The visibility was excellent, the sunlight easily penetrating to the ocean floor forty-five feet below. He smiled, these were ideal conditions to document the site.

Giorgos was already down below him, and pointed to a long depression to the right of where their buoy's anchor rested. The excitement within him growing, Nick pumped his flippers and caught up. Giorgos put a hand out in a stop signal to get his attention, then waved both downward and flat, indicating *go slow, be gentle, and don't stir up the sediment*. Nick gave him the OK sign, and they made their way down to the seabed.

The bottom came into sharper focus. Nick saw where the prop wash of large ships had shifted some of the sediment in the channel, digging out a cavity in a long horizontal row. It seemed it was almost cut out of the hard part of the ocean floor's surface, revealing a soft underbelly. From there the tides and currents had added their perpetual force, eroding it further. Giorgos drifted to a specific spot within the depression, gently fanned away a thin layer of recent silt, and grabbed Nick's hand. *Touch it*, he indicated.

Nick reached out and felt it, an end of a protruding piece of the ship, sticking just barely through the surface. The grain of the wood was surprisingly firm and rough to the touch. Over 2,500 years old, and here he was touching it. There was something thrilling about the very history of it, about the lives of those who made it and fought on it. Their echoes through time rang loudly in Nick's ears.

They set about methodically laying out a grid to show where everything within it lay, in situ. Carefully hammering in a stake to hold the grid, Nick couldn't get it to bite and kept repositioning it. Frustrated, he finally reached down and pulled out a broken bit of pottery. Realizing what it was, he motioned Giorgos over, who fanned where it had sat. The silt drifted away, revealing scattered pieces of broken amphora lying about. Amphora that had contained olive oil and wine for the crew. Elation showed in both their eyes. Not only had an elusive trireme been discovered, but here lay proof of those who had actually manned her.

Nick was so engrossed in taking photographs and meticulously documenting everything, he didn't see Giorgos waving at him. A touch on his shoulder got him to look. Giorgos pointed to his watch and pointed up. Time to ascend.

"It's unbelievable. There's no telling what else may be down there," Giorgos said. "What a time capsule!"

Nick handed a bit of pottery to Dr. Storm.

"That was found in grid C-12 Doc," Nick said, insuring it was properly documented. "What struck me when I was down there was how unprecedented this is. This was all buried and perfectly protected for millennia, by the perfect mixture of non-organic debris. But it isn't anymore, the shipping channel and tides are stripping the protective barrier away. Wood is now lying exposed, soon more will be."

"We can take care of diverting the shipping, but the tides are in God's hands. We need to get the coffer dam built as fast as we can," Stavros said. "Unfortunately, we Greeks spend too much time deliberating and too little time doing."

Dr. Storm was in contemplation of the piece of pottery, turning it over in his hands while looking out to sea. He cleared his throat and looked up at them all.

"You're right Nick. If it stays unburied, it will decompose. If we wait for bureaucratic approval, it will decompose. Even if we build a cofferdam quickly, it will decompose. We simply can't risk that."

"I sense an epiphany coming from my Amerikanós friend," Stavros said. "What is it you suggest, Sir Philip?"

"Don't let it stay unburied. Rebury where it is exposed, to protect it. Until we're really ready to excavate."

"Perks of the office my friends," Stavros said, sliding his ID card and letting them in.

Nick looked at Dr. Storm, smiled, and just shook his head. He could hardly believe his good fortune. He was about to get a personal nighttime tour of the National Archaeological Museum of Athens. By its director of antiquities, no less.

The impressive edifice of the museum was stunning in the evening twilight. Built in a neoclassical design, it sat in the shadow of the incomparable Acropolis, looming above all in the background.

"Just showing some colleagues around," Stavros said to the night watchman, sitting at a bank of video monitors.

"*Apolamváno kyrie*," replied the guard, which Nick understood to mean *Enjoy Sir.*

Stavros ducked behind the desk, hit some switches, and the entire interior of the museum was immediately brilliantly illuminated.

"Welcome my friends, to the history of Greece."

Before them lay a choreographed display of the evolution of Greece, from the Neolithic, Cycladic, and Mycenean periods to the Hellenistic and Roman. Vast rooms were devoted to sculpture, metal work, ceramics, and inscriptions. There were even collections from Egypt, the Near East, and Santorini.

"Simply incredible," an overawed Nick said.

Dr. Storm put an arm around him. "It makes it all tangible, does it not? From the Archaic, to the Classical, to the Hellenistic, it's all right here. The genesis of so much knowledge and advancement throughout the ages."

"Pythagoras, Socrates, Pericles, Aristotle, Plato, even Alexander the Great. The list goes on and on," Stavros added.

They took their time, Stavros a fountain of knowledge, expounding on the documented history, and the myths and origin stories. About an hour in, Dr. Storm reached into a backpack and pulled out a bottle of *Metaxa*, a popular Greek drink made from brandy, botanicals, and wine. Stavros procured Styrofoam cups, and the conversation became even more engaging. Fueled in part by the magical elixir.

Nick stopped in front of a particularly impressive bronze of Zeus and tipped his cup to Stavros. "I've been to the Louvre, the British Museum, the Smithsonian, all the great museums of the world. But I've never seen anything like this."

"Well, as you Amerikanós say, we have home court," Stavros replied.

"You would think, with home court, Greece, or any country, could reclaim their own expropriated national heritage," Dr. Storm observed. "I'm not just talking the Elgin Marbles, Stavros. I'm talking about any significant finds that have been pillaged from the lands that spawned them."

"By nefarious means ending up in the private collections of the selfish or ultrarich. Never seeing the light of day, never being shared with the world," Nick lamented. The Metaxa was loosening all their tongues on common causes they each held dear. They all sighed in unspoken agreement.

"Ah, the Antikythera Mechanism," Stavros announced as they wandered in front of it. "Such a work, such an enigma." The mysterious gear-driven metal mechanism was found encrusted at sea, and dated from 100-200 BC.

"Has it ever been conclusively proven what it was used for?" Dr. Storm asked.

"Let me try that one for size," Nick tipsily replied. "I believe it was to show the movements of the moon and sun through the zodiac, to predict eclipses."

Stavros clapped in appreciation. "Well done. That is the closest science has been able determine. See the replicas over there? We think that is how it may have worked."

"You have so much to show. I don't know where you find room to display everything. Is there much in storage?" inquired Dr. Storm.

"Frankly, we've outgrown it Philip. Plans are being drawn to add new display chambers right beneath us."

"That's fantastic news," Dr Storm said, raising a cup. "How is the fundraising going for that?"

"Alas, these are difficult days for my country. We are in the European Union, yet don't feel fully embraced by it. Debt consumes us. Thus, we look to the private sector. To potential benefactors who might want to burnish their image while doing good works."

"Maybe you can get that tycoon who is funding the trireme dig to pony up?" Nick asked.

"Mr. Kollas? Perhaps. He is certainly one we are pursuing. But working with him comes with, how you say, strings attached."

Meandering toward the front to leave, they found themselves in a room filled with Minoan frescos. Stunning artwork adorned the walls, of youths boxing, antelopes prancing, athletes leaping over bulls, even beautiful bare breasted women in their finery. The images were exquisite, the sophisticated minds of the artists evident in how they saw the world, and themselves within it. The entire exhibit predated the flourishing of ancient Greece, even of the Myceneans.

Nick paused, taking in all its implications. "Do you believe the origin myths were rooted in fact?"

Stavros chuckled. "Now that's a good topic to discuss with a belly full of Metaxa. I'll tell you what I think, but not all would agree with me. That the Minoans we see here played a bigger role than history ever gave them credit for. That they were conquered and absorbed by the Myceneans, and the Myceneans became the Greeks. But in the end, one must ask who really conquered who."

Nick felt the urge to dig deeper. It wasn't often he was in such rarified company. Dr. Storm's eyes twinkled as he tut-tutted. He had been here many times before with his young protégé.

"But what of the myths surrounding the Minoans themselves?" Nick asked. "Do you think it was possible that Santorini was the inspiration behind Plato's story of Atlantis? Or is it just an allegory of the hubris of man?"

Stavros looked around, out of habit for the need of secrecy on certain, sensitive topics.

"Ha, those are big questions Mr. Nick. You wouldn't want to get me in trouble with my sponsors now, would you? I mentioned that our biggest benefactor, Drakos Kollas, had strings attached to his generosity. He is a self-proclaimed nationalist, and defiantly so. Of the faction that believes the ideals and culture of Greece are all organic, grown only from the very soil of sacred Greece itself. Not imported or influenced by other, lesser civilizations."

"But that's preposterous, isn't it? Every civilization is influenced by each that touches it. And influences them in turn. Especially in an area built upon trade like the Mediterranean."

"I don't disagree with you, my young friend. But sometimes we have to dance with the devil to accomplish the greater good."

"The impatience and idealism of youth, I am afraid," Dr. Storm wryly observed. "We both had that disease once, if I remember correctly." He raised his cup toward Stavros.

"Yes, before the reality of life beat it out of us." Stavros laughed, raising his in return.

Nick grinned sheepishly, happy to be the butt of their jokes. He was about to ask another question, but Stavros raised a finger to make a final point.

"Everything that exists today comes from something else, does it not? You, me, the Earth, the sea. The sun that warms us and the stars up in the very heavens. If we take this thought exercise back far enough, I suppose everything ultimately comes from the gods themselves. Wouldn't you agree?"

Nick had no comeback for that, and contentedly nodded his assent. Like Mark Twain suggested, best to keep his mouth closed and let them think him a fool, rather than open it and remove all doubt.

The three walked merrily out, wishing the head guard a good evening. Nick noticed a car discretely parked across the street, away from the street lights.

Odd at this time of night, he thought. *Probably just lovers looking for a quiet moment. But maybe . . . No. I'm just being paranoid.*

They talked and laughed, making their way along the elegant pathways toward the street, the breath of the ancients hanging heavy in the mist of the late-night air.

Nick sipped on strong Greek coffee as the Poseidon made its way out to the dive site. There was a little chop to the sea, but the weather forecast was favorable. He noticed Dr. Storm standing a little unsteadily by the rail, perhaps under the weather from the Metaxa and the waves.

Oh yeah, and the ouzo we got into later, Nick thought.

He smiled inwardly. It had been a good night. An ephemeral night. One he would consciously burn into his memory for future access. There was no telling when the need for future inspiration or solace would inevitably arise.

Stavros went over to the radio and hailed the Hellenic Coast Guard ship that was patrolling the area. He announced their arrival and his thanks. The crew gave a wave then headed back to port, while the Poseidon took its station near the marker buoy.

They all gathered in the pilot house to discuss the day's plans. Dimitris took one look at Dr. Storm and reached into a glove box. He peeled the backing off an object and gave it to Dr. Storm, who nodded his thanks and applied a small sea sickness patch behind his ear.

"Alright gentlemen, the main goal today is to mark off the outer area where the walls of the cofferdam will ultimately go," Dr. Storm said.

Stavros leaned over an image of the seabed below them and pointed. "We are going to fill the depression back in to protect it. Then once we have approval, we can start putting the retaining walls of the dam in."

"When will the fill go in?" asked Giorgos.

Stavros shrugged his shoulders. "Hard to say. We have to get enough of the right kind of fill to pump back down there. It has to be inert, like was down there before it got exposed. Not a small request."

"We have to go down parallel paths at the same time," Dr. Storm explained. "We're scrambling for approval, while trying to procure the fill and the coffer walls. We just need to make sure we are ready on our end for whatever breaks free first."

Assignments given, the meeting broke up. Nick and Giorgos grabbed their diving gear, while Yiannis lugged the tanks over and tested their pressure. Dimitris put down a second anchor to stabilize their position and provide a better dive platform. Dr. Storm and Stavros stayed in the pilot house, strategizing and working the phones. All in an effort to get the slow wheels of bureaucracy to turn a little faster.

Nick, then Giorgos, dropped backwards into the depths, the world going silent except for their own breathing. Nick grinned, the sound always made him think of Darth Vader.

Luke, I am your father.

Once underwater, they couldn't resist a quick look back within the exposed depression, and worked their way there. They both touched the exposed piece of wood for good luck, then hovered for a moment, looking around. They had seen the scans and knew what lay below. It was going to be an awesome excavation.

Armed with bright marking tape and spikes, they went to opposite ends of the perimeter. The slow grunt work of marking out the future position of the cofferdam wall proceeded without incident, the visibility good and the current muted. Nick got lost in the rhythm of the job, occasionally checking his oxygen levels and the progress Giorgos was making.

Eventually he hit an area where the sediment was shallower, a small area brushed by the tides and currents. He tried to tap in a spike, but hit something solid. He tried several other spots, same result. He used his flippers to clear an area, to see what he was up against. Once the silt he stirred up drifted away, he hovered close and tapped at it with his hammer. Small bits chipped off, but it wasn't solid stone or hardpan bedrock. It felt more like coral, yet it wasn't. He worked several pieces free and put them into his tool sack.

As he reexamined the area, he found himself squinting, it had gotten darker. A large shadow was drifting across him, and he looked up.

Not a storm blowing in. That looks like a ship. A big one too, from the looks of it, he thought. *We've got company.*

He checked his tank, and caught Giorgos looking up, then at him. Nick pointed to his watch and pointed up. Giorgos gave a thumbs up, then they both followed an anchor line back up to the Poseidon. As they ascended, a large anchor noisily went in, then a second, both headed a little too close to their work site. They rose a little faster, unsure of what awaited them.

"Ah, there they are now," Stavros said once they broke the water's surface. "Our dive crew."

Nick and Giorgos got out and sat on the flat dive platform extending from the stern, removing their equipment. Yiannis grabbed their tanks, and raised an eyebrow to them without saying anything. Nick looked past him, and saw four men had come aboard. Their dingy was tethered to one side, while an immense yacht sat close by, looming over the Poseidon.

"Your anchors almost hit our work site," Nick fumed, not sure who to direct his wrath at. "What rocket scientist didn't see the marker buoy?"

Giorgos was about to add something, but stopped when he

recognized who had come aboard. An awkward silence followed, until an immaculately dressed man stepped forward and offered his hand.

"A simple misunderstanding. I assure you it won't happen again. Drakos Kollas, at your service."

CHAPTER 9

1646 BC, KNOSSOS, KRÍTI

"Pack my things, we leave at first light," Thálassa instructed. His voice gave no hint of emotion.

Kalli bowed and went into his chambers, putting his possessions into the sea chests. She unconsciously trembled, unable to get the vision of the sacrifice out of her mind. So many young innocents, all fed to that terrible beast. Especially that last pleading face, whose hands she had clasped. She looked at her fingernails. Bits of dried blood remained under them.

I do not understand their ways, she thought. *Do such terrible offerings truly keep them safe from the anger of the gods?*

A whispered conversation in the hallway drew her interest. The word minotaur had caught her ear. That name for the deadly beast roaming the bowels of the palace, far below where she now stood.

Suspicious, she silently edged to the side of the door to better hear. She could just barely make out Thálassa's voice down the hall. She leaned out.

"When you blew on the horn to sound like a bull, I almost ran myself."

"Yes, it echoes well down there. But that last girl got away. There were so many, it was difficult to get to them all quickly," said the captain of the palace guards.

"It may have worked to our favor," Thálassa replied. "The last of the onlookers heard my servant yell, and saw the survivor clinging to the gates. That will spread useful rumors." He laughed lightly. "That will make it easier for the high priestess and the king to control the people."

"Yes sir. But it is hard to see them in the caves, wearing that huge mask and horns," the captain complained. "There were only two of us, we should have had a third."

"Best to keep the circle small, the fewer who know the truth of the labyrinth, the better," Thálassa said. He looked straight into the captain's eyes to make sure he was perfectly understood.

The captain nodded, bowing his head. "The wounds looked real? The bludgeons we carry are made from sharpened bull horn."

"Yes, it looked just like she had been gored. The priestess finished her off. Most convincing," Thálassa responded, slapping the captain on the back and walking him down the corridor. "You did your king proud."

Kalli stood dumbstruck, trying to digest all she had just overheard.

What was real and what was illusion here? *Who controls the fates, the gods or the king?* she pondered.

It was hard to tell, her head spinning with possibilities.

When footsteps started echoing down the hallway toward her, she rushed back to the chests. She folded garments, her heart feeling it might burst through her chest. Its pounding was so loud in her ears she didn't hear Thálassa walk up directly behind her. She jumped when a hand lightly touched her shoulder.

"I didn't mean to startle you," he said. Kalli slowly backed away as he looked at her appraisingly. "You know I am a powerful man, do you not?"

Kalli bowed her head, looking at her feet. "Yes, Kýrios."

He put a finger under her chin, tilting her head up. "I will get what I want. What is due me. Always."

She looked away, avoiding his eyes. Thálassa waited a moment, then nudged her chin a bit higher.

This can be easy, or it can be hard, she remembered him saying. *Serving me has its advantages.*

Resigned to her fate, she sighed in submission.
"Good. We understand each other. Undress."

"Damn, you are a feisty one."

The heavy hammer struck, making sparks. But it had hit slightly off center.

"Hold still, damn you."

The sound made Kalli wince and try to pull away. She struggled against them all.

"Hold her wrist tight lads, or I'll miss and break her arm. And then we'll all have hell to pay with the admiral."

The stout, grimy blacksmith wiped his sweaty hands on his apron. The two guards who had brought Kalli stopped being gentle with their charge, and held her fast. They could not risk returning her to Thálassa injured. Their necks would be on the line. Despite her best efforts, she couldn't budge her arm.

The hammer landed solidly. Then again.

"There, that'll do it. The only way that'll come off is if she takes her hand with it." The blacksmith stood up, admiring his work. "You now have been personally marked with the royal seal," he said, and laughed.

As the guards finally let her up, Kalli raised her left arm. On her wrist was a heavy, ornate bronze bracelet. It was marked with the sacred symbols of her oppressors. Symbols she had seen throughout the palace of Knossos and back on Atlantis. But most discouragingly, the bracelet had a thick ring on it. To attach a chain of bondage.

Thálassa had offered Kalli the chance of giving herself to him willingly. And she had tried, believing it would put herself in his good graces. Which might mean she could eventually ask some small favor of him. Perhaps of getting Demos out of being a galley slave. Maybe he could be tasked with a lighter duty, where he might stand a better chance of survival. That was certainly an honorable intention, the best she could make of her circumstances.

But try as she might, instinct had kicked in. She had tried to picture Demo's face, but it had faded to a different reality. Kalli had resisted, with all her might. *It had all been to no avail*, she somberly reflected. She would not be dealt with so lightly now. The duties would be the same, but not the trust. Nor the bit of freedom he had afforded her.

The guards escorted her briskly back to the dock, anxious to be rid of the troublesome slave. They brought her aboard the command galley, to where Thálassa's chests were stowed, and chained her to the railing. Satisfied she was secure, they wandered off to attend other duties.

Kalli pulled listlessly against the chain, then sat with a great sigh of defeat. Scratching at her wrist, she more carefully examined the bracelet. She had never seen such craftsmanship in her homeland, had never beheld bronze before being abducted. The images on it fascinated her, the symbols of the empire etched in minute detail. Something else was inscribed on the inside where it met her flesh, irritating her wrist. What it was she would never see, unless Thálassa granted it to be removed. Or she somehow stole her freedom.

A flurry of activity amidship gained her attention. Everything for the voyage was stowed belowdecks, and a flag raised upon the mast. The crew came sharply to attention. She saw Thálassa walking purposely up the gangplank, giving orders as he came aboard. The lines were cast, the ship pushed away from the dock, and a shout from the galley master directed the slaves to slide their oars out. They were soon underway, the thump of the drum giving rhythm to the working of the oars. With each stroke, Kríti loomed ever smaller behind them. A flotilla of other galleys, all fully manned with the cream of her warriors, followed in their wake. All to demonstrate to the Myceneans a firm show of strength.

From where she was tethered, Kalli looked out upon the slaves, searching for any sign of Demos. When she saw he wasn't in the same seat, she immediately panicked. Perhaps he hadn't measured up and been sold off, or worse. She closed her eyes and rubbed the neck pendant of her people still hidden under her tunic.

Calming herself, she slowly and carefully reexamined every seat. When she realized he was only two seats away from his former position, she closed her eyes and let out a deep breath. His back was to her, but she was sure it was him. His unmistakable profile was clearly visible. He looked stronger, and seemed to have regained his vision. She had to be careful in case he saw her. His reaction might prove fatal. To them both.

Pondering her dilemma, Kalli looked up and saw Thálassa staring at her from near the stern. He glanced at where she had been looking, and walked toward the slaves rowing there. She immediately looked out to sea, trying to appear disinterested. Thálassa motioned for the galley master, who walked over and bowed before him.

"The new slaves brought aboard, which are they?" Thálassa asked.

"There are only three left my lord. There, over there, and here," he replied, pointing to each in turn.

Thálassa looked down, and recognized the face of a young, handsome, brunette slave. The one whose eyes had burned with defiance. He knelt down and stared directly into the face of the slave, who looked away while continuing to row. Thálassa clearly saw the scar on his neck, the one he had left just a short time ago.

Yes, of course. It must be, he thought. *This slave and Kalli were from the same small nest of pirates. And knew one another. Perhaps intimately.*

Standing, he looked across at Kalli and grinned. She happened to glance back at him, and caught the knowing look. He nodded to her and rubbed the scratches on his face. Tokens of her desperate resistance.

The voyage northward to Mycenae proceeded without incident, the sailing weather excellent. They encountered no signs of the displeasure of the gods. Not an unnatural sight, sound, or scent anywhere along their journey.

Perhaps the sacrifice did indeed please the gods, Thálassa thought. *It is good. Time to focus on the schemes of our enemies.*

They were almost to Mycenae when he called the two ambassadors over. He wanted to confirm their instructions for dealing with the Myceneans before he dropped them off. *There must be no mistakes.*

Yidini instructed those warriors gathered near the bow to move away, ensuring privacy.

"Gather what intelligence you can of their intentions. Confirm our suspicions. If we are right and they threaten war, we need to know when they might act," Thálassa instructed. "The timing is critical."

"I will discretely talk with our spies there," the older one replied. "Preparations of such an undertaking are hard to hide. We have gold to loosen tongues."

"Just make sure you loosen the right tongues. Lies are as easily bought as truth. And can be just as believable," Thálassa said. He looked at the younger ambassador. "What of your sources?"

"We have several who have proven reliable. Atlanteans who have long lived among them." He looked at the dock they were gliding toward. "How long do we have here, sir?"

"Another ship will pick you up within a fortnight. A trade vessel bringing olives, wine, and saffron. The captain knows where to find you."

They saluted sharply and gathered their things. At the dock they disembarked quickly, taking with them chests of gifts for the court. And gold sewn discretely within the folds of their garments. Yidini ordered trade goods removed from the hold, while other items of Mycenean origin were loaded in their place. Before the tides changed, they were back out to sea, accompanied by their impressive escort. The show of force was not lost on the troublesome Myceneans.

In the midst of the bustle of all the activity at the port, one spy had stealthily come aboard. Once the fleet was well away, he was led by Yidini to inform Thálassa what he had learned. He bowed, awaiting leave to speak. Yidini motioned nearby crewmen away, then stood guard so no one would approach.

"Speak," Thálassa said. "What did you observe?"

The spy glanced around, then spoke in hushed tones. "In the taverns, fathers complain their sons have been marshalled, their crops and animals confiscated. Forces gather from near and far, then train away from the villages. I have seen the hoarding of great amounts of grain, animals brought down from the highlands for slaughter. Blacksmiths are busy making arms, which are stashed away. Slaves are being gathered for labor. There is unrest, and talk of war."

Thálassa nodded knowingly, his suspicions further confirmed. "Well done. Lose that disguise, you serve here now."

The spy proudly stood erect with a soldier's martial bearing, bowed, and left.

Thálassa called Yidini and a scribe over, and began to formulate his plans. He would await word back from the two ambassadors, and their network of informants. But he would ensure the armed might of Atlantis would be prepared to do the bidding of his king.

The fleet continued its circuit through the seas of the empire, headed east. Its purpose now was to intimidate potential rivals, and show subdued territories and trading partners that the threat of piracy had been eliminated. Sacrifices of pirate prisoners were left at key ports along the way, suspended by grappling hooks above docks or in the center of villages. A very real reminder of the long reach and power of the Atlanteans and their king.

In those communities settled by Atlanteans, the warnings provided a source of comfort and security. Yet in those areas upon which the yoke of servitude to Atlantis weighed heavily, resentment smoldered beneath the surface. Much like the gods now rumbling deep under sacred Mount Thíra.

At the island of Tinos, a great bull was loaded aboard. Thálassa then had the slave he believed Kalli knew removed from the galley. He was trussed up to be sacrificed, yet uttered not a word. He watched Kalli carefully, gauging her reaction. There was no doubt. She could not mask her feelings. At the last moment he had the slave put back on the galley, and substituted another in his place. It was a cruel game he played, to gain the psychological advantage over one he already owned. Of a mere slave. But it wasn't enough to have her. She must give herself willingly to him. He had found her weakness to exploit.

"Delos off the port bow, sir," Yidini called.

"Well done. The gods have favored our journey," Thálassa replied. "I require some time here to make an offering. The king himself requested it. When I return, we sail for Atlantis."

An armed escort went ashore with the admiral of the fleet. The island of Delos was largely barren, devoid of the ability to sustain itself. Pilgrimages had been made to this spot since time immemorial. It was considered a most holy site, by all the peoples on the islands surrounding it. Even by those from far distant lands. The proper offerings made here could ensure blessings for a person, or a family. Or even an empire.

The magnificent white bull had fought the entire journey from Tinos and had to be hobbled by its feet and laid on its side. Lashed near the mast, it finally gave up the struggle and succumbed to the heartbeat of the waves. Landing ashore, it took some time for the holy beast to regain its footing. But once the ground stopped moving beneath its feet, the bull quickly regained its vigor.

The guards and a group of slaves followed Thálassa upward along a gradual, rocky path. They climbed a small rise, Mount Kynthos, until an altar appeared near the summit. After food, wine, and precious offerings were placed around the altar, Thálassa dismissed them all. He stood alone, looking out at the vista below, holding a rope tied to a bronze ring through the bull's nose. A whiff of rotten eggs, the breath of the underworld, caught his attention. He hadn't smelled that since they had passed through the dead sea. And now, when they drew ever closer to Atlantis and Mount Thíra, it revealed itself again.

What does it mean? Is it a sign of a blessing or a curse? he thought. *Soon all will be revealed. Surely the prophecy will tell.*

The fleet sat idly just offshore, safely at ebb tide on the lee side of the island. There was no sound other than the warm breeze whispering through the objects around the altar. Offerings left over time, many of great value, all never touched nor desecrated. Not by poor fisherman, not even by the pirates who had frequented these islands. Sacred offerings that none would dare disturb and risk the wrath of the gods.

Thálassa had been here before, and well knew the rhythms of the land. Patience was required, even for as powerful a man as he. He absentmindedly poked at the piles of prior offerings with his bronze sword, some truly ancient and decayed. Rusted axes, war clubs, bone-tipped arrows, spears with fire-hardened points. *Primitive offerings*, he mused. *No wonder we are the masters of this world.*

He scraped a little deeper out of idle curiosity. Remnants of every religion under the heavens. Broken jewelry, rain-filled pottery, rotting leather greaves, carved figurines. Gold, silver, pearls, and gems gleamed among the tangle of objects precious to those who made the pilgrimage, yet here remained unclaimed and exposed to the elements. A desolate place where the vane toils of men were inexorably reclaimed by the earth.

The sun nearly setting, he heard the bull snort, agitated. He smelled them before he saw them, shrouded figures silently approaching from an unseen path carrying torches. They were known as the *Graeae*, three ancient women who told the prophecies of the gods. They crept slowly along toward him, crab-like in their movements. Ancient and rotted, their faces hidden by moldy cloaks. One spoke, her breath fetid on the breeze.

"Offerings you bring. Knowledge of the future you seek."

Thálassa stared defiantly at her. He would bow to no mortal but the king. "On behalf of King Mĩnōs and Atlantis, I bring provisions and wine for you. And offerings and this sacred bull for the gods."

The other two women ignored what had been brought when they saw the bull. In a hallucinogenic daze they slowly danced around the bull, leading it before the altar. Caressing it to calm the beast, they chanted softly. As the sun relinquished the day and dimmed on the horizon, torches around the altar were lit. Thálassa noticed for the first time the piles of bones scattered about, of goats, small animals, and fish. Gnawed and broken, nothing going to waste.

"Such a gift is rare indeed," the same ancient hag croaked. "To know the morrow, I must read the signs. What they tell is destiny. Unchangeable. Is that what you truly seek?"

"I seek to honor the gods. That they may bless the king and his empire until the end of time," Thálassa replied.

"Bah, who knows what time the gods keep? Our lives may be but a mere moment to them, while an eternity to us." She cackled so viciously she coughed, then cleared her throat and spat. "Or perhaps our wretched existence is but a play thing for their eternal amusement."

A bellow from the bull startled him, and he saw its throat had been slashed. A bowl was put in front of its gushing neck, quickly filling with blood. The dying beast slowly collapsed to its knees. The two unearthly figures drank greedily, spilling the life-giving liquid about as they fought over the bowl.

The one who had spoken walked over to where the bull had struggled. Laying her hands upon it, with surprising strength, she slashed it open from chest to tail. She reached in and pulled out the entrails, and slowly and carefully felt along their length. She nodded her head ever so slightly, then burrowed deeply in and gathered more. Little by little a steaming pile coiled around her feet, as she sought to divine a clear understanding. To hear the whispers of the gods through the ether. Finally satisfied, she stepped out of the tangle, wiping her hands and arms off upon her cloak.

"What prophecy have you for me?" Thálassa asked.

The ancient one paused, she wouldn't be rushed by a mere human. No matter how powerful in this life. With ancient, trembling hands she pulled back her hood. She looked deep into his eyes, into the depths of his very soul.

"The gods shall grant favor to you, your king, and what you call empire," the raspy voice answered, "until such time as day becomes night."

Thálassa pondered the meaning. The prophecies were known to

be notoriously vague or misleading. "Until day becomes night," he repeated aloud.

Then we are most blessed, for surely that means until the end of time, he thought. *The end of time.*

"Then so it shall be," he said to the three Graeae. He turned and briskly walked back down toward his ship. Away from the ill portents of dream readers and rot and decay. Toward the destiny of men.

CHAPTER 10

JUNE 10, PRESENT DAY, PIRAEUS, GREECE

I don't believe I've had the pleasure," Drakos Kollas said, extending a hand. He puffed deeply on a cigar, and blew the smoke toward Nick's face.

Nick paused a beat, finally remembering the face from the televised interview with Dr. Storm. He took the extended hand and gripped it firmly.

"No, you haven't. Nick LaBounty."

Drakos smiled thinly, then turned his back and walked away to talk with Dr. Storm and Stavros. A large, hulking presence quickly stepped between Nick and Drakos, forming a protective barrier. Between the working peons who dredged the bottom of the sea and men of higher quality. The other two bodyguards, who Nick took for paramilitaries, subtly took up positions on the bow and stern of the Poseidon. He glanced up at the yacht, and saw a couple of men pacing the deck there.

Pretty tight security for a business tycoon.

He went back and took off the rest of his gear. Giorgos was doing the same, and looked up and shrugged his shoulders at Nick. Such was life.

"He thinks he owns the whole damn sea," Nick grumbled. "That's one conceited SOB, in any language."

"Well, in a way he does, *filos*," Giorgos said to his new found friend.

Nick gave him a confused look.

Giorgos lowered his voice and waited for the guard to pace past them. "You don't know, do you? Kollas is funding this recovery. Completely. He insisted on no other sponsors. Stavros is negotiating to have the trireme displayed in the National Museum. But alas, nothing concrete has been finalized yet."

"You mean there is a chance this will end up in Count Dracula's private collection?"

"I don't know where it will ultimately end up. Remember, our job is to excavate and preserve it. For the Greek people."

Nick got up abruptly, but Giorgos grabbed his leg and cautioned him. "Take a deep breath. Honey better than vinegar."

Nick paused and composed himself, then nodded his thanks.

"Easy Mongo, I'm a part of this," Nick said, trying to shoulder his way past Drakos's personal bodyguard. Lykaios cracked his knuckles and glanced at his boss for direction. Drakos subtly shook his head, and Lykaios stood down and let Nick pass.

"Nick has graciously volunteered to be our expert on artifact recovery and preservation," Stavros said, attempting to diplomatically diffuse the tension.

Dr. Storm shot Nick a look.

The sponsor is always right, even when he's wrong. Nick caught it, but withheld judgement. He wanted to see what this Kollas character was all about.

"As I was saying, it is a simple matter for me to cut through all this red tape," Drakos said, snipping an imaginary thread with his fingers. "How much of this special fill would you require?"

Stavros and Dr. Storm exchanged a look, shrugged their shoulders, then looked to Nick.

"How long until we excavate?" Nick asked.

Drakos finally brought himself to look at Nick. "I should hope we will have governmental approval and the requisite materials for the cofferdam within perhaps a fortnight to a month. But one never really knows in Greece, does he?" he said with a small laugh.

"Then we need enough fill to cover an area twenty meters by sixty meters to a depth of three meters. Just to be safe."

"And so you shall have it. If there is nothing else, I have other pressing matters to attend to."

Drakos shook hands with Dr. Storm and Stavros, then clicked his heels and bowed. Turning smartly, he departed for his yacht, accompanied by his bodyguards.

"Of all the . . ." Nick sputtered.

Stavros cut him off with a finger to his lips, then pointed to his ear. Dr. Storm motioned with two fingers walking, and it dawned on Nick. The body guards weren't just for protection and intimidation, although that was certainly part of the intent. They had bugged the *Poseidon*.

"Whose side is he on anyway?" Nick asked.

"Isn't it evident? His own," Dr. Storm said. "I think from here on out it is safe to assume that all is not as it appears."

Stavros had been quiet. "Keep your friends close, and your enemies closer. Sage advice," he quipped.

The three of them slowly meandered the large circular walkway of the *Tinaneios Garden*, located close to the waterfront where the team was staying. It offered a chance for private conversation, since they no longer trusted the boat or hotel rooms. Even the phones were now off limits if they wanted to exchange secure information.

Nick looked around, there was no one within one hundred feet. He pulled an object out of his pocket.

"What is your opinion of this?"

Dr. Storm turned it over and looked carefully, then passed it to Stavros. He in turn scratched at it with a fingernail, and small bits came off. It was light now that the water had dried out of it.

"My best guess is it is a type of pumice. You agree Philip?" Stavros asked.

"Yes. Why Nick?"

"Because the top of the site that hasn't been exposed is covered with it. Then silt above that."

"The geology of this region is fascinating," Stavros said. "Plate tectonics are grinding the African plate against the Eurasia, and we sit right in the middle. Lots of volcanic activity, lots of pumice."

"You've got your own ring of fire going on right here in the Mediterranean," Nick observed.

"Yes, not as big as the one in the Pacific. But it can certainly be just as destructive," Stavros said.

"And just as cataclysmic," Dr. Storm added. "Think of the lives lost by just Vesuvius, Etna, or Thera. Not to mention the hundreds of other smaller eruptions lost to history."

Nick stopped and stood in front of both of them. "The Methana Peninsula is just across the gulf from Piraeus. There are over thirty volcanoes on it. The way I'm reading our site, I'm guessing at some point a large eruption took place and caused a tsunami. That tsunami hit the shores here, and as it receded, it buries our trireme in a landslide of washed down debris. With me so far?"

They both nodded. It wasn't a new concept.

"The eruption continues, and eventually sputters out. But the pumice it produced covers vast swaths of the sea, just like the one near New Zealand in 2012."

Stavros looked it up on his smartphone. "Amazing, that was over 10,000 square miles in size. I had no idea."

"So where does all the pumice go?" Nick asked rhetorically. "Some grinds against shores and turns to sand, or covers low islands, or falls on the mainland and becomes a layer of the geologic record. But much of it eventually gets waterlogged and just sinks. I think that is what is on top of the debris field over our trireme."

"Which encased it, so the protective debris underneath didn't wash away," Dr. Storm said.

"Until dredging tore through the protective crust," Stavros added.

"Tides and currents washed the debris away, until your ship was uncovered and discovered," Nick said. "Think of it gentlemen. If that process happened here, what else might be encased out there, perfectly preserved, awaiting discovery?"

Back at the hotel, Nick took a shower and checked for messages. Heinrich had sent him a purposely vague email, but the implication was clear. He had found something, and was pursuing it. He would update Nick later.

There was also a message from Charlie, touching base and asking how things were going. Nick did some quick mental math, and thought he might catch his brother with a phone call. Evening here, lunch time there.

"Hello Nick, how's Greece treating you?"

"Love it out here man. The country is stunning, the excavation site is unreal. How's things stateside?"

"Status quo little bro. Not much in the news. Have you been keeping up to date on things back here?"

"No Chuckles, I've been spending lots of time underwater. Why do you ask?"

"Well, umm, there's some new rumors popping up in the tabloids. Thought you might like to know."

"Stop dancing man. You know you can always be straight with me. What kind of rumors?"

"The 'my old girlfriend is getting married' kind."

Nick paused. That hit a little too close to home. Even if it was just in some notoriously unreliable tabloid.

"Still there?"

"Yeah, still kicking. Guess I'm not over her yet. Don't want to be."

Charlie laughed softly. "Maybe Greece is the perfect place for you for a little while. Away from all the paparazzi."

"Yeah, best to avoid the white-hot spot light," Nick replied, thinking of an old Billy Joel tune. "Hey, I need a favor."

"Of course you do. What's it this time?"

"I need some background dope on one Drakos Kollas. Big man on campus over here in Athens. But this needs to be discrete."

The multi-billion-dollar hedge fund Charlie was a senior partner at possessed extensive research capabilities. All in the name of prudently vetting domestic and international investment opportunities for their clients by critically evaluating individuals, corporations, and countries, by any and all means necessary.

"Spell that one for me, would you? I'll get our team right on it. On the q.t."

The brothers visited about more mundane things, how Sophie and the kids were doing, and promised to keep in touch. Nick hung up the phone, frustrated at the distance from the cause of his heartache. Yet at the same time grateful for it.

"Seriously, you must have ouzo in your veins over here," Nick said. "I've got to get back to my roots." He ordered bourbon, neat.

Giorgos, Dimitris, and Yiannis laughed at their new American compatriot. Nick could tell he was growing on them. He really appreciated their history, and got frustrated at the same inequities that cut them all deeply. Best of all, he didn't back down when he thought he was in the right. Regardless of who called him out.

They were ensconced at a popular waterfront bar in Piraeus, close to where the Poseidon was docked. They were all happily drinking their dinner, swapping stories, and bonding as a crew.

"I hear Kollas say, 'I don't believe I've had the pleasure.' So Nick goes, 'No, you haven't,'" Giorgos roared.

Dimitris, sitting next to Nick, slapped him so hard on the back he spit out bourbon. "Ha, Mr. Nick, that's a good one! I'm just a, what you say, grunt. I'm just a grunt. I do that to Kollas, I never work 'a here no more."

The three Greeks spontaneously broke into a dirty sailor song, the words foreign to Nick. He hummed and bobbed to the beat, enjoying being a part of their world. These were good men, salt of the earth men. Men who worked with their hands, who lived in harmony with the sea. Who lived as their forefathers had.

Giorgos wandered over to the bar and brought back the food they had ordered. An assortment of lamb kabobs, spanakopita, fried

"Now? The same that has always awaited our empire. Great glory," he replied.

Thálassa motioned to the sky and the sea, speaking loud enough for others to hear. "These are but signs the gods are always with us. It was the same for our ancestors when they first settled the slopes of sacred Mount Thíra. The soil was fertile, the sun smiled upon them. The sea provided bountiful harvest. They learned to navigate the waves, which we in turn now master. This is our destiny." He turned and faced the crew, who tried to appear disinterested in their conversation. "As it shall be for our descendants. Until the end of time."

Kalli continued to look out to sea. She could just make out Thíra in the distance, a whisp of smoke above it. "But what ultimately becomes of us?" she innocently asked. She wondered if a learned man like Thálassa believed any differently than her own people.

He leaned in toward her and lowered his voice. "We are but mortal men. The gods are infinitely patient. The same end awaits us all," he said softly. "Each takes their first breath, screaming to enter the world. Then each takes their last breath, gasping when they leave it. It is only what we do in between that matters."

He stood back up and looked out toward Atlantis sitting below Mount Thíra.

Kalli grew silent. Their beliefs were not all so different, master and slave. She prayed that when she slept forever, she would go to the place of her forefathers and loved ones. She would try to live honorably in this life, as much as circumstances would allow. Then perhaps the gods would favor her in the next, and restore to her that which had been taken away. All too soon.

Arriving at the great port of Atlantis, Thálassa left Kalli onboard and went ashore. Unsure if great damage and panic awaited him, he was accompanied by an armed escort and several handpicked galley slaves. Thálassa carefully surveyed for himself the condition of the docks, streets, and buildings. He was told the ground had continued to tremble with ever increasing violence during his absence. There had been a massive trembling and great exhale of liquid stone and ash from Mount Thíra, but it had stopped abruptly.

The foundations of many structures were badly cracked, some laying in complete ruins. Even many fountains throughout the city, which distributed fresh water to the people, were damaged. Their flow had been reduced to a trickle or had stopped altogether, the clay pipes cracked or severed. Repairs had stopped being made, awaiting a prolonged period of tranquility. Fortunately, despite all the damage, the injuries were relatively few.

He noticed some people taking their leave, mostly those of means or those who had relatives on other islands. They flocked to the port, slaves carrying their most valuable goods and clogging the docks. A steady stream of ships, great and small, made their way out through the harbor. To what they perceived as sanctuary well beyond. This was the normal rhythm of life here, like it had always been. Repairs would eventually be made, and people would return once the gods tired of toying with the mortal follies of men.

The leaders and nobles gathered when they saw the fleet approaching, seeking Thálassa's counsel. It was agreed they should go together to the great sacrificial altar on the slope of Mount Thíra. The High Priestess of Atlantis was summoned and led the procession. They ascended, Thálassa gazing at the summit, which continued to emit a steady plume of white smoke. He had noticed it as they approached by sea. It seemed no greater in intensity now.

They picked their way past a herd of dead goats clustered around the edges of a small pond. Waterfowl floated dead and bloated on its surface, bubbles rising from the depths with the familiar smell of rotten eggs. He had just seen this before, on a much more massive scale upon the Great Sea, but kept it to himself. The high priestess signaled for all to stop when they approached a flat area with a marble altar facing the summit. It sat between the two massive stone horns of the sacred bull. Around it the carcasses and bones of recent animal sacrifices lay strewn about.

Thálassa walked to the altar and turned to address them. He paused, the ground hot beneath his feet, even through his sandals. He noticed barefoot slaves shifting uncomfortably from one foot to the other.

"A most holy offering was made at Knossos. Witnessed by the king himself. Seven young men and seven young women, all pure in body. Then at Delos a great white bull was sacrificed. The entrails were read, the omens were favorable. I heard them myself."

"What fates did they foretell?" asked the high priestess. She held a snake in each hand, their bodies coiled tightly along her arms.

"The gods shall grant us favor, until day becomes night," Thálassa replied.

The nobles murmured among themselves. This was most encouraging. The earth shaking would surely pass. It had always passed. The foul breath of the underworld would fade back to smell of rich soil and salty sea mist. After all, the prophecies had always told the truth.

"Only if a proper sacrifice is made here as well," the high priestess cautioned.

"I agree. That is why I have brought them," Thálassa said, motioning for the slaves to be brought forth. "Choose any you require."

The high priestess uncoiled the snakes and passed them to a priest. She walked over to the slaves, chanting to herself, carefully examining each in turn. She shook her head until she came to the very last one, who was looking down dejectedly at his bound hands. She examined him for scars or deformities, anything indicating he might be impure. Grabbing him by the jaw, she lifted his head. She traced a mark on his neck, recent by the looks of it.

"I gave that to him myself. He was too defiant for a slave," Thálassa added.

"Yes. He is the one. Pure in body, pure in spirit. Place him there," she directed the guards, pointing to the altar. "Quickly."

Demos struggled desperately, but there were too many strong

arms to overcome. He was half dragged, half carried to the altar. His head was roughly thrust down on the stone surface, scratching his face as he fought and thrashed about.

"Hold him tightly," she hissed.

Out of the corner of one eye Demos could see the high priestess held a double headed axe, while invoking an incantation to the gods. Finished, she set the blade on the base of his neck. He could feel the coldness of the bronze, the sharpness of the blade. A trickle of blood ran down the side of his neck. She slowly drew it high above her head, the shadow on his face as she prepared to strike.

Kalli sat against the railing, positioning herself so that the mast gave her some shade from the glare of the sun. The sea was calm and azure in color, gently rocking the ship floating at its berth. The sky above was a crystalline blue, finally devoid of the noisy flocks of birds. Even the clamoring of the crowds had died down, most of their vessels underway and fading into the distance. The fleet lay at anchor just offshore or at the docks, the crews sharing a midday meal, the slaves resting. She sighed, it was calm, almost serene. Her head tilted as she dozed off, for how long she knew not.

She awoke to a sound that had startled her out of the fog of a dream. She had dreamt there was a stampede of grotesquely over-sized bulls thundering down the mountainside, smashing through Atlantis, headed for the ships in the great port. She blinked her eyes hard, trying to shake off the vestiges of the dream, and listened as the noise slowly built in intensity. At first, she didn't hear it as much as felt it in the pit of her stomach. It seemed to come from every-where at once, even deep beneath her, under the ship.

Kalli looked around, confused, to see if others also felt it. They all did, from the dazed reactions she saw from the crew and slaves. Everyone looked around for the source, across the horizon, at the ring of islands surrounding Atlantis, at Mount Thíra looming above them. The sound was all around them, within them, the rumbling growing deeper, impossible to pinpoint. She looked to see where Demos sat, the panic rising in her when she realized he wasn't aboard. Neither was Thálassa.

The gentle waves of the harbor disappeared, the very sea itself shaking. Droplets of water started rising from the surface as if pounded by a heavy rainfall, yet there was not a cloud in the sky. Jets of water started bursting into the air, the mists casting small rainbows all about them. Abruptly the waters went still, and started to recede from the shoreline. The ship Kalli was on started to lean away from the dock. The keel settled, snapping the lines that had held it fast. Fish flopped about in the mud, gasping to breathe. Squid and small creatures groped for pools to hide in.

She tried to stand on the uneven deck and looked around bewildered, but the chain on her wrist held her fast to the railing. Abruptly a maelstrom of sea water in the great port rushed back in, higher than it had been just moments before. The boat swayed then righted itself, floating freely over the dock that had just held it. It was as if the very earth itself was breathing, one moment inhaling and pushing the seas out, the next exhaling and allowing the seas back in, even higher than before. All the while the volume of rumbling was building in an unearthly depth and intensity.

Kalli could now hear screams. The buildings trembled and emptied of people. A flood of humanity started running pell-mell toward the ships. Horses and bulls broke free and joined the teeming masses. Dust started rising as the tallest and flimsiest buildings collapsed. Scattered fires broke out, the roaring voices of the gods reaching a fever pitch that physically hurt.

An invisible and incomprehensibly massive explosion hit everyone and everything at once. Its concussion so loud the world went utterly silent. It blew Kalli off the boat, severing the chain at her wrist, twisting her arm painfully and knocking the wind out of her. As she spun helplessly through the air, she saw ships blown onto their sides, people and animals tossed outward as if by an invisible hand. Even the rising water momentarily retreated as she fell toward it.

Landing hard, she quickly sank, inhaling salt water. She instinctively tried to regain her breath. Disoriented, gagging, and sinking rapidly, Kalli was about to give up all hope when her feet touched bottom. Looking upward she saw sunlight filtering down through the frothy surface. Squatting, she pushed off, swimming hard back toward the light.

The swirling current was too strong, the urge to inhale too great, her lungs near bursting. She flailed about, hitting something, and gave in to the need to breathe. Opening her mouth and tasting salt water again, she hoped the ending would be quick and merciful.

She stopped struggling, the ringing in her ears finally fading, as she drifted back downward. Down toward oblivion.

Demos stared transfixed. The blade was held at its zenith, about to strike the killing blow. Just as the high priestess brought the axe downward with a grunt, the world went utterly black. Standing completely exposed, a massive explosion obliterated her with flying boulders and stone. The same force caused the heavy marble altar to overturn, Demos falling with it, shielded from the worst of the blast. Those around him were blown down the mountainside, tumbling until they were nothing more than limbless corpses.

He lay sprawled on his back, stunned senseless. Hearing nothing, his ears ringing, he felt enormous vibrations shaking the very ground he was on. Regaining his wits, Demos blinked his eyes hard in attempt to clear them, staring at a gigantic column of fire and earth angrily climbing into the sky above him. Blown off parts of the mountain rained down around him, the largest landing in a burst of debris and further shaking the ground. The size of their impacts defied comprehension.

Demos sat up unsurely, blood oozing from his ears and nose. The earth beneath him was so hot he wobbled unsteadily to his feet. Feeling stinging he looked at his forearms, scalded and smelling of burnt flesh. One guard, who was also shielded by the altar, sat up looking at him, about to say something. A large stone whistled down from above and struck him, dashing his brains before he could utter a word.

Not believing it possible, Demos felt the intensity and noise of the thrust of the column increase. He looked at it again with unbelieving eyes, as it reached upward, toward the very gods themselves. The will to survive overcame his initial shock. He looked down below him, at Atlantis and the sea beyond. He started downward, stumbling at first, then with increasing nimbleness and balance as his mind came back into sharper focus.

I must get back, to the ship. To Kalli, he thought.

His single mindedness turned to obsession, blotting out the carnage around him. He became oblivious to the carcasses of man and beast lying about. He lurched ahead. He didn't even see Thálassa and several other survivors working their way downward. An outcropping had blocked the blast from annihilating them. The contour of the land funneled them toward one another until they finally met. Demos felt a hand on his shoulder and turned.

"To the ships," Thálassa yelled at him above the din. He turned to the other survivors with him. "We must save as many as we can!"

Demos dully shrugged and staggered onward. They had just offered his life to the gods. Now he was to help save these very same people. It made no sense, but nothing in this surreal landscape did. They all instinctively headed toward the only possible avenue of escape from this vengeance of the gods.

To the port and ships below.

CHAPTER 12

JUNE 11, PRESENT DAY, PIRAEUS, GREECE

It wasn't just hot, but humid too, with little breeze to bring relief. The Poseidon bobbed lightly on the waves, the crew pleasantly hung over. They lounged about in whatever shade they could find, contented faces all around. Nick sipped on ice tea, sweating out the ill effects of the prior night.

"How did the car run last night Mr. Nick?" Giorgos asked. "Go vroom vroom?"

"Couldn't find a place to park it." Nick joked.

"Most unfortunate," Yiannis said. "I parked mine."

"Yeah, I bet that one went beep beep," Dimitris teased. "You know, like a little clown car."

"No, more like baa baa," Giorgos said. "Like before they're kabobs."

Yiannis just shook his head.

Stavros was on the phone, gesturing with his hands. He smiled and announced that a barge was on the way that should arrive shortly. It was carrying the fill they had requested to rebury the exposed part of the trireme below them.

"Game time," Nick announced, stretching the knots out of his shoulders. He and Georgos walked back to the stern to check on their dive equipment. Yiannis went and grabbed the scuba tanks.

"Say what you want about Kollas. He manages to get things done," Dr. Storm said, following them.

Nick looked up and shook his head. "But at what costs? Think about it."

"I have to see the good in sponsors Nick. Professional hazard I guess."

Nick glanced for eavesdropping equipment near where they sat before replying. "He makes his grand entrance here yesterday. He hears what we need, says he will pull a few strings, and a barge is headed here. Like right now. Fully loaded. No one could make that happen that fast Doc. Not even with a magic lamp."

"You mean he already knew about it?"

"Of course he did. This boat was already bugged. And probably a whole lot more. They've been tracking us all along. Zeus himself couldn't get his hands on that kind of fill in a day."

Stavros wandered back, listening to the last part of the conversation. "That was eating at me when I got the call. I feel like we're being played."

Dr. Storm motioned them closer and lowered his voice. "We can't let him know what we suspect. Let's concentrate on getting this out of the water. Get it safe."

Stavros nodded. "We play along."

The barge arrived shortly after noon, nudged into position by two tug boats. A large oversized hose was lowered into the water at the stern, a powerful pumping station sitting amidship. A second hose was slowly unreeled. It tapered to a smaller diameter, and had a valve that controlled the flow.

"Like frosting a cake," Nick said when first observing the equipment.

Georgos shook his weathered face. "More like aiming an oversized enema."

They both flipped into the water, carefully guiding the hose toward the sea bed. Sea water was drawn in, mixed with the fill on board to make it viscous, then pumped through the hose. It took both of them to control it, since it had a tendency to kick about if the pressure increased too much. By manipulating the valve, they could control the throughput.

The work proceeded slowly as they learned the nuances of the strength of the pump, the amount of back kick it produced, and the ebb and flow of the currents. Finding their rhythm, they positioned themselves on the upstream edge, so the current drifted any over-spray toward the exposed area. And away from their field of vision.

It took hours, with frequent breaks, until the gash in the ocean floor was covered. The fine fill steadily settled, compacting on itself until it was a reasonable facsimile of the original cocoon encasing it. Minus the protective outer shell of pumice that had concealed it for ages. For a final task, they placed weighted floats around the perimeter. These rose about six feet above the fill, and would act as markers when it came time to start construction of the cofferdam.

When the Poseidon finally docked later that day, everyone went their separate ways. It was Friday night, and there were no firm plans on the next stage of the recovery yet. That was awaiting approval and materials for the construction of the cofferdam, which Kollas said might take up to a month. Nick was excited, he now had free time in Greece to do what he loved. Explore with no strings attached.

He went straight back to the hotel, showered, and changed. He sat on the edge of the bed, contemplating his next move. Maybe grab a bite, then go out to the same bar and see if the mystery woman showed back up. It was worth a shot.

I'll just rest my eyes for a minute. A quick cat nap.

Overcome with exhaustion from the day's dive and the prior night's festivities, Nick didn't stir until morning.

Nick awoke early, feeling refreshed from the first really solid sleep he had since arriving. He didn't even remember crawling under the covers. He rolled over and looked at the floor, his clothes in a pile next to the bed. He mentally went through his obligations, and came up empty. Dr. Storm had said he would be in touch, but to feel free to roam about since things were in limbo for a bit. All was good since the dive site was now protected by the fill, and the Hellenic Coast Guard was on patrol to deter any trespassers.

He checked his phone and email, no messages of any importance. Yiannis had kindly offered to play tour guide, but Nick knew he would rather be with his girlfriend, and politely declined. They would see enough of one another working in the tight quarters onboard the Poseidon.

He loaded a light backpack with a couple bottles of water and a few supplies, grabbed a walking map of Athens, and wandered out into the bright sunlight, to see what trouble a solo American tourist with time on his hands could get into.

Hopping on the metro, he headed away from the port area and went northeast to Athens, straight toward the *Acropolis*. When he peered to view it, its meaning was starkly clear, a fortified city on a hill. He wanted to beat the inevitable summer crowds, especially once the cruise ships disgorged their thronging masses of passengers. Arriving just before the dawn, Nick slowly meandered up the pathway. He viewed the silhouette of the Parthenon while the sun rose over it, a breathtakingly timeless landscape.

Nearing the base of the mass of stone, Nick wandered through the oldest operating theater in the world, the amphitheater of Odeon of Herodes Atticus. As the beautifully reconstructed pathway ascended, he marveled at the view ancient Greeks would have had of the city below and Mount Lycabettus beyond. He paused to rub his fingers on graffiti over two millennia old, etched into marble here and there.

Kilroy was here, even back then, Nick thought. *Men always seem to have that urge to say we were here.*

Climbing a jumble of stairs in various states of repair, he paused to look at the Temple of Athena Nike, the patron goddess and protector of Athens. Ascending a final flight, Nick entered through the *Propylaea*, the gateway into the Acropolis that Pericles had rebuilt after the Persian wars. There the massive Parthenon spread out before him, imposing in its grandeur, dominating the landscape.

A few other early bird tourists scrambled about, hurrying to iconic vantage points to take photos of the sunrise. Some posed with selfie sticks, snapping away before crowds obscured their view or cluttered the background. Nick took advantage of the lack of crowds to take photographs too, but of the ancient masterpieces, not himself.

I already know what I look like, he thought. *But I don't know when I'll be back here. If ever.*

He was drawn to a single olive tree, the mythical spot where Athena had struck the ground with a rock. Nearby was where Poseidon had banged his trident and a salty spring appeared, when the two Olympian gods competed for the patronage of Athens. The name of the city clearly showed who had won.

Nick slowly walked around the Parthenon, admiring its gracefully tapered columns. An optical illusion, they were purposely thicker on top to give the appearance of symmetry from the ground below. Much of the great temple had been blown apart when Venetians fought Turks for control of the city. The Turks had occupied the high ground of the Acropolis, using the Parthenon itself as a gunpowder magazine. They believed that the Venetians wouldn't dare fire on a building of such historical significance.

They were wrong.

More damage happened over the years due to neglect and looting. The most famous instance being when Thomas Bruce, also known as the Earl of Elgin, removed some of the best-preserved sculptures. Supposedly with the permission of the Turks of the Ottoman Empire. They were now displayed in the British Museum, a constant point of contention with the Greek government.

There was no admittance allowed within the Parthenon itself, because the restoration work was slowly being done.

Perpetually being done. The ancients only took nine years to build it. We're at forty and counting just to repair it.

When Nick saw the buses pull up and the guides hold their color-coded group flags aloft, it was time to make good his escape. A group of angry looking young men loitered about, talking amongst themselves and eyeing the impending flood of tourists. Pickpockets and thieves, the displaced and dispossessed. A dichotomy of wealthy tourists on holiday and poor locals and immigrants. A single scruffy vagabond such as himself wasn't their mark, but he gave them a wide berth anyway.

Nick exited back through the Propylaea and turned left, following a different pathway down. He went through the Sanctuary of Asklepios, built to honor the god of medicine, which had served as a rudimentary hospital to the ancients. Directly ahead lay the Theater of Dionysus, which could hold over 17,000 and was used up through the Roman period. He sat in it for a moment, transported to a time when the acoustics were still pristine, envisioning the crowd and the actors.

From there it was but a short stroll to the Acropolis Museum. Formerly next to the Parthenon, it was now housed in a recent, purposely built facility. He walked up to the front desk, and asked if a certain person might be in today. Stavros had given Nick the name of his right-hand man who worked here. Shortly after, an energetic young man walked briskly to the desk, extending a hand.

"Jason Calathes, how may I be of service?"

"*Kaliméra,*" Nick replied. Good morning. "Stavros Nomikos gave me your name. I am working on the dive site with him."

"Ah yes, he mentioned a couple of Amerikanós were helping us preserve our sunken heritage. Pleased to meet you."

"Good to meet you too. I wanted to stop by to introduce myself while I was in the neighborhood. Wasn't sure if I would catch you here on the weekend."

"It seems I am always here, one thing or another to be done. Perhaps you might allow me to give you a brief tour?" Jason asked.

"I would be honored. But not if it is keeping you from your work."

"There is always much *ergasía,* much work, but it can wait. I'd rather share professional insight with a colleague."

"This museum is stunning. When was it built?" Nick asked while they walked through it.

"We moved here in 2009. We outgrew the old one next to the

Parthenon long before. But such are the challenges of raising funds. This was much better thought out."

Nick peered down at the ancient ruins under and around the museum, a live dig in progress. Through glass panels in the floor, he saw a woman hunched over working on restoration below. In an Athenian neighborhood over two millennia old.

"Wow, I guess so. The way it incorporates the past with the present. It really brings it to life."

"We hoped that is what people would think," Jason said. "Not dull history, but something real, something you can touch."

They wandered upward, amongst free standing statues and others on pedestals, all within reach of curious hands. Nick was struck by the generous use of glass, allowing a view out to the Parthenon on the Acropolis beyond, and to the ancient ruins below. Truly an immersive experience.

Nick paused when he stood in front of the friezes of the Parthenon, those pieces that had decorated it in antiquity. They were magnificently laid out just as they would have been in antiquity.

"Notice the different colors of the marble?"

Nick blinked his eyes hard, he already suspected what it represented.

"What is pure white is what has been discovered, but unfortunately doesn't reside here. Scattered in many countries around the world."

"Has there been success in repatriating any?"

"Not much my *filos*. If we had invaded Britain and taken the crown jewels, perhaps we would have some leverage." Jason laughed.

They spent another hour together, lost in the intricacies of Greek history, discoveries, and preservation methods. Departing, they exchanged cell phone numbers. Jason made Nick promise to have dinner at his home and meet his family. Ouzo would definitely be involved.

Walking out into the bright sunlight, Nick took a moment to gain his bearings. A hulking dog with a dark face and a brown-gray coat sat just outside, like it was waiting for its master. Nick had noticed many strays around the city, a not-too-subtle problem the locals ignored. Jason had explained to him it was an offshoot of the debt crisis Greece was facing. People were overwhelmed with just making ends meet. Pets simply weren't a luxury many could still afford. The funding for animal control, well, that had dried up long ago with the budgets.

Nick headed across the street, over to the Temple of Zeus. It was well kept, an island of tranquility in the tumble of chaos that was Athens. He angled to put its columns between himself and the Acropolis for a postcard shot. He clicked away and noticed a large dog standing in the middle of it—the same one he had left behind at the museum—cocking his head at him. He thought nothing of it, there were a dozen other strays wandering around the temple.

Nick worked his way a little north to Syntagma Square, admiring the sites and people watching. He found himself enjoying the persona of the Greeks, the ease with which they carried them-selves. Despite hard times, they went about their business, their lives little changed. The bumps in the road of modern times did little to change the rhythm of what they had been doing for thousands of years.

"Amerikanós," Stavros had joked a few nights ago, "always in such a big hurry, off to make so much money. To own a bigger house, drive a nicer car. To drive to work in, to make more money. You should relax, take in life. This is called the old country for a reason. Slow down; we're only here once. Enjoy the journey."

Nick smiled to himself. *A wise man. A wise culture.*

His feet took him to the charming Monastiraki neighborhood, where he decided to take Stavros's advice. He sat at an outside café, ordered a bottle of wine and something to eat, and watched the world of another culture slowly play out in front of him. Young couples strolled hand in hand. Old men played backgammon and sipped Metaxa or Ouzo. Street vendors hawked their wares to tourists. A cacophony of sounds played a background symphony to him. The old country indeed.

Two glasses of wine later, a waiter came up to him with a bowl of water. Nick looked at him quizzically.

"For your *skýlos*, sir. Your dog."

Nick looked around, then behind him. There, the same large dog sat quietly, its head on its paws. Nearly under Nick's seat.

The waiter put the bowl under Nick's chair, and went off to tend another customer, humming an infectious tune.

The dog lapped the water eagerly, then looked up. It put its head on Nick's lap and let out a releasing huff of contentment. Nick stared at the face, the wet jowls damping his pant leg.

"I'm not Greek big fella. It's not like I can just take you home."

The dog raised its head, then set it back down with a thud. Another huff.

Nick rubbed the head, and finished his wine. Finally, he got up to head toward his next destination. Where it was to be, he didn't know.

The big dog followed him anyway.

Nick roamed aimlessly, simply enjoying the sights, sounds, and smells of a foreign city while the sun slowly descended. The spaces between buildings allowed occasional glimpses of the multi-hued sunset, the clouds radiating color far above. The restaurants were busy, tantalizing new smells wafting in the air every time he turned a corner. A faint tune caught his ear, something he recognized, which unconsciously drew him along. Like a moth to a flame.

When Nick looked up, he found himself in front of the Half Note Blues Club. A band was playing in back, a festive Saturday night crowd gathering and mingling. He shouldered his way in, working his way to the far end of the bar. He took the furthest seat, and leaned against the wall. A good place to be alone in a crowd.

He squinted through the smoke and dim light at the bourbon selection. Not all that bad for being in Greece. But maybe there was just something about bourbon and blues, regardless of the location.

He spied a bottle of Woodford Reserve and ordered a dram, neat. His new best friend for the evening. He wasn't going to be alone after all.

Nick looked toward the doorway and did a double take. Had he glimpsed the silhouette of the mysterious Greek beauty from the other night? Then he laughed at his own overactive imagination. Not a chance, not here. He turned off his brain, sipped the bourbon, and listened to a melancholy song. The singer was very good. Soulful. He slowly glanced around the crowd, admiring their mirth and companionship. Finishing his drink, he caught the eye of the bar keep and pointed to his glass.

"*Dýo*," a woman said leaning in, pointing to his glass and holding up two fingers.

She turned and looked at him and smiled. The same smile he had seen reflected in the mirror two nights ago. The beguiling dark-haired temptress that he had unconsciously been hoping he would bump into. And he had, at a blues club in Athens, of all places.

The bar tender returned and put two bourbons in front of them. He nodded at the woman like he knew her, then turned to tend other customers. She picked hers up, swirled a finger around the rim, then raised it to Nick.

"Of all the gin joints in all the towns in all the world," he said.

"She 'a walk into mine," she finished in a stilted accent, quoting Humphrey Bogart from the film *Casablanca*.

They clinked glasses and took a long slow sip, eyeing one another.

"If I didn't know better, I'd say you've been following me."

"Don't feel flattered. I come here often. One of few places hear blues in Athens," she replied. "Right Andreas?"

The bar tender looked up at her and grinned.

There's that accent again, Nick thought. *Greek with a tinge of something else. Yiddish?*

"The music caught my ear, drew me here. I'm a big fan. What about it captured you?" Nick asked.

She sat and put her glass down. "My *bampás*, my papa, played at home all time. Grow up wid it, get in your bones," she seductively said. "Et tu, Brute?"

Nick laughed, she could quote Latin. Funny.

"The same with me. My dad got me hooked, took me to a few shows when I was young. I play a little, but it just made me a bigger fan. To appreciate how hard it is to put your soul into an instrument."

She looked at the band, then back at him.

"Hmm. Not get 'a many Amerikanós wandering back streets. Dey stick to tourist spots. Take picture postcard view and go home. Sad. Never see real Greece."

Those eyes. That accent.

"That's not me. The fun of it is to really go in country. I actually like to get lost, really lost, in a foreign place. Then immerse myself and work my way out. You know, to really experience it."

"Perhaps you not, how you say, so typical."

"I don't know about that. My friends would say I'm pretty typical. In a nerdy kind of way."

The crowd grew denser, people converging on the bar. She drew her stool closer to Nick's, to discourage people from leaning in between them. Their knees interlocked. They each sipped their drinks, listening to the band break into a rendition of *Born Under a Bad Sign.*

"Yassou. I Persa."

"Nick. Nice to meet you."

She looked at him differently for a moment, appraising him, like she suddenly recognized him.

Oh no, don't tell me I'm in the tabloids over here too.

"Ha. You him, aren't you?"

"That depends on which him you mean."

"Him. The *archaiológos.* The famous rock guy."

Nick smiled at her, then got up and signaled to the bar tender. He wanted to cash out and escape. Pretty or not, this was attention he didn't need. After all, part of the appeal of being here in the first place was to be a nobody. To be incognito.

He reached for his wallet and pulled out some Euros. Before he could offer the money, he felt a hand gently on his. She looked at him coyly, batted her eyes, and leaned into him.

"My mistake. I thought you someone else. Stay."

Nick paused, reconsidering.

"It will be *diaskedastiko*."

He looked at her and raised an eyebrow.

"Um, how you say this. Fun. It will be fun."

Nick sat back down, curious and enchanted. "OK. We have fun."

CHAPTER 13

1646 BC, ISLAND OF ATLANTIS

Drifting downward, on the verge of blacking out, Kalli felt something grasp at her wrist. It took hold, jerking her upward, pulling her out of the water. She felt many arms lift her, then set her down roughly on her side. Someone pounded on her back. She gagged, exhaling salt water, coughing in fits. Gasping for air, she realized she was still alive. Blinking through the pain and tears she saw a face hovering above her.

"I thought we lost you," Yidini yelled above the din. "You were blown overboard. I saw the flash of your shackle in the water." He stood up, surveying the pandemonium around them, then glanced back down. "You would have been dead without it." He quickly shouted orders to those still aboard and strode off.

Kalli woozily sat up, comprehending for the first time she had been brought back aboard. Men were in the water, some swimming, others clinging to floating debris. Large and small bits of rock splashed about them, some hitting flesh or bouncing off the deck. Curious and still dazed, she picked one up and looked at it. It was unnaturally light and honeycombed. She watched as several bounced into the water and floated. They seemed harmless, like a light rain.

A new sound caught her ear, rapidly increasing in intensity, its origin unknown to her befuddled mind. Her gaze drifted to a nearby ship trying to get underway. Men scrambled to man the oars just as an enormous flaming boulder tore into the stern in an explosion of fury. The bow jumped out of the water, flinging its occupants near and far. One landed with a sickening thud just in front of her, his maimed body entangling a slave who had reached for his oar.

For the first time she could actually hear the great rumbling instead of just feeling it. Regaining her senses, she looked up aghast at the massive churning column rising far above, spewing ferociously out of Mount Thíra. It reached to the very gods themselves.

"Stroke!" Yidini yelled, pointing to the shore.

Slaves and crew desperately manned the oars. Many benches were empty, their former occupants flailing in the waters around them. Yidini motioned to the other ships still afloat and pointed them toward the shore as well.

"Stroke, damn you," he implored.

The ship started to creep forward. The oars hit both people, debris, and floating stones, seeking purchase in the sea. Yidini ran over to the unoccupied kettle drum and hit it. Trying to get those rowing to work together in some type of rhythm. They floated over the dock they had been tied to, now barely visible below them. It was as if the land itself was sinking into the depths of the sea.

They beached the ship, between storehouses set well above the port. Several other ships did the same. Most of the remainder not sunk or severely damaged also attempted to maneuver toward land. People from Atlantis were starting to stream toward them, screaming for their lives. A ship far to the left, which beached on an unobstructed road, was the first the panicked crowd flocked to. The crew tried to maintain order, but were quickly overrun. People clawed their way aboard, some flinging their children before them. The overloaded galley started to list, and was swamped when even more desperate souls climbed over one another in a frenzy to board it.

Kalli looked out at the terrified masses from her perch on the bow of the beached galley. The crowd shifted away from the swamped ship, and started massing toward the others next to hers.

Several ships working their way to land stopped just offshore, realizing the danger of the mob. She heard yelling behind her, and turned and saw ships headed out to sea with only their crews and slaves aboard.

"Cowards, come back. Help your own people!" Yidini implored. But it was in vain, baser instincts taking hold of even the stoutest hearts.

Again, an unearthly ripping sound caught her ear, and she instinctively recoiled. Another large boulder tore through the sky and landed on the edge of the crowd, sending dirt, cobblestones, flaming rock, and broken bodies in every direction. Other pieces of the mountain, great and small, started pummeling the land and sea with increasing frequency.

The wailing of the mob intensified, its leading edge overrunning the adjacent vessels. Seeing no hope there, the horde started thronging toward the next ship. The one she was on. Looking toward the city, Kalli saw yet another wave of desperate humanity streaming downward. Like the crest of a great wave, it engulfed all before it, an irresistible force headed directly at her. She unconsciously inched backwards until she was against the mast, bracing herself for the onslaught.

Then she saw him, standing on the crest of a hill. Looking down directly at her. Standing right next to Thálassa.

They fought through the stampede of the crowd, and stood atop a small rise, utterly breathless. Thálassa surveyed the contagious pandemonium spreading out before him. His commander's mind quickly assessed the unfolding disaster, just like he would in battling any enemy. But this time the enemy was the very earth itself.

Immediate action was required. Finding a long broken pole, he removed his tunic, and affixed it to one end. He climbed atop a boulder, still hot to the touch. He raised it high in the air, and slowly twirled it. Handing the pole to another he raised his sword high, the signal unmistakable. *Rally to me.*

A few scattered soldiers in the crowd and on the ships noticed it. Some pointed to it, to him. Others looked to see what they were pointing at. More and more eyes drifted to the outcropping, the fluttering tunic, the glint of an upheld sword. To the single beacon of hope amidst the carnage.

As others flocked to him, Thálassa used their numbers to form an escort and forced his way through the masses, down to his flagship. Yidini was already there, while other scattered captains and local military leaders muscled their way in. The soldiers' discipline stiffened with the arrival of their admiral. A protective cordon was formed around the ship. One tiny oasis of order in a sea of mayhem. Thálassa climbed aboard and stood upon the prow, to be clearly visible and heard.

"We can't save everyone. But we must save all we can," Thálassa shouted to those assembled.

He pointed his sword at several captains. "You two, take your ships across to Akrotiri." He glanced upward, and saw the blasting column seeming to reach its apex. It was flattening far above in the sky, spreading outward like spilled ink. It seemed to be drifting more toward the east, steadily darkening the heavens above.

"Load all you can and head to open seas." He aimed his sword at the edge of the great cloud spreading above. "Away from that, toward Kríti."

"Who shall we take?" one asked. "All will demand passage."

"Only those who will help us survive," Thálassa yelled in reply. "Be ruthless. This is war!"

Those captains gathered their own escort and pushed toward their ships. When the crowd refused to part, swords and spears were lowered. Many were slashed before the masses yielded, but the going was difficult. As soon as they gained any ground, the mob closed in again in their wake.

Demos had discretely accompanied Thálassa down to the ship, and climbed aboard to man an oar. He saw Kalli by the mast, their eyes briefly meeting. He smiled despite himself. She was here, safe. Thank the gods he was a useful slave.

His smile quickly faded, his eyes drawn toward the inferno that was Mount Thíra, at the firestorm in the sky. At the rain of death all around them becoming ever more intense by the moment.

Thálassa saw the difficulty at the other beached ships from the bow and jumped down. He grabbed Yidini by the shoulder, and raised his sword high. Captains and soldiers crowded in on them expectantly.

"They need help. Form a rear guard around Yidini," he yelled. "One ship at a time. Fill them. See them off." Yidini's eyes met his. They both knew what he was asking. Thálassa nodded at him, acknowledging his sacrifice. Yidini saluted sharply, thumping his fist to his heart, then raising his own sword.

"On me," Yidini hollered above the bedlam, pointing over to the next ship. The troops hacked their way over, pushing the crowd back, and formed a protective beachhead around the ship. People were tossed off the ship into the harbor, while others were quickly ushered aboard. Once it was filled to nearly sinking, it pushed off. Yidini pointed to the next ship, the process repeating.

Back aboard his flag ship, Thálassa climbed back upon the prow to better command events. He directed ships waiting offshore to beach and take on passengers as cordons could be formed. Several ships that had been fleeing saw some semblance of order restored. They turned about out of guilt, ready to take on their own load of desperate humanity.

Thálassa knew time was of the essence. He noticed the falling of the heaviest boulders seemed to taper off, but the smaller ones blasted higher continued to rain upon them. Worst of all were the molten firebombs that spattered everywhere upon impact, setting fire to anything in their path. Even ships escaping beyond the great port were not immune. He motioned for the last passengers to

lips, down his chest, and stopped at his belly button. He noticed her hand, missing the pinkie. Something gnawed at the back of his memory.

"As you said, we have fun. Lots of fun." She giggled, and wrapped herself around him. "You not 'a remember anything?" She was obviously enjoying his discomfort.

Nick looked at her, slowly shaking his head no. He was still trying to understand her stilted English, her accent, the cadence of her speech.

"Not even your name," he said.

She released him and playfully pushed him away, feigning offense.

"Persa. Pleased to meet you again for first time Níkos."

Nick stared blankly. Her name just didn't register.

"Persa," he repeated to himself. "If you would be so kind, perhaps you could refresh my memory."

She got up, and put on a red silk bathrobe. Opening the window wide, she took a deep breath, then crossed her arms and looked at him. Like she had this conversation before.

"We meet at Blues Bar. You bought me drink. We listen to band. Any'ting so far?"

"No. I've never blacked out before." Nick walked over to the window and leaned out, admiring the view.

"I remember going to the bar, and having a drink. By myself."

A large dog in the corner of the yard heard his voice. It got up out of the shade, and looked at him. Getting no reaction, it huffed and wagged its tail.

"Your dog," Persa said. "He follow you all way here."

"I don't have a dog. I don't live anywhere near here."

"Well, dog, he not 'a know that. But I know all about you. We talk for hours after, well, after we . . ." She looked at the bed and smiled. "After we boom boom."

"I don't mean to be rude, but this is all just so strange."

"Níkos, you 'a tell me you work on dive site. Salvage big piece Greek history. You now have time off. Until next stage. We agree to take little trip."

"Persa, I don't even know who you are. What exactly is it you do?"

"OK. We start again, silly. Pay attention dis time," she teased, walking by and kissing him lightly on the cheek. "I pack bag while we talk. If get to Piraeus soon, we in Santorini by nightfall.

"Santorini?"

"I do ocean research. My father fisherman before me. That why I interested in sea, how I lose dis," she said, waving her left hand with the missing finger.

"What's there for you?"

"Where we map ocean floor. Tectonic plates, yes? You most insistent to come with me. When I say I go Santorini."

Nick rubbed his head, deep in thought. "I did hear from Heinrich. I have a lead on something I need to dig into there."

"So you said."

"If you are an oceanographic researcher, and are headed there anyway, it would be perfect. You really don't mind if I accompany you?"

"I not mind last night. Not 'a mind this morning." She snapped him mischievously with a thong, then threw it in her bag and zipped it up. "We have fun, yes?"

"What was his name Doc? The guy you said was a Vulcanologist?" Nick asked.

"Jim Portmess. He's your man Nick. An American, a crackerjack expert in the field. But a real character too. Stavros said you better strap on your seatbelt if you go out with him."

"I've got an opportunity to bang around the Cyclades for a while. Maybe I can look him up."

"Professional or pleasure?" Dr. Storm asked.

"Both. I met a very intriguing young woman. An oceanographic researcher. I'm accompanying her to Santorini."

"Good, very good. Take advantage of the downtime. I'd so hate to see youth wasted on the young," Dr. Storm replied wistfully.

"Thanks Doc. I'll be in touch."

Nick hung up and looked over at Persa. She was busy concentrating on the traffic, driving a battered pickup truck through crowded streets. They inched along, Persa waving at the people from her neighborhood.

"I maka quick stop before trip, OK Níkos?" she asked.

Nick nodded at her, then gazed out. As they drove toward the outskirts of Athens, the view could have been from fifty or a hundred years ago. Little had changed except for the vehicles driving on streets too narrow for them. A scooter passed them on the wrong side, the girl with her arms around her boyfriend laughing while he grabbed a flower from a window basket for her.

Small cafés and businesses lined the streets. The apartment buildings eventually giving way to small stone houses. Laundry hung on lines, empty spaces popped up here and there, and crops of grapes, apples, and olives became more prominent. The strange newness of it all was enchanting to Nick, like a place he had always longed for but never been for any length of time. Lost in his thoughts, a moist nose poked through the open back window, sniffing him.

"I think I made a friend."

"There worse things, no?" Persa asked.

"There worse things, yes." Nick chuckled.

The truck eventually pulled off and headed down a rough, rarely used road. As branches scratched at the sides, Persa carefully maneuvered around long-neglected potholes. The big dog paced anxiously in back, bouncing in rhythm with the truck bed. They came to a halt in front of a worn stone wall with a broken gate. Above it, between two decayed stone pillars, was a wrought iron Star of David.

"Hope you not 'a mind," Persa said, reaching over and grabbing the flowers she had picked that morning.

The dog bounded down and wandered off, sniffing for game. Nick opened the gate, which protested on its one working hinge. He propped it open, and followed Persa in. Her mood, so buoyant that morning and on the ride out, turned solemn. He stayed a respectful few paces behind her. She walked deep toward the middle of the cemetery. Reaching her destination, she pulled out a Tallit prayer shawl and knelt in front of a series of weathered grave stones. She traced the names and dates with one finger, praying. Her other hand rubbed the tassels of the shawl she wore, like worry stones.

Nick glanced around at the inscriptions, and saw no recent dates. This was a cemetery of the past, frozen in time. He didn't find a single date later than 1944. It was as if the world for these inhabitants had suddenly ended, a place long forlorn and forgotten.

Persa moved on her knees from one grave stone to the next, finally stopping in front of one in particular. It was the single grave that looked recent, the earth overturned, not yet reclaimed like everything else had been. She carefully replaced dead flowers with the fresh ones she brought. Nick thought he saw her sobbing, and walked up behind her. He said nothing, just placed a hand on her shoulder. She took a deep breath, and started praying again. He looked down and read the two names on the marker:

Yitzhak Theocritus 1943-2004
Zelda Theocritus 1953-2021

Nick had several close Jewish friends, and recognized the prayer, the Kel Maleh Rachamim, or Hebrew Prayer of Mercy. He softly joined in, and felt Persa's voice become clearer, her tears subsiding. She reached up and held the hand on her shoulder. Finishing, she composed herself, and got up and faced him.

"My parents. In this place of ghosts," Persa said. "They so wanted children. They tried and tried. Miscarriages. I der only child."

She walked him over to the first grave stones she had knelt at.

"Great grandparents here. They live and die when Greece have, how you say, much to offer. Other relatives too," she said, pointing to names and markers. "Their lives come then go, join soil of this place."

They moved to the next set of markers.

Persa sighed. "My *pappoús*. Grandpa. No body, just eyeglasses buried here."

The enormity of it all dawned on Nick.

"My grandmama, just lock of hair from picture frame. Poor *Giagiá.*" She trembled as she spoke.

Nick's shoulders slumped. He knew what had happened without asking. Even here, so far away from the middle of Europe. Condemned to the fate of the damned.

"Greek Jews, trains take to camps. Jews on Corfu and Rhodes too. All to Auschwitz. None come back here."

She wiped her eyes, and looked across the cemetery. "Few that live, go Israel. Not parents. They stay here, so I bury with family. When time come, I bury here too."

Persa hung her head again, wandering and praying to herself. When she had finally seen enough, they started walking back to the truck. Nick found a broken bit of wire, and worked it into the bottom hinge of the gate. It screeched just as loudly as before, but swung closed and caught on the latch. He then gave a short, two-note whistle, and the dog came running.

"I saw your mother wasn't born until after the war. How did your father survive it?"

"Kind people hid him. Not everyone hate Jüdin. But war eventually kill him anyway. *Ima*, she widow 17 years. Miss him every minute."

Nick was about to ask what she meant about the war killing her father. After all, the grave stone said he hadn't died until 2004. Watching her body language, he decided now wasn't the time.

"You 'a know what Stalin said Níkos? One death tragic. One million a statistic."

They drove back through Athens, arrived at the port, and parked. It wasn't quite so busy since it was Sunday. Other than the arriving tourists being herded onto buses.

Persa's demeanor had changed. The sorrow was replaced with something harder, sharper.

Perhaps anger or a want of vengeance, Nick thought. *Too bad those accountable are gone.*

A nearby poster caught Nick's eye, the face vaguely familiar. He walked up to it to examine more closely. The figure was sitting at a piano on stage in a crowded theater. The Cyrilic text was beyond him.

"Persa, what does this say?"

"Upcoming concert. That Kollas. Think he own everything here. And everyone." Her contempt was palatable.

"He's a concert pianist?"

"Da, performs to raise money for causes. His causes."

Nick thought he heard her swear, but didn't know what a Greek obscenity even sounded like.

"I thought he was an industrialist or something."

"His old money. Just 'a blood money from another time."

"What are his causes?"

She smiled, her demeanor quickly changing back to the playful seductress Nick had first met.

"We no 'a talk politic now. Kollas eat skatá. We go, enjoy trip."

As they grabbed their bags, the dog jumped down expectantly. Persa looked at Nick and gave him sad eyes.

"Dog stay or go? Time you decide."

Nick bent down and rubbed the neck, the dog leaning into him. It was a big breed, some type of Mastiff he guessed from the frame and distinctive face. She was a little thin, her black and white coat was matted, unkept. It was deep and dense around the neck, the skin loose. The evolutionary trait that protected the breed from other carnivores. Nick guessed it had been turned loose by an owner who didn't have the funds to maintain or the heart to kill. Not so very different from his own backstory.

For some reason, of all the lost souls wandering around Athens, she had somehow bonded with him.

"So, what exactly is your story girl?" he asked. She held up a huge outstretched paw. "You were bred to guard something. I guess now that's me."

Persa smiled, obviously agreeing with his decision. She merrily led the way, Nick following. The dog sat, waiting. When Nick noticed it wasn't with them, he gave a quick whistle. The dog bounded after them, then bumped between them with her high hips. To take the lead.

"She hava no tag on collar?"

"None. Do you know what the breed is?"

"Da. Descended from *Molossus*. Friend have one. Good Greek breed, strong like bull. From mountains."

Nick thought hard for a moment. Dogs had always been important to him and his family. Coming up with the right name was no small matter.

"If she were a he, I'd name her *Zeus*. But since she's a girl, I'll go with *Artemis*." The dog turned around, tail wagging. "Good girl, Artemis."

Persa grinned. "I like name. Goddess of hunt."

They walked along, toward the commercial docks at the far edge. Nick smiled inwardly when they passed the Poseidon, berthed nearby. Soon he would be out on her again, diving to reveal secrets hidden beneath the waves.

But not today. Instead, today he would be riding above them. On an adventure in one of the most beautiful places on earth. With a captivating woman he really didn't know.

CHAPTER 15

JUNE 13, PRESENT DAY, DELOS, GREECE

Nick looked all around him, the view mesmerizing. There was just something about the vividness of the colors of the sky, sea, and islands, the smell of salt water spray, the sense of freedom in the wind that energized him. He always wanted to sail the Aegean, but time and circumstance had always conspired against him. But not today. Today he was on a catamaran with his own personal Greek goddess. And it turned out she was a bang-up tour guide to boot.

"You know Cyclades mean? I tell you," Persa said, not waiting for an answer. "All islands around Delos in middle. Like circle. Cyclades, circle. Get it?" She made a circle with her hands for emphasis, then pointed to an island starboard off the bow. "We go Delos now."

"I can't believe I will actually get to set foot there." Nick said. "That was a sacred island to the ancient Greeks."

Persa rolled her eyes, like no kidding. "Wait until you see ruins. Your eyes 'a gonna pop out."

Nick beamed. "Can't wait. For centuries it was sacred to the Minoans, then the Myceneans, and then the Greeks. They made offerings there, left undisturbed."

"Yes, until Mithridates destroy. Then pirates come."

"You certainly know your history," Nick replied. "You should give tours."

"I am," she said proudly. "To party of one."

Artemis had been laying up front on the netting between the twin hulls of the catamaran, her nose to the wind. She heard the bantering and came back, looking for a little attention.

"Hey girl, Delos was the birthplace not just of Apollo, but your namesake Artemis too," Nick said. He got on his knees and rubbed behind her ears. He noticed Persa discretely looking at her phone, something troubling her. When she saw Nick looking at her, she slipped it into her back pocket quickly and forced a grin.

They stopped just offshore and anchored in an isolated lagoon. While the island was uninhabited, it was periodically overrun with tourists, mostly from nearby Mykonos. The Archeological Museum was but one attraction, while the ruins and excavations revealed its long and rich history.

They lowered a Zodiac, a durable inflatable boat, off the catamaran. Nick whistled to Artemis, who gingerly stepped in, unsure of herself. Persa started the small motor and expertly guided them to a vacant beach. Nick stepped ashore, and reached down and rubbed sand between his fingers. Symbolically connecting himself with the ancient land. Artemis bounded off, chasing sea birds along the surf.

"First eat, den explore," Persa said.

She spread an old sleeping bag out on the beach, nylon side down so the sand wouldn't stick. She anchored one end with a cooler and the other with a picnic basket. Nick plopped down cross legged, admiring the view and the feast being laid out. Cold ceviche, grapes, olives, cheeses, pita bread. And of course, chilled white wine. Nick uncorked the bottle and poured them each a generous amount.

They clinked glasses and took a long sip, staring at each other. Cold, crisp and complex, Nick thought he had never tasted a more perfect wine. But perhaps that was the exotic setting and company enhancing it.

"Where is this from? It's fantastic," he asked.

"From where we go. Santorini."

"Ah, volcanic soil. I should have known."

"Da. That why people live there. Even when go boom."

Nick laughed out loud. In a single thought Persa had succinctly summarized the irresistible attraction of peoples, both ancient and contemporary, to geologically unstable lands. The bitter irony was that volcanos created rich soil that yielded the richest crops. History was littered with the corpses of those who couldn't resist the lure despite the risk. At places such as Vesuvius, Mount Etna, and Krakatoa. And of course, Santorini.

"Oceanographic researcher, eh? What exactly am I getting myself into?"

Persa passed him a heaping plate.

"You see on ship tomorrow. Today, we explore."

They finished lunch, then worked their way up off the beach. Artemis romped around them, exploring, but never far away. Nick got the feeling they were being guarded, the herding instinct of the breed showing through. It made him miss Nanook, Soba's dog who had bonded so strongly with him. Who had so loyally died protecting them.

His pulse quickening, Nick crested a rise. Before him the magnificent ancient mysteries of Delos revealed themselves. Persa, excited to show him its wonders, took his hand and pointed.

"There Mount Kynthos. We climb later. First see important secret."

"What secret?" Nick asked.

Persa put a finger to her lips and leaned into his ear to whisper. Nick bent down and listened hard. Suddenly she roared, startling him. She giggled, and kissed his cheek.

"Lions. We see lions!"

As they hiked upward from the beach, a pier and cruise ships gradually revealed themselves off in the distance. Tourists in brightly colored outfits and a scattering of sun umbrellas wandered about. Here and there tour guides held up flags to gather their flock before a particularly interesting site. Persa had carefully chosen her anchorage to give them the illusion of privacy during their lunch. For here among the ruins, there was none.

"It appears all of Mykonos has landed," Nick joked.

They made their way through an ancient marketplace, known as an agora, then skirted the Sacred Lake. It was the legendary birthplace of the god Apollo and his sister Artemis. Drained long ago to prevent malaria, it was one of the few areas with any vegetation.

"Ta-da!" Persa announced.

Arrayed before them was the most recognizable view on the island, the iconic Lions of Delos. Gifted by the Naxians in the seventh century BC, those that hadn't been plundered stood in a row, still protectively facing the Sacred Lake.

"Magnificent. This is better preserved than what I ever thought." Nick gazed all around him, at the temples, the House of Dionysus, the theater, buildings great and small. "It's overwhelming."

"Many come here. Build on what others build. Ideas grow. Greece flourish," Persa observed. "Now, we climb."

They took the most direct route, avoiding the circuitous path the crowds of tourists were following. Steadily gaining elevation, it took them past the Temple of Isis and then the Temple of Hercules. They found a well-worn ancient pathway, Artemis instinctively leading the way. Nick could only wonder at whose footsteps had tread here over the millennia.

While only four hundred feet high, Mount Kynthos was the highest point on the island, affording a panorama of the entire landscape. A hot breeze rose toward them. Nick slowly circled around to take it all in.

"What a view! Let's take a selfie."

He took his phone out and put his arm around Persa. "Say feta!"

Persa expertly slipped from his grip, and gingerly took his phone.

"Me here many times. Take you," she said. She stepped back, Nick kneeling down with Artemis.

"Say Ya mas!"

"Your mama!" Nick replied.

Persa snapped a shot, looked at it, and handed the phone back.

"I think she's shy girl. What do you think?" Nick whispered to Artemis as he gave her a rub.

They explored other sites on the way down, Nick lingering at certain ones. Persa would point to her watch and drag him away. But like a magnet he was inexorably drawn to the Archeological Museum.

"Thirty minutes only," Persa said before letting Nick enter. "Three-oh. Hear me?"

"That's cruel to an archeologist. Why are you so mean?" Nick joked.

"Must make Santorini today. Work tomorrow."

"If I take more than thirty, we have no fun?"

"No." she said, arms crossed with a pout face. "You hava no fun."

"OK, thirty it is. Gotta run."

With that Nick sprinted into the museum, snapping pictures at a furious pace to review on the sail to Santorini.

He sat looking at the photos, bouncing to the cadence of the waves, then gave up. The view around him was simply too sublime not to enjoy. What had Stavros said about Americans, they never live in the moment? Here was one to live in. He glanced over at Persa, holding the wheel of the catamaran, hair flowing in the breeze, bronzed skin shimmering in the late afternoon sun.

He had made it back in thirty minutes. Thirty-two to be exact, but she said close enough for an archeologist. Which was promising. Perhaps they could still have some fun, yes?

"You. Steer."

Nick was startled out of his daydreaming. She was giving him the wheel. He jumped up, anxious to actually be doing the sailing, rather than just being ballast. Although in this setting, being ballast wasn't all bad.

He grasped the large wheel, which handled tighter than he

would have guessed. They were making a good fourteen knots, a pretty fast clip for this class of catamaran.

Persa stood behind him, and guided his hands. She gently kicked at his stance.

"Spread feet. You fall, wheel spin."

"Let me guess. Wheel spin, we lose momentum. We lose momentum, Persa get mad. We no want 'a that," he said, teasing her accent.

She let her hands slide off the wheel, and held him around the waist. She hugged him tightly, her flowing hair tickling him.

"No. We no want 'a that."

It was just before sunset when they sailed into the old caldera that had been Mount Thera. Scattered islands were all that was left, Santorini being the largest and most prominent. Persa was at the helm, carefully watching the depth monitor. The port in sight, she showed Nick how to bring in the sails, and switched to the engine.

"What are the main ports here?" Nick asked.

"Old port under Fira. Too busy, tourists there. New Port under Athinios. Ferries there, busy too," Persa answered. She navigated toward the crescent-moon-shaped main island. "We go 'a here instead."

Nick saw they were headed to a smaller port on the north side of the crescent. They pulled into the anchorage, a sign on shore announced they sat beneath Oia. Persa dropped the anchor, and went below while Nick admired the view. He picked up the nautical map to orient himself. Looking west, the sun was just setting on *Thirasia*, the other island-remanent rimming the caldera. A small volcano jutted up in the very middle of the caldera. A reminder of past cataclysms.

Santorini

Persa emerged from the galley with two chilled shots of Ouzo and a light dinner. She smiled and handed a shot to Nick. They sat silently, listening to blues music playing on the sound system. She leaned into him, and watched the sun finish its downward arc, sipping and savoring the strong licorice flavor of anise. They nibbled as the air cooled, the sky turning from red to purple, then finally to black. When the pinpricks of stars started winking above, Persa got up and sat on Nick's lap.

"You good Amerikanós at museum today. Not take 'a too long."

"And hey, not a bad sailor either, right?"

"No, not 'a too bad," she said, kissing him deeply. "Tomorrow we in bunk room. Wid others."

"And tonight, we have this whole catamaran to ourselves," Nick observed.

Persa started giggling. Artemis was licking at her toes.

"Well, almost."

Later, Persa rolled over and gently woke up Nick. He didn't know how long they had lain there. Her skin was cool to the touch. The stars above were brilliant, galaxies and constellations clearly visible. A shooting star arced gracefully through them. The soft rocking of the waves and the lingering euphoria conspired to lull him back to sleep.

"I get 'a ready for work tomorrow. Morning come early," she said, getting dressed.

Nick checked his cell phone for signal strength. "I've got a call to make. I'll be down in a little bit."

He dialed a number, and unconsciously walked to the side of the boat facing where he was calling. Like they could see him if he looked that way. He realized what he was doing and laughed at himself. Strange habits in this day of seamless, everywhere connectivity.

Artemis followed and sat by his feet. Getting no attention, she plopped on his foot, huffing. Nick sat down and started rubbing behind her ears with one hand.

"Hallo, wer ist das?"

"Heinrich, it's Nick."

"Ah, Nickolas, Ich been trying to reach you. Ich have huge news for you."

Nick wanted a private conversation, and glanced around to see where Persa might be. Not seeing her, he turned his attention back on Heinrich. Artemis's ears perked up, hearing something. Curious, she wandered off to investigate.

"Lay it on me Heinie. I could sure use some good news."

The research vessel, or RV, was docked below Fira. It certainly wasn't the newest or biggest one Nick had ever been on. But it was well outfitted with the latest equipment, and manned by an efficient and experienced crew. The *Serafina* was one of several in the Greek fleet. She had been built in 1986, was 98 feet long at the beam and displaced 143 tons. He was impressed by the array of scientific equipment onboard, including the multibeam and side scan sonars, remote operated vehicle (ROV), underwater cameras and sledges, sediment traps, draggers, and trawls.

"Níkos, this Captain Rouvas," Persa said, introducing a trim man who appeared to be in his fifties, with a neatly clipped white beard and impeccable uniform.

"Pleased to meet you Captain," Nick said, feeling his hand engulfed by a massive mitt. The strength of the grip betrayed this was a man who didn't just delegate the work.

"Alekos, but please, call me Alek. Welcome to our humble little ship. We do hope to tease some secrets out of the depths."

"She is not so humble. This is the real deal. Very impressive. But tell me, why is the ship named the Serafina?"

Alek smiled, finally relinquishing his grip. "Our mission is to research the fire below. Before it becomes the fire above. And does great harm."

"Serafina Hebrew," Persa added. "Mean fiery one. Appropriate, no?"

It was Nick's turn to grin. "Appropriate, yes."

"Our Persefoni here tells me you are a professional archeologist, working with Stavros and his team up north. That is a significant discovery. We are most pleased to have you aboard."

"And honored to be here. Your English is better than mine sir. The connection?" Nick inquired.

"Study abroad in my youth. I did my PhD in Geodynamics in England. I do tend to speak the King's English when I'm not speaking Greek."

"As George Bernard Shaw said, 'England and America, two countries separated by a common language,'" Nick joked.

"Well said. I'll let you get settled, and look forward to dining with you in the mess tonight."

Alek tipped his cap and turned his attention back to the bridge. Persa gestured toward the narrow passageway. Nick grabbed his backpack and followed her through a hatch, down a ladder, and to the crew's quarters.

"How many aboard?" he asked.

"Six crew. Two scientists. You," Persa said.

"And you are one of the scientists?"

"Da. Used to crew other ship. Did studies so can do research. More money. More, how you say, interesting."

"I'm looking forward to seeing you in action."

"Ha. You see enough action already Níkos."

Nick blushed slightly and smirked. *A real firecracker, this one.*

The Serafina weighed anchor and cruised out of the port. They slowly passed the larger volcano in the middle of the great caldera to their port side. It was known as *Nea Kameni*, the new volcano. A smaller one behind it then revealed itself, *Palaia Kameni*, or old burnt volcano. Once the outer rim island of Therasia slipped by off to the stern, they emerged into the broad expanse of the Aegean.

Nick peered over Persa's shoulder as she stared intently at a screen, monitoring their progress. The task for the day was to record a small stretch of where two enormous floating pieces of the earth's crust, tectonic plates, were grinding against one another. The subduction of the African plate under the Eurasian plate created a large volcanic arc, with Santorini firmly in the middle.

"We go straight. Turn, come back straight. Turn again," Persa pointed out on the screen. "Do all day. Map carefully."

"The ships I worked on called that mowing the lawn." Nick replied.

"Good analogy," Captain Alek commented. "Not as exciting as diving for treasure, but it does a good job of turning up anomalies."

"See how far plates move. Too much stress, bad things happen," Persa added.

Alek leaned over her other shoulder. "The greater goal is early warning to shoreline communities. If the plates keep sliding just a little at a time, that is good. Like a pressure valve. If they build up too much stress, they could release all at once."

"And create undersea earthquakes, which produce tsunamis. And all the collateral volcanic activity, I assume," Nick said.

Persa sat up and rubbed her eyes from staring too long. "Big booms dangerous. If no warning."

Alek looked at Nick and winked. "This process does tend to occasionally turn up more interesting things. Let me show you."

He walked Nick over to another bank of monitors. Alek queued up an old video feed, which showed ghostly footage of several ribs of a sunken ship. Large clay amphora lay strew about, several unbroken. Intermingled were other smaller containers, and what appeared to be ingots of some type of metal.

"We came across this over toward Crete just last month. It's over a mile down, had never been seen. Showed up as a dark anomaly when we were, well, when we were mowing the proverbial lawn."

Nick looked closer, and touched the screen. "Bronze Age?"

Alek nodded. "That's what our scientists think."

"Tin and copper. None of that was native to Crete. They had to import it to make bronze weapons."

Alek clapped him loudly on the back. "Stick with that archeology thing young man. I think you've a future in it."

The crew worked in shifts, the methodical scanning of the ocean floor never ceasing. The captain and first mate carefully guided the navigation with pinpoint GPS, compensating for wind, tides, and currents. No drifting was allowed. Persa and her scientific counterpart also constantly rotated, one always on duty at the monitors. Ensuring every piece of equipment was perfectly capturing that section of the ocean floor. If anything exciting or out of the ordinary was found, Captain Alek got a call. Day or night.

In the mess the following evening, Alek sat at the traditional head of the table, flanked by Persa and Nick. Those crew not on duty joined them, good naturedly bantering back and forth. So far it had been a good cruise, the weather favorable. Perhaps they were even a little ahead of schedule for a change.

"Thank you, Captain, for your hospitality," Nick said, raising a glass to his host.

"You are most welcome. I trust we didn't bore you too badly."

"Not at all. It's been an education. More than I could have asked for."

Captain Alek drank, then set his glass down. "A man such as you sees different pieces of things. Then puts them together. Sometimes in ways others wouldn't have the intuition to. So tell me, what do these pieces tell you?"

Nick frowned for a moment, deep in thought. "You know we are working on recovering a trireme, and that had absorbed most of my thoughts. As it should, it is such a big part of Greek history."

Two of the crew heard the word trireme, started talking, then mimicked rowing and chuckled.

Persa saw Nick's confused look. "They joke. Say good news. Lunch time. Then bad news. After lunch, captain of trireme want to water ski."

Alek couldn't suppress a smile and shook his head.

Nick laughed out loud, then continued. "But seeing your work here, all the footage of other ancient wrecks you showed me, the museums I visited, my own research. It makes me want to dig into certain myths, to see if they are based on any historical reality."

"Particular myth?" Persa asked.

"Yes," Nick said, looking at Persa then Alek. "I'll let you all know if anything comes of it."

"To the myths of the sea," Captain Alek toasted, raising a glass.

"Ya mas," came the reply from around the table.

Before Nick dozed off in his bunk, he connected his cell phone to the ship's wireless to check one last detail. The captain had called Persa by her full name, Persefoni. She had never used her formal name around him. He actually didn't even know it until then. A subtle detail, but now he was curious. He plugged it into a search, and the meaning popped up. It didn't make sense to him.

He tried a different search, just to be sure. Same result. It was a girl's name, of old Greek origin. As he lay there, it troubled him. Who would possibly name their little girl that? Perhaps more importantly, why? There was certainly no gray area in the definition of what it meant.

Bringer of death.

CHAPTER 16

JUNE 16, PRESENT DAY, SANTORINI, GREECE

Nick got off the tender at *Skala*, the port that catered to cruise ships and private tour boats. It was not a deep-water port, and other tenders were busily shuffling passengers from the large ships anchored offshore. Above it all loomed *Fira*, the beautiful capital of Santorini.

He had spent two days aboard the Serafina, eagerly observing the deep-sea mapping and research being conducted. Captain Alek had been most gracious, allowing full access to their mission, while also sharing insight of anything even remotely archeological in nature. He had caught a ride back in when repair items and provisions had been brought out.

Persa would be aboard until she rotated back out, at a yet-to-be-determined date. Perhaps they would get back together if their schedules allowed. Time would tell. Nick grinned, reflecting on the time he had spent with her.

We have fun, yes?

Artemis whined and nudged him back to the present with a moist nose. She saw donkeys lined up at the landing to give the tourists rides up the steep cliffside. The quintessential Santorini experience. Or so the vendors hawking the rides claimed. Nick shook his head in disgust, and watched several of the sure-footed animals struggle with overly heavy loads.

A picturesque cable car provided alternative transportation up to the rim. Tourists in a long line jostled for position while yet another cruise ship pulled in just offshore.

"We've been sitting for too long girl," he said to Artemis. "We're going old school."

Artemis looked up at him and tilted her head.

"You know what they say." He laughed, giving her a rub along the thick fur of her neck. "Old school's the best school."

They slowly worked their way up the steep path, pausing at the switchbacks to let donkeys pass in both directions. Nick's heart pounded hard until he found his rhythm, and gradually adjusted to the exertion.

Funny, the guides seem to have no trouble climbing this. Too bad a few more of the tourists didn't skip the buffet line to give it a go.

They carefully sidestepped the gifts the donkeys periodically deposited along the route, avoiding the accompanying swarms of flies. The view became ever more spectacular as they gradually gained elevation. It was a vista unlike any he had ever seen. Finally cresting the ridge, he found a shady spot to take in the spellbinding panorama. While Artemis lay panting, Nick caught his own breath.

"1650 BC buddy. This is not where you wanted to be."

"I don't know about that. It would have been one hell of a show." A hulking bear of a man walked up to Nick and extended his hand. "Damned pleased to meet you."

"Jim Portmess? How the hell did you know it was me?" Nick asked.

"Well, how many tourists actually take the time to climb up here? With a dog, no less. You said meet at nine. I figured it had to be you."

They walked over to a nearby tavern and grabbed a table on the veranda, under a bright blue umbrella. Jim sat down like he owned the place. Nick set his sweat-soaked backpack down, Artemis finding shade under the table.

"*Karáfa Assytriko sas parakaloúme,*" Jim called out to a pretty, dark haired waitress. He whistled softly as she walked away.

Jim grinned and looked at Nick, like they had known one

another all their lives. "Assytriko, you know? Santorini's best known dry white wine. Grown right here, from the rich volcanic soil. A taste of Thera, as it were."

Déjà vu, thought Nick.

The waitress brought it back quickly with a flourish and a sly glance at Jim. There were few other customers this early in the day. She also thoughtfully brought along a dish of water for Artemis.

"Hair of the dog," Jim toasted to Nick, then took a long drink and poured himself another. He looked down at the large dog at their feet and laughed. "No offense."

Nick sipped at his, then set it down. Stavros had been right about this character. Strap on your seatbelt.

"I'm sure none was taken," Nick replied, petting Artemis.

"Hey, by the way, congrats on that Aztec discovery. You actually don't look anything like I had pictured," Jim said.

"You mean how the tabloids pictured."

"Yeah, that. Enjoy your fifteen minutes of fame?"

Nick smiled. There was no escape.

"I could do without it. You must lead an adventurous life as a Vulcanologist." he said, purposely changing the subject.

Just like Stavros had mentioned he would do, Jim took the bait and chance to talk about one of his favorite subjects. Himself.

"I think every Vulcanologist does. It's in the job description," he joked. "The more eruptions we study, the more we are going to understand how they behave. But I lost a dear friend, crazy story. You ever hear it?"

Nick shook his head no.

"Mark Dumas. Best friend I ever had. We worked together in the field for years. We were in Japan back in '11, at Mount Unzen. The site was hot—you know, active. We had been carefully monitoring it. Mark switched shifts with me so I could give an interview. A fricking interview."

Jim paused, composing himself. Nick could tell the wound still cut deep, all these years later.

"A pyroclastic flow killed over forty people that day. Including Mark."

"Damn. Sorry to hear that," Nick said.

"Yeah, well I saw you've had your own losses. You get it."

They sat in silence for a few minutes, each lost in their own thoughts. Nick soaked in the view, playing various ancient scenarios out in his mind's eye. Of what it really might have been like to have actually been here—at this very spot—when Thera erupted and collapsed in upon itself, back into the sea.

"*Igne natura renovatur integra*," Nick finally toasted in Latin, curious if Jim would get the reference.

"Through fire nature is reborn whole," he replied thoughtfully. "Cheers to that."

Two carafes later, Nick realized he was more than a little buzzed. Jim was just getting warmed up. Nick ordered food to maintain some sense of equilibrium. He wanted the conversation to be productive, and wasn't sure he could keep pace with Big Jim.

"What I need is to learn more about the mechanics of eruptions, the underlying forces that generate them. I have a theory taking shape. But I need to vet it, to see if it holds water. Because when I announce it, I suspect some important people are going to get pretty upset."

"Well, you've certainly got the right guy. And hey, I'm right in the middle of something very relevant."

Jim took a deep drink and frowned at the empty carafe. Two Ouzo, he signaled the waiter. "Say, I can always use a wing man. How long you got?"

"A week, more or less. I'm on call for an underwater recovery that could break loose anytime."

"Sounds perfect. We can always get you back if needed."

"From where?"

"From the best place to learn all about plate tectonics and vulcanology," Jim said. He chugged the rest of his wine and slammed the glass down. The waiter dropped off the two shots, and Jim raised one to Nick.

"On a live volcano!"

"I feel like the frickin' tin man," Nick said, flexing the arms of his silver suit about unsurely. He was sweating buckets, and they hadn't even descended into the crater yet. He looked through the visor of the silver cone on his head, getting his bearings.

"Welcome to Hades my friend," Jim said. "Let's not keep Charon waiting, shall we?"

Great, I'm melting and he's joking about the ferryman taking our souls across the River Styx.

They were on the nearby island of Milos, where a stratovolcano had been slowly stirring to life. Most famous for the Venus de Milo, which had been found here, the island was being closely monitored to give early warning to its inhabitants. Jim, with Nick's assistance, was going to place additional sensors beneath the rim.

Jim led the way down the faintest hint of a trail. Nick trailed closely behind, walking mechanically. Trying not to lose his footing on the loose bits of scree and pumice. Jim turned around and put a hand up. "Stay at least seven or eight feet behind," he cautioned. "If you fall, I don't want you taking me with you."

They had put headbands around their foreheads to keep the sweat out of their eyes. It seemed a losing strategy to Nick. The visor slit was starting to fog, and he blinked hard in an attempt to see clearly

"Got it," Nick replied.

And thanks for the vote of confidence, he thought.

They each carried a half dozen sensors in a reflective pouch. Jim pointed around to where Nick should place his. The warmth he had first felt at the rim was just from the suit heating up in the bright Mediterranean sunlight. Down below the rim, the real heat arose from the bowels of the earth. Nick peered, and caught a glimmer of lava bubbling far below. The breath of Hades. The gateway to the underworld.

This isn't sweating. This is cooking.

He looked to Jim, who appeared to be going about his business nonchalantly. When they both completed their placements, Jim gave him a thumb's up, then pointed to a ledge. They both carefully walked over to it. The spot afforded an unobstructed view into the chamber far below. At least Nick hoped it was far below. It was hard to tell through his stinging eyes. He tilted his head down, then instinctively backed up and looked away.

"Pretty typical reaction for first timers," Jim yelled over to him. It was loud where they stood, sound you felt more than heard. "Man up buddy. Take a good look into the soul of Mother Earth."

Nick screwed up his courage and walked a few tentative steps forward. He leaned back instinctively, finally forcing himself to look downward. He shuddered involuntarily. Searingly hot thermals vented directly upward, blasting at his suit and headgear. The heat shot by him like a solar wind, the surface of his suit crinkling from the intensity. He stood there, mesmerized by the bubbling caldron of molten stone. A thought gnawed at the back of his mind, just out of reach. Of what this glimpse into Dante's inferno meant, a mere taste of the devastation a volcanic eruption could unleash. He closed his eyes, and it came to him. What Robert Oppenheimer thought when he witnessed the first detonation of an atomic weapon. A piece of Hindu scripture.

Now I am become Death, the destroyer of worlds.

He felt a hand on his shoulder, gently tugging him backwards.

"That's no lava lamp," shouted Jim. "Time to vamoose."

They worked their way back up, Nick refusing to even look back over his shoulder. He wouldn't do anything to throw his equilibrium off, even in the slightest. Jim periodically stopped, turned around, and took another reading. They crested the rim, Nick not stopping until he was where he couldn't possibly roll anywhere but downhill, away from the mouth of the crater. He sat and pulled off his headpiece with shaking hands. While he always had what he felt was a healthy respect for the sheer force of volcanos, the reality of this completely dwarfed it. He had stared into the abyss, and blinked.

"Man alive," Nick stuttered. "It wasn't even erupting."

"Don't be so hard on yourself. You're nuts if you don't fear it," Jim said, slapping him on the back.

"So, you were afraid too? The first time?" Nick asked, looking for common ground.

"No, of course not. I'm no pussy. Let's get a drink."

"Congrats. You've seen the elephant, and lived to tell about it," Jim said, raising a glass. It was a term soldiers used to signify the first time they had faced actual combat.

Nick looked at his forearms, tender to the touch. "I feel like a toasted marshmallow. Crinkly." He raised his glass back.

Jim rubbed his own leathery arms. "Not so bad. You get used to it."

"I'm not sure I could ever get used to being cooked. But there is something hypnotizing about looking into it."

As he sipped on his drink, Nick noticed Jim refilling his again. Already.

"Ya mas," Jim said, smiling.

"Hey, help me get a fundamental thing straight. What is the difference between magma and lava?" Nick asked.

"They are the same thing, it's just a question of location. Think magma in middle earth, lava on land."

"Mnemonics. Love it."

"Tell me, did Captain Alek treat you well?"

Nick grinned. He had taken an immediate liking to the captain. "Top shelf guy. Really went out of his way to show me things he didn't have to. They are doing good work out there on the Serafina."

"That they are," Jim replied. "I've spent quite a bit of time on her myself. My expertise comes in handy to them in certain, shall we say, situations."

"I suspect their data comes in handy to you in your research, too."

It was Jim's turn to quote Latin. *"Manus manum lavat."*

"Truly," Nick said. "One hand washes the other." It was fun to have another history nerd to banter with.

Nick had one other question on his mind, and Jim must have sensed his reticence.

"For chrissakes. Out with it man." He wasn't one for the subtlety of playing games.

"There was a woman scientist working on the Serafina. She's the one who introduced me to them. Her name is Persa. You don't per chance know her?" Nick asked.

"No, can't say that I do. I've been aboard most of the Greek research vessels at one time or another. Never came across anyone named that. Why?"

"I don't know. Attractive woman, fun. Really knows her stuff. Maybe it's just a hunch. Something tells me she just isn't quite what she seems."

Jim tipped a glass at Nick. "Women. They all are a bundle of secrets and contradictions. But it sure would be boring without them."

Dinner that night was at a restaurant looking out to the sea, with the volcano they had climbed in the background. Nick stared at the slight smoke wafting out of it with a sense of wonder. *Wait until Charlie hears about this one.*

"Pretty amazing, isn't it," Jim commented.

"I never tuned into just how much volcanic activity is always going on."

"Right now, there are probably twenty erupting somewhere across the globe. Usually, we get fifty to sixty different volcanos going off in a typical year."

"You're kidding. I've got a lot to learn."

"OK. Let's start with the basics," Jim said, pushing everything to the side. "The earth isn't as solid as people think. Its dynamic, ever changing. It's no coincidence the continents fit together like a jigsaw puzzle. A German, Alred Wegener, first proposed it like a hundred years ago."

"Pangaea," Nick said.

Jim chuckled. "Pangaea. One huge supercontinent. But the

pieces drifted apart over time. On plates that float on a sea of molten rock."

"Continental drift?"

"Exactly. And while they drift, the plates bump and grind against each other, like this." Jim put two napkins flat, and rubbed them together. "Think San Andreas fault line."

Nick nodded.

"When they have similar mass, you get mountains." He pushed the two napkins against one another and they bunched upward. "Think Himalayas."

Jim then pushed one napkin beneath the other, the one on top folding upward. "And when they don't have similar mass, one goes high, one goes low. That's when we get subduction. Think around the edges of South America and the Pacific Rim. The Ring of Fire." As he warmed to his subject, Nick found his enthusiasm infectious.

Jim then slowly pulled the napkins apart, leaving a growing space between them. "But this is a zero-sum game. If some plates are colliding, others are gapping. Where the plates drift away from each other, the sea floor spreads. This thins the surface, and new crust forms undersea ridges."

"That's a lot of movement going on everywhere at once," Nick observed.

"It is, but it's a very slow process. Mother Earth has all the time in the world."

Jim hooted at his own joke, and Nick had to laugh too. At him, not with him.

"Anywhere a plate is sliding, grinding, buckling, or spreading, there exists the possibility of volcanic activity. Just like you saw today."

"Thanks. That helps to put it all into context. This is a complex science."

"That it is. But today man, you were tip of the spear."

"I felt like it. Pretty wild. Those little devices we planted, how will they help?" Nick inquired.

Jim leaned back and stretched. "There's more than one way to skin a cat. To decipher what *might* happen, we monitor earthquakes, ground movement, rock and water chemistry, use rovers in hot spots, and utilize remote satellite analysis. Anything to detect a surge on the land's surface. Our supercomputers run prediction algorithms based on all of that. We need to be able to order evacuations if gas concentrations become too toxic. Hell, we even use drones. I lost my last one to a lava bomb."

"A what?"

"A lava bomb. Had my drone getting perfect video, and up burps a molten blob. Think it would land anywhere else? Nope. Straight down it came. Right on top of my drone."

"Nailed by an incandescent projectile. Wild."

"Yeah, well I've got another on order. Amazon delivers, right? But what we spread out below the rim today, in military jargon, think of those as boots on the ground."

"First line of defense?"

"Yeah. A kind of trip wire. All battery operated, so a finite life span. They all triangulate with everything else we have on the ground and in the sky. If there is a magma buildup below ground, or the slightest movement or change of temperature, we'll know. In real time."

"How often do you have to replace them?"

"Once the batteries start winking out. Typically, every couple months. Why? Wanna give it another go?"

Nick pondered for a moment the emotions he felt as he had stood awestruck, gazing into the fiery depths. "No, this moth is good. Once near the flame is enough for me."

The adrenaline from the day finally wearing off, Nick decided to check his messages. He sat on the edge of a cot, Artemis contentedly at his feet. Jim was outside smoking a cigar and singing to himself. With what may or may not have been his last nightcap.

Nick scrolled through the messages, stopping on one that caught his eye. It was a text conversation between Dr. Storm and Stavros that they copied him on. It concerned the bit of pottery Nick had brought up from the dive site before they had filled it back in to protect it.

Dr. Storm had done some analysis, and felt the piece predated the trireme it had been found on. It was only a fragment and contained no organic material, so it couldn't be carbon dated. But the symbols were not Greek from that time period. So far, they had proven indecipherable, and would require additional study. Stavros felt that it could have drifted to its location, which with the currents was a real possibility.

But that didn't jibe with what Nick observed when he was diving and had picked up that particular pottery shard. It had seemed imbedded, almost like concretion. There were other fragments strewn about, other items, things that could reveal the secrets of the trireme. At least once it was completely rescued from its undersea entombment. He mentally filed that bit of information, and decided to make an overdue call.

The phone rang four times, no answer. Nick prepared to leave a message, trying to come up with something witty to say. Just before the next ring, a familiar voice answered, recognizing the number.

"Nick, how are the beaches and babes treating you?"

"Hey Charlie, all good. Too busy for the beaches so far. On the babe front, a little more interesting."

"Good to hear. I dug around like you asked, into that industrialist you wanted more info on. Turns out—"

"Hold tight bro. Thinking our communications might not be so secure."

"Gotcha. I'll put it in the shelf. You know how to access."

"Roger that, thanks. I've got some info for you too. I'll do the same. Turns out I need to step carefully."

"What is it with you anyway?" Charlie joked. "You wouldn't think bones and old shit would be so controversial."

"I always appreciate the cerebral way you look at my profession. Helps me see the bigger picture."

"That's what I'm here for. So, what's up on the babe front?"

"I met a lovely oceanographer. Pretty. Bright too. She got me aboard a research vessel. Watched them map a section of the ocean floor for a couple days."

"Hmm. Really fascinating stuff. Sorry I missed it," Charlie replied sarcastically. "Anyway, guess who I just heard from?"

"An old girlfriend seeking alimony?"

"Close. *Your* old girlfriend. Soba was wondering how you were doing. If she should reach out."

Nick was silent, thinking of the implications. Of the last time they had talked.

"What is it man, you playing Odysseus over there in Greece? The sirens singing to you?" Charlie asked. "Or maybe that oceanographer?"

"It's complicated Chuck. You know that."

"I know. But Soba's still my favorite ex-Miss Nick."

"Let me think on it. I'll be in touch."

"OK. But never say never little brother."

CHAPTER 17

JUNE 18, PRESENT DAY, MILOS, GREECE

The lab on Milos was sparsely furnished, the small building it resided in a remnant of an earlier time. It sat above *Lagada Beach* and the port, looking out at the volcano directly across the bay.

Jim had insisted Nick sleep in the one folding cot, while he threw a sleeping bag on the hard concrete floor. Artemis lay protectively next to Nick, occasionally giving Jim a sniff and lick. Jim took it in good stride, affectionately stroking the big dog until he finally dozed off, snoring loudly.

In the middle of the night Nick heard Artemis get up, whining softly and becoming agitated. She nuzzled him until he got up too. Slowly shaking off his slumber, he took her outside to a crystal-clear night. A sliver of the moon shown above, the stars brilliant over the bay. He thought he could see just the slightest hint of color reflected out of the cone of the volcano. The breath of Hades. Or maybe it was just his overactive imagination.

He relieved himself, but Artemis refused to follow suit. She looked around alertly, pawed at the ground, and scanned for something Nick could neither perceive nor detect.

"What is it girl?" he said kneeling down, methodically rubbing behind her ears.

She stayed alert, tilting her head and sniffing at the breeze for a few more moments. Finally satisfied there was no threat, she got up and led the way back in. Nick was fast asleep on the cot before she did her customary two circle routine to bed down.

"You crash here often?" Nick asked Big Jim the next morning.

"When you're bouncing around the field like me, you'd be surprised where one sleeps. Sometimes you just kinda live in the lab."

"Sounds like the life of a low-paid archeologist. I can relate."

"It wouldn't be logical to sleep anywhere else." Jim laughed loudly at his own witticism, waiting a beat to see if Nick got it. "Logical. Vulcanology. You know, Spock was Vulcan."

Nick shook his head and chuckled. "I get it. Funny guy."

Jim got up and went over to the folding tables with various pieces of equipment scattered about. He checked calibrations and readings, making sure everything was in perfect working order. A large, well-used seismograph sat directly on the concrete floor, specifically situated to get an accurate reading.

"Our sensors are all online, looking good. And get a load of this," Jim said, holding up a long paper print-out. He let out a long, slow whistle. Artemis heard it and stared at him.

"Looks like an EKG," Nick said.

"It is. Of Gaea. You know, Mother Earth. There was some serious activity overnight."

They both looked closely at the readings from the seismograph, which showed some subtle tremors, leading up to a significant one at 3:10 a.m.

"Never felt it, I was out like a light," Jim said.

"Ha, that explains it," Nick replied. "Artemis woke me up in the middle of the night. I thought she just had to pee. I went out with her. I never saw or felt anything, but obviously she did."

"Yeah, well, they are a little more attuned to pick up on things like that. Things you and I can't even hear or feel."

"You're my own canary in the coal mine, aren't you girl?" Nick leaned down and rubbed her belly. "Who's a good dog? You are."

Jim spent an hour making phone calls and banging out emails. Obviously not his favorite part of the profession, but a necessary evil. After making another final check of the equipment, he looked at Nick expectantly.

"Ready Freddy?"

"For what?" Nick asked, gun shy as to what he might be getting into now.

"Yesterday you had a good look from below. Time to see from above."

Nick adjusted his headphones tighter, to further dampen the noise of the rotors. He peered out the bubble-shaped canopy of the helicopter while Jim tilted it toward his side.

This cat is the ultimate adrenaline junkie, Nick thought. *It's like hanging with a war correspondent with a death wish.*

"Look into that bad boy," Jim instructed. "Different perspective from up here, isn't it?"

Nick glanced down, instinctively reaching for the grab bar in front of him. He had the sensation of being at the very top of a huge roller coaster, the instant before free fall.

Fasten your seatbelt, Stavros had warned.

"When enough pressure builds, a volcano can explode and eject rocks at a velocity of two- to three-hundred meters per second." Jim tilted the chopper even further on its side, and went into a steep dive screaming toward the cone below. "That's over ten times faster than this."

Nick fought the urge to spray his breakfast around the entire canopy. He swallowed hard, the taste of bile burning the back of his throat. Just as he was about to lose control, Jim leveled off. Nick glanced over, his knuckles white from holding on for dear life.

"What the hell Portmess? You fly like Maverick!" Nick yelled. Referencing the daredevil pilot in the movie *Top Gun.*

"Hey, this is a full-service flight. Just trying to give you the complete experience. You know, in sensa-round."

Nick couldn't help but laugh along with him. Jim was like that one crazy friend everyone should have in their lives. Just once. The one who egged you on, pushed your buttons, stretched you to your outer limits, then just for good measure kicked you in the ass to extend them a little bit further. Who dared you to get comfortable with being uncomfortable. Someone always fun to have around, if you could somehow survive it.

"From here you can see how it formed. Look into the water around it. This whole region was volcanic, rising from the depths."

"And looking to rise some more?"

"Could be. Let me show you the rest of the area. You'll get a good read on the topology and geology from up here. Pretty indicative of most of the islands in these parts."

They flew over Anitmilos, Kimolos, Poliegos, then finally back over Milos. Jim took them toward its north shore, to *Sarakiniko Beach.* He picked a spot to land off to one edge, away from the sun bathers and frolicking kids. Once the rotors slowed then stopped, he took off his headset and turned to Nick.

"Perks of the job. Grab that cooler behind you Goose, let's go check out the beach babes."

They spent the afternoon drinking the local beer, Mythos, and periodically jumped in the water to cool off. Nick draped a towel over his forearms, not wanting to sunburn them. They were already a little chafed from his encounter in the crater. Jim snickered at his tenderfoot companion, and dug into the cooler. He pulled out links of a Greek sausage called *Loukaniko,* flavored with fennel seed and orange peel. He also produced flatbread, goat cheese, grapes, and olives. A veritable feast, perfect for an afternoon on the beach.

"This theory you're working on, what other insight do you need?" Jim asked, draining a beer.

Nick sat up, anxious to pick the brain of one of the foremost experts in the field. "Once a volcano's eruption peters out, what happens to the column it thrust upward?"

"Depends on the force of the eruption, the duration, weather, and wind conditions. Lots of factors."

"What about with something like Thera?" Nick asked.

"That was a massive one man, maybe the biggest ever witnessed by we homo sapiens. Over *14 cubic miles* of dense rock material was ejected. That's before any of it even expanded like pumice does. Think of all that coming back down."

"It's hard to fathom."

"It is. But you can model it on some assumptions, based on hard science. Like the depth of the ash layers found from Crete to Turkey. Stunted growth in tree rings around the Mediterranean. Or core samples of the ocean floor that show pumice over 250 feet deep. And that reading was taken fifteen miles away from Thera. Fifteen fricking miles! Simply mind-blowingly massive.

"Has mankind ever witnessed anything on that scale?" Nick asked.

"Krakatoa killed over 35,000, and this dwarfed it. The Mount Tambora eruption in Indonesia might have been the only thing approaching it. But that took place where it was lightly populated."

"Wasn't that the year without a summer?"

"Yeah. 1816. Crops failed and livestock died all over the globe since there was such tonnage of particulates in the atmosphere. They had the equivalent of a nuclear winter. It caused the largest famine of the century."

"So, can you give me your scenario? Based on what you've learned?" Nick asked.

"There's no lack of them, or theories floating around the internet. Hollywood has had their take. Hell, you can even catch a movie at the museum in Santorini postulating how it played out."

Jim paused, and stuffed a sausage in his mouth. A couple of kids walked by, pointing and admiring the helicopter. He waved, and took a long, slow swig of beer to wash it down. Then he got on his knees, and made a large mound in the sand.

"Here's my take. There was a smaller, earlier eruption, which we can tell from the ash deposits. Just the volcano clearing its throat. That probably scared some people off. But repairs were being made, we can see that at Akrotiri. Today we can monitor concentrations of quakes, seismic swarms, to tell of an impending eruption. But they didn't have that luxury. There were people still around when this monster blew its top."

Jim scooped out the top of the mound he had made and threw the sand into the air.

"Kablam! Krakatoa was heard thousands of miles away. This was much, much more powerful. Think how loud it must have been. The energy of two hundred atomic bombs released in a fraction of a second."

Nick watched the dust from the sand Jim threw in the air drift away on a breeze.

"And then the collapse?" Nick asked.

"Yeah, the collapse. The collapse of the column, and of their civilization. After all, what goes up, must come down."

He scooped more of the sand out, leaving a large hole where the top of the volcano would have been obliterated.

"There were two things going on now. The eruption finally slows once the magma chamber completely depletes. The weight of the column collapses on itself, gaining mass and speed. That hits what's left of the volcano, and starts a massive pyroclastic flow. It's so big and superheated it spreads out in all directions, skimming across the sea while it evaporates it. We've found evidence of the flow on the ocean floor *25 miles out*. Simply amazing.

"What was the other thing going on?"

Jim leaned back down, and dug deeper, leaving a broken circular rim with a divot in the middle.

"There was so much magma built up under the surface that once it was ejected into the atmosphere, the caldera collapsed and left a huge depression in the ocean floor. That's why you see the ring-shaped islands of Santorini today. The ocean rushed in and filled that super-hot caldera. Can you possibly imagine what that must have looked like?"

"No, I can't," Nick said, raising a beer toward Jim. "But I think you're bolstering my theory."

Nick picked up Artemis back at the research station. A kindly assistant of Jim's had watched her, enjoying the company. Gathering his things, Nick caught the short ferry ride back to Santorini. He wasn't about to subject the dog to any of Big Jim's flying exploits.

On the ferry, Nick started thinking about his plans. Agenda item number one: Grab a bite. Item two: Find a place to crash for the night, preferably with access to Akrotiri. He wanted to visit the famed ancient town from the time of the eruption. Persa was still on duty on the Serafina, so no need to reach out there. Which made him think about his real muse.

I owe Charlie a call about Soba, he thought. *Even here, with all this, I miss her.*

An old grizzled fisherman sitting nearby befriended Artemis, giving her a scrap of his sandwich. Artemis leaned into him, and was rewarded with a heavy-handed stroking. From tough calloused hands, shaped from pulling heavy nets over many years. Nick noticed that others on the ferry seemed to avoid the fisherman. A caste system even here, in the scattered islands of the Aegean.

"Mastiff, good breed," he said with a twinkle in his eye. "Strong. Loyal."

"Same as Molossus?" Nick asked.

"Da. Molossus ancient time. Mastiff now."

"She seems to have adopted me."

"Will serve you well," the fisherman said.

They struck up a light conversation, Nick with his few words of Greek, the fisherman in his stilted English. Nick learned what fish were most plentiful, the best bait, how to take advantage of changing tides and seasons. Of the travails of being a simple fisherman. He was fascinated by the man and the lore of the stories he told.

"Come. I buy you drink. I tell you of sea. You tell me of Amerikí."

Nick noticed a subtle lilt to the man's accent, different than the Greek he had heard in Athens.

"Your Greek sounds different. Is it a regional accent?" he asked.

"Ha. It what called Cretan Greek. You know, from Crete."

elements, the site allowed easy access to tourists. Nick beamed, his pulse quickening like it did anytime he was in proximity of profound history. It was both an ancient museum in situ, and a live archeological dig.

The Minoan version of Pompeii, Nick thought. *What a time capsule!*

He left Artemis in a shady spot away from the wandering crowds, paid his admittance, and walked into the vast complex. It stretched even further than he had imagined. To gain his bearings, he found the scale model of the entire site. Snapping a quick photo on his phone, he fell in behind a tour group with an English-speaking guide. They were mostly Brits, Americans, Canadians, and a few Aussies. Along with a scattering of others who didn't speak Greek, but could perhaps understand a little English.

"Unlike Pompeii, this site was never looted. It has followed a planned excavation from the start," the young guide explained. Nick guessed he was a university student paying his dues and working for tips.

"The earliest people living here predate even the Minoans, arriving in the Neolithic period around the fifth millennium BC. The Minoans here and around the Mediterranean reached the height of their power and influence during the Bronze Age."

Nick stopped and gazed at a recently unearthed mosaic. So fresh it wasn't completely cleaned yet, but the image was unmistakable. It showed a massive, bulging mountain.

Perhaps Thera pre-eruption? Could it be?

He pictured it in his mind's eye, filling out the contours of the caldera Santorini sat in. It all made sense, it seemed to fit. He snapped several photos with his phone for future reference.

The guide walked backwards while addressing them, pointing out areas and objects of interest. The process of tagging along was slower than Nick would have liked, but he found himself drawn to the story the young man wove. Who seemed like an earlier, more innocent version of himself.

"Everything here was well preserved because it was buried in a protective layer of ash and pumice. A Greek Archeologist, Spyridon Marinatos, oversaw the work. He thought this was the right place to find an ancient settlement, and in only a few hours of digging was proven correct. What you see before you are the fruits of that labor."

Nick could no longer contain his enthusiasm and worked his way to the front of the group.

"The same Marinatos who was Director of the Heraklion Museum on Crete? Who found where the battles of Thermopylae and Marathon took place?" Nick asked.

"Yes. One and the same. I see we have a student of history among us. Welcome sir," the guide responded.

The tour continued over those acres which had been methodically uncovered. The paths wound through the timeless streets themselves, and to strategically situated overlooks. An immersive experience for those so attuned.

"Notice how well the frescos have been preserved. The brighter colors are where preservationists have added missing detail, to show what it would have looked like in all its former glory."

The tour group stood in awe of the artwork. The whimsical style of birds flitting above colorful fields, antelopes romping, two boys boxing. It reached across the gulf of time and connected on a very human level.

It's not just that this is exquisite, Nick thought. *It shows how they viewed themselves. Their interpretation of their world.*

Nick purposely held his questions back, not wanting to derail the young guide's carefully rehearsed descriptions. He instead meticulously examined the buildings and artifacts, amazed at the state of preservation. Parts of multistory buildings remained, elaborate drainage systems, some of the first indoor lavatories ever discovered, pottery, trade goods, even furniture survived the cataclysm. Right here, safely ensconced by insulating layers of ash. At the very edge of ground zero.

The tour over, Nick hung around and waited for the tour group to disperse. He noticed a man with a baseball cap pulled low trailing the tour group, who constantly buried his head in a guide book.

Maybe just a shy tourist, Nick thought. *Or doesn't speak the language well.*

Nick sidled over to the guide and gave him a generous tip and words of encouragement. "The same stylized frescos like at Knossos?" Nick asked.

"Yes, and I have seen both with my own eyes," replied the guide. "We worked sites around Crete last summer. I got to really explore Knossos. The artwork, the building styles, even the drainage. It was all from the same people. But it is strange, isn't it, that no bodies have been found here?"

"Not if this was the high rent district," Nick said. "The rich could afford to leave at the first signs of trouble."

"Yes, as others have speculated. That would make sense. You saw the repairs that had been made here, before the great eruption. They must have had warning."

"I hope to see Crete for myself soon, to compare," Nick said, looking at a message on his phone and smiling. He shook the guide's hand and patted him on the shoulder.

"But first, I have a trireme to excavate."

CHAPTER 18

JUNE 20, PRESENT DAY, AKROTIRI, SANTORINI, GREECE

Nick intended on taking the ferry back to Athens. But after checking on Artemis and getting her water, he had wandered back into the excavated passages of Akrotiri. Where he found himself drawn to the echoes of a different time. He explored the site deeper, taking photos and notes. He was so immersed in his task that he was startled when a guard tapped him on the shoulder. The complex was closing, time to leave. Too late to catch even the last ferry out.

"Oh well, we missed out on that one girl," he said to his canine companion.

The big Mastiff jumped up to greet him, nearly knocking him over.

"Yeah, I know. Looks like it's under the stars for us tonight."

The sun was setting, the evening sky clear. They made their way a short distance due south, to a stretch of beach. Off to one side sat a hotel catering to those who came by water to see the wonders of Akrotiri. Nick found a series of cabanas that tourists could rent for the day. He plopped in the one furthest from the hotel, Artemis patrolling, then laying protectively by him. A warm gentle breeze and the sounds of the waves lapping the shoreline lulled him to sleep.

A young couple strolled onto the beach, thinking they were

alone. Giggling, they lay in a cabana not far away. Nick heard them through the fog of a dream, their whisperings and giggling becoming a part of it. When Nick heard the girl scream, he awoke, leaned up on one arm, and whistled. He thought he briefly caught a glimpse of two partly naked figures running toward the hotel, as Artemis proudly came bounding back.

"Yeah, way to scare a couple lovers away. Wouldn't want anyone having more fun than you," he laughed.

Artemis circled several times, finally laying down. She huffed contentedly, her work done. All was safe, the beach secure from any interlopers. Human or otherwise.

They were up and out early, before the hotel staff came to put out fresh pillows and towels and to rake the beach. They caught the earliest ferry, the Blue Star, and settled in for the eight-hour ride back to Athens.

"Glad you could tear yourself away from whatever temptress had you so preoccupied," Dr. Storm joked while he looked at the dinner menu. They sat at an outdoor terrace overlooking the port of Piraeus, preparing for the next day's work.

"Who's this new friend?" Stavros asked, stroking the dog under the table.

"That's Artemis. Evidently, she took pity on me and took me in," Nick said.

Stavros rolled his eyes.

"Oh, the woman. Her name is Persa. She's an oceanographer. I got to spend some time on a research vessel she works on, the Serafina. They were mapping the ocean floor out along some fault lines."

"From good Greek family? What's her last name?" Stavros probed.

"Hmm. Let me think. I know it, really."

"Ah, the indiscretions of youth," Dr. Storm mused. "At least you were gentlemen enough to remember her first name." He tut-tutted and shook his head.

Not really. Not at first, Nick thought.

"Theocritus. Yeah, it was Theocritus," Nick said, remembering his trip through the cemetery.

"Sure you aren't just making that up to get these two old fossils off your back?" Stavros teased. He looked over at Dr. Storm and grinned mischievously.

"No sir. Honest."

"Well, a pretty name, in any language," Dr Storm said.

"Hey Doc, that pottery fragment I brought up from the dive site. It had inscriptions on it we couldn't make out. Any headway deciphering them?" Nick asked, trying to steer the conversation in a different direction.

"Funny you should ask. We took them to the specialist at the Acropolis Museum. I believe you met him. Jason Calathes?"

"Met him? He was kind enough to give me a personal tour. On a weekend no less."

"That would be just like him," Stavros said. "I couldn't do my job without him. He is, how you say, my righthand man."

"Turns out the script on it is Minoan," added Dr. Storm. "Religious writings we suspect. But no way of knowing for sure. It's all in Linear A."

"Still undecipherable. Even after all these years," Nick said. "But what is an ancient Minoan shard doing on a Greek trireme?"

Dr. Storm reached out and pat Nick on the shoulder. "It could have gotten there any number of ways. No telling until you get back down there."

"Tomorrow we start on the trireme again," Stavros said. "Much work to be done. Exciting work!"

"So what's the game plan?" Nick asked.

"Start the cofferdam, before the sediment drifts away," Dr. Storm replied.

"The materials are here already?"

"Enough to get started. Seems our benefactor pulled a few

strings," Stavros commented, lowering his voice. "I have it on good authority he greased the wheels of bureaucracy."

Nick leaned back and took in the view over the bay. "I suspect bribery is right up his alley."

Dr. Storm shushed them, glancing around the veranda. "We can't be too careful. Discretion gentlemen."

Stavros and Nick nodded, and finally noticed the waiter standing directly behind them. Patiently awaiting their order.

Nick went back to the same hotel he stayed at the last time he worked aboard the Poseidon. He registered, then discretely slipped the receptionist a ten Euro note. There was no way Artemis would get in unnoticed. The young woman gave Nick a sly nod, then put a finger to her lips while looking at the dog.

"*Kane isychia.*"

Nick smiled his thanks, and discretely took the back stairs to his room. He took a hot steamy shower, sand-blasting a few days' worth of accumulated grime out of his pores. Artemis sniffed every corner of the room, finally settling in front of the doorway. With nothing to herd, she instinctively blocked the only entry point.

Finally clean and relaxed, Nick sprawled across the bed, his phone connected to the hotel wireless. He accessed the secure server where Charlie had posted a confidential dossier on Drakos Kollas. He grabbed a notepad and quickly jotted down bullet points, summarizing key information. Even with the secure server, he didn't want to be online any longer than necessary.

Great Grandfather, Christos. Archeologist, discoverer of several minor archeological sites in the Peloponnese and Asia Minor. Married heiress and inherited fortune upon death of her brothers. One under mysterious circumstances. Newfound wealth allowed him to pursue his passions. Became noted within tight knit Athenian intellectual society of the time.

What was it Persa had said? Nick thought. *Oh yeah. Old money is just blood money from another time.*

Grandfather, Theodoros. Noted international expert on ancient Minoan, Mycenean, and Greek civilizations. Collector of antiquities, significant benefactor of Athens Museum. Went missing at end of German occupation in 1944. Started the family industrial empire. Questionable fortune amassed during turmoil of German occupation. Rumored use of forced labor and expropriating Jewish assets and properties. Possibly fled to South America with escaping Nazis and collaborators. Suspected of utilizing same ratline as Adolf Eichmann and Josef Mengele. Was never located. His son and sole heir survived in postwar Greece.

Father, Aimilios. Consolidated holdings during postwar chaos through strongarm tactics. Accused of selling military arms to both sides during civil war of 1946-49. Charges never stuck, cleared family name. Became leading industrialist while Greece expelled Communist influence and became member of NATO. Expanded beyond industrial manufacturing into shipping and export businesses. Influential with military regime which was in power until 1974. Became increasingly involved in national politics. Operated in background. Peddled influence, played king maker.

Drakos Kollas, The Dragon. Took a more visible role than his predecessors. Didn't avoid spotlight. Aggressively grew family empire via questionable business practices. Leveraged financial crisis to crush or buy out competitors. Charges of coercion, bribery, and blackmail all settled out of court. Suspected ties to Greek Mafia, the Godfathers of the Night. Avowed Greek nationalist, active contributor to Greek first causes. Revisionist who denied Armenian and Jewish holocausts ever took place. Famous concert pianist in his own right, proceeds to charity. Very concerned with personal and corporate image and perception. Successfully sued press for libel and defamation of character. Even tabloids steer clear, especially after an investigative reporter disappeared.

This is one mendacious character, Nick thought. *With some type of deeper, well-financed agenda. What it is, I don't know. Yet.*

He checked his messages, none from Heinrich, one from Persa.

Nick immediately dialed Heinrich, again no answer. He left another message, growing increasingly alarmed at the lack of response, which was completely out of character for his friend.

He then listened to the message from Persa. Nothing major, she was just reaching out and wondering where he was. Perhaps they could get together when she came back to port.

Thunder boomed in the distance, Artemis lifting her head and tilting an ear. Rain started to patter off the window. A storm was blowing in.

Nick fitfully fell in and out of sleep. The sound of the storm, the confidential information on Drakos, the lack of response from Heinrich, and Persa's accent all played in his mind. His last thought before he succumbed to sleep was the end of her message to him.

When I see you, we have fun, yes?

The shoreline is higher than the last time I was here, the dockworker noticed.

And it wasn't from just the tides. Greater forces were at work, global warming steadily melting the ice caps, the seas inexorably rising. He and his young son wandered along the shoreline, along the north edge of the Port of Piraeus. They went past the tomb of Themistocles, looking for small sea creatures in the surf, picking up interesting looking seashells.

It was always fun to go out the morning after a storm, the sea churning up and washing different flotsam and debris along the water's edge. The father had made a habit out of doing it, the chance for an intimate bonding experience. The father with his son, his son and the sea.

He hoped for a better future for his son, one that offered more opportunity than simply operating cranes and hauling freight at the docks. Not that he was complaining. It was good work. Honest work. Yet he hoped for better opportunities for his progeny, just like every generation did. Perhaps someday his son would even captain one of the ships that came into the port he worked. Perhaps.

Each time out they explored a different area of the peninsula, slowly working their way around the great port that provided the father's livelihood. Today's exploration took them to a stretch that faced out to where the currents were strongest. A recent storm had stirred things up. The father was hopeful.

"You know, for thousands of years fathers have walked their sons along these very shores," the father told the young boy proudly. "From here, great wooden ships had set out and saved Greece. Saved all of civilization. Just out there, by the harbor police ship, one such trireme is being rescued from the depths. Right there, can you believe it?"

"Yes papa," the youngster said eagerly. There was nothing he loved more than the lore of the sea and the stories his father told.

A sparkle caught the boy's eye. Just a brief glint of sunlight, reflecting off something in the surf. Curious, he tip-toed in as the water receded with the waves. Whatever it was, it was gone now, or covered by sand trickling back to the sea. He dug with his toes, feeling around. Nothing.

The waves came back in, the water rising. There it was again, a sparkle just under the water's surface, just a few feet away from him. He squealed with delight, his joy so loud the father looked up from his own search. The boy skipped over to the spot, and stepped on the sparkle. The water receded again, burying his little foot with sand.

He felt it with his toes. Another wave washed in and receded, burying his foot a little deeper. He reached down with both hands. When he tugged at what was underneath, he couldn't pull it free. He tried again and grunted as he pulled, to no avail. He looked at his father with pleading eyes. The older man came over with a grin, proud of the enthusiasm and innocence of his son.

"Let's see what treasure you've found this time, son."

He got down on one knee to investigate. The water came back in and covered the object again, but he saw a bit of it protruding. He grasped at it, and still it held fast. Patiently he dug deeper around it with strong, callused hands. He found the shape fit his hand, and with a firm tug, the suction released its grip.

The man gasped when he saw what he held. It was a very old dagger, the metal greenish in color. It had jeweled inlays, several of which were missing. In spots the green tarnish had rubbed off from the friction of the surf. Odd symbols were inscribed on it. It couldn't have been here in the surf for long.

"Thank the gods," the father said in a prayer of thanks. Zeus himself must have stirred up the storm, and delivered this from the depths.

He smiled at his son and proudly showed him the ancient dagger. He stood fully erect and pointed it out to sea, to where the trireme was being excavated. Proof of the great ships that had departed from this very soil so long ago. All in the name of sacred Greece.

"Make sure the placement is exact. Once we build the walls, we can't expand the area," cautioned Stavros.

The crew of the Poseidon was gathered around him, looking at the maps and diagrams laid out on the charting table. They had all been eagerly awaiting this very moment. The start of building the protective cofferdam around the buried ship site. Once that was completed, it would be pumped dry, and the real work of excavation could begin.

"Any troubles with trespassers?" Giorgos asked. As a Greek marine archeologist, he was protective of the site, and its history.

"None that we could tell," Stavros said. "Our Hellenic Coast Guard was on patrol the whole time. That should have kept any looters away."

"Since we reburied it, I suspect you'll know if it was disturbed when you get back down there," Dr. Storm added.

"I think it would've been hard for anyone to get at it," Nick said, looking toward the shore. "With that circus around. Unless they had divers or a submersible."

A crowd had gathered, the media with telephoto lenses and drones, the curious with beach chairs and binoculars. Vendors peddled drinks and food to those assembled. Even the occasional helicopter flew over the site.

Stavros straightened up from bending over the maps. He looked stressed, the heavy burden of expectations and scrutiny on him. On them all.

"That's not even funny my friend. Time you and Giorgos had a firsthand look."

Dimitris maneuvered the Poseidon into position and dropped anchors fore and aft. Yiannis helped Nick and Giorgos with their equipment, and grinned sheepishly when Nick asked him if he had checked the hull for barnacles. Giorgos elbowed Nick while Yiannis bent over with the air tanks, motioning like he was spanking him.

Hairy spiders.

They both laughed.

A huge barge with a towering mechanical arm slowly moved to a point on the outer edge of the dive site. It was loaded with long beams and sheets of interlocking steel plates. The team had decided to take a page out of the playbook of the recovery of the *La Belle*. It was one of Robert de La Salle's ships, with which he intended to start a French colony. In 1685 it sank in the shallow waters of Matagorda Bay, southwest of Houston. The conditions and depth were similar, so there was no need to reinvent the wheel in terms of protocol. They knew exactly what needed to be done.

Nick and Giorgos dove in, this time with Giorgos guiding a drone tethered to the Poseidon. It would allow a direct, live video feed to those anxiously awaiting above. They quickly located the undersea floats they had left to mark the perimeter. Using hand signals they split up, each headed a different direction around the perimeter to carefully examine the site. The fill that had been put atop the wreck appeared to be undisturbed, other than slight erosion from currents and tide. Nick gave Giorgos a thumbs up. Underneath, the trireme awaited them.

After Nick carefully documented the site with a camera, they went back topside to report.

"What's the weather forecast?" Nick asked.

"Favorable, at least for a few days," Stavros replied. "Let's guide in the internal ring of pilings. Then the barge crew can attach the sheets between them."

"The outer ring will take a little time too," Dr. Storm said. "Then they will fill between the two walls to give us a working surface above the dig pit."

Stavros put an arm around both Nick and Giorgos. "With a roof over it all to keep out the sun and rain. What do you say men? Let's dig into some history!"

Yiannis swapped their oxygen tanks, and Nick and Giorgos splashed back under. One by one the vertical beams were placed, as they double checked the distances between to ensure an exact fit. A piledriver on the end of the barge rhythmically hammered each firmly into place, the surface of the silt stirring with each blow. The team of divers off the barge attached horizontal crossbeams, and the oval skeleton of the cofferdam took shape. When the last crossbeam was in place, everyone exited the water. Tired but excited. The dream was getting real.

The sound of a fork clinking quieted down the assembled group.

"Gentlemen, on behalf of Greece, I want to thank you all for your efforts." Stavros raised a glass to those assembled around the table. "Well done."

"Ya mas" came a chorus of replies, with a few "Here, heres" mixed in.

It had been over a week since the construction of the cofferdam had commenced. The critical work was done, the walls themselves welded together and secured. There was still much to do, including filling in between the two walls to create a walkway above the dig, and adding the protective roofing. That would take another four or five days, and then the real work of archeology and preservation could begin.

The crews of the Poseidon and the barge, plus select dignitaries and press, were in a festive mood. The food was excellent, the drinks flowed freely, and their work had the adulation of the Greek people. Not to mention the rapt attention of the international archeology community.

"And now a word from our sponsor," Nick whispered to Dr. Storm, nudging him with his elbow. He glanced at several figures standing in the background, and saw one glaring back at him. The hulking bodyguard he had crossed once already, back aboard the Poseidon.

True to form, Drakos Kollas rose and stood next to Stavros, patiently waiting for him to resume his seat. He wasn't a man to share the spotlight. Stavros lowered his glass and gave an awkward nod to him, then sat. Drakos waited a moment longer, until all eyes were focused firmly on him. This was a man practiced in the art of being noticed, of being in control.

"I am honored to be the sponsor of this sacred undertaking. For what an opportunity we have in front of us. To show Greece, to show the whole world, a true symbol of the very birth of democracy. I intend to remind everyone how the roots of the concept of self-rule and freedom sprang from this very soil and these very seas. How our ships triumphed against despotism and slavery, shining a beacon of light that oppressed peoples have reached for ever since."

Dr. Storm raised a subtle eyebrow to Nick. Kollas was taking a lot of credit for something he didn't own, or for that matter, even discover. Nick nodded back just as discretely. He likewise saw Kollas wrapping himself in the Greek flag for his own glorification. And something else that he couldn't quite put his finger on. At least not yet.

"When this excavation is complete, I will create a new complex devoted to not just this trireme, but to everything that went into spreading the concept of democracy across the entire world. A monument to the glory and ideals that *were* ancient Greece. From the Myceneans to the Spartans, from the Athenians to the Macedonians. To more recent times and the brave Greek resistance fighters who fought against the Ottoman Turks, and then the Nazi's. For only in Greece could the Olympics have been born. Only in Greece could tyrants fall and dictators meet their demise. Only in Greece could the enduring blueprint for democracy emerge."

Kollas raised his glass to the crowd. An assistant behind him dramatically unveiled a model of a vast business, entertainment, and living complex. It featured sprawling shopping and business centers designed to mimic the Agora and the Acropolis, replicas of ancient theaters, towering condominiums, and in the center, the new museum. It featured a model of the trireme as its central focal point. All situated over the ancient ruins scattered between Piraeus and Athens.

"Only in Greece," Kollas said, tilting his glass. He then took a sip of champagne.

"Ya mas," came the roaring reply. Opportunity for work and a better life beckoned for all.

Nick glanced at Stavros, shifting uncomfortably in his seat. The planning council had been out maneuvered. Or on the take. This had been the end game all along, the Disneyfication of a World Heritage Site. The quest for ever more wealth, power, and control. Designed to ultimately benefit one man, and one man only. Perhaps even to the point of fulfilling his highest political aspirations.

Bring prosperity to Athens, you bring prosperity to Greece. Bring prosperity to Greece, the possibilities were endless. To a man with the vast resources of Drakos Kollas, the presidency would be but a heartbeat away. And heartbeats could be fragile things.

Kollas wandered off to hold court with the handpicked media that had been invited. Nick could faintly hear him talking about repatriating stolen and looted Greek artifacts, how the new museum would be greater than even the Louvre, that it would signal a rebirth of the tourist industry, employ many thousands before and after construction, and reinvigorate a moribund Greek economy.

"Sad business, this. I thought Athens already had a world class museum," Nick said, dejectedly shaking his head and offering his hand.

Dr. Storm clasped it solemnly. "Yes, it does. One that is a tribute to a whole people. Not to a single man's ego."

Nick looked around, and saw many getting caught up in the excitement, in the man's vision. These were hard times, and he offered hope. But that hope would come with a price.

"Crumbs from the table," Nick commented.

"Quite. But even a drowning man will grasp at straws if they believe that is all that is available to them."

Nick glumly grunted in agreement. "Well, I'm off for a few days Doc."

"You won't be missing anything here young man. We'll just be putting the finishing touches on the cofferdam. You've got some time."

"Unfortunately, I've something I need to attend to."

"That pretty Greek oceanographer, perhaps?"

"No. My friend Heinrich in Germany. He's gone missing."

CHAPTER 19

JUNE 29, PRESENT DAY, HAMBURG, GERMANY

H e turned the key over in his hands. It was silver, small, and had a number stamped deep within it. The kind used where there were lots of lockers, like at a bus or airport terminal. Places easy to get to, where things could be hidden in plain sight.

Nick had flown directly from Athens back to Germany. He rented a car in Hamburg, and paid cash. That made the attendant at the counter raise an eyebrow, but he didn't care. He picked up a burner phone at a nearby kiosk catering to tourists. No sense in making it easy for anyone to track him.

He sat in a nondescript Volkswagen in the parking lot, purposely waiting ten minutes before even starting the engine. Looking to see if anyone had followed or lingered about. While he sat, he replayed in his mind the last message Heinrich had left him.

Nick, diese Heinrich. Finden something most important. Think others haben interesse too. Call me schnell, ja?

He did call him, many times in fact. But he was never able to connect after that last message. With no recourse, he finally reached out to Heinrich's employer, the *Ministerium für Vermisste Soldaten.* They were likewise perplexed as to Heinrich's whereabouts, and could offer no help. He had never failed to show up to work or check in regularly. It was most unlike him, most unprofessional. Most *ein-Deutsch.*

Nick took a last look around, and saw only a few service attendants going about their business. Nothing suspicious. He checked his watch, nearly rush hour. Perfect. He carefully pulled out, drove to an address on Hachmannplatz, and parked the car. Grabbing his backpack, he checked over his shoulder. Then he quickly was lost among a throng of people, coming and going at the crowded Hamburg Train Station.

Nick nonchalantly grabbed a bratwurst and worked his way to a far corner of the terminal. He ate slowly, watching the crowd mill about. Glancing up, he saw security cameras blanketing the terminal. Self-consciously, Nick quickly looked away.

It doesn't seem anyone is tailing me, but what the hell do I know? he thought. *I'm not trained in spy craft.*

The locker number was 1979. Heinrich had been very specific that should anything go wrong, should they ever lose touch, Nick was to go retrieve something there. What it was, he had no idea. But it was time to find out.

He walked between people putting things in lockers, and those taking them out. A single row of benches separated the lockers, the paint worn, the floor sticky in parts. A harried looking mother juggled two young children and crammed a bag in. A tourist looked at his key and wandered bewilderedly, trying to make sense of the numbering system. Two teens, sporting florescent colored mohawks and neo-Nazi skinhead tattoos, appeared to be conducting a little business transaction. Nick soon found what he was looking for, just below eye level. Locker 1979.

Glancing left and right, it seemed no one was paying any attention to him. He inserted the key, which fit easily, but the lock wouldn't turn. He tried to force it, but no luck. Trying again he grunted and turned so hard the key bent slightly. Still the locker wouldn't budge. Frustrated, he pounded on it with one fist, which got a passing security guard to glance at him. Nick looked away, absentmindedly rubbing his head. After the guard walked past, he tried to pull the key out. Instead, the locker swung open.

A single envelope was tucked inside. Nick grabbed it, then felt carefully around to make sure he missed nothing else. The rest of the locker was empty. He suddenly realized it would be easy for someone to simply tear his backpack away. Since the envelope was small, he folded it and put it into the safety of a front pant pocket.

He made his way cautiously toward the incoming train platform. Unconsciously patting the pocket, he avoided looking anyone in the eye. When a train of commuters pulled up and disgorged its mass of passengers, he melted into the crowd.

Nick drove away from the train station, over the Kennedy Bridge, searching for a private place to look at the contents of the envelope. He didn't have a definitive plan in coming to search for Heinrich. He didn't really know much about his family, only the name of the ministry he worked for. But he had the key to the lockbox, and now he had its contents. He would simply have to react to information and events when they presented themselves.

He turned onto Tier Garten Straube, found a parking lot, then retreated into a large urban park. Looking around, he walked past a rose garden, an open-air stage, and finally a wilderness area of many trees and manicured lawns. Nick ducked off the path and doubled back a short distance to see if anyone had followed him. He carefully peered out from the side of a stand of trees. The coast seemed clear, only the same scattering of people as when he entered. All casually going about their business.

Paranoid. I'm fricking paranoid, Nick thought. *But still, Heinrich is missing. I'm not making this shit up.*

He sat with his back to a copse of trees. The only writing on the outside of the envelope said *Schließfach 1979*, in a hurried scrawl. Locker 1979. The envelope was sealed, so he cautiously tore it open. A single folded piece of paper was inside, along with a matchbook. The implied message was clear. Burn after reading.

Now he *was* nervous.

Nick unfolded the note with unsteady hands. It contained a one-word name, and an address:

Wessel, Ebelingstraße 19 Ostberlin

Hmm. Someone named Wessel. Could it really be? The same Wessel that Pavlus and Zorba just told me about? I don't believe in coincidences, this is leading to someone. Someone very real. Living on a street in Berlin. No, East Berlin. And the writing's hard to read, like it was written in a hurry. Like Heinrich was running out of time. Or running away from something.

Nick turned the note over. Nothing was on the back. He held it up directly to the bright sunlight, squinting through the front and then the back. No trace of secret or faint writing. He tore open the envelope completely, so he could examine it inside and out. There was nothing other than the locker number on it. He held it to the sunlight in the same manner. Again nothing was revealed.

A sound in back of the trees startled him. He clutched the message to his breast and crouched lower. The same noise again, this time coming closer. Nick looked around, seeking an avenue of escape. There, he could sprint through the trees, get back to the open-air stage, where he had seen people. Nobody would want witnesses.

Get to where there are witnesses.

He got on all fours and peered around the base of the tree trunk. Digging in his heels, he put one hand on the trunk for leverage, ready to flee. He craned his neck just a little further, trying to get a look at his pursuer.

A startled duck looked back at him, eye to eye. Beak to nose.

Quack. Quack quack quack.

It bit at him and flapped its wings defensively. Instinctively putting itself between the nest and Nick. His heart leaping from his chest, Nick fell backwards with an awkward thud. The duck nipped at him before he could get up. Nick arose, any chance at secrecy lost. Children in the park pointed to him, before their mothers could protectively grab them. Away from the peeping tom sulking in the bushes.

Artemis, where are you when I need you? Nick thought. *Maybe I shouldn't have left you with Dr. Storm.*

Nick mustered what dignity he could, and strode off briskly.

Government many years as translator. Then for our reunified country, as administrator. Now, I hier. Of no use to anyone other than Papa, I am afraid."

"Stasi?" Nick blurted out before he could even catch himself. Meaning the brutal secret police that enforced every aspect of living in the former Soviet puppet state.

Otto was unsurprised by the question.

"Let us say I evaluated and translated sensitive information, and leave it at that. Ja? You must understand, times were different then. Harder. There wasn't much, much . . ." He struggled to find the right word.

"Freedom?"

"Freiheit, yes, you could call it that. The war gutted Germany. Then the Russians occupied us. We had to start over, with a government not of our choosing. Children of the war paid a heavy price." He shook his head in resignation. "They still do."

Nick nodded sympathetically.

"Your father, he served on a U-boat?"

"Yes. U234. Only two survivors." Otto looked him sternly in the eye. "Tell me, Mr. LaBounty, why do you seek it?"

Nick had been rehearsing in his head for this potential moment. Since he knew he would have to find out what happened to Heinrich. He decided the best way to play it was short and direct.

"A friend of mine was working on it, who invited me to help him. He's gone missing. The only clue he left me was this address. And the name Wessel."

Otto stared at Nick, evaluating him with a practiced eye. He looked over at his father, then around at the apartment. At what his life had become. He sighed deeply.

"What is your background Amerikaner? Why should I trust *you?*" Otto asked.

"I'm a simple archeologist. The man who left me this address was a colleague. A good friend," Nick replied, leaning closer. "I find the meaning of the past. The truth in it," Nick stated matter-of-factly.

Otto tilted his head. A slight glint of recognition. He arose quickly, and went to one of the many stacks of magazines and newspapers. He dug through them, looking for something specific amid the chaos of the piles.

Nick knew where this was headed. He took the opportunity to get up and look closer at some of the items about the apartment. Badges from the Kriegsmarine on a mantle. A picture of a handsome young submariner next to them, standing proudly in uniform. He took another look at the old man sleeping in the chair. Hard to believe it could be the same person. He picked up the group photo of everyone on the deck of a submarine. There was a signature on it. He walked over to the window for light, and squinted at it closely. Then he noticed movement.

Casually glancing out the window, Nick saw someone across the street. A man quickly peeked up at him, then looked away. The solitary figure turned, and headed down the street.

"Dönitz."

Nick heard it, but was still preoccupied with the man he saw walking out of sight.

"Großadmiral Dönitz," the old man in the chair behind him muttered.

Nick turned and looked at him. He was awake and stared back, then bowed his head ever so slightly toward him.

"Papa says that was signed by Admiral Dönitz. He met him once. The day that photo was taken," Otto said without looking up. "Ja, here it is."

Otto walked briskly back to the table, then waited for Nick to join him. He set a magazine on the table, and pointed to an image.

"Diese you?"

An unflattering photo on the cover of a German Archeology periodical stared back at him.

"Yes."

"Then you are more than a mere archeologist. You have fame. Fame brings influence. The ability to get things done."

"Perhaps," Nick said. "But it is worth repeating. Whatever I do, whatever quest I undertake, I always seek one thing only. The truth."

"Wunderbar. Perhaps we *can* help each other."

"The only reason my friend would have given me this name and address was he was onto something. Something that narrowed his search to U234, from the five U-boats we researched," Nick explained. "Is there any reason you can think of why he would point me specifically to your father?"

Otto mulled Nick's words over, and the implications of what might happen if he revealed too much. He looked at his dad, snoring softly again. Nothing to lose there, his days were numbered. As for himself, he really didn't care. What mattered was the truth, and the dignity of saving his family name. The world must know what really happened.

This Amerikaner, he could stir things up. He would have to be ready for that. His old training kicked in. Give him enough to act on, but hold something back. For leverage, for control. In case he found he needed it.

"Perhaps because of what was on U234," Otto replied. He walked over to the TV and picked up the scale model. He returned to the table, and handed it to Nick.

"Or because of who," Nick said.

Otto raised an eyebrow. He better be careful not to underestimate this foreign archeologist. He was obviously clever. The water ran deeper than his innocent face let on.

"It was called the Type X. The largest in the fleet." Otto said. "Only eight were ever built. It could carry a huge amount of cargo. And go virtually anywhere."

Nick closely examined the model, turning it over in his hands. "Before we go on, I have to ask. Why do you want my help? What's in this for you?"

Otto smiled. Despite his suspicious nature, he liked this man. Direct, to the point. Yes, perhaps they could do business.

"Papa survived the sinking. He was rescued near Santorini. Then taken to Crete to wait out the end of the war."

Nick's eyes widened faintly at the mention of Crete. Otto's trained and ingrained instincts picked up on the subtle change.

The old man in the chair sat up for a moment, put his arms out to fend something off, yelling words Nick couldn't understand. After seeing where he was, he calmed down. Soon he was snoring again.

Otto shook his head. "He's still fighting the war. Still battling his demons." He took a moment to check on his father, and tucked a blanket over him before continuing.

"After the surrender, he made his way back home, back to Germany. Home was now in the Soviet Zone of Occupation. He told his story, that he survived the sinking of U234. That he saw fantastic things. But the U-boat was never found, no other survivors lived to corroborate his story. Officials dismissed his claims; he was discredited. Others who served in the Kriegsmarine jeered him out of the beer halls. A crazy man trying to cash in on a fable."

"That's why you think I could help?"

"Ja. Because I believe what he went through was real. I want you to prove it. I want his honor restored."

"I can understand that." Nick stood and paced. "You said he saw fantastic things. Like what was onboard?"

Otto nodded. "Archeological treasures. Things destined for the Reich."

Nick wrung his hands, then sat back down. "Somehow the disappearance of my friend is tied to this. If I can find the U-boat, perhaps I find him."

Otto wrote on a piece of paper and slid it across the table. "Maybe this gives you a place to start."

Nick looked at him questioningly.

"What is this?"

"It's the name of the man who escaped with him."

CHAPTER 20
JUNE 29, PRESENT DAY, BERLIN, GERMANY

Despite Otto Wessel providing him with the name of the other U-boat survivor, Nick felt he was holding something back. There was more to the story. To find it out, he would have to do his own research. With the disappearance of Heinrich, the clock was ticking.

He checked into a downtown Berlin hotel. He wanted to get into the mindset of postwar Germany. He grabbed a walking tour map from the Concierge, had a quick meal, and caffeinated himself. After circling some highlights on the map, he set out to step back into the not-so-distant past. To place himself into the militarized fervor of an Aryan people so filled with hate they didn't just set out to rule the world. But to eradicate parts of it.

Nick started at the Französischer Dome, then paused to admire the Konzerthaus and the nearby Deutscher Dome. All remnants of a less controversial and more cultured past. He walked down to Checkpoint Charlie, the former Cold War hot spot. Ground zero for East vs. West. He shook his head at the carnival-like atmosphere, while tourists snapped selfies at the former Allied checkpoint. With a museum and gift shop conveniently located nearby, no less.

He was in a more sober state of mind as he worked his way through the Holocaust Memorial, then found himself standing in front of the Brandenburg Gate. Newsreel footage played in his mind of Hitler and his motorcade rumbling through it. Of grainy films of the horrors of the concentration camps. Of the Nazi emblem on the Reichstag blowing up at war's end.

The bitter irony of the proximity of the Holocaust Memorial to the Brandenburg Gate was not lost on him. There would be no denial or revisionist history here.

Nick took his time wandering from the Reichstag to Palace Square, the former headquarters of both Prussian kings and the Communist Regime. Finally, he finished his self-guided tour at a famous section of the Berlin Wall. Where everything came full circle, to the present day. To where East Germany was still trying to be integrated and accepted by the West. To where a WWII Kriegsmariner stubbornly clung to life, hoping to clear his good name. And to where Heinrich had disappeared into thin air.

Back at the hotel, Nick went directly to his room, pulled out his laptop, and logged onto the wireless network. Time to learn what he could about this Günther Wessel.

He plugged the name into a search engine on the chance there might be a direct hit. No such luck. East Germany, while in the Soviet Bloc, had tightly controlled information and kept a lid on dissidents. He tried various combinations of words and names, racking his brain for some connection that might have made its way to an article or news item over the years.

Nick finally plugged in *Verlorenes Unterseeboot, Griechenland,* and *Wessel.* Lost U-boat, Greece, Wessel. A hit!

It was an old newspaper article from Der Speigel. Günther had been mentioned by the West German newspaper. He must have somehow smuggled notes to them. Only now was it digitizing back issues, enabling Nick to stumble across it.

That couldn't have gone well for him back in East Berlin. Not with the Cold War on, Nick thought.

It was dated 1952, before Otto was born. Before Günther had a family that could be threatened. Nick hit the translate button, and read on with mounting interest.

Man Claims Survived Sinking of U234

Petty Officer Günther Wessel claims he and one other man survived the sinking of U234 in the Sea of Crete. Records show the U-Boat left Athens shortly before the Allies took procession of the city in October 1944. It was lost, presumably with all hands. Its exact location has never been determined. No manifest was ever reported. It had been rumored to have carried key personnel, war material, Nazi sympathizers, and a variety of archeological treasures bound for the Führermuseum to be built in Linz. Wessel also asserted to have seen scattered remnants of an ancient civilization on the sea floor during his escape. Efforts to contact and substantiate these claims with Mr. Wessel have been unsuccessful.

Nick looked up, beads of sweat forming on his forehead. Otto had never told him about any of this. That his father had seen other things on the ocean floor during his escape. Der Speigel dismissed it as the manic rantings of a traumatized survivor. A German who now lived behind the Iron Curtain, perhaps looking for a pay day for an exclusive, or a way out.

Yet that didn't make sense to Nick. Günther had willingly gone back to Berlin after the war, back to the Soviet Zone of Occupation. To where his family had been, to his roots. He had married, started a family, lived there even yet. Money didn't seem to be the motivating factor, he could have easily monetized it once the wall came down. He was out to prove something greater, that what he had seen was real. His son was trying to help him, with his limited means. But Günther had been unable to do it. The technology to find U234 didn't exist when he still had his mind and his health. Now he had neither.

But then I came along, Nick thought. *Someone with the expertise who could help them clear their good family name. No wonder Otto held this back. He was afraid I would think Günther was mad or had PTSD. That there was no truth in any of it.*

Nick thought back to the apartment, to the piles of newspapers and magazines. The research laying scattered about. The obvious obsessiveness of their search. When Otto had excused himself to go to the bathroom, apologizing about his prostate, Nick had sprung into action. He had taken pictures of every item, of absolutely anything that might prove useful, laying strewn about the apartment. Of everything Günther and Otto had collected over the years. Framed articles and newspaper clippings glued to posterboard. Things that had never been digitized, and so weren't searchable. Until now.

He reached for his phone, scrolled to a picture, and zoomed in. It was all there at his fingertips. If only he could decipher the cryptic clues.

Nick awoke early the next morning, and realized he had overlooked a critical clue. He had been so enthralled with what he had found out about Günther Wessel, he forgot to search for the other survivor. The name Otto had slipped him on his way out of the apartment. He reached into his wallet and pulled out the slip of paper.

Karl Schultze.

He quickly plugged it into the same searches he had done for Günther, along with various combinations and permutations. Nothing. It was as if he never existed. He put the slip of paper back in his wallet; it would have to wait. Yet another mystery for another time. Right now, he had a meeting to attend to.

Nick raced to Heinrich's employer on the outskirts of the business district, the Ministerium für Vermisste Soldaten. While he had talked with them by phone already, he had made no headway. Nick felt it was time for a face-to-face meeting to see if he could break anything loose.

Ironic that he works for the Ministry for Missing Soldiers, when he has gone missing himself.

He was shown in, and sat and waited in a baren reception room. There were others there, younger people, perhaps descendants looking for clues or closure. He didn't see any old women or widows. Too much time had passed. The world was closing the final chapter on those who had participated in WWII.

"Joachim Müller. Gut to meet you in person," a middle-aged man in a rumpled suit said, offering a hand. He walked Nick back into a small office, pulled out a chair for him, then sat behind his desk.

"I appreciate you talking to me the other day, and seeing me now," Nick said. "Heinrich was a colleague, and a dear friend. We went to school together. He asked me to help him on a project, and then he went missing. No communication whatsoever, which is so out of character for him. Have you heard anything?"

Joachim shook his head no. "Most strange. Heinrich was very fachmann. Very professional. We have heard nothing. Diese so unlike him."

Nick decided to play the one card he had on Heinrich. It was confidential, but his disappearance called for drastic action. He didn't know if the connection was known, but there was only one way to find out.

"We went to Cuxhaven together. Researching a lead he wanted my help with. When we were there, he said something I never knew. That his grandfather was in the SS. Obergruppenführer Schmidt."

Joachim put a finger to his lips, and walked over and closed the door softly. He pat Nick on the shoulder and walked back to his desk and sat.

"Diese not common knowledge. I know because we good friends. What you call drinking buddies. That is why he works here. His part to right past wrongs."

Nick shook his head slowly in contemplation. It all now made perfect sense. It explained why a man of such talent and drive would toil in relative obscurity in a forgotten ministry. All to make up for the sins of his grandfather.

"Was he working on anything controversial? Anything that would have put him at risk?" Nick asked, changing tact.

"Nein. His assignment recently changed, from finding missing soldaten in Russia to finding missing U-boats. But nothing unusual about that. Assignments change all the time."

Nick frowned. He was running out of possibilities. "No one else has inquired about him? Not even his family?"

"No family, his parents passed. He was only child."

"Not even friends?"

"Few friends. Only du inquired. His work was his mistress."

"Damn. There must have been someone else," Nick pondered aloud. "A girlfriend perhaps?"

Joachim closed his eyes for a moment in concentration. "Ja, now I remember. There was one other inquiry. From a woman."

Nick leaned in close. "Did she leave a name or number?"

"Nien, but a most unusual accent. Greek perhaps."

For Nick it felt good to be back out on the Autobahn, exhilarating even. Or perhaps it was simply the need to get away from an increasingly claustrophobic Berlin and its many ghosts of the past. He arrived in Cuxhaven midafternoon, and made his way back to the Deutsches U-Boot Muséum. It was the last place he and Heinrich had been together. Possibly there might be a connection he could pick up on.

"*Kann ich dir helfen?*" a handsome young man asked. standing sharply as Nick entered. He was dressed neatly in a business suit. A new recruit doing his volunteer duty, Nick suspected.

"Amerikaner. Sprechen Englisch?" Nick asked.

"Ja. How may I be of service?"

"I was here earlier in the month, with a colleague. We spoke with an older gentleman. He supplied us with some documents for research."

"Ah, you haven't heard then. Klaus, the last Kriegsmariner who worked here. He passed just recently."

"I'm sorry to hear that," Nick said sincerely. "He seemed a wealth of knowledge. Was it unexpected?"

"I don't know. He seemed in good health for one his age. He—"

Another man walked up from in back of the counter. He was brusque, and dismissive of his younger companion. He motioned him away, and turned to Nick with a look bordering on contempt.

"Now it's time for next generation to take the lead. Klaus and his brethren will judge us. To see what we will do with our inheritance."

Nick raised an eyebrow, but didn't immediately reply. He was being challenged, but wasn't sure why. He sized up this interloper, and decided offense was the best defense.

"My colleague, Heinrich Schmidt, has gone missing. We talked with Klaus. He helped us with a search we were doing. Has anyone here seen or heard from him?"

As he spoke, Nick flipped open the register, to see if Heinrich had come back since their last visit. To see who else may have been here, perhaps looking for him. There were no new entries. Even stranger yet, there was no record of Nick and Heinrich having been here. Ever.

But that doesn't make sense. I know we signed in.

"There nothing for you here," the angry man sneered, gripping the register and closing it. "Leave. Schnell."

Nick looked as the hand closed the register, and noticed the ring. It was the Totenkopf Death's Head ring. Worn only by members of the SS. Or their loyal descendants awaiting the arise of a Fourth Reich.

Nick lay in bed, getting his bearings. He had been in so many places in such a short time he was disoriented every time he woke up. He wasn't in Berlin, that was the other night. The room didn't look like his Cuxhaven hotel, yet it was familiar to him. Greece. He was back in Greece. Back near the port of Piraeus.

He rolled over and looked at the face staring back at him. Artemis sat beside the bed, her huge head tilting, waiting for Nick to stir. Direct eye contact got the tail thumping, then a face licking. Dr. Storm had been kind enough to watch her when he flew to Hamburg. Now she was back with her favorite human.

Nick wiped his face and rolled onto his back, staring at the ceiling. Reality flooded back in on him. There was much work to be done.

First order of business, call his brother. With Heinrich missing, and threats from unknown quarters starting to swirl around him, Nick needed somebody to have his back. Who was friend and who was foe was getting ever harder to distinguish. He knew exactly where Charlie stood. He checked his watch, did the time zones in his head, and dialed hopefully.

"Hey Chuckles, it's me. How's things?"

"All good here bro. Everything's copacetic. How about with you? Was the info I got you useful?" Charlie asked.

"Spot on. Exactly what I needed. It answered questions for me, and raised new ones. Those I need to work on from this end. But there was one other thing."

"Of course there is. There always is. What is it this time?"

"What do you mean there always is? When is the last time I asked you for something?"

"The last time you called."

"Oh, yeah. Well, I could use you over here Charlie. I need someone to help me unravel something. Something that gets bigger the deeper I dig. I need someone I can trust, someone to cover my six. Just for a few days. Maybe a week at most."

Silence.

"Still there Chuck?"

"Yes."

"What do you think?"

"I always wanted to go to Greece."

"Does that mean you're in?"

"I always wanted to go with my wife."

"Hmm. Well, can you make it over here?"

"Believe it or not, I've been waiting for you to ask me. I figured it was inevitable. But there is just one problem."

"Yeah. What's that?"

"I'm going to miss you."

"Why would you miss me if you're coming over here?"

"Because Sophie's going to kill you."

Nick hung up, excited that his brother would be joining him. He checked his messages and email, and quickly gathered his things. Then he and Artemis headed down to the docks. To the Poseidon.

There were backslaps all around, since the next phase of the excavation could begin in earnest. Nick smiled, it was good to be back in the company of these men. Even the normally reticent Yiannis was grinning, as Giorgos and Dimitris teased him. This time it was about his taste in clothing. Evidently his bright Hawaiian shirt was deemed out of place on a good Greek ship. Naturally his latest nickname graduated from hairy spider to *kefáli ananá*. Pineapple head.

As they pulled near the cofferdam there was tangible excitement in the air. Powerful industrial pumps had been installed, which had been working methodically day and night ever since. Already the water level within had dropped nearly fifteen feet. Nick stood on the packed earth between the retaining walls and stared down at the internal waterline. He could see it move ever so slightly. They would be mucking around on the bottom in no time.

Stavros and Dr. Storm were already there, under a specially constructed awning. It was situated above one end of the cofferdam to protect the crew and equipment from the merciless sun. Nick ducked under it and looked at a large monitor. It was connected to a camera that zoomed in on the steadily ebbing waters within.

"At this rate we should be to the bottom in no time," Dr. Storm said, putting a hand on Nick's shoulder. "You'll soon be getting your fingernails dirty with some real history."

Stavros looked up when he saw Nick, and walked over with a colleague.

"I believe you two have already met," Stavros said. "This is my good man Jason. Nothing gets done without him."

"Nice to see you again Mr. Nick." Jason reached out and shook Nick's hand. "I've something for you."

Jason handed Nick the fragment he had recovered from the dive site. From grid C-12.

"We were able to run some tests, to reveal more of the writing on the fragment. We can't decipher any of it, but we were able to carbon date some residue found stuck to it."

"How old?" Nick asked.

"1500 to 2000 BC."

"Whew," Nick whistled. "That would be older than any trireme."

Stavros carefully handed Nick an item wrapped in cloth. "A dockworker just found this in the surf over there. He brought it by the museum, to Jason. What do you make of it?"

Nick gingerly took it, and slowly unwrapped the protective cloth. Within lay a bejeweled dagger.

Nick looked at Stavros, then at Jason. "Found after the last storm?"

"Yes," replied Jason.

Nick looked below at the receding waters of the cofferdam, then back toward the shore, judging the distance and the tides. He turned the dagger over in his hands, carefully examining the remaining jeweled inlays and the craftsmanship. He picked up a magnifying glass and squinted at the symbols etched within it. "This script is Linear A. That means it predates the Myceneans, who predated the Greeks."

"Who built the triremes," Jason added.

Nick looked at Dr. Storm, who knowingly nodded agreement. He then looked closer at the monitor, the bottom of the waters in the cofferdam coming sharply into focus.

"If this dagger washed ashore from the wreck below, then that raises possibilities," Nick said. "Either it is an older artifact that was brought aboard . . ."

"Or it is an older wreck than any of us suspected," Stavros said, smiling broadly.

Nick was so excited that sleep eluded him. They were on the cusp of a discovery, perhaps even a tremendous discovery, and the possibilities were endless. What lay beneath the remaining sediment could be anything. The overactive imagination of an archeologist was a dangerous thing. Especially at night.

Maybe it is a trireme, just like we've thought all along. And the dagger was brought aboard by someone. Someone of importance, Nick thought. *Yeah, that was probably it. Occam's Razor, dummy. The simplest solution is always the most likely.*

He tossed in his bed, punched his pillow, and hung an arm over the edge. Artemis nuzzled it, until she got a rub out of the deal. She rolled on her back, playfully nipping and pawing at him.

But what if it wasn't brought aboard? What if it was part of the wreck itself, part of something more? Linear A was used by the Minoans. That script still has never been cracked. Could it all be that old? Minoans traded here. Was a ship of theirs lost in a storm?

Nick rolled over onto his stomach, pulling the pillow over his head. Sleep was hopeless.

Artemis suddenly stopped playing, and sprang on all fours. She let out a low growl, which alarmed Nick, so he stumbled out of bed and turned on a light. The protective canine instinctively crept toward the door, the hair in the middle of her back raising. Nick glanced around and grabbed an umbrella from the corner, the only thing close at hand.

He stealthily approached the door from the side, in case it was forced open. There was a gentle knock, and he jumped at the noise. So forcefully the umbrella sprung open in his hands, scaring him even more.

"Níkos?"

He tossed the umbrella aside and stepped over Artemis to look through the peep hole. Her tail started thumping forcefully against him once she recognized the voice and scent. Nick spied an exotic face looking back at him hopefully.

"You there? We have fun, yes?"

CHAPTER 21

JULY 2, PRESENT DAY, PIRAEUS, GREECE

I finally had a little time off. It get 'a so lonely on big ship with all dos men, but no you." Persa pouted. She sat on the edge of the bed, a sheet discretely pulled over her. She gently stroked Artemis, who leaned into her.

"We've been busy. The pumps have drained almost down to the seabed. I can't wait to excavate," Nick said.

He didn't provide any more insight of what new discoveries may lay beneath. Seductive though Persa was, he didn't completely trust her. At least not anymore.

"Yes, precious trireme. I hear Kollas want to make big buildings to house it. Big man, with 'is big plans."

"Well, I'm not sure I agree with them," Nick said. He grabbed a couple of water bottles from the mini-fridge, and handed her one. "There's the subtle detail that he would be building on sites of historical significance."

He sat back down next to her. Artemis put her head on his knee, huffing until he rubbed behind her ears.

"By the way, how did you know I was even here? I've been traveling around a bit."

"Yiannis told me," Persa replied with a shrug.

Nick looked at her and raised an eyebrow. "Hmm. How do you know Yiannis?"

"I find Poseidon on web site. It show crew. I friend Yiannis. You know, on Facebook. He say he recognize my photo. You show crew my photo Níkos?" she asked, flirting and rubbing his leg with her foot.

Nick grinned unsurely at her, saying nothing.

I did show them, he thought. *But it's creepy she searched out the crew. Found Yiannis. Friended the weakest link. Gotta be careful. I have a black widow in bed.*

Persa turned off the light, and pulled Nick back into bed with her. She curled in his arm, her hair across his chest, and soon was fast asleep.

Nick lay there, trying to doze off. Normally he would have no trouble after being with a beautiful woman. But visions of the excavation played in his mind, of what may lie beneath the silt. And of what lay right within his arms.

It was just before the dawn, and Persa had lain awake for over an hour. Yet she never stirred, and stared straight ahead into the darkness, forcing her breathing to be measured and regular. She focused on her safe place, methodically calming herself, slowing her heartbeat. To appear to be sound asleep. Just like her rigorous training had taught.

She heard Artemis nuzzling Nick. He slowly awoke, sighed, and sat on the edge of the bed, petting the big dog. He quietly got up and slipped out, careful not to wake her.

Such a nice man, she thought. *I don't like deceiving him.*

She rolled over and looked at the bedside clock, and the things he had left strewn about the room.

He could be gone a few minutes or an hour. Let things play out a little more.

Twenty minutes later, Nick gently opened the door, and carefully put down a couple cups of traditional Greek coffee and some fresh fruit. Artemis put two paws on the bed and huffed in Persa's ear, then gave her a lick for good measure. He smelled of fresh air and briny sea.

"I tried not to wake you."

Persa rolled over and smiled seductively at him. "Da, but dog not get memo."

He handed Persa a cup, and she breathed in the strong brew, then tasted the *kaimaki*, or foam, on the top. The brew would provide a good jolt to jump start the day, especially if she drank any of the unfiltered grounds at the bottom.

Nick playfully ruffled Persa's hair, then gave her a light kiss on the cheek.

"Gotta run. Big day today." He grabbed his things and headed out with Artemis, winking as he closed the door.

Persa patiently waited ten minutes, sipping on the coffee and nibbling on the fruit. Finally satisfied, she crept out of bed. She wanted to make sure he wasn't coming back for anything, and peered out the curtain. Nobody was around. The coast was clear.

She slid the chain lock back on to the door, put on snug plastic gloves, and started to methodically go through his things. There had to be a clue or two left lying around here.

His backpack and wallet had gone with him, so she rifled through his clothes. She checked all his pockets for any receipts, ticket stubs, or match books, anything that might indicate where he had been or who he was with. Coming up empty, Persa examined his toiletry travel case, under the mattress, in each dresser drawer. Nothing. It was as if he suspected her, yet he had never indicated any distrust. Not until last night. She knew. She always knew.

Her handlers had always been impressed with her ability to extract information from even the tightest lipped sources. Her exotic good looks and cunning made her an invaluable intelligence asset. She could read people like an open book. Nick had been one, but something had changed. No matter. It would barely delay her efforts. If at all.

There was one final thing left to check. She sat at the desk and opened his laptop. It booted up and asked for a password. She took a small thumb drive out of her pocket and placed it in the USB port. A box appeared in the middle of the screen, numbers and letters whirring by too fast to read. Like a jackpot machine on speed. Suddenly it stopped, a code locking in, appearing in large letters.

Persa smiled. Eight character minimum, alpha numeric, with at least one special character. She could have guessed this one by herself with no trouble.

AlbertJosie1984!

His parents, the year they married, exclamation point. Funny. And so predictable. She checked her watch. She needed to be out of here soon. Time to dig into the data and dash.

Artemis bounded aboard the Poseidon, followed closely by Nick. Dr. Storm and Stavros were already aboard, mapping out the day's activities. Dimitris was warming the engines, while Giorgos and Yiannis checked the gear. The crew was primed, excitement hung in the air.

Yiannis walked over to Nick, and showed him a picture on his phone. It was of Persa and her Facebook account. His new found friend. Yiannis gave him an elbow and a wink.

She knew exactly who to go after. No doubt about that, Nick thought.

As the Poseidon approached the cofferdam, they all saw that the pumping was completed. A technician explained a specially installed pump would now run when any seepage or rainwater accumulated. The careful and tedious work of excavation could now commence in earnest.

Nick and Georgos descended to the bottom to examine the site. After conferring, several grids were agreed upon, and Nick looked up and gave the thumbs up. Yiannis directed people to a specially constructed pulley and basket system, powered by whirring electric motors. He made sure it wasn't overloaded, lowered the helping hands down, and raised any collected debris up. Stavros had recruited staff from the various museums and universities under his purview. Word had spread quickly, and working on a live excavation of this magnitude held great appeal.

Nick took charge of the manpower on the seabed, ably assisted by Giorgos. Stavros, with the help of Dr. Storm, managed operations from above. The work proceeded quickly at first, as the remaining loose sediment was collected, examined, and disposed of. Teams worked in assigned grids, an informal competition developing between them. Within a few hours, a rhythm had developed with filled buckets going up to Yiannis and Dimitris, and empty ones returning. Once the teams reached firmer layers of packed earth, the work slowed. Trowels, picks and magnifiers became the order of business. The awning above provided relief from the direct sunlight, but not the humidity.

Artifacts from the suspected landslide that had originally buried the wreck started to emerge from the protective cocoon. Bits of shaped stone used for building, fragments of pottery, pieces of forged metal, even bones of small animals and birds. All were carefully photographed in situ, bagged, tagged, and labeled by grid. These were then packed in boxes and raised out of the pit. Nick carefully examined a piece of a tooth that could be human. He used a magnifier to peer closer.

"Nick, I said what do you think?"

Nick looked up, lost in his work. Dr. Storm knelt down next to him, and touched the tip of the partially exposed prow. The same dull piece of wood that Nick had touched on his first dive. There was now over two feet of it exposed, twice that of when it was discovered.

"Incredible, isn't it Doc? Do you feel the history in it?" Nick replied. Doc nodded back, grinning broadly.

"But we're not going to know the timeframe until we get a whole lot more of this exposed."

"I'd say with all the manpower Stavros has rallied, that shouldn't be too terribly long in coming."

"Yeah. At least we don't have to hack through that layer of sunken pumice," Nick said, pointing at the jagged exposed outer edges around them. "The currents, tides, and prop wash did that heavy lifting for us already."

Dr. Storm ran his fingers along the grooves in the wood. "We have guests above. It would be good if you could come up and press some flesh."

"Let me guess. Drakos?"

"Among others."

"Absolutely necessary?"

"It would be good for all of the American delegation involved to make itself known."

"Do they suspect what we think we may find?"

Dr. Storm shrugged. "For all we know, Drakos has heard every conversation we've had. But if he has, he's not letting on."

Nick waved at Giorgos and pointed up, then headed topside. As he ascended, Nick saw the working space at the end of the cofferdam crowded with dignitaries. He shook his head in disgust. He wouldn't be getting anything else accomplished today.

"This is Dr. Storm's colleague, Nick LaBounty. Nick has extensive experience in marine excavation," Stavros said, introducing him to the assembled group.

"Ah, the famous Mr. LaBounty. So nice to have you aiding our quest," replied Petros Morakis, the prime minister of Greece. Drakos Kollas stood next to him, smoking a cigar, unsmiling. A reporter and cameraman angled for a good shot. Four others were in the group, all well dressed and evaluating the unfolding excavation. The top Greek brass.

Nick flinched at the comment, preferring anonymity. Obviously, word of his prior exploits had circulated. He shook the proffered hand.

"I am honored to be involved in such a worthy endeavor. May what we unearth bring much good fortune to all of Greece," Nick said, looking at the prime minister. He glanced at Drakos, who stared back, betraying nothing.

"Perhaps you could enlighten us on what today's efforts have yielded?" the prime minister asked. A camera zoomed in on Nick's face.

"Today's work was all preparatory. We have removed the protective layer of fill. Now begins the task of excavating through the detritus of time. To find out the state of preservation of the wreck, and what secrets it may contain."

The reporter translated his comments, then the camera shifted to the prime minister, Drakos, and the dignitaries. Nick could hear Drakos expounding on what this would mean to the working people of Greece, and how his sponsorship had made it all possible. Nick edged away, over to the equipment bank. He and Dr. Storm looked at a screen, monitoring the activity below. Artemis came out from her cool place under the table and leaned into Nick.

"He's a well-connected man, isn't he?" Nick observed.

"You don't become a powerful tycoon like him without friends in high places," Dr. Storm said.

"No, I don't suppose you would. But I suspect he leaves a trail of enemies too."

Their photo op complete, the dignitaries made their way to a transfer boat, Stavros escorting them past. Drakos paused and looked at the screen Nick and Dr. Storm were huddled by. His hulking bodyguard, Lykaios, stood protectively behind him.

"Discoveries can often have different interpretations," Drakos said to them both. "It is important the right version be told from the outset. We wouldn't want less-educated people getting confused and misinterpreting the past."

Artemis let out a low growl and started nudging past Nick, toward Drakos. Lykaios immediately reached under his coat. Nick grabbed the canine by the collar, restraining her, but didn't scold her. She continued to emit a deep-throated growl, her hair raising.

"Isn't it most important to get the truth out, whatever it may be?" Nick asked. He felt Dr. Storm lightly touch his elbow. "Even if it doesn't fit neatly with a preconceived narrative?"

"No matter how well intentioned," Dr. Storm added, trying to diffuse the growing tension.

Drakos glanced to make sure the group was well out of ear shot. He turned to Nick and glared.

"You arrogant Americans, you think yourselves so righteous.

What do you know about history? You've been around for a few hundred years and think you invented democracy," Drakos said, the veins in his neck bulging. "We gave birth to great ideals when your country was nothing but wilderness and wild beasts. There is no original thought in America that you didn't import or steal from something we came up with thousands of years ago."

Nick held Artemis tightly, and walked directly toward Drakos, until they stood face to face. Lykaios stepped toward him, and he let Artemis go. The dog crouched as if to leap, and Nick snapped his fingers. Artemis froze. Drakos gestured to Lykaios to stand down. He couldn't risk a confrontation here. Not with all these witnesses.

"We didn't invent democracy, but we sure as hell perfected it when the world was still ruled by kings," Nick said, his blood up. "Do you even remember the meaning? *Dēmos*, the people. *Kratiā*, to rule. Don't forget, that has always been when Greece was at its greatest. When the will of the people ruled."

Drakos wasn't about to be lectured by this young, impetuous academic. He leaned in and hissed, "You try to measure greatness in centuries. We measure it in millennia. America is nothing but the rejects and strays from every country on earth. Just like that useless dog." He pointed his finger like a gun at Artemis, and clicked his thumb down. "Here in Greece, we know how to take care of strays."

"I thought that went well," Nick said.

He meandered through a park with Dr. Storm and Stavros near their port-side hotel. Artemis followed behind them, discouraging any eavesdroppers. Stavros was clearly agitated, not finding anything about the confrontation the least bit funny.

"They must have ears everywhere. He knew we might find something different once we excavated," replied Dr. Storm.

Nick rubbed the stubble on his chin. "He wants to control the narrative, truth be damned."

"The irony is we really don't know what lies beneath. At least not yet," Stavros said. "It would have been best to not agitate him until we had the facts. I still have to work with Kollas. He is, you know, the——"

"The main sponsor. Yeah, sorry about that. But I can't un-ring that bell. Consider this his opening gambit. A preemptive strike to set the tone, for whatever is discovered," Nick responded, then checked his watch. "It's been a long day gentlemen. If you'll excuse me."

Nick left them while they strategized, and went back to his hotel. He let Artemis in, who sniffed around the room. There was a note on the desk. It was in Persa's flowing handwriting. Scented with her distinctive perfume.

Last night most lovely. Now duty call.
I go back to ship. Miss you. Me.

He looked around the room. Everything appeared to be exactly as he had left it. After satisfying himself that nothing had been disturbed, he sat at his laptop. Looking carefully at the closed lid, he froze. He leaned in closer and squinted. It was there, right on the side. A tiny black hair from Artemis, one that he had carefully left closed in on the side of the black lid. It now sat atop the black desk, nearly invisible. A little trip wire to tell if anyone had been on his laptop.

Busted.

He crawled into bed after he jammed a chair under the door handle. A little added protection, just in case.

Like that would do any good, he thought. *I am clearly in the crosshairs of Drakos. I still don't know what Persa's game is. What will we uncover tomorrow? Where the hell is Heinrich?* Nick sighed. *Will I ever get any sleep?*

It seemed he had just nodded off when the alarm on Nick's phone beeped, startling him. He was so disciplined he always awoke before it ever sounded. But not today.

Nick rolled over and hit the snooze button, and saw Artemis looking at him, nose to nose. She tilted her head in confusion or concern—he couldn't tell which—then gave him a lick.

"Don't be too disappointed in me girl. I've got a lot on my mind."

Even though it was a Saturday, they were on site with the rest of the crew before 7 a.m. To see what secrets might be revealed today. And to beat the unrelenting heat.

Nick directed the teams at the bottom to concentrate in the very middle of the dig site, fanning out to the surrounding grids. They would work at it from the inside out. Space was tight, and the larger workers ended up on bucket brigade while their smaller counterparts huddled in the dirt, scraping inch by inch.

The number of artifacts started to diminish the deeper they burrowed. There was just compacted earth, which was counterintuitive. Stavros and Dr. Storm descended, and huddled with Nick. What was going on?

"From the debris field, it is evident this was buried by a landslide," Dr. Storm observed. "Everything being recovered is from land, not sea."

"And then encased on top with a sunken layer of pumice," Stavros said, slowly rotating a piece of the honeycombed stone in his fingers.

"But the artifacts are fading out the deeper we go. We've found very little since we got below the looser debris level. We're at packed earth now. If the ship had been near land or at a dock when it was buried by a landslide, there should be random artifacts throughout," Nick said.

Giorgos and Jason were working in a nearby grid. They called out for Nick. Stavros and Dr. Storm followed him over.

"What do you make 'a this?" Jason asked.

They had worked down to a distinct solid layer of earth, hardened on top, covering their entire grid. There were imprinted round shapes, four to five inches in diameter, dotted across the surface. It was eroded in spots where the currents had carved into it.

Where something of value might have drifted with the tides. Like a piece of pottery, or a dagger perhaps? Nick thought.

He took a trowel and flacked away the hard dirt, down deeper, into yet more-compacted earth. Stavros knelt next to him, rubbing the circular indentations on top. Dr. Storm paced back and forth, stroking the point of his beard in contemplation.

Nick slowly stood, and looked around the entire site. It appeared the ground was tapering downward along the edges, a slightly higher mound in the middle. The look of puzzlement dissipated from his face.

Dr. Storm noticed it first and looked at Nick. "What have you got young man?"

"It wasn't out to sea, or tied to a dock. Remember how much the sea levels have risen? I think this might have all been dry land," Nick replied.

"But why would it be on land? How can you even tell?" Stavros asked.

Nick knelt down to where he had been digging. "This has been compacted on purpose. Before the landslide ever happened." He crumbled a bit of the dirt between his fingers, watching it fall back in the hole. "Don't you see it?"

Dr. Storm squinted in concentration for a moment, then let out an unconscious grunt of satisfaction. He held his arms out with one hand above the other, like he was holding a pole. He then made up and down motions. "They tamped it down to compact the earth, to preserve it. That's why there are all the circular indentations."

"But why would anyone bother to do that?" asked Giorgos.

Stavros now smiled too, in on the mystery.

"Because they wanted to preserve it," Nick said, looking up. "This wasn't a sunken wreck. It was a burial mound."

CHAPTER 22

JULY 4, PRESENT DAY, PIRAEUS, GREECE

Everyone wanted to be in on the action at the bottom of the dig site, but there needed to be room to work. Stavros limited who could go down into the pit. Even the media crew would have to shoot from above, on the walkway of the cofferdam. At least for the time being.

Nick decided to personally work from the middle outward. From the telling rise of tamped earth that seemed to be hiding something from them. The original survey imaging had indicated ship ribbing and a mass along the keel, which was thought to be ballast stones. He now had an intuition it might be something else.

"OK. Let's see what the gods have left for us," Nick said, nodding at Jason, who had the other set of hands he most trusted.

After documenting, they removed a large piece of hardened, tamped earth from the top of the center mound. It contained the circular indentations, and would be examined in minute detail under the controlled conditions of a lab. The work proceeded slowly, the surrounding grids likewise being painstakingly excavated, inch by inch. The ancient soil was filtered for any fragments, then hauled up in buckets.

Nick and Jason methodically scraped their way downward on the center mound. It had partially eroded at one edge, the bottom of the exposed area filled with drifting sea shells and bits of broken coral. Bucket after bucket was filled, sifted, then removed. Despite the shade from the awning far above and strategically placed tarps, the heat and humidity steadily rose. The bottom of the pit soon smelled of a fishy tang mixed with sweat and brine.

After nearly five hours, Nick and Jason started to hit a flat, hard surface. Clearing revealed a single piece of flat stone, about six feet by two and a half feet in size. It soon became apparent it sat roughly atop a hallowed out stone box. One side was broken, near the eroded and exposed part of the mound. They started removing sand, shells, and compacted coral that had drifted and accumulated there. Jason lifted a last bit of shell with the point of his trowel, exposing something underneath.

"Nick, look here," he said.

They both used their trowels to widen the hole. Nick knelt down with a fine brush and dusted away some of the dirt. They looked at each other with widening eyes, and cautiously picked at the edges. Others around them, diligently working their own grids, were oblivious to the unfolding drama just a few feet away.

Nick knelt in and gently pumped a blow-out bulb, removing the sand particles. It was visible now, distinct. He looked back at Jason, raising an eyebrow. Jason nodded back. It had to be. More picking away around it, until first one, then two, lay exposed, side by side. Finally satisfied, Nick and Jason sat back, smiling broadly. Nick looked up above until he caught the eye of Stavros, who tapped Dr. Storm on the shoulder.

"What have you got?" Stavros asked.

"Remains," Nick said. All heads turned toward him. The camera crew above zoomed in.

"It's a roughhewn sarcophagus. Broken in on one side."

"What can you see?" asked Dr. Storm.

"Two fingers of a hand. With a ring. We have a body down here."

It had been Stavros's idea, once the actual excavation started, to have a camera crew on hand to document the unfolding events. If the find turned out to be significant, it could be compiled into a documentary to accompany any future exhibit. Kollas had naturally objected, but even he realized it was a futile argument. Word was out, and a fascinated public demanded real time information. But if he couldn't control the documentation, he would try to influence the interpretation.

Jason and Nick stood before the camera crew, Jason answering questions asked in Greek, Nick fielding those asked in English. Jason was much more in demand.

"We have no idea who may be inside, or what the state of preservation might be. We have to proceed carefully. Everything around the sarcophagus could yield clues and needs to be analyzed. We don't want to damage anything in rushing to open it," Nick said. After thanking his interviewer, he wandered over to where Dr. Storm sat. Looking at close-up images and discussing options.

"The quickest solution would be to open it in situ Philip," Stavros said. "Think of the excitement it would generate."

"Or, you could lift it completely out and put it on a barge," Dr. Storm replied. "Then examine the contents in a more controlled setting."

A sudden flurry of activity made them all turn their heads. Several officials cleared a path from a tender to where they sat atop the wall. A small entourage made its way to them, and stopped under the awning. The excavation's sponsor had returned.

"I just heard. Most magnificent news. May I see?" Drakos rhetorically asked.

Nick led them all down to the cracked sarcophagus. Drakos examined it, and looked disappointed. His ever-present body guard handed him a handkerchief, which he put on the ground. He knelt gingerly on one knee, and peered at the ghostly exposed finger bones. He arose and turned to Stavros.

"Origin?"

"We won't know until we remove the lid and examine the remains."

Drakos looked at the position of the sun, then at his watch. "What are you waiting for?"

"We don't want to rush into this. There are many factors to be considered. We have to—"

"You have until tomorrow," Drakos interrupted. "I will be by with the prime minister at 4 p.m. Don't disappoint me." He turned sharply on his heel and headed for the lift out of the pit.

"Every once in a while you have to kiss a—" Nick said.

"We know, we know," replied Dr. Storm.

Stavros frowned for a moment, then wiped the look of frustration off his face. "Let us not lose sight of the fact we have a tremendous discovery on our hands. In situ it is. Let us prepare."

Further excavation was done around the site until the crews were exhausted. When evening descended, fresh hands rotated in and continued the work under bright halogen lights. Slowly the outline of the perimeter of the ship emerged from its entombment, random pieces pointing skyward. Dr. Storm joked it reminded him of dinosaur ribs from an excavation he had done in the bad lands of South Dakota.

The sarcophagus was cleared down to its hard stone surface. Nick covered the exposed cracked side to protect it, where they had first discovered the protruding finger bones. When no one was looking, he discretely slipped something into his pocket. A clue he didn't want falling into the wrong hands.

At midnight Stavros called an end to it. Sharp minds and bodies were needed for the morrow. Nick and Jason were the last to come up, emerging grimy and sweat-stained.

"How are you holding up young men?" Dr. Storm asked.

"Exhausted. And exhilarated," Nick said. "We're so close. So very close."

Jason bobbed his head in agreement.

Everyone was going to have a hard time sleeping tonight.

"Are they still alive?" Dr. Storm asked.

Giorgos cradled the head of the guard in his lap. He was moaning softly, disoriented and unconscious. Yiannis did the same with the second guard. Giorgos examined him closely, and pulled out a small dart from the back of the guard's neck. He held it up for all to see.

"Yes. But drugged."

"Thank the gods," Stavros said. "They must have snuck up out of the water." He stood looking at the sarcophagus, then started fuming, swearing in Greek. "I can't believe anyone would do this."

"Afraid so. See for yourself." Nick stood aside, handed him a flashlight, and let him peek deep into the sarcophagus.

The cracked side had been forced open, broken wider, whatever lay inside taken. The contents completely ransacked.

"But why Stavros? Why now, on the cusp of such a tremendous discovery?" Dr. Storm asked.

Stavros leaned on the edge of the sarcophagus, the weight of expectations and the inevitable firestorm of media scrutiny upon him. "I don't know. It makes no sense. Not with the eyes of the world watching."

Dr. Storm rubbed the back of his head, searching for answers. "You can't fence any of it. Everything is too hot."

"Maybe someone wanted it for themselves?" Jason said.

Nick held up a finger to his lips, then tapped his ear. Careful, their conversation was probably being monitored

Stavros nodded, and spat on the ground. There would be much to answer to today.

The police came out, halting the excavation while examining the site in minute detail. A no-nonsense inspector and several detectives closely questioned everyone involved with the project. All official photographs of the dig and the film from the media crew were duplicated for review.

Drakos arrived early afternoon, immediately accusing Stavros of gross negligence and the police of incompetence. He was irate at not being allowed to question the guards himself. When told the excavation was being halted for the time being, he left in a huff for the prime minister's office.

Stavros and the team were escorted back to shore. The crew went their separate ways, Stavros, Dr. Storm, and Nick then headed to the nearby park to talk in private. Each had had plenty of time to digest the looting, and formulate their own conclusions. Artemis, ever alert and intimidating, roamed about them as they walked, insuring no prying ears.

"A burial ship for the ages. And the body disappears on my watch. Right before we reveal it," Stavros lamented.

"Not your fault," Nick said, patting his shoulder. "You took the right precautions. You had security posted."

"Only a handful even knew we were opening the sarcophagus today," observed Dr. Storm. "They struck before the contents could be revealed."

"Who could benefit from this?" Stavros asked.

"There is another game afoot here. That is why I took the precaution of taking this," Nick said, pulling an object out of his pocket and holding it close.

Dr. Storm huddled in and grasped the object. "From where? How did you get it out?"

"Fantastikós," exclaimed Stavros. He closed in too, so no outside eyes could see what they beheld. "Anyone else know?"

"No," Nick said. "It was on the wrist, covered in debris. I slid it out when I was alone, when no one was looking or filming. I had a bad feeling, a premonition, that there were too many eyes watching everything unfold. I took it for safekeeping. Just in case."

"What do you make of it? Mycenean?" Dr. Storm asked, handing it to Stavros.

"No, earlier," Nick said. "The symbols on the outside are clear, definitely Minoan."

Stavros looked at it briefly, then slid it into his coat pocket. Nick made a very visible display of putting something back into his own pocket. Just in case anyone was looking. They all continued to meander along in the park.

"I couldn't read what was on the inside, concretion covered it,"

"But I do, I need to say it. You've been loyal while I haven't. While I have been courted."

"Maybe not completely loyal."

"That doesn't matter to me Nick. Does it to you?"

"No. C'mon, we're adults. We were apart. Now we're not."

Soba smiled and put her arm in his. They were at the waterfront now. The water below lapped at the retaining wall. Nick pointed out into the distance, the cofferdam well-lit and patrolled.

"That's where all the magic has been happening."

Soba squeezed his arm tightly and continued. "For generations my forefathers had carried on the bloodline. I struggled with betraying that heredity. But I think they accomplished what they set out to do. The treasure of the Aztecs was found and preserved. The bloodline of Montezuma carried on to me, and will carry on past me. With you."

"You mean you're willing to be with a commoner?" Nick joked.

"Yes, the Princess and the Pebble."

"I see Charlie has gotten to you."

"Funny what fifteen hours of flight time in confined quarters with someone will do to you."

The sound of laughter and music drifted toward them as they approached a portside bar. Charlie was inside, sitting with Dr. Storm and Nick's new companions.

"I hate to say it, but get ready for some more travel. Tomorrow morning we hop on a ferry," Nick said.

"Dare I ask to where?"

"First stop, Santorini."

CHAPTER 23

JULY 6, PRESENT DAY, AT SEA

Might as well get comfortable. I've done this ferry route before. It takes about eight hours," Nick said. Artemis paced around them, ever herding her little flock.

"I don't care how long it takes. I've never seen seas and islands so beautiful," Soba said. She was more used to the stark beauty of her homeland of the Desert Southwest.

Nick could see the look of enchantment in her eyes. It was warm despite the early hour, the sun shimmering diamonds off the sea. On the port side, the islands of Kea and Kithnos slowly slipped by. He had the same reaction the first time he had been here. A blend of awe and fascination, mixed with a little anger. Anger that it had taken him so long to discover this corner of the world. A well-kept secret no one had thought to tell him.

"Yep, Sophie's going to kill you when she sees what she's been missing," Charlie joked.

"Great. The wrath of yet another woman to contend with," Nick replied.

Soba gave him a stern look like she was offended. "We're not all bad, you know. It's just hard always being right." She kissed Nick lightly on the cheek.

"So, we've got lots of time to catch up, right? Bring us up to speed bro. What's the plan?"

By the time Nick had given them the highlights of the excavation of the trireme, the theft from the sarcophagus, and the disappearance of Heinrich, they were just over an hour from their destination. While the ferry threaded between the islands of Sikinos and Ios, the trio stayed outside to admire the view. They found a spot in the shade, the heat partially mitigated by the breeze.

"I now see why Odysseus took ten years to get home," Soba said.

"Only because Penelope awaited him," Nick replied. "Otherwise, I don't think he would have ever gone home again.

"OK, enough quoting Homer you two. You're not the only ones who ever read the Odyssey," Charlie said, rolling his eyes.

Approaching Santorini, the ferry slid in past the rim of the old caldera, past the emerging cone of Nea Kameni, and into the busy port of Athinios. Charlie wanted to take the gondola to the top, while Soba lobbied for the unique experience of a donkey ride. Nick insisted they walk up the switchback trail. While ascending Soba realized the conditions of the donkeys and gave Nick a look of understanding. Nick squeezed her hand, then snickered as he watched Charlie start to sweat profusely from the exertion and the heat.

"I see what avoiding the stairs has done for you brother," he chided.

"Bite me," came the gasping reply.

"Ah, skewered by your rapier-like wit yet again. I guarantee the view will be worth it. And speaking for all the donkeys of Santorini, they thank you for not having to haul your pale white ass on their ass to the top."

Soba giggled out loud at the brothers' light-hearted bantering. How she missed it.

Nick had made a call beforehand. Here was an opportunity to reconnect with his new found daredevil friend, and introduce him to Soba and Charlie. Jim Portmess was only too happy to meet them for dinner.

"You should have seen him, it was like he was standing on the edge of Mount Doom in Mordor. You know, Lord of the Rings,"

Jim said, regaling them with stories of Nick's baptism to vulcanol-ogy. "Thought I was going to lose him there, right off the precipice!"

"You actually looked down into a live volcano?" Soba asked.

"Who would have thought. My little brother. Playing with fire," Charlie chimed in.

"It was as if Earth is a living, breathing thing," Nick said. "I still can't comprehend the sheer power of it. Awesome. And terrifying."

"Cheers to Mother Earth," exclaimed Jim, raising a shot glass of Ouzo.

"Ya mas," came the reply from around the bar.

"Still crinkly," Nick said, smiling and rubbing his forearms.

"So, how long are you here?" Big Jim asked.

"A day or two. I'm following up on a lead related to my friend who disappeared. It may be nothing, but I've got to check it out."

"Say, if these two have nothing to do while you look, I could give them a peek into the inferno."

Soba and Charlie sat wide-eyed listening to the conversation, fidgeting in discomfort.

"I can actually use them. But hey, thanks for the offer," Nick said, winking at Soba.

They talked into the night, swapping tales of adventures and derring-do. The view from the veranda was especially stunning to Soba and Charlie, who had never been there. The sun slowly set, bathing the cliffs below and everything around them in soft hues of pink and orange. To the west, the cone of Nea Kameni and the outer island of Therasia darkened against the horizon. The sea turned pink, then purple. Everyone watching broke out with sponta-neous applause as the sun finally winked out.

Nick glanced around, admiring the communal spirit of the crowd. He noticed a stranger sitting nearby at the bar, sipping a drink. When they made eye contact, the stranger quickly got up and walked away. The abruptness of the departure caught Nick's atten-tion, a nervousness like the stranger had been caught doing something.

K. Schultze
1921 – 1944

"He was telling the truth. No one else could have possibly known the name of the other survivor," Nick said.

They sat in the ferry terminal, awaiting a ride from Santorini to Crete. While a high-speed ferry would only take two hours, they decided to enjoy the ride on a conventional ferry. It would give them six hours to plan and prepare. And to take in the spectacular view and sunset.

"What does it all mean?" Soba asked.

Nick furtively glanced around, making sure no one was too close or paying undo attention to them.

"Before I get into that, are your phones all the way off?" Nick asked. "We've been one step behind every time. I don't want anybody tracking us."

"That's why you've been paying in cash, isn't it?" Soba asked.

Nick nodded.

"Look, go through your luggage. All of it. Top to bottom, carefully. Make sure *nothing* was planted."

The three of them discretely unpacked, thoroughly examined their belongings, and repacked. Nick checked the backpacks and duffle bags themselves, then sat back, unsatisfied. Artemis sensed something was amiss, and nuzzled him.

"Yeah, I know girl," he said stroking behind her ears and under the collar. "I'm missing something."

As he stroked her neck, the back of his hand rubbed against a bump under the collar.

The collar. It couldn't be. Who had access to that? Only Kollas, Persa, the excavation team, the news crews, anyone and everyone, he thought.

Nick unbuckled it, and felt carefully along its length. He felt a small bump in the middle, and noticed a bit of thin wire protruding at the end. He tugged at the wire, and the bump moved slightly.

A tracker and an antenna.

His heart sank, that was dirty pool. Someone had gotten to him through his damn dog.

He walked over to the edge of the dock and waited a moment. A fishing boat soon glided by, its hold wide open in anticipation of the day's catch. Nick tossed the collar, which hit the deck and slid, teetering on the edge of the hold. He watched nervously, hoping a crewman wouldn't see it. The boat rose as it plowed into a wave, then settled again. The collar wobbled for a moment, then slipped away from view. Deep into the hold.

"Good luck tracking that around, you bastard," Nick said. "Whoever you are."

They boarded the ferry and took seats near the stern, away from the crowd. The noise of the engines would drown out their conversation. Charlie and Soba sat in rapt attention, anxious to understand why they were headed to Crete.

"Heinrich discovered critical information about a missing U-boat, and left me a clue just before he disappeared," Nick explained. "It was the name of someone who claimed to have survived the sinking, a man named Günther Wessel. I met him, and his story was unbelievable. Literally."

"But the grave marker we just found, what does that prove?" Charlie asked.

"It proves he was telling the truth, at least about getting off the U-boat with one other person. Which makes me think he may be telling the truth about what else he saw," Nick replied.

Soba looked at him with expectant eyes. "What else did he see?"

"I wish I could tell you. But I think it's safer if you both don't know. At least not yet." Nick knew if anything happened, if Charlie or Soba somehow became pawns in all of this, ignorance might be the only thing keeping them safe.

"Well, can you tell us why we are going to Crete at least?" Charlie asked.

Nick brightened. That was on a less nefarious front. More like the type of archeological escapades he liked to get swept up in. An ancient enigma to solve.

"Yes, certainly. The shipwreck we are excavating holds secrets. Secrets so important to someone that they were willing to risk raiding the sarcophagus and all it held."

Nick paused, weighing how much information he should give.

"I have a theory about the origin of the shipwreck. One that won't conveniently fit the narrative being crafted by certain parties. We're going to Crete to see if my theory holds water."

"Sounds exciting! Where on Crete are we headed?" Soba asked.

"We land at the port at Heraklion. But our ultimate destination is the ancient palace of Knossos."

Pello sat quietly, gazing through the scope of his high powered Kefefs sniper rifle. It had been pilfered from the armory of the Greek special forces. An ironic twist, but it would be put to better use here.

It wasn't so hard tracking them, trying to always be one step ahead. The Amerikanós were getting better at deception, perhaps they knew they were being followed. Yet their primitive attempts at stealth were of little use. After all, Pello's people were here, ingrained into the very fabric of every aspect of society. They had always been here. And always would.

The organization he worked for had discrete eyes and ears everywhere. A secretive and nebulous network, constantly feeding him information. They were not like the Greek Godfathers of the Night or the Sicilian Cosa Nostra, who were messy and visible. Pathetically driven only by money. His was an organization that had endured for millennia, and was driven by higher ideals and longer-term ambitions.

Pello's highly attuned eyesight caught movement in the distance, the curtain in a window above the port parting. He looked back at the ferry, and saw a crowd of tourists disembarking. The three Amerikanós were toward the back, separate, with a large dog. They got off last, watching the departing tourists to see if any lingered about. Not bad for amateurs.

He glanced down at the photo he had been given, temporarily taped to his forearm. It was of the younger man, the one called Nick. The instructions had been very specific. He was the one.

He focused the crosshairs on the target. This would be just like his grandfather had taught him when he was young. Learning to hunt in the rocky and unforgiving hinterlands of Crete.

The patient hunter was always in control. Let the prey come to you, unknowing. Right toward the instrument of their own demise.

He carefully set the hair trigger. It was a clean shot, no wind to contend with. Breathe in. Breathe out. Just like his *pappoús* had said. One. Two. Three. Tap.

The recoil shook the scope off center, and he shifted it back to make sure he had taken out the target. The curtain in the far window fluttered, a red stain now along its edge. Pello eyed the would-be assassin, slumped over in the chair, a rifle in his lap and a growing red dot in the middle of his forehead. He looked down the street, and saw the dog staring back up. The assassin had fired wildly when he was hit, but no one had noticed. No damage had been done.

It was proving most difficult keeping this Amerikí alive. But Pello had been specifically instructed to protect him at all costs. The archeologist was on the right track of discovery, and nothing must be allowed to interrupt his work. Because as Zorba had told him, Nick was searching for the same thing they all sought.

Even if he didn't know it. At least not yet.

Artemis heard the two silenced shots and a nearby ricochet. She instinctively looked up at a far window, the barrel of a rifle disappearing from view. She crouched and crept ahead of Nick, Soba, and Charlie, letting out a low growl.

"Easy Artemis, easy" Nick said, unsure of what set her off.

Maybe it was the backfire from a scooter he thought he had heard. He patted his thigh as he walked, signaling for her to follow.

"C'mon girl. We've got a lot to do."

CHAPTER 24
JULY 8, PRESENT DAY, HERAKLION, CRETE, GREECE

They sat outside enjoying the view and fresh air at a café near their hostel. It was still early morning in Crete, just after sunrise. The air was fresh and crisp, too early for the humidity to build. The cruise ships were not yet in the port of Heraklion, and the streets had more of a local feel to them. At least for the moment.

"It says here the Minoan civilization faded as the Myceneans conquered and absorbed them," Soba said, putting down her tour book. "The Myceneans were the earliest Greeks?"

Nick leaned back from his breakfast and sipped the foam from the top of a strong cup of Greek coffee. Charlie saw an opening and reached over and grabbed a *bougatsa*, a crispy filo pastry filled with warm custard and drizzled with icing and cinnamon, from Nick's plate,

"You gonna finish that bro?" he asked, then took a big bite. "Man, you can't get that at home."

Nick laughed. "Sure, just help yourself."

He was always amazed at the prodigious amounts of food his brother could consume. No wonder he had the nickname Chuck Wagon. He looked back at Soba, certainly more appealing with her sparkling green eyes, tanned skin, and long black hair. A radiant Amerindian if ever there was one. Enhanced by the excitement of her first time in the Mediterranean.

"Yes, the Myceneans were the earliest recognized Greeks. They were warlike, and took advantage when they saw weakness. The Minoans were an empire built on trade. Although they weren't afraid to protect it," Nick said. "You'll learn all about them this morning at the museum."

Charlie looked at Soba and rolled his eyes. "Oh boy, another museum. I can hardly wait."

Soba smiled back and shushed him.

"Seriously. Who the hell were the Minoans? Who cares?"

Nick shot him a look. "History cares, ignoramus."

A television screen set back under the awning had the news on, and a voice caught Nick's ear. It was Drakos Kollas being inter-viewed, with subtitles in English for the tourist set. Nick leaned forward, trying to catch the gist of the segment.

It was plainly evident from the footage. Kollas stood in front of a large crowd, haranguing them that Greece should be for Greeks only. Images showed the recent boat exodus from North Africa, beleaguered refugees being turned away or herded into desolate and overcrowded camps while water cannons turned on protesters. Other images played in the background, of climate change causing coastal flooding, drought laying waste to farmland, and raging fires destroying large swaths of land. Famine, pestilence, war, and death. The four horsemen of the apocalypse appeared to be charging upon the very shores of sacred *Hellas*.

Kollas demanded lucrative jobs go to Greek nationals only, a break from the European Union and all the debts owed, even a restoration of Drachma over the Euro currency. He railed against immigration, banged the drum of Greeks being priced out of their own backyards. He had struck at the raw nerve of nationalism during turbulent times, and many were flocking to his banner. It was steadily escalating. Unless calmer heads prevailed, there could soon be blood in the streets.

"That's the knucklehead you were telling us about?" Charlie asked. "Seems like a real *Seig Heil* kind of guy."

"Yes, a loud man with small ideas for complex problems. Still, he carries real weight around here. But the hell with him. What say we go see something really fascinating?"

The Heraklion Archeological Museum was just blocks from the port. It didn't open until 9 a.m., but Nick was granted early access as a professional courtesy. They were escorted in by a colleague of Stavros, and given free reign. The museum was deserted except for a few wandering security guards and the cleaning crew.

Nick led them on a chronological tour, from the Neolithic to the early Bronze Age, then from the Golden Age of the Minoans to Roman times. A span of over 5,500 years.

"Those Minoans weren't so bad, eh?" Nick asked rhetorically.

They stood in front of a stunning fresco which showed bull leaping done with a stylized, contemporary grace. The large panel had been rescued and restored from the palace of Knossos, and was now one of the focal pieces of the museum.

"That's beautiful. It seems I've seen that style used elsewhere," Charlie said.

"That you have. Much of what you see is so timeless it's been widely emulated."

They wandered past sacred bulls with golden horns, snake goddess figurines, sculptures, pottery, luxury objects, burial goods, and metalwork. The famous Arkalochori Axe, discovered in a cave on Crete, inscribed in symbols thought to be in Linear A. Whimsical frescos of dolphins leaping, a man somersaulting over a bull, and bare-breasted women with dark kohl eyes. All remnants of Europe's first highly developed civilization. Finally, they stopped in front of a famous gold bee pendant, indicative of Minoan artistic crafts-manship.

"Incredible. How long ago did they flourish?" Soba asked.

"3,500 years, give or take. They were ahead of their time, and then disaster struck," Nick said, still amazed at the capricious whims of nature. "Just think where other civilizations stood 3,500 years ago. If Thera hadn't erupted when it did, history might have been unfolded very differently."

They continued to wander and marvel at the exhibits. The museum opened and tourists started to stream in. The noise level slowly built with the increasing crowd. It was evident the cruise ships were disgorging their day trippers and tour groups.

Nick felt his phone vibrate, and checked the screen. It was a burner phone, whose carefully guarded number he had given only to Dr. Storm and Stavros. He looked at the images on it and smiled. They were of the bracelet he had found and surreptitiously taken out of the sarcophagus. Stavros had his right-hand man, Jason, work at removing the concretion that had formed on it. The inside of the bracelet was now fully visible.

Nick enlarged the interior images and tried to make sense of them. There appeared to be a series of random lines and shapes, with a single inlaid stone, flush with the surface. Puzzling, it gave no hints of its meaning. The exterior had Minoan symbols on it, which even modern science had never been able to decipher. Another mystery for now.

He would remove the card and toss the phone as a precaution now that it had been used.

"What is this?" Soba asked, breaking the spell. She was looking at a round clay disk that was starting to draw a crowd.

"Kinda looks like prehistoric pizza," Charlie wisecracked. Nick grinned. It kind of did.

"That's the famous Phaistos disk. See the different symbols on it spiraling out from the middle? There are 45 unique symbols making some type of message 240 characters long," explained Nick.

"Early Twitter," Charlie joked.

Soba raised an eyebrow. It simply didn't look like much, until one considered its age.

"Famous for what?"

"For never being deciphered."

It was only a fifteen-minute ride to Knossos, once Nick could find a driver willing to take the three of them and Artemis. Her intimidating size and protective nature didn't make it easy. Eventually, an extra ten Euro note did the trick.

"I see Muttski is costing you," Charlie joked. "You must really like her."

"You know how it is when they claim you," Nick said, looking at Soba. "Like penguins, right? Mates for life."

They drove through the crowded outskirts of Heraklion, up winding roads through vineyards, to the remnants of the vast palace complex in the hills beyond. Once portions of the structure came into view, Nick could barely contain his enthusiasm.

"This was the very center of Minoan civilization. Three times bigger than Buckingham Palace, it has been called Europe's oldest city. Its construction was so elaborate that the legend of the minotaur was born here."

"You should give tour," the driver laughed. "I hear tourists tip good."

As they pulled in, Nick took the hint and gave him a few more Euros. Artemis was left in the shade, then they paid their entrance fee and walked in. They immediately spied an iconic part of the palace, the terracotta pillars and restored frescos standing out against a crystalline blue sky.

"Wow, this must have really been something back in the day," Charlie said. He walked over and looked at a rendering of the complex in all its former glory.

"Think of it," Nick pontificated, walking hand in hand with Soba. "There were over 100,000 people at this palace and the surrounding city before disaster struck. Can you imagine what the king was thinking when he looked across the sea and saw the heavens billowing above Thera?"

They explored throughout the palace, lingered at the throne room, admired the frescos, and gazed out through a massive set of bull horns. Nick focused on the icons and symbols, the complex layout, the stylized artwork, even the plumbing. All of which flourished and faded before other civilizations had even started to take hold.

"It's not hard to step back in time here," Soba observed. "This place is just so, so . . ."

"Timeless," Nick finished. "There is a certain symmetry to it. Every dominant ancient civilization, whether Minoan, Egyptian, Greek, or Roman, rose from its own origin myth, flourished, then fell. To make way for the next."

They sat in silence admiring the former spectacle, imagining the hilltop palace at the peak of its glory. It wasn't too difficult with the short films and pamphlets they viewed.

Soba pulled a lunch out of her backpack, and they retreated to the shade to eat.

"I see the wheels turning Nick. What are you thinking?" Charlie asked.

"I'm walking a fine line here Chuck. Between not telling you too much to keep you both safe, and needing your help. Because maybe you could see things from an angle I don't."

"Can't you compartmentalize it? Just have us help with a piece of it? We don't need to know everything." Soba said.

"Yeah, keep us in the dark on other parts. How it all fits together," Charlie added.

"I suppose so. But the question is, which piece."

Nick nibbled at his gyro, lost in thought while mulling the possible ramifications. After a few minutes of silence, he brightened up and looked at them with determination etched on his face.

"OK, here is something I am struggling with. Somebody looted the wreck site, cleaned out the sarcophagus. But I took this first. I had an uneasy feeling something might go down. This was a little insurance." Nick inserted the memory card he had saved from a burner phone into his camera. He scrolled until he had images of the bracelet, both the inside and the outside. "I recognize some of the symbols on the outside, they match what we've seen on Minoan artifacts. We don't know what they mean, but many match. Like on the Phaistos disk we just saw."

"But if no one has ever cracked that code, whatever you called it, what makes you think we can?" Charlie asked.

"Linear A. Yeah, so far that has proven unbreakable. Even to those devoting their careers to it. We don't have to crack that. We just need to figure out if the inside of the bracelet means anything. I have a sneaking suspicion it does. Otherwise, why go to all the trouble to put it on the *inside*, where no one will ever see it?"

Charlie and Soba looked at the images closer, trying to decipher any possible clues. There were three separate images to encompass the entire inside, and another three for the outside.

"What's the ring sticking out on the side?" Charlie asked.

"We're not sure yet. It may have had something to do with bondage, like they put on a slave. But this person was buried with honors. It's puzzling," Nick replied.

"They're fragments, squiggles. It makes no sense," Soba observed, looking at the inside. She had a natural inclination to wrestle with and solve puzzles. One of the reasons she and Nick were soulmates.

"I know. But somewhere in here is a clue, and I think it ties into everything else I can't tell you. Let me know if either of you get any ideas about it."

They walked among the ruins, seeking inspiration and insight. The size, scale, and sophistication of the site amazed them. Especially Soba and Charlie, who had no real prior knowledge of the Minoans. They were both still incredulous at how long ago the Minoans had thrived, given the advanced state of their civilization.

With no epiphany's forthcoming, the trio went back to the bull horns and gazed at the hills beyond.

"Do you think Atlantis was just a simple myth? You know, something that really happened and then got exaggerated?" Charlie asked.

"Could be. But Troy was a myth too, and that turned out to be real. There are just too many interconnected loose ends to easily dismiss."

Soba turned and looked at Nick. "What kind of loose ends?"

"Ice core samples and tree ring dating that show a tremendous eruption took place. Rock strata showing the same. Stories in the bible telling of plagues and darkness. Pieces of history scattered across cultures around the globe that mention it. And Plato wrote about Atlantis. Supposedly he heard about it from his grandfather, who learned of it from an Athenian stateman named Solon, who was told by an Egyptian priest."

"That's a whole lot of ifs," Charlie interjected.

"It is, but just look at Pavlopetri. That was discovered in the late '60s off what would have been Sparta. A whole Minoan city, preserved underwater. You can swim among the buildings, tombs, and streets."

"That's my point bro. If Atlantis was real, wouldn't it have been discovered already?"

"Not necessarily. And great discoveries have been made on flimsier evidence. Plato wrote that Atlantis lay between the pillars of Hercules. Scholars have always taken that to mean the Strait of Gibraltar. But that could also have meant it lay between Greece and Asia Minor. There were major shrines to Hercules on both. And you know what lies right between them?"

"Santorini," Soba and Charlie replied in unison, now completely caught up in the quest.

"I can't read this menu man. It's all Greek to me," Charlie said, frustrated but trying to be funny.

"Seriously, try the *souvlaki* Chuck. It's basically a Cretan kabob," Nick advised. "Or the seafood. It doesn't get any fresher than here."

Their orders placed, the waiter hurried off to the next table. The deck of the restaurant they sat at looked northward, out over Heraklion, to the island of Standia and the sea beyond. The sun had just set, the waters dark and faint stars just emerging. A slight breeze wafted upward from the shore, Artemis sniffing it eagerly. Another perfect Mediterranean night.

"You mentioned the legend of the minotaur originated here," Soba said. "I've heard of it in passing, but don't really know it."

Charlie grunted and shook his head, knowing what was coming.

He poured himself another glass of wine and leaned back, taking in the view.

"Ah, the minotaur. I'll give you the Reader's Digest version, or we'll lose Charlie," Nick joked.

Charlie tipped his glass toward Nick.

"Athens had offended the Minoan king, and had to ship off boys and girls as tribute every few years. To right here, where they were brought up to Knossos. There they were led to a labyrinth under the palace, to be devoured by the minotaur. A hideous beast with the head of a bull and body of a man."

"Sort of like Charlie over there," Soba quipped.

"Yeah, bullheaded, just like him. Anyway, the prince of Athens, Theseus, decides to put an end to it. His dad, the king, agrees but asks he change the sail from white to black when he returns, so he knows if his son survived. With me so far?" Nick asked.

Soba bobbed her head eagerly, caught up in the tale and the enchantment of her surroundings. Charlie stretched and yawned, petting Artemis. He had heard this one before.

"When Theseus reaches these shores, the Cretan princess, Ariadne, falls for him. She agrees to help if he marries her and takes her back to Athens. Theseus agrees, and Ariadne brings the builder of the labyrinth, Daedalus, to him. Daedalus tells him to bring a spool of string so he can find his way out of the maze. Theseus ultimately finds the minotaur, slays him in vicious battle, and follows the string back out."

"What happened to the princess?" Soba asked.

"You can't rush him," Charlie advised. "He tells stories like the grandpa in *The Princess Bride*. C'mon Nick, tell her what happens to Princess Buttercup."

Nick feigned hurt feelings, then stopped his tale.

"Nick . . . ," Soba pleaded.

Nick glared at Charlie, then continued.

"Theseus rounds up the Athenian youths, and escapes on a ship with Princess Ariadne. But he loses interest in her, and drops her off on the island of Naxos."

Nick saw the look of disappointment on Soba's face.

"Don't worry, she did OK for herself. She ends up marrying Dionysus, the god of wine. Which for my money, isn't a bad god to be married to. But in all the excitement Theseus forgets to change the sail to black. When the king sees the white sail, he is so distraught he throws himself in the sea and dies. Thus, Theseus becomes king. Triumph and tragedy, all in one tidy myth."

"So very Greek," Soba observed.

"Or maybe the Greeks were so very Minoan," Nick replied.

"Theseus fell victim to one of the classic blunders," Charlie joked, quoting from the Princess Bride. "Never get involved in a land war in Asia, or go in against a Sicilian when death is on the line."

"Or against a Minoan, evidently," Soba added. "Hey, do you think the Sicilian's traded with the Minoans?"

"Yes," Nick said, doodling on the paper tablecloth as dinner arrived. Soba and Charlie knew they had lost him, and chatted while enjoying their meals. Nick's sat getting cold, while he became more and more immersed in the depths of a puzzle in his mind.

"I said how's it going Einstein?" Charlie repeated.

Nick looked up and tore off the piece of the paper tablecloth he had been working on. He held it so Soba and Charlie could see it. It gave a view as if the bracelet were broken open and laid flat.

"This is the entire inside of the bracelet. It's trying to tell us something, I just can't seem to get my head around it."

Soba unconsciously rubbed her Native American necklace, a circular design which represented the continuous cycle of life and death, the eternal path of the sun, moon, and stars. She abruptly stopped, and looked at Nick.

"What was that clay circle we saw? With all the symbols on it?" she asked.

"The Phaistos disk?"

Charlie leaned in, interested now. "Why, what are you on to?"

Nick pulled a guide book from the museum out, and flipped to a photograph of the disk. He put it next to his sketch of the bracelet on the table.

Soba walked behind Nick and looked over his shoulder.

"We Indians have used swirls to indicate the passage of time, to show the old turning to the new, to tell stories."

She put her two index fingers on the photo of the Phaistos disk, and started spreading them further apart in a line.

"What if this disk is just a chronological story, told in a swirl?"

Nick slapped the table, finally catching up with her insight.

"And what if the inside of the bracelet was originally a swirl that was instead made to fit the piece?" Nick said, his voice rising. "The disk in reverse."

"Start with the jewel. That has to be the center," Charlie said, proud that he was keeping up with them.

"Paper won't work," Nick mumbled distractedly, looking around the restaurant. He spied the dessert cart being wheeled around to show the diners. He jumped up, saw what he was looking for, grabbed it, and came back to the table. The waiter stood dumbstruck, unsure of what just happened.

Nick took the *Xerotigana*, a spiral Cretan dessert bun dipped in honey, unrolled it, and laid it flat. He put the sketch he had done above it, then used it as a guide to carve a replica of the lines and symbols onto the unrolled bun. Soba pushed a small date in where the jewel would have gone.

"Here goes nothing," Nick said, licking the honey off his fingers.

Starting with the date, he slowly rolled the bun back into a spiral along its edge. The marks he had made started to line up. The three of them stood and looked down at it, trying to make sense of what they were seeing.

"I don't get it," Charlie said.

"But they clearly fit together. What do you think it is?" Soba asked.

Nick slowly walked around the table, viewing it from different angles, He suddenly stopped and stared at it.

"Well, I'll be . . ."

Several patrons had noticed the commotion and were starting to look on with curiosity. The waiter from the dessert cart started to wander over. Nick glanced around, took a quick picture of his creation, and smiled at Soba. He grabbed the pastry and mushed it into a ball and tossed it to Artemis. He then nodded to his brother. Charlie picked up the sketch and held it over the table candle, until it was nothing more than ash.

There would be no evidence of their epiphany left behind for wandering eyes.

"Charlie, do me a solid and pay this gentleman for a most enlightening meal," Nick said, flipping him a room key.

"You get your own room tonight brother. Soba and I've got some celebrating to do."

The lights slowly dimmed inside the magnificent Greek National Opera house. Located in Kallithea, the southern suburb of Athens, the rich, famous, and well connected gathered for a highly anticipated performance. The chatter of the packed audience faded with the lights, and a solitary figure strode purposely across the stage. He turned and faced the crowd, stiffly bowing from the waist. With a flourish, he sat at a bench in front of a specially crafted Steinway piano, then adjusted the tails of his tuxedo.

The stage lights went out, and the spot lights swiveled to him. He seemed to float in the ether, the anticipation building. It was a practiced theatrical entrance. He knew from experience how to work a crowd.

She sat far above, safely ensconced in the shadows toward the back. With her connections she could have sat anywhere, but she preferred to remain anonymous, incognito in the crowd. It pained her to be here, yet she really had no choice. Her training had instinctively kicked in, overcoming not so much her fear as her revulsion. Revulsion that a man who should be reviled was met with such acclaim. Revulsion that he was viewed as a forthright member of the aristocracy, and was becoming an increasingly powerful figure in national politics. Perhaps with his own grand ambitions.

If you know the enemy and know yourself, in a hundred battles you will never be in peril, she remembered. The quote from Sun Tzu had been drilled into her and came back to her now.

Know your enemy.

The first notes drifted through the perfect acoustics of the concert hall, rising to even where she sat, far in the back. She recognized the music of Mikis Theodorakis, the most famous of Greek composers.

Appropriate for Athens, she thought. *Smart. Always play to the audience.*

She watched the performance through opera glasses, despite herself. The music rose and fell, reaching crescendos that filled the opera house. Even she had to admire the pure talent, the gift to envelop one's self in the mind of another and passionately project their vision. The crowd expressed its acclaim between pieces, while they were subtly led down a specially planned pathway. The cadence of the pieces chosen quickened, the energy building, all leading to a final, specifically selected piece.

Hmm. That's not by Theodorakis. Not Greek at all.

She concentrated harder, trying to place the song, to put a name to the composer.

No, it couldn't be. Opera translated to piano. Wagner, the Ride of the Valkyries.

She gasped at the sheer audacity of it. Wagner, a German and well known anti-Semite. Hitler's favorite composer. Being played here, on Greek soil. It was as if it was happening again. Did her oath mean nothing?

She couldn't breathe. The air was suddenly heavy, the walls closing in. Her head spinning, she rose and stumbled out of the row, tripping over legs, nearly falling down. She squinted in the dim light, groping her way to the back, to the stairs, to the ground floor, to the street beyond. To sanctuary.

She ran across the street, gasping for air, lungs heaving, hands on her knees. Even here she could hear the music, the song carried beyond the hall, ending with a flourish. The crowd cheered loudly, lustily, hailing the performance. From one of their very own.

She looked down at her missing finger, rubbing the stump, the phantom pain excruciating from the sheer proximity of her tormentor. Her very soul ached. For her, her father, her grandparents. For her people.

No, not while I still draw breath, she thought. *I will not let this define me.*

She slowly stood up straight, composing herself. Carefully arranging her hair and straightening her dress, she stared directly at a street poster of the evening's featured performer. Drakos Kollas.

"Masada shall not fall again," she said aloud, quoting the vow of all Mossad agents. She walked up to the poster and stared. At a face that had haunted her dreams for years.

Persefoni spat upon it.

"Nor shall Greece."

CHAPTER 25

JULY 9, PRESENT DAY, HERAKLION, CRETE, GREECE

S oba's head rested on the pillow, her green eyes staring over at
Nick. She breathed softly, patiently waiting for his to open. It
had been a wild night, with the thrill of possible discovery hanging
in the nighttime air. Not to mention the thrill of making up for lost
time apart. Nick's eyes fluttered, then gradually opened. He gazed
across at Soba, and smiled.

"That was nice. Missed you," she said.

"Mmm. You too. Let's not let the world get in our way again,
shall we?"

Soba giggled playfully and rolled back on top of him, tickling his
face with her long hair. She had playful thoughts, then felt a nudge.
Artemis nestled her huge head between them.

"My turn. I'll take her out."

She pulled a robe around herself, and opened the door. She was
startled to see a reporter loitering just outside. He flicked his
cigarette away and stuck a microphone in her face. His cameraman
started recording the proceedings.

"Is it true you have reunited with the archaiológos?"

Soba stood there speechless, taken completely unawares.
Artemis crouched and growled, then pushed by her and jumped out
the door. The reporter and cameraman fled, Artemis nipping at

their heels. She only stopped when she heard Nick whistle from within.

"Good girl," Nick said, getting up and stroking her massive neck as she pranced back in. He looked at Soba and gave her a kiss.

"Good morning, Princess. So it begins. Let's grab our things and get the hell out of here."

They managed to retreat to the docks with no further paparazzi on their trail. Charlie joined them on the upper deck of the high-speed ferry, headed back to Santorini. Time was now a factor, Nick opting for the quicker ride. There was much to accomplish.

"You really think that was a map on the inside of the bracelet?" Charlie asked. "I'm not sure I'm buying it."

"It definitely was. I manipulated the photos with editing software, and created this. Basically, the same thing you saw last night made out of dough."

Nick showed them the high-resolution image of what he had created from the three photographs. There was no doubt about it. The inside of the bracelet, when wrapped around the jewel in a swirl, formed an outline of the eastern Mediterranean.

"And I believe that is Atlantis at the very center. The jewel of their empire."

"If I'm reading the map right," Soba said, comparing the photo to her tour guide map, "You're saying Santorini was Atlantis?"

"Close. More like Santorini was Thera. And Atlantis was *on* Thera," Nick replied.

"But why would it be on the inside of a bracelet?" Charlie wondered. "That no one would ever see?"

"Who knows. Pride? Hubris? To show ownership? What I do know is that whoever gave it, very much valued the person who wore it. The craftsmanship is exquisite."

"You and every arm chair historian believe Atlantis was more than a myth," Charlie said. "Why is your argument any more convincing?"

"Because I have a witness. And I intend to prove it."

The scarred and gnarled hands of the fisherman worked expertly at repairing the worn net. It was his most valuable tool, one he took a great deal of pride in. It had been mended so many times he doubted there was any of the original left in it. There were parts his father had repaired, even his grandfather. But that was the timeless way of the sea, the way it had always been. The way of his forefathers, since time immemorial.

He sensed a presence before he even saw it, and never bothered to look up. Artemis thudded up over a nearby dune, sniffed the air, then headed down to him. Her tail wagged and she leaned into him, to be rewarded with a heavy-handed petting. She would only ever have one true master.

Nick followed in her wake, standing over him now. Charlie and Soba stopped and sat at the top of the dune, taking in the view of the great caldera from their perch on Santorini.

The fisherman dusted off his knees and stood. He offered his hand to Nick.

"I expecting you."

Nick took the powerful hand in his and shook it, looking him in the eye.

"She's your dog, isn't she?"

"Da. Good Cretan breed. Most loyal creature," Zorba replied.

"Don't you mean Atlantean?"

Zorba chuckled, then motioned to an empty stretch of beach. They wandered down it, Artemis pacing a broad perimeter around them. Waves from an impending storm pounded at the shoreline. A shore that had once been a part of a vast volcanic mountain slope.

Nick stared out past the island of Nea Kameni, to the gap in the great caldera rim beyond.

"It really existed then, didn't it?" Nick asked.

"Da. No myth."

"And you've been leading me to it?"

Zorba silently nodded. He stopped walking and looked out to the sea, hands clasped behind his back.

"Why? Why not find it yourself?"

"Because I only suspect. Not have means to prove."

"But Pavlus knew."

"Pavlus rescue man, hear story. Only tell few of us. We never tell anyone else."

Nick shook his head in amazement and sat on the beach. Zorba grunted as he sat and joined him. Artemis came over and lay between them with a huff of contentment.

"What's her real name?"

"Skýlos. Dog, in Greek."

"Really? Dog?" Nick said, shaking his head. "Clever. So she'll answer to anything?"

Zorba grinned as Skýlos lay her head in his lap. "Da."

"You knew Heinrich and I were on the trail of finding the missing U-boat. And the survivor from that very U-boat told Pavlus he saw something underwater when he escaped. Marvelous things, things that looked like a sunken city. I didn't find that out until I tracked him down in Berlin. I don't think I really believed him, not until we found the grave of the other survivor."

"Believing not finding," Zorba said.

"No, I suppose not. But I have a theory. Before we go there, I have to ask you something. Why is finding this so important to you?"

Zorba picked up a small piece of driftwood and started whittling. The words came to him, hidden deep inside. Words that echoed down through the centuries. Words never shared with outlanders.

"We have here, what you call it? A caste society. My ancestors never go away, we always here. Call us Cretans, Minoans, Atlanteans. All same. Greece grow from us, from others. Best of many. We defeat Persians, democracy begin. Turks not stop it. Nazis not stop it. Democracy strong tree, deep roots. Survive to this day."

Zorba paused, turning over the figure he was whittling. He looked back out to the caldera, to the sea beyond.

"Being Cretan hard. We treated second class. Like what you call

Roma, or Gypsies. Not 'Greek' enough. I want to prove former glory, prove it help all Greece. Hold our heads high again."

He continued whittling, concentrating on the small piece he held. "Why you seek?"

It was Nick's turn to reflect. He had many motivations, all of them mixed and complex. The thrill of the hunt, the lure of the unknown. His insatiable wanderlust and thirst for knowledge. His fear for Heinrich and how his disappearance must somehow be tied into this untold history. But he owed this honest, simple man a straight forward, simple answer.

"Truth. It always deserves to be told, unvarnished and unfiltered. I firmly believe that understanding the past is always the key to our future. There is a great untold story here. I intend to tell it truthfully, no matter how distasteful that may be to some."

"Ha!" Zorba exclaimed, slapping Nick on the back. "That why choose you. We seek same thing!"

The two men arose and made their way back, retracing their footsteps. Soba saw them coming and waved from the top of a dune in the distance. Nick stopped, deep in thought.

"One more thing. I found a tracking device in Artemis's, I mean Skýlos's, collar. Is that how you've managed to keep tabs on me?"

Zorba furrowed his eyebrow and stroked his chin.

"No. We have different ways. We everywhere, but always out of sight. That mean someone . . ."

"Someone else is tracking our efforts," Nick finished.

As they crested the dune, Zorba handed Nick the whittled figurine.

"For you. Atlantean galley. When we rule the sea."

Zorba smiled at Charlie and Soba, then walked back toward the kantína. Skýlos followed at his heels.

"Where is Artemis going?" Soba asked.

Nick didn't reply, he was too busy turning over the figurine in his fingers. The lines seemed familiar, even the curve of the prow.

Just like on the wreck they were excavating back at the port of Athens.

"How we narrow down?" Zorba asked in his stilted English.

They sat in the far back corner of the kantína. A rugged looking young man Nick hadn't seen before ensured no one invaded their space. He was introduced as Pello, while Skýlos lay nearby. It was safe to talk here.

"Yeah, if Günther really saw something when his U-boat sank, how do you know where it went down?" Charlie echoed.

"Let's back up first, so we have context," Nick said.

He reached into his backpack, and pulled out a leather-bound notepad he kept for any search, a habit he had picked up from his father. He pulled it out and flipped to a specific page.

"Let me read this quote from Plato."

"But afterwards there occurred violent earthquakes and floods; and in a single day and night of misfortune all your warlike men in a body sank into the earth, and the island of Atlantis in like manner disappeared in the depths of the sea."

He started sketching in his notepad before continuing. "Envision the whole caldera back in time. A single, massive mountain, like this. On one side it goes down to a plain, where the city sits. And in front of it there is a bay, circular in shape and protected. The great harbor of legend."

Zorba's wife tottered over, and placed drinks around the table. This time she stopped in back of Nick, and leaned down and kissed his head. She gave Zorba a playful cuff on the ear as she went back to the bar.

"No pressure now," Soba grinned. "You can't disappoint *her.*"

Nick sighed and took a deep drink.

No, I can't disappoint her. Or any of them.

He pointed back to the notepad.

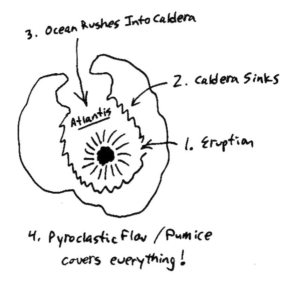

3. Ocean Rushes Into Caldera

2. Caldera Sinks

Atlantis

1. Eruption

4. Pyroclastic Flow / Pumice
covers everything!

"The magma chamber beneath fills, pushing the mountain ever higher. Even the harbor rises, pushing the seawater out of it. The volcano finally erupts, sending over *14 cubic miles* of debris into the atmosphere. All the while, the surface of the sea is filling with millions of tons of floating pumice. After all that magma is ejected, the volcano itself starts to collapse. So much so it sinks down below the surface of the sea, into the empty magma chamber. It creates a massive divot, the waters rush back in to fill it, the collapsed column falls and—"

"Simple Nick," Charlie reminded him. "Keep it simple for us non-scientists."

He was caught up in his theory, and having a hard time dialing it down. Dr. Storm and Stavros would understand the complexities of the detailed version, would expect it, but not this audience. He took a deep breath and recalibrated before continuing.

"Think of it. Akrotiri was just a fringe trading village. It was but a glimpse of what once existed here. Atlantis sank into the sea and was buried where it sat. In a collapsed caldera under mountains of ash and pumice that coated the sea floor for miles around. Not just coated it but truly buried it, where it was thickest, right at ground zero. It's out there, protected, cocooned. Buried so deep under so much debris so long ago it looks just like the ocean floor."

"Hidden in plain sight," Soba reflected.

"Sounds feasible," Charlie said. "But I'm no vulcanologist."

"No. But I am," said a gregarious voice from the bar.

A large bear of a man swiveled around and looked at them, raising a glass.

"Probable, who knows. But possible, absolutely. Got your call Nick," Jim Portmess said. "Ya mas."

Nick raised his glass back, smiling. This was the right type of reinforcement to have on hand for what he had in mind.

Nick introduced Jim to Zorba. Skýlos went over and leaned into Jim, giving him a big, slobbery kiss. They all sat silent for a moment, looking out at the great caldera, weighing the evidence.

"That maybe tell the how," Zorba said. "Not the where."

"I think you know where," Nick said.

Zorba looked at him with puzzled eyes. He thought for a moment, and came up with nothing. He raised his eyebrows and spread his hands open quizzically.

"Perhaps where you keep losing something," Nick said. "Like your fishing nets."

"When I talked with Otto about where his father said the U-boat sank, he pulled out a diary. It was written when Günther was still young and his memory fresh. Just after the war. He was insistent it went down *inside* the caldera," Nick explained. "He described drifting past the islands of Nea Kameni and Palaia Kameni after he surfaced. In enough detail to give a rough idea of where we should search."

They were outside now, all the way to the edge of the cliffs. The remnants of the caldera spread out before them, the edges giving a hint of the size of Mount Thera in ancient times.

"Where lose nets, sometimes little oil bubbles," Zorba said. "Never thought U-boat. Maybe just small wreck, like fishing boat."

"Oil?" Nick asked. "Every square inch of the caldera floor has been probed and scanned. All the wrecks identified, all anomalies investigated. If we knew what type of oil, it may confirm my theory."

"Or refute it," Charlie said. "So how do we tackle this?"

Nick looked out at the small fishing vessels bobbing offshore. The wind had picked up, the skies threatening. There would be no fishing today. Maybe not tomorrow either, unless the storm front veered off.

"I've got an idea. It involves investigating a specific grid of the caldera. But you're not going to like it," Nick said, looking Soba in the eyes.

"Me? Why possibly not?"

"Because I will have to call in a favor."

"From who?"

"From Persa."

"It would be best if it looked like a fishing charter. I don't want to draw any unwanted attention. Think you can come up with something like that?" Nick asked.

"That no easy. Need to ask around."

"You sure you're OK with this? What with my girlfriend being around and all?"

"I big girl Níkos. Plenty others to have fun with," Persa replied. He detected a distinct coolness in her voice.

"I'm sorry it worked out this way. I didn't know she—"

"Meet tomorrow morning where Serafina docked," Persa said, cutting him off.

"OK, thanks. I really appreciate this." He was at a loss for what else to say. He was about to add something, but the line went dead.

Charlie waited until the conversation ended, then walked over.

"What's the good word bro?"

"We're on. But cover my back for me," Nick whispered. "We're about to have two alpha females in close quarters."

Charlie laughed at Nick's obvious discomfort. He gave Nick a slap on the back and a hug around one shoulder.

"Sure thing. I can always use a little entertainment!"

CHAPTER 26

JULY 10, PRESENT DAY, SANTORINI, GREECE

It was early Saturday morning at the small port, on the north side of the crescent beneath Fira. The dock where the Serafina lay was not as busy as on weekdays. She was in for some slight repairs and refitting. The timing of Nick's call to Persa was coincidental and fortuitous. The crew was on shore leave, taking full advantage of the lull in operations. A heavy weather front continued to build, discouraging smaller craft from going out.

Nick and his entourage of Zorba, Jim, Charlie, and Soba stood beneath the bow of the Serafina. The breeze picked up while a few random raindrops fell. Nick looked at his watch and started pacing.

What if she's just blowing me off? She seemed pretty pissed. Maybe this wasn't such a good idea after all, he thought.

Nick looked at the others and smiled, trying to project confidence. They were looking at the sky and their cell phones, gauging the weather. He shrugged, he would give her a little more time. He resumed his pacing.

A half hour later, he decided he must have been set up. Time to go, to cut his losses and regroup.

Just as Nick was about to gather the others and leave, a ship slowly came into view, gliding past the stern of the Serafina. Persa waved from its deck. Another person he couldn't quite make out guided her in.

As they docked, he finally recognized him. It was Alekos Rouvas himself, captain of the Serafina.

"Permission to come aboard Captain?" Nick shouted.

"Permission granted," Captain Alek said, looking down from the bridge of the sixty-five-foot *Neró Mágissa*, or Water Witch. "I heard you could use some help probing the depths."

Nick led everyone aboard. Persa was unexpectedly cordial when greeting him. She gave him a quick kiss on the cheek, and shook hands as Nick made introductions all around. When he came to Soba last, Persa embraced her.

"You muse from States," Persa whispered. "I see why he like you."

"Thank you?" Soba replied.

"Captain Alek," Jim said, giving him a hearty handshake. "It's been too long."

"It has Jim," he said. "We've been out mapping along the fault lines near Crete. I've got some interesting data to share later."

"What do we have here to work with Captain?" Nick asked, looking around the ship.

Captain Alek spread out his arms, obviously proud of the vessel they had managed to commandeer on such short notice.

"I present to you the Neró Mágissa. A beauty, isn't she? All the latest electronics and detection equipment, twin 650 horse power diesels, and most important for you, commercial deep sea diving equipment."

"But how did you manage this? Whose ship?" Nick asked, looking at Persa with raised eyebrows.

"Not what know. Who know," she said with a coy smile.

"This ship was between assignments. I may have taken liberties with my position," Captain Alek said. "I had nothing to do while the Serafina was laid up for repairs. Persefoni here told me what you were after. How could I say no?"

"I can't think of anyone I would rather have help us out. Your expertise is most welcomed."

"Weather turning. Where we go?" Persa asked, cutting to the chase.

Zorba walked over to the maps scattered on a plotting table. He pulled one on top, of the inside of the caldera, and pointed to the deepest waters within it.

"Here, between Oia and Nea Kameni. We lose nets for years."

"Right along the Kameni fault line," Jim said, looking closely at where Zorba pointed. "In the volcanic arc of the Aegean Sea Plate. What else have we got?"

"I am triangulating in on a few bits of information," Nick explained. "Lost nets. Occasional oil bubbles. The story of a U-boat survivor drifting past these islands who claimed he saw fantastic things. Ancient texts describing the port below the city. And this, a map showing the jewel of their empire. Right here, on Mount Thera."

Persa and Captain Alek looked at the manipulated photograph of the inside of the bracelet. It was crude, but clearly showed a map of the eastern Mediterranean. With a jewel marking where a city once stood. Crafted all of 3,500 years prior.

"My god. Where is that from?" Jim asked.

"That little gem is from the wreck we were excavating outside of Athens," answered Nick. "Before the sarcophagus was ransacked. Very few know of its existence."

"How deep fault line there?" Zorba asked.

Jim squinted at the map and ran his finger along a line. "800 to 1,000 feet deep in this area."

"Anyone know the world record for a free dive?" Nick asked.

No one answered, while several shook their heads no.

"830 feet. By an Austrian guy named Nitsch. You know where? In Santorini, of all places."

"Maybe what Günther saw was real," Charlie said. "He actually could have survived."

They all stood silent for a moment, daring to believe they were on the cusp of a great discovery. To either prove the existence of a fabled myth, or finally lay it to rest.

"When Persa told me where you were looking, I grabbed this from our prior mapping expeditions," Captain Alek said, finally breaking the silence. He produced a portable hard drive and plugged it into a computer.

"Let's see if it helps narrow the search area."

The Neró Mágissa quietly slipped from its moorings and glided out from the docks. A few seagulls dove in its wake, looking for anything stirred up by its propellers.

"Do you think anyone will buy it?" Charlie asked. He finished putting the fishing poles in the tubes scattered about the research vessel, to provide the illusion of a fishing charter.

"I don't know. Maybe," Nick said. He looked out at the darkening skies. "If a storm kicks up, anyone who sees us will think we're nuts."

Charlie slipped the last two poles into tubes and turned to his brother. "This U-boat we're looking for. What can you tell me about it?"

Zorba and Soba wandered over to listen in.

"Pretty damn amazing for its time. Nearly three hundred feet long, only eight were ever built. The one I hope is here, the U234, was the last ever built."

"What made it so special?" Charlie asked.

"It was the biggest class of U-boat the Germans ever built. It could lay mines or act as a large transport. It was 2,700 tons fully loaded, and could travel over 18,000 nautical miles. The Allies were worried these would be used to transport key Nazi leaders, bullion, and biological or nuclear material to South America. Stuff that would lay the foundation for a future Fourth Reich."

"I've read about rumors of U-boats turning up in obscure places," Jim said. "Leading to lots of speculation about who may have gotten away. Did any ever really make it?"

Nick shook his head no, thinking of his missing friend. "Based on what Günther said, at least not this one."

"A Fourth Reich, that's pretty damn frightening," Charlie said. "In this era of ultra-nationalism, it doesn't sound so far-fetched."

Nick watched the gulls scatter back toward shore. Soba sidled up to him and leaned in for warmth against the chill of the evening breeze. Zorba grabbed the railing, flexing his hands in silent frustration.

"I'll tell you something for sure brother. Men die, but hate and money live forever. We can't allow another Reich to arise from the ashes."

The tedious task of scouring the search grid commenced, with the Neró Mágissa slowly towing a magnetometer on a preprogrammed GPS heading. Persa watched while Nick, Captain Alek, and Jim reviewed the hard drive data, previously complied using multibeam sonar. With few anomalies on the sea floor visible, the decision was made to concentrate along the Kameni fault line within the caldera itself. Where currents would have caught a young Günther Wessel and drifted him by Nea Kameni and Palaia Kameni, to eventual rescue by Pavlus and his father.

The ship slowly turned and headed back the way it came, overlapping the edge of the prior route. Mowing the lawn over a stretch of seabed that seemed to hold the most promise. Persa kept a trained eye on the readings from the magnetometer, ignoring the smaller hits. Any debris field from something as large as a U-boat, even if covered with silt from the currents, would cover a large area. It was an exercise of patience and endurance.

"Take a break," Jim suggested, looking over Persa's shoulder. "You've been staring at that damn screen all day."

Persa rubbed her eyes, then stood and stretched. She couldn't argue.

"You can handle dis?"

"Yeah, no problem," Jim replied. "I'm pretty good at this type of stuff. Fault lines, tectonic plates, and anomalies are all in my wheel house."

Glancing around, Persa saw Captain Alek, Nick, and Zorba huddled over the plotting table. Debating drift and wind current patterns. Charlie came up from the galley with a platter of sandwiches to pass around. Persa yawned, then headed out for some fresh air.

"Any luck?" Soba asked.

Persa saw Soba leaning over the railing, admiring the view. The sun had just set, the stars obscured by cloud cover. The lights of Santorini flickered high on the cliffs off in the distance. She walked over to the railing and leaned over too.

"No. Not 'a yet. Dis slow process. Take time."

Soba looked over at Persa, then back out to sea.

"I don't know what you know about me, but back home I'm known as a shaman. Someone who can read spirits, and people. I can tell there's more to you than meets the eye."

"Da. We all like to think that," Persa said dismissively, trying to change the subject.

"I see there are two of you. One very vulnerable, who was deeply hurt. Still in pain. The other who is very controlled, who seeks something. Who would do anything—"

"Careful Miss Shaman," Persa said, cutting her off. "You not know what lie beneath."

Soba was about to say something, when a shout from the cabin made them both turn.

"Persa come read this," Jim yelled from the console screens. "We've got a hit. At that rise on the ocean floor."

The whole group huddled around the monitor. Persa zoomed in on the image from the magnetometer. A dark mass was visible, distinctly cylinder shaped but short in length. No conning tower, a distinct submarine feature, was apparent.

"Could be. But long enough?" Persa asked.

"If it hit the ocean floor with force and disintegrated, there would at least be a debris field," Captain Alek said. "If not, the reading should show a longer object."

"None of that is above the surface?" Jim asked.

"No. All buried, except little piece," Persa replied.

On another display, Nick zoomed in on the exact same area, at images captured from the multibeam sonar. The seabed rose in a hump covered in a couple of indistinct outlines. He zoomed in further, and adjusted the contrast.

Zorba tapped the screen.

"Nets?"

"Only one way to tell," Nick said. He looked over at Captain Alek. "Mind if we take the *AUV* for a spin?"

Nick and Persa walked out to the back deck, and prepared the *Autonomous Underwater Vehicle* for launch. With no cables to the mothership, it was a highly maneuverable and unmanned way of exploring the depths. A drone for the deepest ocean floor.

Once ready, Persa gave the thumbs up. Jim gently lowered the unit into the sea via an onboard crane and winch. While the AUV slowly descended toward the sea bed, GPS and remote thrusters kept the Neró Mágissa on station with a minimum of drift. It could drop the AUV on the proverbial needle in a haystack.

The team returned to the monitors in the control room to watch the descent. Jim aimed to place the AUV just down-current of the dark magnetometer reading. Ensuring any disturbed silt wouldn't interfere with their vision field.

"Six hundred feet, seven hundred, eight hundred," Jim read aloud. He slowed the descent to a crawl. The bright lights and camera of the AUV stared out into nothingness. He deftly manipulated the toggle, allowing the unit to touch down softly on the seabed. "Contact. Reading 858 feet deep."

A slight amount of silt rose in front of the camera, then quickly drifted away. Jim waited a moment, then swiveled the camera in a slow arc. Nothing of significance was visible, until the camera panned to the far right.

"There, that dark patch. Zoom in on it," Captain Alek instructed.

Jim adjusted the lighting and zoomed the camera lens in. What looked like gray blurry spider webs came into sharp focus, cross-hatched shadows dancing on the seabed.

"Drift nets," Nick said. "They must have caught on something."

They were scattered on the sea floor, some rotted and decayed to mere threads. A few in a small clump looked more recent, the tides and current not yet scattering them about.

"Need closer look," Zorba said.

"Careful Jim. We don't want the AUV to get fouled in those nets," Captain Alek advised.

Jim paused, and handed him the controller. "You drive from here Cap. I'm not the one who borrowed this bad boy of a ship."

"Weather check?" Captain Alek asked.

"Good next six to eight hours. Then get rough up top," Persa said, consulting a satellite feed.

"I'm going to have to reposition the AUV," Captain Alek said. He used one toggle to engage thrusters to lift the unit, and a second toggle to propel it forward. "I've got to get a bit closer. To where the mechanical arms can reach."

He went slowly, leapfrogging a bit at a time, getting a feel for the strength of the current. Finally satisfied with the position, he let the AUV settle with a thud on its sled, and waited for the silt to drift.

"See that?" Nick asked. "There, leaking up. Just a few drops. Am I the only one seeing this?"

"I see it," Jim replied, tracing the path on the monitor with a finger. "Oil?"

"The weight of the AUV must have dislodged it," Charlie said.

A mechanical arm extended out with robot-like precision, pinchers gripping at a tangle of netting. It gently pulled up, making progress until the tangle stuck fast. Captain Alek then extended a second arm, equipped with several built-in tools, and activated a small circular saw. He pushed it against the netting, back and forth, as small bits drifted away.

Nick noticed sweat beads forming on the captain's forehead.

The tension was building in the control room, the banter subsiding. "How we doing Captain?" he asked.

"She's like a fine woman lads. Needs a bit of coaxing and persuading before she's willing to give it up, I'm afraid."

The men snickered nervously. Nick got an elbow in the ribs from Soba, and a look that said, "Good luck the next time you try to persuade *me*."

"Done cutting."

Captain Alek pulled again at the tangle with the pinchers. A slight movement, a little give. Silt shook loose from the netting, creating a cloud that obscured vision. It drifted away, revealing a torn net.

"Let's see what this thing can do," he whispered to the silent room. He pulled harder this time, the arm recoiling, the dust again kicking up.

The cloud of sediment swirled slowly for a moment, then completely dissipated. The camera revealed a gray hump-shaped ridge, completely covered in jagged bits of concretion. Torn and shredded bits of netting hung from it, waving in the current like grass in a breeze.

"Do you have something that can knock a bit of that off?" Nick asked.

Captain Alek smiled as a hammer extended from the Swiss Army mechanical arm. He positioned it closely, and flicked the toggle. The hammer snapped down sharply, and bits of concretion filled the field of view. The sound came over the audio feed, reminiscent of a muffled bell. The debris drifted away, oil bubbles in elongated shapes wobbling past the lens. Six inches of a smooth surface lay revealed, leaving no doubt as to its origin.

"That *has* to be a propeller," Jim exclaimed.

Persa's eyes met Nick's, her expression incredulous.

"Could it really be?" Captain Alek asked.

"I'll be damned. Günther was right. About everything," Nick said, shaking his head.

Zorba pounded the chart table, smiling. They were one step closer.

"What does it all mean?" Soba asked.

"I think we've found the U234," Nick said, touching the image on the screen. "And maybe a whole lot more."

"She must have struck at a sharp downward angle and burrowed in somehow. That's why the magnetometer reading didn't show much length," Captain Alek observed.

"It hit at a soft spot in the fault line," Jim added, comparing the live video feed with the side scan sonar readings. "Right in the middle of the volcanic arc of the Aegean Sea Plate."

"Can you imagine the force of the impact? To bury itself like that?" Nick asked. "What could cause that?"

Captain Alek shook his head sadly. "Depth charges I suspect chap. Catastrophic damage, loss of control, pressure implosions."

"It must have hit a pocket beneath the crust," Jim said. "It's the only explanation for burrowing so deep."

"Now tomb," Persa muttered to herself. "Hold secrets."

Nick paced back and forth in front of the displays. "We need definitive proof. Right now, all we have is conjecture. Ideas?"

Captain Alek maneuvered the AUV to view different angles, but there was nothing more to see. Just scattered nets and a bit of an outcropping that hid the outer edge of a massive propeller. "The proverbial ship's bell would be nice," he joked.

"What would really identify it?" Charlie asked.

"Identification numbers on the hull. On the conning tower, or the bow," Nick replied. "But she went in bow first. Everything's buried."

A red warning light and alarm went off, startling everyone. Persa looked at the video feed for the rear-facing camera of the AUV.

"Trouble Captain. Net caught," she said, pointing to the AUV's propeller guard.

A loose bit of net had drifted into the propeller guard, and wound around the propeller shaft. Captain Alek halted the AUV, then attempted to reverse it to unwind the net. It worked for a moment, the net spooling out. Without warning it caught again and doubled back over on the shaft, dragging the unit to the sea floor like a winch. They all watched helplessly as currents slowly wrapped some of the drifting nets about the AUV, entangling it.

"Damn it. I knew that was a risk if we got too close."

Jim walked over to two specially constructed lockers. He peered inside. "Cap, this ship works on deep sea platforms? Mineral exploration, oil rigs?"

"Yes. And deep-sea recovery."

Jim opened both lockers wide, revealing two ungainly, otherworldly suits. Each Deep-Sea Exosuit looked like an outsized body of armor, with a bubble helmet and robot-like articulating arms and legs. The self-contained and self-propelled units allowed the user to descend to tremendous depths, without the need to decompress. The trade-off was limited movement and dexterity.

Nick looked at Jim and nodded. They were on the clock now. There simply were no good alternatives.

"How about Nick and I take a dip?" Big Jim asked rhetorically.

There was a flurry of activity as the two clunky suits were rolled on specially constructed dollies to the aft deck. It was already dark outside, but that didn't matter where they were going. The weather forecast called for the storm front to arrive in six hours. Just enough time to do a descent, untangle the AUV, take a quick look around, and ascend.

Nick crawled into an Exosuit, stood up, reached his arms out and got a feel for the confines of the unit. Claustrophobic and a little tight, but it would do. Jim tried to squeeze in, but his imposing stature wouldn't allow it. He tried multiple angles, attempting to force himself in, but he couldn't change his size. It was no use

Persa tapped him on the shoulder.

"Hey *megálo távros*. Move. I do."

Jim looked dumbly at Persa, then at Captain Alek.

"She called you a big bull, and she's right," Captain Alek said. "She's certified for this. Let her have at it."

Jim paused a moment before finally stepping aside while Persa pushed by him. Nick had been right. There *was* something about her.

Persa easily crawled in and stretched out to reach the controls with her hands, manipulating them and articulating the elbow joints. When Jim bent over to clear the deck in front of them, she toggled the mechanical gripper and gave him a pinch.

Jim jumped and hit his head on the bottom of the crane with a dull thud.

"Work good. Ready," Persa said through the internal comm link, clicking the gripper in front of him. "Let's go."

"Yeah, chop chop big guy," Nick chimed in, enjoying Jim's discomfort for a change. "Let's get this show on the road."

Persa and Nick were hoisted aboard a small platform that would be lowered to the sea floor. While the suits they wore were bulky, they allowed some limited movement to get from one point to another. But most importantly, they were self-propelled. A great expedient at the depths they would be working at.

With a mechanical arm, they each gripped the cable, and slowly descended into the depths. The lights from the Neró Mágissa above faded to a dull glow, then blinked out altogether. Their helmets illuminated their faces with a bluish fluorescent sheen as they looked around, then stared at one another. There was nothing else to see in the otherworldly void they were suspended in.

"Five hundred feet down," Jim said over the comm. "You both doing OK?"

"Check," Nick replied.

"Da," Persa said.

They stood in silence, the platform swaying ever so slightly, the cable playing out deeper and deeper.

"Six hundred feet."

Nick mouthed the word *local*, and they both set their comm system to talk with each other only.

"How many times in one of these?" Nick asked.

"Three, four time," she replied.

"Seven hundred feet."

"Good. This is dangerous. We need to work together, and be careful."

She stared at him inquisitively. "Da. What else?"

Nick paused, formulating his thoughts.

"Someone is very interested in all this Persa. In everything we're doing. We've got to have each other's back. In case anything unexpected happens. OK?"

She managed a slight grin. "You no worry Níkos. Persa have back."

Nick was about to reply when he felt a jolt.

"850 feet," Jim said. "You should be down soon."

They both switched their comm system back to open channel.

"Thanks Spock. We already are."

"How are things looking down there?" Captain Alek asked.

"All good Cap. We're going to have a little look around."

"Don't dawdle. That storm front is coming in faster than we thought."

"Roger that."

They saw the glow of the lights from the AUV about one hundred yards away. They had drifted a bit off course on the way down, the impending storm strengthening the deep-sea currents.

Each tried their propulsion system, testing it to get a feel for how it performed at these depths. They carefully navigated toward the AUV, more resembling bounding astronauts on the moon than undersea divers on a fault line. Each time their feet touched down, little tendrils of silt arose, which were then swiftly swept away by the currents. As they mastered their propulsion controls, they stopped bouncing, and hovered over to the AUV.

"Good thing this isn't an ROV," Nick commented. "We would have had a hard time avoiding the umbilical to the surface. Here, hold it steady."

Persa stood in front of the AUV, and clamped onto it with her mechanical hands. Nick moved to its back, and gripped the net wrapped around the propeller shaft. He pulled on it, softly at first, then with increasing force.

"Try it in reverse Captain. Slowly."

Far above, Captain Alek toggled on a joystick, the propeller moving in fits and starts, until it spun freely. Nick staggered backwards, the net finally giving way. He and Persa spent the next ten minutes clearing away other random pieces that had become entangled around the AUV, until at last it floated freely.

"She's all yours Cap."

"Roger that. We'll hover it away from the nets while you two take a look around. In case you need a hand with anything," Captain Alek replied, glancing from one display screen to another. They provided a panorama to the surface of the events unfolding far below them.

"Jim, weather update?"

"Front looks like its shifting directly towards Santorini. I'd say you've got twenty minutes to look around, tops."

"Hear that?" Captain Alek repeated. "Twenty minutes tops, then you both get back on the platform to ascend. No delays."

"That's an affirmative."

Nick signaled to Persa, pointing to the protruding ridgeline about forty feet away. They both leaned forward and hit their propulsion buttons. The current drifted them off their mark, which they compensated for with extra bits of thrust. They came in obliquely, puffing up bits of sediment as they landed. Purposely updrift of all the floating netting.

Nick descended at the protruding bit of metal he saw. It was enshrouded in a coral-like mass, the reflective glint in his lights betraying a hint of what lay below. He reached out and touched the edge of the massive propellor with the hand of his Exosuit. Being here was surreal, yet when he touched it, everything became real. Heinrich's hint of the name of Günther Wessel had led him to this very spot.

If only he could be here to share this moment, Nick thought.

Persa shuttled over next to him, the look of excitement on her face bathed by the fluorescent glow of her helmet. Nick smiled back, then noticed her expression abruptly changing. Large blobs of oil rose between them. Persa started to say something, her face contorting. She mechanically reached toward him, but fell away before they could touch. Into an abyss opening below them. The lights on the sides of her helmet swung about wildly as she spun downward and the glow of her headpiece faded to nothingness.

Nick felt the seabed below his feet crumble away. He looked where his pincher gripped the exposed bit of propeller, precariously holding him in place. A strong updraft suddenly hit him, a blast of released hot thermal water and oil spinning him until his grip broke. He hit his propulsion but too late, and tumbled downward into the abyss.

Yelling helplessly into his comm system, he spun out of control, following Persa into the bottomless depths below.

Soba and Charlie stood quietly outside, getting a bit of fresh air. They would go back in once Nick and Persa reached the ocean floor and started to look around. The slow, controlled descent would take a while.

Jim stood by the stern, counting off the depth marks into his headset. The ship rocked in the increasingly turbulent waves, the sky now starless from the cloud cover moving in.

"See that?" Charlie asked.

"What?"

"There, right there.

A gush of liquid bubbled to the surface, its sheen reflecting in the lights of the Neró Mágissa. The smell was sharp, distinctly different from the salty sea air.

"Oil?" Soba asked.

"Smells more like diesel."

They heard shouting from the cabin, something was wrong. Charlie grabbed her by the arm. They turned and rushed back in.

"Nick, Persa, do you read?" Captain Alek asked over the comm system. His voice betrayed increasing alarm.

"Do you read? Over."

Only silence. Captain Alek turned up the volume to pick up any sound. Still nothing. He adjusted the squelch setting to increase sensitivity. The speaker crackled sharply with interference, but no voice answered.

Soba frantically grabbed the microphone from him.

"Nick can you hear me?"

She looked at Charlie with terror in her eyes.

"Nick!" she screamed.

Deafening static was the only response.

CHAPTER 27

JULY 10, PRESENT DAY, SANTORINI, GREECE

Freefall. Spinning crazily downward. Bouncing off something, ricocheting. The headlamps briefly reflecting, giving a surreal strobe-like feel of the descent to a crack in the earth. Deeper and deeper, seemingly to Hades itself.

Impact, then complete and utter silence.

Nick blinked his eyes. Hard. It was claustrophobically quiet. He tried to orient himself while he gasped for air. The only sound he heard was his own muffled breathing, as he realized he had been holding his breath throughout the fall.

He was still stunned from the impact. It happened so quickly, so unexpectedly. He had just been standing there, on seemingly solid ground, touching the propeller. Persa descending and standing next to him, then everything giving way, both of them tumbling into the abyss.

He shook his head, trying to regain his senses. For a moment he thought he was back diving on the trireme site. He stared out. His helmet was buried in something, making him blind to his surroundings.

Nick looked at the positioning indicator on his heads-up display. It showed he was lying flat, face down.

What happened? Am I buried alive? he thought.

He swallowed hard, forcing back bile. And fear. He squinted and looked at the oxygen gauge. One hour and fifteen minutes left. He stared at it for a moment longer, to ensure he wasn't bleeding any O_2 from the impact. The reading was steady. Which meant his Exosuit had maintained integrity, despite the fall and whatever he had hit.

Thank God. OK. I've got time. Think. The comm system. Try the comm system.

"Neró Mágissa, do you read? Do you read? Over."

There was no reply, only silence.

"Captain Alek, this is Nick. Do you read?"

He waited. Still no reply. Panic started creeping in.

What am I forgetting? Oh, yeah. Her.

"Persa this is Nick, do you read?"

Silence.

"Can anyone hear me? Over."

He closed his eyes, concentrating on the sounds. All he heard was his own breathing and the pounding of his heart. He held his breath, his heightened hearing picking up a slight humming from his headpiece. Not even any static.

Shit, not good. Maybe my comm system broke from the fall. I'm on my own. Now what?

"Can anybody read me? Anyone?"

Nothing.

Lying here whining isn't going to solve anything. Pull yourself together man. Take action.

He looked at his displays again, then gently toggled his thrusters to see if he was pinned down or not. Feeling slight movement, he fired them to try to stand the Exosuit upright. Still blind to the outside, he used the head's-up display to gauge when he was vertical. He felt his feet settle, unsteadily at first, then solidly. He closed his eyes and waited a moment.

Slowly the silt around him drifted away and the water cleared. Something was in front of him, something massive and foreboding, but he couldn't make it out. He tilted his head backwards, the twin lights on the sides of his helmet fading the higher up he looked.

Something above, maybe lettering. Faded, his lights just barely illuminating it.

I can't make it out.

Nick remembered he had a powerful underwater lamp, an integral part of the Exosuit. Captain Alek had bragged about it, that the 20,000 lumen LEDs could illuminate anything he might encounter. Blindingly so.

Did it survive the fall?

He mechanically reached down. It was there, still attached to him. With a clamp and a tug, he released it, then raised it. After turning it on, he was blinded for a moment from the reflection, until he angled it upward. Nick gasped when the outline of a U-boat came into focus. It was suspended before him, nearly vertical, the bow buried thirty or forty feet deep into the very seabed he stood upon.

He played the lamp higher. Faded letters appeared. Still legible. Large letters on an undamaged part of the U-boat.

By God it was true. It's really right here.

U234.

"Níkos that you? I see light below. Níkos you read?"

There was an edge of hysteria in her voice.

"Persa this is Nick. I hear you clearly. Where are you? Over."

"*Dóxa to theó*," she mumbled. "I hit, what you call, conning tower. Fell in big hole. Into sub."

Nick craned his neck upward, and saw where the hull had been imploded. The hole was at least twenty feet across. A depth charge must have exploded close to it. No wonder the U-boat had struck the sea bed with such force.

"Use the light attached to your leg. Wave it."

A moment later Nick saw a bright beam reach out from within the confines of the hull.

"I see it. Are you hurt at all?"

"No, me just shook. You?"

"I'm OK. It's good to hear your voice."

"Da. You talk ship above?"

"No, I can't raise it. Can you?"

"No raise."

"That crust we fell through. It must be blocking transmission. I can only talk local with you."

Nick looked further above, to where the U-boat had broken through some type of layer of sediment. The stern still hung there, surrounded by it. Nick aimed the light there, and squinted at the small opening they had fallen through, right next to one blade of the propellor.

He played his light above on the underside of the crust. Made of sunken and solidified pumice, he guessed. Forged from time and pressure, they were in a sort of water-filled cavern beneath it, the high point near the stern of the U234. It tapered down around the edges, eventually meeting the sea floor.

We're trapped between the crust above and the sea floor. And can't communicate with the surface.

He looked at the external water temperature. It was a good twenty degrees warmer than when he stood by the propeller.

"Where we Níkos?"

"We're in a pocket of some kind. Judging from water temperatures, this was probably formed by thermal vents from the fissure below us."

"How?"

"It warmed the sea water within it, pushing the crust of solidified pumice upward. Maybe drawing in more water through cracks. Over time, it must have created all of this."

"Den sub crash in?"

"I think so." He looked at the head's-up display. "Listen, I've got seventy minutes of air left. You?"

"Uh, seven five."

"OK. We've got to get the hell out of here. Get back to the lift. Stay there. I'll come up to you."

Nick pushed his thrusters on. He lifted off slowly, just a few feet, and started spinning. Something was drastically wrong, he could rise no further nor stop the spin. A warning flashed on his head's-up display. Damage Sustained. He decreased power, and landed with a thud.

Seriously? What else can go wrong?

He gently tried again, this time nothing at all happened. His Exosuit had maintained structural integrity and not bled O_2, but it had taken a beating from the fall. Nick wasn't going anywhere. He tilted his head back and looked at the imploded side of the U-boat, a good 150 feet above.

Even if I can't get out, she still stands a chance. She can propel herself back up to the lift.

"Persa, I'm afraid you need to go solo. Do you read? Over."

No reply. He waited a moment, still nothing.

"Persa, do you read?"

Silence.

Fricking great. Does anything work down here?

He looked more closely around the sea bed upon which he stood. At the contours of the surface, at the size of the cavern in which the U-boat had struck. At what would now be his tomb.

Nick shuffled his feet and slowly turned around, taking in the landscape he would be spending eternity in. He noticed silt-enshrouded rectangular objects scattered about the sea bed. Probably items that fell out of the hole in the U-boat.

Curiosity getting the better of him despite his predicament, he looked at one right next to him. He pounded it once with his metal fist. The silt rose in a plume, then drifted away. There were markings visible, stenciled in black beneath a German eagle perched upon a Swastika:

Minoische Artefakte
Museum Linz

He examined several more of the large crates, each labeled either Minoan, Mycenean, or Greek artifacts. There was no doubt about it. The Germans had pilfered the priceless treasures when they abandoned Athens. Intending to put them, along with everything else they had plundered from across Europe, Russia, North Africa, and the Balkans, into a special museum. It was designed by Hitler's favorite architect, Albert Speer. To be built in Hitler's hometown of Linz, Austria.

The Führermuseum.

He laughed aloud at the absurdity of his situation. An archeologist, surrounded by treasures he would gladly spend a lifetime examining. All out of reach, taunting him, destined to become offerings in his grave.

Ironic. But somehow appropriate.

The head's-up display read fifty-eight minutes of air left. He sighed, and glanced around one last time. Just off in the distance, a slight glow appeared. With nothing else to do but count down to zero, he shuffled over. Something lay on the seabed. Something man made. He recognized it and felt a glimmer of hope. It was upside down, stuck from its own impact. The AUV.

They must have seen us fall, and sent it in after us. And then it lost communication and plummeted. Right down to here.

Nick bent down, and with a strong mechanical lift, flipped the AUV over. The faint glow became brighter, the lights no longer buried in sediment. He saw controls on it. Designed for local, manual operation.

He gripped the rear-mounted handles and squeezed them. It took a moment to get a feel for it, but now he understood. The harder he gripped either handle, the stronger the thrust. Tilting the handles in any direction steered it, including up and down.

Here goes nothing.

He gripped tightly, the powerful AUV immediately whisking him upward. Gaining control, he circled once to better manage his ascent. That's when he finally saw it. What Günther Wessel had seen escaping the U-boat. What Plato wrote of two and a half millennia ago. What the bracelet indicated was the center of the world.

Indescribable and overwhelming, spread out below was the unmistakable outline of an ancient city.

He squinted through disbelieving eyes as streets came into sharp focus, remnants of buildings, statues, fountains, even what looked like massive stone bull horns. All vestiges of a once mighty empire and people. Encased and preserved beneath the sea by the very pumice and pyroclastic flow that had annihilated it.

Atlantis.

Persa pointed the brilliant lamp outward so Nick could see it. Out of the hole in the hull she had tumbled into. He would be up soon, she had to look around now. It was her only chance to do so, before she would have to explain herself.

Perhaps Nikos understand, she thought. *No, I no risk it. Too much at stake.*

She snapped the lamp back to her suit. It was too bright for the confines she was in. Moving as quickly as her suit would allow, she searched the blast area with the lights on either side of her helmet. There were crates strapped to the floor, some of which had broken loose. She looked upward toward the stern. The watertight doors above her had held, despite the implosion.

They survive little while up there, only to die here. Sea bottom.

She picked up a transmission.

"Persa, I'm afraid you need to go solo. Do you read? Over."

Ignore. He done for. Focus. Find what came for.

"Persa, do you read?"

He dead now. Concentrate.

The bulkhead below her had been blown apart, the way down toward the bow open. She clanged through it, and was suddenly among debris and bodies. Lots of them. Skeletons drifted from her movement, shrouded in the uniforms of the Kriegsmarine. She saw one who might be the captain, judging from his insignia.

One I seek important. Should be near Captain.

She edged further in, ghostly bodies reaching for her, bouncing off, disturbing others in a domino-like cascade. Their movements cast spectral shadows in the vast metal sarcophagus of the U-boat. A dance of the dead.

One body floated toward her, until the skull met her helmet. Other bodies drifted with it, creating a tangle. She tried to reach to brush the skull away, but her rigid arms wouldn't reach. It stared at her, accusing her. Of what so many of her people hadn't been able to do. Of surviving.

"Get off 'a me!" she screamed.

Persa flung her arms about desperately, skeletal bodies moving, disintegrating, mixing with one another. The skull slipped away, and tattered bits of uniform and dust obstructed her vision. She calmed herself, stood still, and waited for the water to clear. When it did, he was right there by the captain. Back by the periscope. Dressed exactly as she had been told. In the same distinctive black suit favored by his descendants.

Persa moved toward him, and gently put one hand against his forehead. She pressed him against the bulkhead to hold him steady. With the other hand, she extended a clamp-like claw, and reached for the lower jaw. With a sharp twist she broke it free and glared into the empty eye sockets. Carefully she deposited it into a container built into the Exosuit, and snapped it shut.

Proof positive *he* had been here. Of who he was. A collaborator of the worst kind.

Nick slowed the AUV as he approached where he had seen Persa shine the light out. Now he saw first-hand the catastrophic damage inflicted by the depth charge. A massive hole had been blown into the hull, the innards of the U234 laid bare.

He shined the bright lamp in, searching for some sign of Persa. There was nothing. Just more of the same crates secured to internal decking, along with scattered debris.

Maybe she made it out of here. Couldn't hear me and took off, Nick thought. *I hope she got through.*

He stared at the damage for a moment longer, pondering what the U-boat was transporting, the civilization it had crashed into, and how time and circumstance had brought them together.

The lamp picked up movement on the fringe. Something in the bulkhead below had been disturbed. He stared closer. The skeletal remains of an arm drifted out. Then a partial skull. A light shone out, then the helmet of an Exosuit looked through.

"I hear you now Níkos."

"Thank God you're OK. The bulkhead must have interfered with transmission."

"You suit not 'a zoom no more?"

"No, but I found the AUV."

"You find what you look for?" Persa asked.

"Yes. And a whole lot more."

"Me too."

Persa led the way, the thrusters on her Exosuit working perfectly. Nick followed up behind her, propelled by the AUV, ensuring she made her way safely. They slowly worked their way up the length of the U-boat, to the hole by the propeller they had fallen through. They easily rose past it, in part riding the warmer water trapped below as it escaped upward.

Like birds riding thermals off the cliffs, Nick thought. He glanced at his head's-up display.

"Time left?"

"Gotta one five."

"I've got eight," Nick said, eying the lift off to the side, drifting in the current. "There's not enough time for that."

They both pondered their choices, and their chances.

"What we do Níkos?"

"Hope the AUV has enough juice left. Grab and hold on."

As Nick hung onto the handles on the back of the AUV, Persa clamped on tightly to him. Squeezing the throttles as hard as he could, the AUV revved and headed toward the surface. The extra weight and non-aerodynamic shapes clinging to it taxed the AUV's motor and batteries.

"Seven hundred feet to surface," Persa read.

"Four minutes of air left," Nick said.

"Six hundred feet."

"Three minutes left."

"Four hundred."

"Two left."

"Two hundred."

"One."

"One hundred."

The AUV started to struggle, losing momentum.

"Hit your thrusters," Nick gasped through his oxygen-depleted helmet.

Above, a crowd stood by the edge of the ship, shining bright lights onto the water's surface. They looked at a monitor that showed the forward camera of the AUV, then looked back at the sea. The images showed the AUV was losing its power when abruptly it started ascending again. Breaking the surface, a crane grabbed the first visible Exosuit while the second breached nearby. The AUV bobbed for a moment, then sank back into the depths.

Nick started coughing and gasping for air once his helmet was removed. He was barely conscious, his lips and skin blue and cyanotic.

Persa was lowered down right next to him in her own Exosuit. The helmet was also removed, but her breathing not labored. Her oxygen supply had lasted just long enough.

Nick took a deep breath, his panic subsiding. It was night, the sky was dark. But he was safe. Back onboard.

He dimly perceived somebody walking into his field of vision. The person was blurry at first, lights in back of him, then came slowly into focus. Lykaios leered at him and cracked his knuckles. Nick was about to say something, when a big fist flew at him.

Then his world went black.

CHAPTER 28

JULY 11, PRESENT DAY, ATHENS, GREECE

He sensed he was suspended, his arms and shoulders achingly numb. His toes were touching the floor, but just barely. He spun slowly, aimlessly in the air. He tried to open his eyes, but couldn't. His eyelids felt too heavy, his mouth dry, his mind fuzzy. Something was off. He didn't feel like he controlled his own mind, much less his body.

What's going on? Where the hell am I? Nick thought.

There were voices in the background, but they were faint, unintelligible. He felt his arms release, then hit the concrete floor with a thud.

Funny, that didn't hurt. Should it have?

He was finally able to crack open his eyes. A clinical looking bald man in a white apron was carefully putting needles and vials away. The small glass containers clinked as they were placed into an aluminum container, which closed with a snap. The bald man was seemingly a professional at this, detached. Humming contentedly while he finished his work.

Hmm. That's a nice tune. I wonder what it is?

"Anything?"

Nick tried to turn his head to see who was talking, but couldn't.

"No. He doesn't know anything about the body found onboard. He is what he says he is. Just a do-gooder archeologist. Chasing ghosts of ancient myths. Trying to find things for 'the greater good.'"

"Are there any more left to do?"

"No. He was the last. I'm done here."

"Excellent. You will be well compensated, as always. Lykaios, take the archaiológos to the others. I'll be with you shortly."

Nick felt himself dragged down a corridor. The heels of his shoes bumped over the cracks of the rough-cut stone floor. A heavy door was unlatched, creaking under its own weight. It grated along grooves in the floor as it was manhandled open. He felt himself flung through the air, about to hit again.

"Sýllipsi!"

Charlie and Jim grabbed him before he smashed face-first into the floor. They set him gently down while the door clanged shut. Lykaios and two others could be heard talking and laughing, their conversation echoing then fading as they walked away.

Nick blinked hard, his senses slowly coming back. He felt he was in someone's lap, and looked up and saw Soba's concerned face. She leaned down and kissed his forehead.

You look so pretty. Why are you crying?

Charlie and Jim were right there, and Captain Alek, Persa, and Zorba too. He smiled weakly. The whole gang was back together, ready for another adventure. A familiar face wandered over and looked down at him.

Are we back on the ship? Hey, I know you. Your name, what is it? It will come to me . . .

"Willkommen back Nick," Heinrich said, reaching down and clasping his hand.

Nick stared up at him. He didn't look so good. He was bruised, busted up. Come to think of it, none of them did.

"Afraid we've all had a bit of a go at it," Captain Alek added, sensing his confusion. "Seems we found something they didn't want found. Bloody business, this."

Nick looked up again, and saw concern in Soba's face. She was softly stroking his hair. It felt nice, and he was so very tired.

His heavy eyelids shut, and the world faded to black again.

"We saw and heard everything, right through your cameras and communication system. Simply amazing what you found down there. Too bad you won't be around to get credit for it," Drakos Kollas said.

They were all sitting on the floor, leaning against the wall of a dungeon-like room. Ensconced deep beneath the Kollas family mansion. Four armed guards and Lykaios loomed over them.

"What's your game, you bastard?" Nick asked.

"Ah, the idealist speaks. Well, since there's no chance any of you will get to tell the tale, I shall share it with you. You are, after all, a captive audience." Drakos chuckled at his own joke.

"*Panáthemá se*," Zorba growled through clenched teeth.

Drakos glared at him. "You and your Cretan scum will be put back in your place soon enough."

"You fool yourself, but *oi theoí xéroun*." The gods know.

Lykaios stepped behind Zorba and hit him hard on the head with a truncheon. He rolled over, unconscious.

"Anyone else care to interrupt? No? Good. I will tell you a little story, about a family who lived right here for generations. They struggled, but worked hard, and believed in the dream of a resurrected and united Greece. In the late 1800s, they got into the chemical business, and expanded into munitions during World War One."

"Selling to both sides, no doubt," Captain Alek said.

Lykaios made a move toward him, but Kollas raised his hand.

"Yes, like any good arms merchant, they sold to all those in need. They prospered during turbulent times, and employed hundreds of Greeks. Soon they were employing thousands. Then World War Two erupted. The Germans occupied us. You have to understand, it looked like they would soon be masters of all Europe. My family made certain, what you would call, concessions, to them."

"Since you're telling us this little fairytale, define concessions,"

Nick said. He noticed that Persa had tensed up, and tried to make eye contact. She flexed her fists and averted his gaze, keeping her eyes downcast.

"It was really quite simple. There was a war on, and it was expanding. The Germans invaded Russia, and they now needed munitions on a massive scale. We provided them war matériel, they provided us labor. What you Amerikanós like to call quid pro quo."

"Unless you're Jewish. Then you're worked to death," Jim said disgustedly. "I've heard the stories."

"They would have been shipped to the concentration camps anyway. We bought them time. Gave them hope."

Kollas paced as he talked, his hands clasped behind his back. "My grandfather Theodoros owned the munitions plant. He had a great love of archeology and history. Of the purity of his people, much like the Nazis. He and his forefathers collected great artifacts over time. Proving the ascendency of Greek culture. The very superiority of it. Even the Germans saw the truth in it. Theodoros worked with Speer, even met Hitler himself. To make sure the great treasures of Greece were preserved forever, safe from the ravages of war. He chose what to take, to have them transported before Athens fell to the Allies. And then he accompanied them aboard U234."

Nick looked at Heinrich, then stared at Drakos. It all made sense now, why Drakos would go to any lengths to find the submarine. Because it was proof of his family's use of Jewish slave labor. Of their working hand in hand with the Germans to expropriate their own heritage. All to be displayed at the Führermuseum in Linz.

"Your grandfather was a collaborator. Your family fortune was built on the blood of innocents," Nick said.

"No, Theodoros was visionary. He saw the future, even if he was a bit premature. I will see his dream through."

Drakos reached into a satchel bag and removed a jaw bone. "I have you to thank for this," he said, walking up to Persa. "Why you took this from my grandfather I don't know. My interrogator said he could get no reason out of you. But no matter. This will be buried here, with honors."

He reached back into the satchel and removed a journal. He tossed it disdainfully onto Nick's lap.

"Here, I don't need this anymore. You and Heinrich should appreciate it. Günther was most meticulous."

Kollas walked toward the door, then turned around. "We'll go back to the U234, and dispose of anything we don't want coming to light. Like the inconsequential Minoan artifacts. And, of course, retrieve my grandfather's body. I will then announce to the world the discovery of U234, and the recovery of cultural treasures expropriated from Greece by the Nazis. That will cement my family's legacy. And since I will be recognized as a great Greek patriot, I will be free to pursue my political aims," he said disdainfully.

"There's no need to involve all these innocents," Nick pleaded. "I'm the one who stirred this up."

"Yes, you did. And for that I will be forever thankful. Tomorrow the headlines will say the Neró Mágissa was lost at sea with all hands during a storm. Most tragic."

He looked at Lykaios and sneered. "*Oi nekroí den léne paramýthia.*"

Lykaios gave a satisfied grunt, understanding that dead men told no tales. It would be his pleasure.

From the Journal of Günther Wessel

October 10 1944.

The streets are chaos, Athens is bedlam. We finally received our orders to evacuate. Bombing of our positions and the docks of Piraeus has intensified. Where is our Luftwaffe? Crates are being loaded tonight, markings indicate they are destined for Linz. We have to be underway before daylight. I heard our captain arguing with the Wehrmacht and Gestapo on priorities. Even though this is our largest U-boat, we only have room for so much and so many. It seems everyone who helped us wants to get out before the city falls.

They aren't worried about the enemy. It's the revenge of the Greeks they fear.

October 11 1944.

We had to wait for some high-ranking Greek ally to board. He must be a big shot, but he almost got us all killed. We were strafed while loading the last crates brought aboard with him. We submerged once we were deep enough. God knows what will happen to those we left behind. We will head toward Crete, still held by our own reliable Wehrmacht troops. Thank God it's not the Italians or Romanians, they would have surrendered already. We will top off fuel and provisions. Where we go from there will depend on circumstance. This U-boat is built for it. We can go to South America if necessary.

October 12 1944.

Scuttlebutt is Athens fell. We travel underwater by day, surface by night. The British and American patrols are heavy. We aren't well armed to fight them off, this is a cargo U-boat, made for long-distance transport and mine laying. We only have two stern torpedo tubes, which is what I man. I help defend our floating city, but stealth is our real strength. We now take an indirect path to avoid patrols. The crew is starting to settle into a routine. The aisles are crowded, the hammocks are stowed, we sleep atop crates of food. We will gain room as we eat our way through provisions. The big engines are running smoothly. This is a magnificent machine, the pride of the Kriegsmarine.

October 13 1944.

We passed between islands of Sikinos and Ios. An enemy patrol plane sited us at dawn before we could dive. They now know we exist. We continued to head south while submerged, hoping to avoid them. Two hours passed before we heard the screws of a ship. Then the pinging of their sonar started as they sought us out. We dove deeper and changed course to evade them.

The captain chose a route between the islands of Thirasia and Santorini, to a depression within an old caldera. We dove below our maximum depth and stayed there. The U-boat holds up well, springing but a few pressure leaks. We feel we have lost them, but the pinging started again. We drift deep, silent, eventually running low on air. Another ship with a different acoustical signature glides far above, two hunters searching for their prey. We hear splashes, depth charges exploding, seemingly far off. More splashes, the explosions creeping steadily toward us. Close enough to feel the vibrations. New leaks burst forth, but the captain changes course and lets us drift silently, even deeper. The pinging gets louder, the splashes now on top of us.

A tremendous explosion hits us amidship on the starboard side. We feel the bulkhead crumble, and immediately know it is fatal. Our U-boat starts to nosedive, grinding and imploding in its death throes. The ship is nearly vertical, hurtling downward. We feel a tremendous impact, and know the nose has hit seabed. There is a great compression of air in our compartment, despite the watertight hatch securing us in the stern torpedo room. My ears feel they will burst and my eyes pop out. Leaks spring through equipment and seams in the hull. Knowing we are soon to die, my mate and I take our one chance. We don primitive aqualungs and goggles, put flashlights around our necks, and open the inside doors of the torpedo tubes. We stand looking at one another, the water in the torpedo room rises past our waists, then to our necks. We take a last gulp of air and put our mouthpieces in, and open the outer torpedo tube doors. A crash of water fills our room, the tubes completely open to the sea.

He enters one tube, I the other. I struggle to crawl its length, my breathing labored. I finally emerge out the stern, the U-boat resting on its nose. I start to descend, the water pressure crushing the air out of my lungs. Before I descend too far, I finally find where to pull on my vest. It inflates and I start to float upward. An after explosion near the bow lights the bottom surface, and I glance down. I see straight lines, what looks like streets. The remains of collapsed buildings are next to them. I see an ancient city, sunken and preserved beneath me.

I drift upward along the length of U234, toward the propellers. It had burst through a layer of sediment on its descent, through a crust of some type into a deeper cavern below. The U234 rests vertically in this a pocket, only the tips of the propellors above the surrounding sea bed. Light filters in around them, guiding me upward.

I float up past the conning tower, near where we were fatally hit. The aqualung saves me on the ascent. While I struggle to breathe, it is enough. I go through the opening around the propellors, into brighter waters, and reach the surface. I spit out my mouthpiece and remove my goggles, and look frantically for my mate. Oil and debris rise around me, stinging my eyes and gagging me. I see two destroyers fading into the distance. All is silence now, just wind and waves after being with so many of my countrymen. I hear a faint shout, and when I rise on a wave, I see Karl floating fifty meters away. I swim to him, he isn't in good shape. He took too long to get up, his breathing is ragged. He has the bends, even worse than I do.

October 14 1944.

I take off my belt and loop our life vests together, in case I fall asleep. They are starting to lose air. Like our lungs, they were crushed by going too deep. If they go flat, we will slip below the waves and be with our comrades one final time. We drift through the evening and night. Karl is getting worse. He exhales bloody air bubbles. With dawn comes a fishing boat. I yell and wave desperately. It slowly comes our way. A man and his young son take us aboard. They give us strong coffee and blankets and take us to shore. A priest there shows us kindness and takes us in. Karl dies within a day, suffering terribly. I recover, and am taken to Crete. I wait out the end of the war with the other Germans who hold the island. We will never surrender, until Germany surrenders.

. . .

May 12, 1945.

We heard the news, the war is over for us. Germany has surrendered to the Allies. I long to see my family, to know what has become of them. I heard Berlin is now occupied by the Russians, but that is where I shall go. It is my home, and whatever comes, I will make my life there.

I will never abandon the Fatherland.

Nick finished listening to Heinrich translate the journal entries. He looked at the map Günther Wessel had drawn, slowly tracing the path of the U-boat with his fingertip. It had been written in November of 1944, while he was on Crete. While his recollections were still fresh. Günther's estimation of the location of the sinking was unerringly accurate. It was within a half mile. Yet his story had been dismissed as the lunatic rantings of a madman. Such an incredible tale of survival, and loss.

Nick set the journal down and looked over at Heinrich. "Otto had told me there was a journal, but wouldn't show it to me. At least not yet. He wanted to have some leverage. His old Stasi training kicking in, no doubt."

"Ja. They drug me, and find out. I could not hide what I know. They tail you to Berlin. Go to Otto and Günther after you. They took Otto and journal with them. Killed Günther, make it look natural," Heinrich said. "He was old man. No one would suspect anything."

"What happened to Otto?"

Heinrich shook his head and looked away.

Nick thought back to the day he had first visited Otto and Günther in their East Berlin flat, in the old Khrushchev slums. Where he met an old warrior and his son looking to clear their good family name. Of looking out the window and seeing a man staring back up at him, who turned and walked away. He was tailed, but had thought nothing of it. Too caught up in the tale Otto was telling him.

Footsteps could be heard echoing down the hallway toward them. Nick got up and stood protectively in front of Soba. She clasped his arm and steeled herself. Whatever they were facing, at least they would face it together.

The sound of the latch on the heavy door lifting caught everyone's attention. They stared as it was forced open by burly guards burnishing automatic weapons. Lykaios entered between them, and stared at Nick.

It was time to meet their fate.

CHAPTER 29

JULY 12, PRESENT DAY, ATHENS, GREECE

They were hustled down a long, dark corridor, deep under the Kollas family mansion. They stumbled, yet couldn't reach out, their hands bound by zip ties behind their backs. Security was tight, with Lykaios leading the way. Nick, Soba, and Heinrich walked behind him, prodded along by a guard. Charlie and Persa followed with another guard, while Jim, Zorba, and Captain Alek brought up the rear, with two more armed guards behind them. Eight bound prisoners and five guards. Drakos was taking no chances.

A large black van awaited them. They stood there nervously for a moment, the van door sliding open. One guard discretely brushed past Persa, her hand grasping something. Nick saw the exchange and looked away, betraying nothing. They were all forced in and sat on the floor. One guard got in the driver seat, Lykaios in the passenger seat beside him. Two guards sat against the rear door, while one sat with his back to the driver and Lykaios.

The van pulled out from the garage, three guns pointed at the prisoners. They were so disoriented it was a surprise to see it was nighttime. They had all lost track of time in the confines of their dank cell. Nick noticed the other men evaluating the situation, contemplating action. When they tried to whisper or give non-verbal clues to one another, rifle butts swung their way.

"*Isychia!*" a guard in the far back shouted.

Nick glanced at Persa, who had her head down. Their eyes briefly met. Nick gave a subtle nod.

Wait, her eyes seemed to say. *Be still just a moment longer.*

The van hit a small bump in the road, jostling everyone about. The guard with his back to Lykaios turned to the front, as if to discuss something. In the practiced motion of a trained assassin, he put his gun to the head of the driver, aimed down and fired before anyone could react. The van swerved wildly, driverless, out of control.

One guard in the far back put a hand against the wall to balance himself, while inadvertently raising his short barrel assault rifle. Persa seized on the momentary confusion and leapt at him. The small blade she used to cut her zip tied hands free expertly slashed across his exposed throat. In the same instant Nick and Jim bull-rushed the other guard sitting next to him. They wrestled for his gun as it fired again and again, bullets ripping through the ceiling and bodies alike. Charlie and Zorba piled on, while Heinrich shielded Soba with his body.

Lykaios instinctively reached for the steering wheel and steered toward a wall alongside the road, which would toss its occupants. Before he could, a gun pressed against the base of his skull.

"*Káne stin ákri!*" the guard behind him said.

The momentum of the van slowed as the dead driver's foot fell from the gas petal. Rather than pulling over, Lykaios jammed the steering wheel hard to the left. There wasn't enough momentum to roll the van, but it pitched everyone in back against one wall, Captain Alek at the bottom of the pile. Lykaios threw his door open and jumped out, rolling when he landed.

The van went off the road and ground to a stop. The back door swung open, bodies tumbling out. Persa quickly started cutting off everyone's zip ties. Nick looked at the tangle of bodies and heard moaning. He stared for a moment at Heinrich; it didn't look good for his friend. Grabbing what looked like an Uzi, Nick ran out, looking for Lykaios. A single shot rang out, whizzing past his head. He ducked and ran across the road, crouching against bushes, looking and listening for movement.

He heard something off to the side, and crept toward it. By the time he realized it was a ruse, it was too late. A strong fist knocked his gun away as the warm barrel of a just-fired pistol was thrust up under his chin. "You mine now Amerikanós," Lykaios whispered into his ear.

Nick was forced behind an outcropping, struggling desperately while being dragged.

If Lykaios uses me as a hostage, he can have this whole area sealed off with a phone call, Nick thought. *The others would stand a better chance if I could get him to shoot me.*

Nick reached for the gun, but Lykaios anticipated it and brought it down sharply on the back of his head. Nick slumped onto his knees, dazed.

Lykaios looked out over the top of the rocks, and yelled toward the van. "I have the one you call Níkos. You hear?"

Before there was a reply, Nick heard a dull thud, and the sound of a body falling.

"I 'a hear you," said a uniformed guard, looking down at Lykaios on the ground.

As Nick regained his senses he recognized his savior as the guard who had shot the driver in the van. The guard stood over Lykaios, kicking away his pistol. He carefully kept his gun trained on Lykaios, and looked at Nick. "Nice job. You keep him busy. So I could track."

"Yeah, that was my intent," Nick replied uncertainly.

With the adrenaline fading and the fear of a close call taking hold, Nick started trembling. He reached down and picked up the pistol while Lykaios sat up. The pent-up anger of their abduction, the torture and beatings, their intended execution, all came out in a blind rage.

"You son of a bitch! You'll never do that to anyone ever again. Damn you to hell!" Nick cocked the trigger and aimed it with shaking hands.

Those able to walk had gathered around them. Soba looked at Nick with pleading eyes.

"Easy bro," Charlie said. "Let the authorities handle it."

Persa walked over and gently put her hand over his, and lowered the gun.

"Don't. If anyone has reason, it us," Persa said, looking over at her accomplice. "Justice slow, but justice come. For everyone."

Nick was about to walk away, when he noticed Lykaios smirk. There was no reason to think he wouldn't get out of this yet. Kollas would no doubt get him released, and he would be back on the street in no time.

"*Axiolýpitos erasitéchnis*," Lykaios muttered under his breath.

"What did he say?" Nick asked.

"Pitiful amateur," Persa said.

Nick wound up and swung around, coming down hard with the butt of the pistol. Flush on the bridge of the nose. There was a cracking sound and Lykaios collapsed, knocked out cold, his nose smashed and bleeding profusely. It would bear a permanent reminder of his encounter with the pitiful amateur Amerikanós.

Persa looked at Nick with a sardonic grin.

"There bigger fish to catch. We go. Now."

Nick looked around the interior of the van. It was bullet ridden, bloody, and cluttered. Yet it was perfectly functional for what they intended.

Big Jim had taken a bullet to the abdomen rushing a guard, Zorba one in the shoulder, and Captain Alek had snapped a collarbone when the bodies tumbled on top of him when the van swerved to a stop. But none of their wounds appeared fatal. That wasn't the case for Heinrich. His body lay by the side of the road, his face covered by a bloody cloth. He had been killed instantly by the spray of automatic rifle fire when he dove to shield Soba.

As the finality of Heinrich's death sunk in, Nick collapsed to his knees. His shoulders slumped as he sobbed, the grief pounding him in waves. He removed the cloth to gaze at his friend one last time.

"I'm sorry man, so sorry. I was too damn late. I should have known, when I saw that stranger outside Günther's window. I'm so sorry Heinrich."

Soba knelt down and put an arm around Nick. He leaned into her shoulder and sighed, drying his eyes with a sleeve. "I should have known."

Charlie put a hand firmly on Nick's shoulder. "We've got work to do bro."

Nick took a deep breath and stood, regaining his composure. "I won't let you down again. I'll expose that bastard Kollas and whatever he's hiding in the caldera. I'll make sure the world knows you were the real hero here."

A plan was quickly formulated. Soba would stay behind to tend the wounded. One tightly bound guard was also left there. Help would arrive soon.

Nick and Charlie stripped the two dead guards for their uniforms, and slipped into them. The collar of Nick's was doused with blood from the slashed throat. He tore an undershirt off one body, and patted at the blood around his neck. It wasn't perfect, but it was night and would have to do. The bullet holes in Charlie's were easier to conceal. They climbed into the back of the van with a still-unconscious Lykaios and sped away.

"This Malachi," Persa said, turning around from the passenger seat as her partner drove. "He undercover many months."

Nick looked at his neck in the rearview mirror. He dabbed it once more and tossed the blood-soaked rag.

"I get it now. The way he shot the driver, he didn't want to blow out a window. You needed the van to look normal. To get back in."

Persa nodded at him.

"You learning. We go back to garage, like nothing happen. Need get Drakos now. While still have blood on 'is hands."

"Why bring Lykaios?" Charlie asked, nervously fingering the bullet holes in his shirt.

"If we need to get by security," Malachi replied coldly.

Persa saw their confused looks, and tapped her head with a knife. "Might need eye or finger. For scanner, yes?"

Nick grinned. There was just something charming about her.

Even when she talked about dismembering a live, fellow human being.

"Níkos, pull hat down. Sit here."

They traded seats, Nick sitting next to Malachi, who drove toward the Kollas family mansion. Persa passed the short-barrel assault rifles to Nick and Charlie, and made sure they knew how to use them. High rate of fire and simple to operate, good for the untrained. Malachi was armed with the same, while Persa held Lykaios's pistol. She frisked him roughly, found more ammunition, and chambered a round.

"Do two teams. Need uniform in each, throw 'dem off. Níkos you go Malichi, Charlie go me," Persa instructed.

Nick turned and looked at her.

"You want him alive?"

"Da. But don't die trying."

Malachi slowed the van as they turned up a long, winding driveway. He stopped outside an ornamental gate, which concealed its real purpose. Heavy security. Even a bomb-laden truck would have difficulty crashing through it. A remote camera trained on them from above a speaker box.

"We disposed of the bodies as instructed," Malachi said in perfect Greek. "It went off perfectly."

The camera rotated, focusing on Nick. He looked away, acting disinterested. The camera panned back to Malachi. A voice came over a speaker next to the camera.

"Where's Lykaios?"

"We dropped him off at his favorite bar. I think he needed some female companionship. He was a little worked up over that pretty Greek whore we just buried."

There was a click, and the gate slowly slid open. Malachi tipped his cap to the camera and put the van in gear. He carefully drove up the driveway, the gate clanking shut, then locking behind them.

"Pretty Greek whore?" Persa whispered, cuffing Malachi behind the head. He looked over at Nick and raised an eyebrow. What was one to do?

There was a second gate just before the mansion. It was a simple weighted bar next to a concealed sentry box. This one was purposely designed to blend into the landscape. The real deterrent were the posted armed guards. The eye of another discrete camera peered at all traffic. Tonight there was only one guard on duty since several had accompanied the van out.

Malachi stopped and waited. A serious looking, thickset security guard walked out. He nodded at Malachi, recognizing him.

"Yassou Remis," Malachi said nonchalantly.

Remis squinted at Nick in the passenger seat, and aimed a flashlight at him. Satisfied nothing was amiss, he lowered the flashlight and went to raise the gate. Then he paused, and walked back. He pointed the flashlight again at Nick, at a smudge above his collar. His eyes widened and he reached for his earpiece to transmit a warning.

The flash momentarily blinded everyone in the van. Remis staggered backwards, collapsing to the ground.

"Cover's blown," Malachi yelled as he lowered the gun. "Hang on."

He backed up twenty feet and floored it, the van gaining just enough momentum to smash through the gate. All four tires blew out, an unseen tire barrier popping up with the forcing of the gate. The van tore up the driveway on disintegrating tires, racing to the front entrance. Before it even halted, Persa jumped out, followed closely by Charlie. They ran up the front steps, while Nick followed Malachi around one edge of the mansion.

Persa tried kicking the door in, but it held fast. Her pistol wouldn't do it either. She grabbed Charlie's automatic rifle and sprayed the lock. They both kicked, and still the door wouldn't yield. It had been built for just such an eventuality.

They ran down the stairs and circled the mansion in the opposite direction of Malachi and Nick. The windows were too high to reach, there seemed no way to force their entry. They rounded a corner, Persa spying where several trees grew close to the mansion. One had a high branch overlooking a window. She nimbly scrambled up the trunk, Charlie struggling to follow her. She shot out the window, then swung in. Despite his best efforts, Charlie couldn't make it up. She was on her own.

Malachi led, Nick crouching behind him. They worked their way around toward the back. They stopped at a spot overlooking the garage entrance below. The large doors were closed, but would be the likely avenue of escape if anyone evaded Persa and Charlie. Malachi motioned for Nick to stay on this side, while he covered the other. He patted Nick on the shoulder, then crept across the open ground. Reaching the other embankment, he took a position opposite Nick. He pointed to his eyes, then at the garage. *Watch it like a hawk.*

Inside, Persa landed softly on her feet. She glanced around the room, getting her bearings. It was a bedroom, empty, faint light glowing under the door. She felt pain, and looked at her left arm and hip. They had been badly cut by jagged glass in the window frame. No major arteries severed, she would deal with it later. She ran to the side of the door, cracked it open, and peered down the hallway. Noise came from the far end. She ran on tiptoes to another doorway halfway down, and hid within it. She listened again, more sounds, voices. Drakos yelling at someone. Her prey was close.

She leaned out and saw movement. Instinctively she pressed herself into the corner formed by the door in back of her and it's recessed opening. A burst of shots rang out, ricocheting off the walls and splintering the door jam. She tasted blood and spit out bits of wood. Footsteps ran toward her then stopped, more shots tearing just past her, one so close it nicked flesh.

She took a deep breath, it was do or die. She jumped out onto the floor, rolling as she did so. Completely exposed.

Outside, they heard the shots, and Malachi looked across at Nick. He held a hand up, indicating to stand fast. It was a burst of automatic rifle fire. It could have come from Charlie supporting Persa, there was no way to tell. A second burst echoed, and still Malachi held his hand up. Signaling, *Wait. We need more intel. Soon.*

What, no pistol shots? Come on Persa, Charlie's no soldier! Nick thought. *Cover his ass!*

There was movement off behind Malachi. Nick saw it and was about to shout a warning, just when a single shot rang out. Malachi's head snapped forward, his body tumbling down the embankment. It landed with a sickening thud in front of the garage, sprawled at an unnatural angle.

The shirt color, it couldn't be, could it? Lykaios!

Persa gracefully rolled into a one knee firing position. The suited guard had just paused, moving to the side to get a better angle to administer the coup de grâce. She fired at the broad target of his torso, then at his head. Heart and brain. He was dead before his body crumpled to the stone floor.

More sounds came from the end of the hall. Persa grabbed his assault rifle and sprinted down toward the last doorway. She stopped just before it, pressing flat against the wall. She cocked the hammer on the pistol until it clicked. Holding her breath, she counted in her head.

Enas, dýo, tría!

She crouched low, then threw the pistol hard against the opposite wall in front of the doorway. It hit loudly, then fired when it struck the floor. As a burst of gunfire sprayed out of the open doorway, she leaned out and fired the automatic rifle at the exposed figure. A bright red slash stitched across his chest, his gun firing from clenched hands until the clip emptied. As he doubled over, Persa rushed the room, not knowing what awaited her.

Nick ducked down from his spot overlooking the garage, wondering if Lykaios had seen him. That was a trained killer, on his home turf. He held his breath and strained hard to listen. Both to hear if

Lykaios was moving about, and to figure out what was going on inside.

If Lykaios took out Malachi, what chance do I have? This shit is getting real!

He heard a single shot go off somewhere in the mansion, then a string of automatic shots in reply. One more quick burst, then silence. He peeked back out, no signs of anything.

What the hell? Where is Malachi's gun? It was just down there next to him.

He heard the gun bolt being pulled in back of him. Then a gruff laugh.

"Not so hard to escape from empty van," Lykaios said, grabbing Nick's rifle and tossing it aside. He glared at Nick as he felt at his shattered nose.

"I get gun from dead guard at hut. Dog Malachi die quick. You not so lucky. You will die slow Amerikanós."

Lykaios raised his rifle, aiming the end of the stock at Nick's head. Before he could bring it down to knock Nick unconscious, a burst of automatic fire tore through Lykaios. Blood and viscera sprayed on Nick.

"I don't think so," Charlie said, the smoke curling from the barrel of his automatic rifle. "I'm the only one who gets to beat on my little brother."

Persa squatted low and swung her gun side to side, glancing around the room. It was a corner office, with a huge mahogany desk and bookcase-lined walls. Elegant tables with rare artifacts and reading chairs were scattered about. A massive globe sat on a pedestal, a telescope aimed out a window, exquisite sculptures and carefully lit paintings graced the room. In one corner sat a specially crafted Steinway piano. All the trappings of wealth, privilege, and power. With only one way in or out.

She checked under the desk and behind the furniture. There were three windows along each wall, one cracked open, the curtain fluttering from the breeze. She cautiously approached, hearing a slight grunting coming from outside. She stood directly in front of the window and looked down.

Fingers desperately held tightly to the window sill. Long fingers. The accomplished fingers of a concert pianist.

Drakos Kollas hung on, gauging the distance, deciding if he dared let go. He noticed a shadow above and looked up. The light blocked out the face, only showing a figure in silhouette. He couldn't tell if it was friend or foe, but his grip was slipping.

The window suddenly slammed down so hard it shattered the glass panes. It crushed his fingers and trapped him there. He hung, writhing in pain, unable to rise or fall. He screamed in agony, cursing at the world and his tormentor.

As the window opened and he flailed through the air, he knew. He had always known it might happen.

Vengeance had found him.

He felt himself suspended, slowly spinning, drifting above his own pain somehow. His hands, God how they hurt, even through the fog he was in. Only his thumbs felt like they hadn't been pulverized. He sensed aching in his shoulders, but that was almost pleasant. It took his wandering mind off his crushed fingers. His toes brushed against something below, just barely. He started to drift back into unconsciousness, but felt the sharp jab of a needle in his arm.

Who is that I see below? Is it me? Funny, that's how the prisoners looked. When we drugged and beat them to make them talk.

His mind slowly came back into focus from the chemical rush of the injection. He looked at the figure before him, withdrawing the long needle from his arm. Under normal circumstances he would have found her attractive.

As the fog lifted, the pain came back in waves. He felt nauseous, started to throw up, but the convulsions only made the pain in his shoulders worse. He tried to swallow his bile, choking on the pain.

"There, there, now. I need you conscious Mr. Kollas. So I can have a little talk with such a big man," a pretty woman said in perfect, unaccented Greek. "Such an important man as yourself. This time *I* get to ask the questions. Every time I don't like your answer, I will take one of these."

She showed him the stump of her missing finger. He looked back dully.

"Well, let's give you a little shot of this too. Since you so graciously gave it to all of us."

The woman stuck another needle into his vein, and pushed the liquid into him. Staring into his eyes and smiling.

"Seems it makes secrets go away. We wouldn't want to have any secrets between us now, would we Mr. Kollas?"

She waited a few moments, then clasped his face with one hand and shook it.

"Would we?"

"No, we wouldn't."

She pushed his face away. He started to slowly spin again.

"Good. Now you get comfortable, and I'll tell you a little story. Kind of like the story you told us not so long ago. But this time it will be from a different perspective. One I think you will appreciate."

She reached out and stopped his spinning so he faced her.

"My grandfather was named Ephraim Theocritus. Theocritus, you remember that name, don't you?"

"Yes. Know name."

"Good, it means Judgement of God. Keep that in mind while my little tale unfolds. Ephraim was leading the Greek resistance during the war. Right here, in Athens of all places. Ephraim got thousands of Jews out, right from under the very noses of the Nazis. You know who the Nazis were, don't you?"

"Yes. Yes, I know."

"Well, it turns out *your* grandfather was also very busy during the Second World War. Collaborating with the Nazis. Working

Jews to death to make munitions for them. Stealing everything they own. Clever, and ironic. Using what they had to finance their own doom. Do you know what else your grandfather was busy doing?"

"No. No, I don't."

"He was busy stealing our cultural heritage. Every kind of antiquity. Minoan, Mycenean, Greek, Macedonian, he stole it all. Why? Because he sold out to the Nazis. He personally chose every piece, and earmarked them to go to Hitler's new museum in Lintz. Do you know what else he did?"

Drakos looked at her dully. His capturer shook the chain he was suspended by, the sharp pain bringing him back into focus. She looked at him with a raised eyebrow.

"What? What else?"

"Your grandfather pointed out any Jews he saw. Some to work in his factory, some to deport. And to prove his loyalty to the Nazis, he identified my grandfather. Right when he was trying to get his own family out. He watched as my pappoús was executed, while his whole family was sent to the concentration camps. Can you imagine such a thing?"

Drakos slowly shook his head no.

"But the Nazis, they made a mistake. Most unusual for them, being so very precise and meticulous. They missed one. My father. He was just a baby. A sympathetic family took him in before he could be found and taken away. Wasn't that kind in the midst of so much horror? The wife's baby had been stillborn. A life for a life, yes? After the war, when he was old enough, this kind Greek family told my papa exactly what happened. You knew him; do you remember him?"

"Was it, was it Yitzhak?"

"Yes, Yitzhak. Yitzak Theocritus. Now we're getting somewhere. Well, he grew into a man, and knew his family history. And knew of the corruption in yours. He set out to prove it, to expose the truth. But you couldn't let that happen now, could you?"

Drakos started passing out, his head drooping to one side. The pretty woman took another vial and injected it into him. It took a few minutes to take effect, but she was patient. She had all the time in the world.

"Stay with me. We're not done with our little fairy tale just yet. What was my papa going to do?"

"Expose. He was going to expose us."

"Very good. But he never got the chance, because of you. You didn't kill him, because he had gone to the authorities. That would look too suspicious, and might lead right back to you. You needed him to change his story. So, you threatened him with the single most sacred thing to him. Me."

Persa reached into his coat pocket and found a cigar cutter. She pulled it out and held it before him.

"My father married later in life. He met a younger Jewish woman, and they only had one child. I was just a little girl when you used me to intimidate him. To control him. To make a point for him to not cause trouble. So, you used this on me. To show how you could punish his child for his transgression. Anytime. Do you know what that did to him?"

Drakos's eyes came into sharp focus. He had forgotten the little girl from all those years ago. It was her, right in front of him, all grown up. Talking right to him. He would never forget those eyes. So full of innocent trust when he took her little hand in his. Then pain. Then hate.

What was her name? Persa something, Persepolis, no that wasn't it. Persa, Persefoni. Yes, Persefoni.

"He had survivor's guilt already. Of being the only one in his family to escape the Holocaust. Then you went after his only child. You proved he couldn't even protect her. He committed suicide, you know. Just as surely as if you had pulled the trigger yourself."

That name meant something. I looked it up once. What was it? Old Greek. Something about death.

Persa grabbed his face hard, and held it firmly.

"I vowed my revenge. I went to Israel, joined the Mossad, and was trained. I lived to find your grandfather, to prove he was a collaborator. To avenge not just my father, but all my people."

She let go of him in disgust.

325

"That is why I seduced Nick. I drugged him at the bar, and learned of his intentions. I found he was on the track of the very U-boat your grandfather escaped on. That is why I took the jaw bone from the submarine. To match dental records and DNA. To prove the Kollas family empire was built on blood and lies. To prove that even time and distance cannot erase the sins of your fathers."

Ah, now I remember. Persefoni, Bringer of Death. I always thought it odd a father would name his little girl such a thing.

"Now you and your family will be judged. Not by me, not even by the souls of my brethren crying out from their graves. But by the good people of Greece."

Persa carefully placed his crushed pinkie finger in the cigar cutter. The same finger she had lost. She held it up before his face.

"You know what having a finger cut off feels like to a little girl?"

Drakos tried to focus on the hand before his face.

"Like this."

CHAPTER 30
JULY 19, PRESENT DAY, ATHENS, GREECE

An amazing find. Simply amazing," Dr. Storm said, stroking the point of his salt and pepper beard. The excavation of the ancient vessel from the cofferdam near Piraeus was nearly complete. The pieces were being carefully removed and transported for preservation. Soon to be reconstructed and featured at their own special exhibit, adjacent to the National Archeological Museum of Athens.

Stavros slapped him heartily on the back, overjoyed at the wealth of archeological knowledge coming to light.

"All this time we thought it might be a trireme, Philip. I never dreamed it would be so much older. The gods have smiled upon us my friends. They have seen fit to pull back the curtain on a lost chapter of history."

"Even we archeologists can be blinded by our own prejudices and preconceptions," Dr Storm reflected.

"An *Atlantean* galley. Who would have ever thought it possible?" Nick said, fingering the whittled figurine Zorba had given him. "If it hadn't been protected in a burial mound, it might never have survived. The design was revolutionary. When the Myceneans conquered and absorbed them, it became the blueprint for their fleets."

"Sad, in a way," Dr. Storm said, slowly shaking his head. "Such a magnificent people. A natural disaster of a magnitude never seen cripples their civilization. Their technology falls into the hands of those they traded with, then is turned against them."

"But isn't that the way of it, Doc?" Nick said. "The best ideas absorbed, the worst discarded. Incremental improvements made on the shoulders of those that came before. Everything and everyone blended together in the name of progress. Civilization marches on."

"Quite so young man," Dr. Storm sighed. "I just wonder though, what the world would be like today if Thera hadn't exploded. Would the idea of democracy have ever evolved in Greece?"

"Maybe, maybe not," Nick reflected. "I can't believe the idea of freedom from tyranny wouldn't have flickered to life eventually. It had to, some time. Somewhere."

"Well, that's the fun of counterfactual history, isn't it? One thing's for sure," Dr. Storm said, then chuckled lightly. "We wouldn't be standing here having *this* conversation."

Stavros walked between them and put an arm around each. "Tell me Mr. Nick, how is everyone recovering?" he asked.

"Recovering. Oh no, I'm going to be late." Nick shook hands and hustled down to a tender, ferrying people to and from the cofferdam. He jumped aboard just as it was departing. Narrowly escaping an unexpected dip in the Aegean. Just like another young man named Demos, over three and a half millennia earlier.

As Nick ran into the lobby of the hotel, he saw Soba standing off to the side, glancing at her watch. He muttered to himself, it wasn't like him to be late. Especially for something this important. She looked up at the sound of his approaching footsteps.

"Sorry I'm late Princess. I got a bit absorbed by things."

She smiled and feigned disinterest.

"The absent-minded professor is late. How completely unexpected."

"Yeah, Well I—"

"Well nothing. Let's go see how he's doing."

The cab dropped them off at the front entrance of the *Evangelismos Hospital*, near the heart of Athens. Nick and Soba nodded to the guard posted outside the room. He recognized them from prior visits, and waved them in.

Nick rapped lightly on the door and went in first. Persa was seated by the bed, gently holding Jim's hand. He looked and grinned, gamely making an effort to sit up. He grunted in pain, and lay back down.

"Easy big guy. Don't tear out any stitches on my account," Nick said, walking over and sharing a fist bump. Soba followed and fluffed his pillow, then gave him a kiss on the forehead.

"He not such a good patient," Persa said, shooting him a scolding look. "But he make 'a me laugh. I give you some time." She leaned in and gave Jim a deep kiss on the lips. Rising, she glanced at her phone, took a call, and started talking animatedly in Hebrew as she left the room.

"What 'ya going to do?" Jim said. "She's a real pistol, that girl is. And she thinks vulcanologists are sexy."

"Ha. Two words that don't belong in the same sentence. Vulcanologist and sexy," Nick said. "So how you feeling man?"

"Christ, they got me under lock and key here. I could heal just as well back in the field. I've got shit to do, you know?"

"Really?" Soba asked. "Just as well in the field? I don't think so Jimbo."

Jim flushed a little, then let out his signature belly laugh. Which made him wince, making Nick and Soba laugh too.

"OK. OK. Maybe I'm not quite ready yet. But I'm going stir crazy here. Give me some dirt, will ya? What's going on outside? How's everyone doing?"

"You're the one everyone is worried about," Nick replied. "Captain Alek is fine, not much you can do about a broken collarbone. He's already back at work. Said he's too busy to sit around on his ass all day like you."

Jim put his hand up and laughed again, signaling for mercy.

"By the way, he sends his regards. Looks forward to getting you back aboard to chase some fault lines."

"Nice! What about Zorba?"

"We'll know more tonight," Soba answered. "We're having dinner with him."

They brought Jim up to date on the excavation and the most recent finds, exchanging small talk until Persa came back in. Jim asked them one last question before they left.

"What about that SOB Kollas? What happened to him?"

"He's being put on trial. Really his whole family history is too," Nick answered. "Turns out there is such a thing as too much publicity."

As Persa walked them out, Nick turned back toward Jim. "And I'll tell you one other thing. With those crushed and missing fingers, he won't be giving any more piano concerts."

Persa closed the door behind her and waved her thanks to the guard.

"I wanted to talk with you both, alone," she said, slowly wandering down the corridor with them. "I want 'a you both to understand." She took her time, obviously deep in thought. "When I grow older, I spend life researching Kollas. I learn what he did to my family. I seek, what you call it?"

"Vengeance," Soba said, with a hint of sympathy and understanding.

"Da, vengeance. I see him game system, never get hands dirty. Too smart. Too rich. But I know truth. Know why Papa kill self, what happened during war."

They all stepped aside when an orderly with a patient on a gurney hurried past them, followed by a nurse and a doctor.

Nick turned to Persa as they started walking again. "You learned I was onto finding the U-boat. The U234. The one you suspected his grandfather escaped Athens on."

"Mossad well informed on suspected war criminals. We know what you and Heinrich working on. I 'a learn things important to you. History. Latin quotes. Blues music. Good bourbon. Make you like me. Easier to seduce. You were my mark."

"It makes sense now. You drugged me that first night, didn't you?" Nick asked, trying to make sense of their initial encounter.

"I slip something in drink at bar. Give truth serum at my flat."

Persa looked at Soba. "He not bad guy. Honest, trusting. Not his fault."

"Hmm. Maybe too trusting. But yeah, not so bad," Soba said. She leaned into Nick. He had been specifically targeted by the world's foremost secret service. And an enchanting professional to boot.

"It always just business Níkos. I after greater truth. After justice."

Nick shook his head, his ego taken down a notch. He thought he had done the seducing. After all, wasn't he that irresistible?

"Just business. Tell me Persa, do you find the ends always justify the means?"

Persa looked back at him, a single tear of regret trickling down her cheek. But the torment in her eyes, and her soul, was gone. Justice had been served.

He had his answer.

The big dog came running at them, circling excitedly. She leaned affectionately into Nick, refusing to budge. Until he got down and gave her a good, deep rubbing behind the ears.

"Good girl Skýlos. Missed you buddy."

Soba frowned, confused.

"I thought her name was Artemis. Doesn't Skýlos just mean dog in Greek?"

"It does. Long story. I'll tell you later. Let's go see Zorba."

Nick walked into the now-familiar kantína, looking through the crowd for his friend. It was good to be back on Santorini, among these timeless people. When the patrons looked up, a round of applause spontaneously broke out.

Here was the man who had uncovered the existence of Atlantis. Who proved definitively that the Minoans and Atlanteans were one and the same, sharing their bloodlines with modern Cretans. Those ancient traders and settlers who had scattered their lineage across the islands and shores. Nick was championing their contributions to the civilizations ringing the Mediterranean, especially that of ancient Greece. He was now counted as one of their own.

Zorba spied Nick and Soba at the entrance, walked over, and put his one good arm around him in a hearty embrace. His wife followed with shot glasses, smiled, and gave Nick a peck on the cheek.

"To our friend from beyond the sea," Zorba toasted in Cretan, raising his shot high.

"*Eviva do*," showered the replies.

Old men tottered up to shake his hand, young men embraced him, women kissed him. Soba became the object of their affections too, as the toasts continued to flow. It was a night for celebration. Ancient spirits were in the air.

Nick soaked in the joy and well wishes of these proud people. It was impossible not to share in their happiness and zest for life. Yet a part of him still ached for his friend Heinrich, who should rightfully be here celebrating with him.

Pello came up and hugged him hard, and pointed to a newspaper tacked to the wall. Nick squinted at it, and saw a photograph of himself on the cover of a Greek tabloid.

Great, he thought. *Is there no escaping it?*

"You famous here now Amerikí. No pay for drink!"

Music started when two men picked up their traditional Cretan lyres and broke into song. Nick found himself grabbed as everyone able got up and danced. He was gleefully twirled from one partner to the next. Soba was caught up in the same frenzied whirling of bodies, until she and Nick found themselves facing one another.

A circle formed around them, hands clapping, feet stomping, voices singing and gayly laughing. They exchanged a brief kiss, before being pulled apart and passed from partner to partner again.

Finally overcome by the alcohol, music and spinning, Nick raised his arms to free himself. He staggered over to Soba, grabbed her hand and led her out of the melee.

"Uncle already," he yelled to her.

"Agreed," she giggled back at him.

No sooner had they found a table in the corner than drinks were dropped off. Zorba waved to Nick from across the room, and worked his way over through the crowd. He sat, smiling at the two exhausted, but exhilarated travelers.

"Ah, my friends, good to see you," Zorba said, patting Nick on the shoulder. "Glad you make trip."

"Your people certainly know how to celebrate," Nick replied, admiring the traditional music and dance.

Soba leaned in and kissed Zorba on the cheek in greeting. Before she could utter a word, arms dragged her back to the dance floor. Who wouldn't want to dance with the beautiful young woman with the exotic looks? She shrugged at Nick and laughed, twirling away into the crowd.

"It is good. Times been hard. People with ties to Crete, back to Atlanteans, feel validated. We do what we do when times good. Or bad. We live life. We celebrate."

Nick saw Zorba's arm was still in a sling, to immobilize the shoulder wound.

"Tell me, how are *you* doing?"

"Never better. People think this old fisherman hero."

"They're right, of course."

"Bah, if I know I get this attention, I shoot myself long ago."

They both shared a laugh and sat silently for a moment.

"By the way, I have something for you," Nick said, breaking the silence. He slid an object wrapped in cloth across the table.

Zorba raised an eyebrow, then unwrapped it with his one good hand. It was a bejeweled Bronze Age dagger, the one discovered recently by a father and his son on the shores of Piraeus.

Zorba's eyes grew wide as he examined it. He couldn't suppress a smile and looked at Nick. Was this really for him?

"Don't worry, it's all above board, I assure you. I talked with Stavros. He cleared it on his end. From the inscriptions, we believe its Atlantean. We all thought it should be back with its people. With you."

Zorba ran his fingers along the symbols, their meanings lost to time. But still no less sacred. Nick noticed the tattoo on Zorba's chest matched one on the dagger. He realized he had seen it on others here, on Pello. Like a Mason's handshake, it was a silent, secret symbol, bonding the brethren together.

"It should be in museum. In Heraklion. Where all can see it."

"If that is what you believe, I'll let you deliver it personally."

Zorba held it, felt its balance, admired its craftsmanship. He flipped it up in the air, and watched it come down, imbedding itself in the table. Simply timeless.

"That what I believe."

Nick raised a glass to him, Zorba returning the gesture. They both sipped on their drinks, eyeing the reveling crowd. Soba caught Nick's eye briefly, waved, and was lost back in the mass of whirling bodies.

"Do you think all this recognition will make a difference," Nick asked, looking at the festivities. "You're not like the lost tribes of Israel anymore, lost to time. Your roots to a great ancient people are now fact."

"No, it won't," Zorba replied, reflecting on the trials and tribulations of his people over the years. Of the subtle and overt discrimination, of being the wrong caste. "We never care what others think of us. We always know connection. Here, where matter," he said, thumping his chest. "In heart."

"Well, there's no such thing as bad publicity. I'd bet you a case of Raki that interest in all things Cretan and Atlantean will explode. Your people will be hauling tourists everywhere, telling them of your myths and legends. You should be proud of your heritage, and tell the world all about it."

"*Eviva do* to that my friend," Zorba said.

"*Eviva do*," came shouts from throughout the kantína.

It had taken over three months for the big day to arrive. Nick, Giorgos, and specially trained archeologists qualified in deep sea diving had scoured the U234 and the surrounding debris fields. The treasures pilfered by the Nazis and destined for the Reich were recovered, piece by piece, case by case.

Those in pristine condition were immediately repatriated, filling museums in Istanbul, Kusadasi, Rhodes, Nicosia, Beruit, Tel Aviv, Cario, Tripoli, Tunis, and Catania. But most prominently, the collections swelled in the National Archaeological Museum of Athens and the Heraklion Archeological Museum of Crete.

Many of the other priceless artifacts would require more careful restoration, and be returned in due course. The blanks in the archeological record, of whether the Minoans and the Atlanteans were the same people, and what had triggered the collapse of their civilization and the rise of the Myceneans, were filled in. Atlantis took its proper place among the great civilizations of the ancient world.

"It looks magnificent, does it not my friend?" Stavros beamed. He stood in the National Archaeological Museum of Athens, in front of a specially constructed exhibit explaining the trading relationship between the Atlanteans and Myceneans, and the eventual absorption of the Atlanteans into the Mycenean empire. Recovered treasures from U234 filled up the better part of the hall, shedding new light on this epoch of history.

"That it does," Nick replied, gazing at the sarcophagus he had helped discover. The body found within it was displayed immediately adjacent, dressed in period garb and clasping a sword to its chest. While wearing the bracelet that had helped unravel the entire mystery. The bracelet that showed the Atlantean view of their world.

"Just wait until the galley has been restored. It will rival the great Viking Longship in Oslo when it is done," Stavros enthused.

"It will surpass it," Dr. Storm said. "My god, it predates the longship by two and a half millennia. The story it tells is incredible. The pathos of the collapse of a whole people, its simply heartrending."

"Ready gentlemen?" asked the photographer.

They all gripped the oversized pair of scissors, and counted out loud along with the gathered crowd of well-wishers and dignitaries.

"Enas, dýo, tría!"

The ribbon to the exhibit was cut, toasts were made and champagne flowed.

Charlie's wife Sophie looked over at Nick, then pointed two fingers at her eyes and then his with a serious face. Eyes on you mister. "Charlie always said he wanted to bring me to Greece. So nice of you to invite me along," she said, finally breaking into a smile and elbowing Charlie.

"And to think this is just the first dedication," Soba said, arm in arm with Nick. "It's all a bit overwhelming."

"Tomorrow round two, right bro?" Charlie asked as the entire crew of the Poseidon wandered over, clinking glasses and singing a favorite sea ditty. Persa and Jim joined them, along with Zorba and his wife.

"Right, round two tomorrow," Nick replied. "But today let's all enjoy this. Everyone here has earned it. To great things!"

"*Se spoudaía prágmata*," showered the replies. To great things!

Later that evening, Nick and Soba left the festivities. A crowd of paparazzi had anticipated their exit, and blocked their path. Cameras flashed and microphones were thrust in their faces as they attempted to leave. Nick tried to shield Soba as best he could, but when an overly aggressive reporter grabbed at Soba, his temper flared. When he drew his arm back to retaliate, he heard a gentle voice in his ear.

"We take care of dis Níkos," Persa whispered.

He realized there were now a half dozen well-muscled agents around them, cordoning off the journalists and clearing a path.

After Nick got in his car to drive away, he looked back and nodded his thanks to Persa. She smiled and waved, then discretely punctured the tires of several motorbikes awaiting their drivers.

So much for the would-be pursuers.

Nick fingered the map he had drawn, orienting it in his mind with what he saw below. The seaplane circled high over the great caldera that was Santorini. He could see it all now, how it all had laid out, how it conformed with the remnants below. How the jagged cliffs and islands below were once joined together. And where Atlantis would have sat, beneath the great mountain of Thíra.

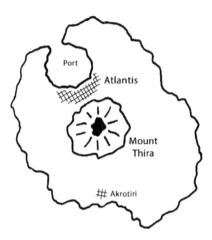

What they were looking for was barely visible from above, and the plane swooped in lower for a closer view. If the sunlight hit a certain way, they could just make it out. A small, dark depression under the shimmering surface of the sea lay there. Right where the U234 had punctured through the crust of the ocean floor. The exposed propellor caught a glint of sunlight, revealing itself.

"Hidden in plain sight," Nick observed.

"I'm not sure so plain," Jim said. "That hole was completely encrusted, invisible. If fishing nets hadn't snagged and oil leaked up, we still might not know it was ever there."

Charlie had his nose pressed against the window like a kid flying for the first time. "I can't wait to see it. This is going to be wild."

"It will be to anyone who hasn't seen it yet," Nick replied.

He and Giorgos had the advantage of spending much time at the U234 wreck site working on the recovery of artifacts. But even Nick hadn't ventured as far afield as they were going today. Everyone who had been abducted by Kollas would be on this maiden voyage, accompanied by Stavros, Dr. Storm, the Greek prime minister, and the prefecture of Crete, just for good measure.

The submarine they would be taking down could hold ten passengers and two crew, each squeezed into confined quarters. Nick sat up front in the nose next to the helmsman. In a row on the left were the prime minister of Greece, Stavros, Zorba, Captain Alek, and Soba. On the other side sat the prefecture of Crete, followed by Dr. Storm, Jim, Persa, and Charlie.

The submarine was specially constructed to provide nearly unlimited viewing, with each person sliding into a sort of glass bubble on either side. The strap-in seats were fully rotating, allowing riders to even hover face down if desired.

"I feel like the tail gunner in a B-17," Charlie quipped, swiveling around.

"Or like Jacques Cousteau," Captain Alek said. "Exploring a virgin sea."

The newly christened *Atlantis* was lowered from the Serafina, and glided along the surface for several hundred yards. Once in position, she started to gently submerge, immersing everyone in the filtered sunlight of the Aegean. Visible directly below, the back propellor of U234 came into focus, as well as an excavated and rein-forced opening through the crust of pumice. The opening was large enough to allow the curious to see what lay below, via a small fleet of specialty submarines—if one could afford the ticket.

The Atlantis hovered over the U-boat propellor and the opening for a moment, allowing everyone a bird's-eye view of where they were going. It then slowly descended through the punctured hole in the crust. Once through, the Atlantis followed the nearly vertical body of U234 downward. Upon reaching the place amidship where depth charges had shattered the hull, the descent paused.

Despite the excitement of the moment, everyone remained respectfully silent. They eyed the catastrophic damage. The external depth charge explosions had imploded the U234, leaving a ragged, gaping hole. Good and bad men had died here, taking their dreams and aspirations with them.

A mechanical arm extended from the Atlantis, about to deposit a wreath inside the U234. Which would officially memorialize it as a war grave.

"This is for you Heinrich," Nick said aloud.

He knew Heinrich had spent his life making amends for the actions of his own grandfather, Obergruppenführer Schmidt, who had served in the SS. He released the control that held the wreath.

"May all who died because of the war, past and present, rest in eternal peace."

Amens echoed throughout the confined quarters they all sat in.

The descent continued, until the Atlantis hovered directly over the sea bed. Edging forward, its brilliant lights were turned on. Powerful beams provided direct and oblique illumination, some reflecting off the bottom of the overhead crust. The world before them lay fully exposed.

"My god, it is all there. Complete as it ever was," the prime minister of Greece said. "The video feeds do it no justice."

"It is an underwater Pompeii, is it not?" echoed Stavros.

The prefecture of Crete sat speechless, enraptured at what lay before him.

Nick, who had already seen it firsthand, provided a detailed narrative. He used a high-powered laser pointer from his seat in front to call attention to certain details.

"And there are the ceremonial horns of the bull, overlooking the main plaza. The temples are off to the side, this one escaped much damage. Note the fountain in the middle, and how they used aqueducts to bring water into the city . . ."

They spent nearly an hour exploring, hovering within the confines of the vast undersea cavern. Tantalized by what they couldn't see, where the edges of the ceiling of pumice met the seabed.

"I clearly see how it all happened now," Jim said. "You with me Captain Alek?"

"Yes, the fault line. The friction."

"Please tell us," Soba said, "in layman's terms"

"There, do you see the crease? Where the ground drops about

ten or fifteen feet?" Jim pointed out. "That's a fault line. Literally two tectonic plates grinding against one another."

"After Mount Thíra erupts and implodes, the sea floor is covered in pumice. In some places very deeply," Nick said.

"Absolutely! Fast forward a thousand years, and the plates shift," Jim went on, completely in his element. "Cracks appear in the pumice-covered sea bed. Hot vents along the fault warm sea water, which rises and creates a small bubble. More warm water escapes, cold water seeps in, and the cycle continues. The bubble expands, gradually exposing this part of the city beneath. Think of it as a big blister."

"And then the U234 punctures through it like a missile. Günther survives, sees a bit of the sea floor, and lives to tell the tale." Nick shook his head. "Simply amazing."

"And here we are," Stavros said, looking at all that lay before them.

"Here we are, indeed" echoed Dr. Storm.

The Atlantis turned around, and began its ascent. While rising past the implosion on the U234, Nick reflected on their collective journey.

"Greed, cruelty, prejudice, intolerance. We've experienced some of the worst of mankind in this discovery. And yet, also some of the best. The Atlanteans were ultimately absorbed and assimilated. The best of their culture survived, was adapted, built upon. Time seems to ensure the blending of the best of all cultures, the best of humanity. Even regardless of the religion or race."

"Maybe someday they not matter," Zorba added. "Too much blood spilled in name of religion. Too much hate because of race."

They all sat silently in contemplation as the Atlantis finished its ascent, breaking through the surface. Crystal blue skies shone above, the sun sparking off the waves around them. They headed back toward the Serafina, the Greek prime minister's voice finally breaking the spell.

"I forgot to mention. I just heard from the International Criminal Court at the Hague. They believe what the Kollas family did constitutes a crime against humanity. I suspect Drakos and his family empire is about to get publicity and scrutiny they never wanted."

"Should be like when the Israeli's kidnapped Eichman from Argentina," Nick said. "The world will be watching."

"That good," Persa added, excited at the prospect. "Their empire built on blood. Now dead can rest in peace."

"Let's hope it turns up where monies were stashed for any future Fourth Reich," Stavros said. "Before the world gives rise to another Hitler or Stalin."

Dr. Storm grunted his agreement. "Unfortunately, you can see the world polarizing before our very eyes. Prejudice and xenophobia disguised as patriotism by silver-tongued demagogues. It's always us against them, never the greater *we*. The world can certainly do without another arms race."

Nick, ever the optimist, was more hopeful. "Perhaps what we've discovered here, what we've learned, will help enlighten people. Who knows, with a little luck, maybe someday we'll all figure out that the only race that matters is the *human race*."

EPILOGUE
1646 BC, AT SEA

The salt stung her eyes and parched lips. Her scalded scalp and back throbbed from the exposed burns, the pain awakening her. Kalli blinked hard, trying to make sense of her surroundings. Her befuddled world refused to come into focus. It was all disorienting, and she was so very tired. She felt like she was floating, yet something was solid beneath her. The gentle rocking motion lulled at her, beckoning her to submit and give up the struggle. Sleep, and the pain would go away. Sleep, and see your loved ones again. Sleep.

Loved ones. I do miss my parents, she thought. *It would be so good to see them again. It has been too long. I'll tell them of Demos, how he has become a man, how he has proven himself. Perhaps he will ask Papa for my hand,* she thought.

A scratching sound rose and fell with the gentle undulations of the waves. Kalli slipped away from the twilight of consciousness, the rhythm of the grating intertwining with her feverish dreams. Of creatures of the underworld clawing their way to the surface through great cracks in the land. Seeking the souls of the living, to drag back to the depths of the inferno from which they came. She could feel the heat, smell the stench of their fetid breath. Felt their fingers on her ankle, grasping at her, beckoning her to follow.

"Demos!" Kalli yelled, startling herself awake. "Do you live? Demos!"

Panicked, she sat up and frantically looked around. A flood of memories overwhelmed her, of the catastrophe that had engulfed them all. She tried to stand, but hadn't the strength. She gingerly sat down, in the half-swamped galley of the Atlanteans. The mast had snapped, the sail burned away. She felt gently at her head, the hair gone, burns about her face and body. She smelled the bloated bodies and decay of men and sea creatures about her, her own singed hair and burnt flesh. A corpse floated in front of her, his hand wrapped around her ankle in a death grip. She shuddered and kicked him away.

The sudden urge to vomit was overpowering, and she retched to the side. Odd, it wasn't revulsion that caused the reaction, not after all she had seen and experienced. She felt a twinge deep within her abdomen, and grasped at her belly. Was it really possible, in the midst of all this carnage and the end of days?

She heard the scratching again. Against the side of the galley the sea was filled with floating stones, rubbing relentlessly against the hull. Singed birds lay upon them, some still alive and vainly trying to regain flight upon featherless wings. They had been blown before the tempest, and then were overcome by it. She watched in morbid fascination, their struggles causing some to slip beneath the carpet of stones, to the depths below.

Eventually regaining her senses, Kalli looked farther out. The sea was covered in a floating mass of gray stones to the horizon, thick as far as the eye could see. She lifted a single, honeycombed stone and beheld it. It was just like those she saw raining lightly in Atlantis when she was being prepared by the slave girl. Was it just a few days, or a lifetime ago? The girl's words of advice came flooding back.

Be strong, you do this. You endure. Survive.

Kalli felt a twitch in her abdomen again. An instinct stronger than any she had ever known suddenly possessed her. She would not succumb to the whisperings of the dark gods of the underworld. Not now, not after all this. She would survive, whatever the costs. With him.

Does he still live? Where is he?

343

"Demos!" she yelled, beseeching the gods of her ancestors.

But the only reply was the desperate cries of dying birds, the moaning of wounded men, and the cacophony of the grinding sea of floating stones.

Kalli didn't know how long she dozed, she had lost all track of time. Her skin itched and was wrinkled from laying in the water. Her back hurt terribly. She blinked hard, and looked up for the position of the sun. A massive dark cloud hovered far above, blotting out the light, drifting off in one direction. She thought she saw the sun within it, or was it the moon? It was hard to tell.

Will the gods ever stop toying with me? she thought.

She needed a better vantage point. She half swam, half stumbled along the water-filled hull of the galley. Pushing aside floating stones and bobbing bodies, she reached for the broken mast. A scorched body clung with one arm wrapped around its base, facing the stern of the ship. Toward the direction of the great cataclysm that had struck them. The other hand still grasped a sword, to lead his men and fend off the dark forces of the apocalypse. She recognized the bronze chest plate he wore, and reached down to turn his head toward her. The face was gone, but the man was still unmistakable. *Thálassa.*

Kalli sighed, and stepped over him. She grasped the remains of the mast for balance, scorched on one side, the black coming off on her palms. Such fury, this breath of the gods. Everything facing it had been seared or torn away. She remembered gazing at it until the last moment, when she had instinctively huddled down and turned away.

That's why my back hurts so, but why I can still see. Everyone rowing looked directly into it.

She pulled herself fully erect, wobbled, and beheld an eerie scene of devastation and desolation. Of the great flotilla of ships she had beheld escaping from Atlantis, only a few were still visible.

They lay smoldering and entrapped within the vast sea of floating stones. All the other ships, with thousands of souls aboard, had simply disappeared. Swallowed whole by the very sea.

She looked closely at her own ship, sluggishly riding low in the waves. There weren't many bodies about, they must have been blown overboard. Where no doubt they drowned beneath the suffocating floating carpet of stones. Several men in the galley were shaking off their stupor and sitting up, just as surprised to find themselves alive as she had been. She noticed the moans of the wounded, those few who hadn't been knocked unconscious and drowned where they sat.

Where they sat. He had just been there, working the oar desperately. Which bench was it?

She frantically looked to where Demos had last sat, the bench empty, the hull sloshing with water and stones.

"Demos!" she called out again, her voice hoarse. A few slaves and soldiers turned toward the sound of her voice, looking through blinded eyes, uncomprehending.

Kalli pried the sword from Thálassa's dead hand, and used it to balance herself. She worked her way back toward his bench, turning over the floating bodies, one by one. She heard something muttered near her, the speech muffled. Listening closer she heard it again, and approached a scalded body, half hanging over the side.

"K-k-kalli . . ."

She dropped the sword and tenderly pulled the body back in. She turned him toward her, his upper body blackened and blistered from the blast. His face was raw, the skin peeling off, the eyes sightless.

"You l-l-live?" Demos asked.

"I do. The gods have blessed me to behold you one more time." She hugged him tightly to her breast.

Demos tried to talk, but coughed up blood and blackened flesh.

"Shhh, be quiet my love. I am here. I am with you."

She felt the urge to cry overwhelming her, but stifled it. She could cry later. Now, at this moment, she had to be strong. For him.

"It-it-it is good you will live."

He coughed again, so hard he struggled to breathe. His hand gripped her harder, his breaths coming in ragged gasps. It was if he had held on only to be with her one last time. She had to tell him, before it was too late.

"I am with child, Demos. Your seed will live on in me. Our son will be a great man, and have many children. We will be immortal, you and I. Our blood will flow forever."

Demos looked at her through unseeing eyes, the corners of his burned mouth forcing a pained smile. Kalli leaned in and kissed what was left of his lips. His body shuddered and then went still.

"Until we meet again in the green fields of our home," she whispered into him, inhaling his last breath. "Under the tree where you gifted to me a son."

Kalli allowed herself only a moment of grief, then straightened with determination. She gently lifted him until he sat teetering on the very edge of the galley. Balancing him carefully, she swung his legs outward. She held him from behind and gave a last, lingering embrace. Finally, she let go. The body quietly slipped through the floating stones, leaving no trace of its passing.

"Before I join you again my love, there is much yet to do."

Kalli carefully picked among the bodies, seeking any survivors. She tended the wounds of those she found as best she could, learning their names. There were but twelve of them, nine slaves and three Atlantean soldiers. All badly injured to one degree or another, two grievously. Few could see, and of those that could, it was only through one eye. Brave men all, they had rowed desperately, turning their head's away only at the last moment.

She pondered her predicament. The sail had burned away, the mast shattered. They didn't have enough manpower to row, but it mattered not. The carpet of floating stone was so thick it wouldn't permit crossing, even if their oars could penetrate to gain purchase.

Think. The gods didn't spare me only to cast me away now. Surely, they left everything needed to survive. Just think woman. What would Thálassa have done?

Her thoughts drifted back to when they had been marooned with the king in the middle of the Great Sea. Surrounded by a mass of dead sea creatures that refused to allow passage. Thálassa had taken charge then, inspired his men, led them forward. His voice rang in her ears now.

Restore discipline. Keep them busy. Give them hope, even when there is none.

She gathered scattered helmets from the living and the dead, and set the survivors to work bailing with them. When the water within the hull was lower, she helped toss the light stones overboard. She looked for anything useful, including unburned cloaks, clay pots, provisions, and tools. Finding a spar with a hook, she picked birds and fish off the floating stones about them, before this bounty of the sea slipped away. Finally, she helped push the dead overboard. The bodies were already starting to fester, best to remove them before disease corrupted the living.

Fresh water was now their greatest need, and there was precious little of it in unbroken amphora. She alone doled out what they had, and to the two most wounded, she gave none. When one who was a slave expired, his body was unceremoniously dumped over the side. The other, who was a soldier, survived longer and demanded drink. His two fellows voiced their support, threatening her.

"You own us no longer," Kalli said, brandishing Thálassa's sword over him. "Water is only for the living. And you no longer live."

With that she thrust the blade with two hands into his heart.

"Tinásso," she directed. Toss.

The slaves pushed aside the two remaining soldiers, lifting the limp body and dropping it into the sea of floating stones. They would all survive or perish together. But it wouldn't be a man who led them. Or an Atlantean.

On the third day of drifting, a light rain pattered about them. Kalli showed how to use the cloaks to funnel water into their bailing helmets. At first the rain water was murky, filled with the dark residue of ash washed from the skies. Undrinkable, they reluctantly poured it over the side. Later in the day the rains ran a little clearer. The coarse fabric of the cloaks filtered out the largest pieces of grit, and they learned to let the water settle within the helmets for a time.

Those with patience slacked their thirst, while those with none coughed up violently.

Kalli sparingly doled out their reserves of food, and supplemented them whenever possible from what floated around them. The stones embracing the galley were gradually drifting away or sinking. She had the sense that they were moving, imperceptibly, although there was no landmark to gauge it by. One by one the ships she had seen surrounding them in the distance disappeared. Whether they drifted away above the sea or slipped beneath it, she could tell not.

The days dragged on, blending into one another, the occasional rains continuing to slack their thirst. When food became scarce, they were reduced to eating rancid flesh and gnawing at old bones. First one slave, then another passed. Solemnly she consigned them to the depths.

One of the Atlanteans, who had been so vocal and intimidating, succumbed to his wounds and hunger the next day. About to have him tossed overboard, Kalli paused. It was unthinkable, but they were desperate.

"Keep the body here, for now."

Even his companion didn't object.

She heard words spoken, in the cadence of her people. Soft voices, women's voices, reached her ears. Voices that betrayed a mix of awe and admiration. Tinged with horror. Her eyes fluttered as she fought to awaken. It seemed she had been dreaming forever, of drifting and rocking on the sea. Of hearing men praying in weak voices, stones scraping against the hull, waves lapping endlessly. Now there was only the soothing sound of women softly talking.

"Surely, she was delivered by the gods. Why else would she alone survive?"

"She must be marked for some special purpose. If she lives."

"Look at the bracelet she wears. She must have married a

nobleman."

"That's not a bracelet, but a shackle. Perhaps she belonged to someone important."

"They ate human flesh? I could not have done it. I would rather have died."

"You say that sitting here in the safety of our village. Who knows what one is capable of when your life, and the life you carry within you, is at stake."

Kalli lay with one arm draped over her eyes. When she moved it, the light was bright, even through her eyelids. She leaned up on one elbow, and raised a hand to shield her vision.

"H-h-how long?"

The talking suddenly stopped, and one woman ran out of the hut. Kalli could hear her yelling that the dead woman had awakened. A kindly old face kneeled down in front of her and stroked her hair. She rested a hand on her belly and grunted knowingly.

"Two moons dear. Rest, and grow strong. You are with child. A child consummated by fire, destined for great things."

"Two moons. But the blink of an eye to the gods," Kalli said. "You live Demos, in me. You live."

Comforted, she drifted back to sleep, to the familiar recesses of her mind and dreams of home.

When she awoke later, the air was cooler, the light no longer in her eyes. She guessed it was evening, and kept her eyes closed and breathing steady. To better learn of these people and their intentions. Of from whence she came. Excited voices, just outside the hut, discussed what had happened. And more importantly, what it might portend.

A fishing boat with two men had spotted the drifting remains of the galley, and went to see if any valuables survived. They were shocked to find a woman and one of their brethren yet alive, hidden from the sun beneath frayed and faded cloaks. Laying among scattered corpses and glistening bones. They had been brought back ashore, with much rejoicing since the male slave was of the village. He passed of his wounds, but the woman stubbornly survived. And miraculously, today she had awoken.

The priestess had cared for her, convinced her surviving the great inferno far to the south was an omen from the gods. A talisman of good fortune for their people which they must care for. Her fevered speech had betrayed she was from some nearby tribe, of kindred spirits who toiled under the yoke of the Atlanteans.

Kalli heard all she needed. She was among friends, she was safe. She opened her eyes and spied a young girl sitting in the corner, pulling on a thin rope. She followed its course, and realized the bed she lay upon was being rocked back and forth.

"Why do you sway me child?"

The girl had been daydreaming, and her eyes opened wide in surprise. She was in the room alone with the woman everyone was talking about, part human and part demon. A she-devil, an eater of the dead. Before her trembling mouth could answer, the priestess ducked in with a bowl of broth. She handed it to Kalli, and motioned for the youngster to leave them.

"You were tormented when you lay still. Because you drifted in the galley for so long. You calmed only when I held and rocked you. It seemed the best way to get you to rest. To regain your strength."

Kalli sat unsteadily on the edge of the bed, the earth moving beneath her feet. The priestess pulled up a chair and guided her to it. Kalli grasped at the arms, swaying slightly. In danger of falling, she closed her eyes. Sighing, she sat still.

"I am afraid the sea moves within me yet."

She sat silently for a moment, then slowly opened her eyes and stared at the priestess. She was older than Kalli had thought, the wisdom of many years etched upon the wrinkles of her face.

"You and your people have been most kind. How may I repay you?"

The priestess looked at her and smiled. She heard children outside giggling, thought of her people, flourishing along the coast. She reached over and touched Kalli's belly. Perhaps the future of her people.

"The gods have punished the Atlanteans. They no longer come to demand tribute or collect slaves. We have been repaid already."

1603 BC

A father and son stood away from the seashore, on the edge of a hillock overlooking the village and the docks. The breeze shifted, the sounds of men hard at work reaching their ears. The man took a deep breath and looked out with pride. So much had been accomplished. Someday his son would rule here in his stead.

"But I don't understand Father. Why would she never remove it?" Atreus looked up at Pelops, confusion on his young face.

"Your grandmother was a proud woman. Strong, determined. She would not shirk from her past. She wore the bracelet as a reminder of her abduction. Of those who would have enslaved us all."

Pelops looked at the worksite below. A ship was being dragged on rolling logs up from the harbor, toward a natural depression in the ground. The shouts of long lines of men could be heard when they pulled in unison, heaving the craft a few feet at a time.

The boy could barely contain his excitement. He had seen the ritual of burial many times, but never like this. People from near and far away were streaming in to pay their respects. After all, it was his father who ruled these lands.

"Why bury her in a ship?" Atreus asked. He had never heard of such a thing.

"It isn't just any ship, son. That is the very galley she was found upon all those years ago. An Atlantean galley. We copied it, and now it is us who rule these seas."

A soldier in burnished bronze rode up on a horse, dismounted, and bowed. Atreus hid behind his father until he recognized the face. Pelops gestured for him to rise.

"All proceeds according to plan, Your Highness. The ship will be in position by sundown. Tomorrow we shall put the sacred soil of Mycenae upon it. That it may endure for all time."

"It is good, Anatole," Pelops replied to his most trusted general. "She would have preferred to slip away unnoticed. But I, and the people of this land, owe her much more than that."

In the morning, the perfumed and oiled body was brought down from the temple by the high priestess, then gingerly placed in a rough-hewn stone sarcophagus in the middle of the galley. Kallistra was dressed in all her finery, a look of contentment upon her weathered and wrinkled face.

Pelops placed a piece of gold in her mouth, to pay Kharon, the ferryman of Hades, to transport her soul safely across the River Styx. He then crossed her arms over the very sword she had been found with all those years ago. The sword of her oppressors, and ultimately the sword of her freedom and redemption. Finally, he reached under his cloak and removed a dagger. It had bejeweled inlays that even the best Mycenean craftsmen couldn't recreate. His mother had stolen it from Thálassa himself, she had told him. It would now accompany her to the land of her ancestors.

He stared at her face one last time.

Rule with dignity and fairness, he remembered her saying. *Listen to wise counsel. Respect the people. You rule only for their good, not yours.*

He had, and the collection of villages by the sea prospered. Others from the surrounding area flocked to his leadership. There were stirrings here, perhaps of something even greater.

The work the next day proceeded apace. An endless procession of men carrying wicker baskets of earth built a mound over the galley, until a small hill formed and appeared as part of the landscape. Men with heavy, fire-hardened poles tamped the earth down until it was rock hard. In the end it was if nothing had ever been buried here. An invisible tomb for the ages.

Pelops walked alone to the top of the mound and knelt. He put a hand to the ground, to commune with her one last time.

Rest easy Mother, you are with Father now in Elysian Fields. I will follow your advice, your example. I will do my duty honorably.

He arose and looked back toward the harbor. Toward the sea that had born her back to these shores. He couldn't suppress a smile as one last thought came to him.

And may the gods be prepared for you. For they have never seen your like before.

PRINCIPLE CAST OF
CHARACTERS

PRESENT DAY

Alekos Rouvas – Greek captain of the research vessel Serafina
Charles (Charlie) LaBounty – Nick's older brother
Dimitris Bakos – Greek marine engineer of the research vessel Poseidon
Drakos Kollas – Greek business tycoon and industrialist, heir to family empire
Dr. Philip Storm – Nick's college professor, mentor, and friend
Eddie Sullivan – Paleontologist, Nick's friend
Ephraim Theocritus – Grandfather of Persa
Giorgos Ioannou - Greek marine archeologist of the research vessel Poseidon
Günther Wessel – WWII German U-Boat crewman
Heinrich Schmidt – German forensic archeologist, former classmate and friend of Nick
Jason Calathes – Deputy of Greek Antiquities, key aide to Stavros
Jim Portmess – American vulcanologist, renowned expert in the field
Lykaios – Bodyguard of Drakos Kollas
Nick LaBounty – Archeologist and adventurer
Otto Wessel – German administrator, formerly worked for Stasi
Persefoni (Persa) Theocritus – Greek oceanographic researcher

Petros Morakis – Prime minister of Greece
Soba (Altsoba) – Navajo medicine woman, Nick's girlfriend
Stavros Nomikos – Head of Greek Antiquities
Theodoros Kollas – Grandfather of Drakos Kollas
Yiannis Kostas – Greek crewman of the research vessel Poseidon
Yitzhak Theocritus – Father of Persa
Zorba Balaskas – Cretan fisherman living on Santorini

AGE OF ATLANTIS (1646 BC)

Atreus – Son of Pelops, future ruler

Cletus – Leader of Mycenean seaside village

Demos (Demotimos) – Shepherd, boyfriend of Kalli

Kalli (Kallistra) – Young woman, name means *most beautiful*. Slave, then Ruler of Mycenean coastal tribes.

Keos – Personal servant to King Mínōs

King Mínōs – King of the Empire of Atlantis

Pelops – Son of Kalli, ruler of Mycenean coastal tribes

Rusa – Advisor to King Mínōs

Thálassa Iremi – Commander of Atlantean fleet, hand of the king

Xenophon – Village elder, father of Kalli

Yidini – Thálassa's second in command

ABOUT THE AUTHOR

A graduate of the S.I. Newhouse School of Public Communications and the Whitman School of Management at Syracuse University, Jay LaBarge spent his professional career growing companies in the networking, telecommunication, and consumer electronics industries. A businessman by profession but historian by passion, he and his wife Sandy raised their daughters Ashley and Kara in the Central New York area, with frequent trips to his childhood home in the Adirondack Mountains.

He continues to pursue his love of history and travel with his wife to out-of-the-way places both domestically and abroad. His lifetime of curiosity and wanderlust ultimately led to the creation of Aztec Odyssey, and now Apocalypse Atlantis.

You can find him at:

Jayclabarge.com

Facebook.com/HistoricalActionAdventure

Amazon Author Page

ALSO BY JAY C. LABARGE

Aztec Odyssey: Available On Amazon

A treasure lost to time, a string of stolen artifacts, and one archaeologist determined to expose the truth.

The year is 1521. Wracked by plague and war, the majestic Aztec empire begins to crumble. As their beloved capital city falls to the ruthless Spaniards and hordes of vengeful tribes, the Aztecs make a last-ditch attempt to secretly save their heritage before it's lost to the sands of time forever.

Meanwhile in the modern day, a string of high-profile robberies lays waste to archaeological sites and museums across Mesoamerica. Rumors say the artifacts hold the secret to a legendary myth—The Seven Cities of Cibola —which has concealed countless treasures for centuries.

Faced with unravelling the mysteries of both the present and the past, aspiring archaeologist Nick LaBounty embarks on a dangerous mission to solve a long-held family mystery and discover the truth behind the stolen artifacts.

He soon finds his fate irreversibly entangled with a civilization from over five hundred years ago. But time is running out, and the future of both a fabulous treasure—and all Central America—teeters precariously in the balance.

Nick LaBounty's First Discovery: Available on Amazon or

Author Website (for free).

Hopelessly lost and in danger of freezing to death, three young boys fight for their very lives against a freak storm in the wilds of upper Michigan.

What started on a lark as a journey of exploration takes an ominous turn, as they discover more than they ever bargained for. Both about secrets buried deep beneath the frozen ground, and hidden within themselves.

This coming-of-age tale follows Nick LaBounty and his friends as they try to persevere their ill-timed expedition, and their own adolescent frailties. A hunting cabin hidden deep in the woods, the rumor of a lost trapper, and the lure of relics from the ancient past prove irresistible, and possibly fatal.

Through trials and tribulations, both physical and mental, the boys attempt to prove themselves to one another. Often with unexpected, and perhaps fatal, consequences.

Printed in Great Britain
by Amazon

83858807R00215